AWAKENING ALICE

by
Kira Kenley

Kira Kenley © 2014

Disclaimer: This is a work of fiction. Names, characters, businesses, places, events and incidents are either the products of the author's imagination or used in a fictitious manner. Any resemblance to actual persons, living or dead, or actual events is purely coincidental.

Published by Kira C. N. G. Kenley.

To Rosanna:
With me from the beginning and in
my heart until the end.

'*What you are seeking is seeking you.*' Rumi

'*And more than anything, I want to love. As if my life depends on it. Because actually it does.*' Sid Harris

Table of Contents

ADAM I

My whole life changed yesterday: my mother died. Now I'm an orphan. I'm alone. No longer a boy, but not yet a man – caught somewhere in between. And now alone.

My father died before I could know him, before I had the chance. 'You missed out' – that's what my mother was forever telling me. He was a great man, she said, and I believed her. She said I reminded her of him and she had no doubt that I would grow up to be the fine man that he was. She said they don't make men like him anymore (you only have to look at my sisters' husbands to see that), but maybe I would be the exception.

I'm the youngest in my family. My siblings are all years older than me. They've all been married and leading their own separate lives since I was a small boy. An incredible age gap exists between me and the others. Mammy always said I was hiding at the end of the barrel, that the best came last, but I wasn't to repeat that to the others – it was our little secret. There are many secrets in my family. Some she told me, but I've a feeling she took many with her to the grave.

Mammy got really sick only nine months ago and her suffering was intense. Cancer: the disease that's killing everyone these days, according to Bernie, the younger of my two sisters. By the time Mammy was diagnosed it was too late. She was dying and that was that. It was Bernie who told me, while Mammy and Marie, my eldest sister, sat in silence. That was the day I had to grow up, like it or not. After Bernie and Marie had left, I sat for a long time with Mammy saying nothing. Eventually, she broke the silence. She told me she would be glad to be with my father again but she was sorry to be leaving me. She would have liked another ten years to see me married and to meet my children. I wanted the same – that was, until she got really sick. Then I wanted her gone, out of her suffering, even if it meant she was away from me.

My heart is broken, and my insides feel like they've been taken out and put back in again by someone who knows nothing about human anatomy. I'm all over the shop.

Spoiled, I am – that's what Marie tells me. She's the one who likes me the least. The feeling's mutual. Marie is the bad egg in the family, the hardest to crack. She's forever complaining and she gave Mammy the hardest time, even when she was ill. I don't know how she can live with herself. She's married to a saint, Mammy always said, and they have no children because John has his hands full taking care of her. Then there's Bernie. I get on great with Bernie, which is just as well because now I have to go live with her and Tommy and their son Aidan. But first we have to get through the funeral. It's the second funeral in this family. I had been at my father's funeral but I was in Mammy's belly then. This is my first real funeral and the hardest I'll ever have to attend, so I was told by some old woman at the rosary last night. Everyone feels so sorry for me. I'll always be the baby of the family.

Right now I feel nothing. I think maybe I'm still in shock because even though I knew Mammy was dying, I wasn't ready for her to go just yet. And when she took her last breath, it finally hit me – I won't ever see her again. I don't know what to do with that. How will I cope? I love her so much it hurts. Literally.

I haven't cried since it happened and for some reason I don't feel like crying. I feel mostly angry, especially with Marie. She just seems to be causing problems left, right and centre. I don't understand why. She's a grown woman but you'd swear she was the teenager. Last night, she had a right go at me. Bernie butted in and told her to stop, to leave me alone, for God's sake. Marie really doesn't like me, but I try not to take it personally because she really doesn't like anyone.

I've always felt like I don't fit in with these people, like I'd been thrown from a great height and just landed here. I told Mammy that's what I felt like, and she said it was probably because I'd never met my father and because of the age gap between me and my sisters. But I don't know. It feels like it's something more than that. I've a way of looking at life that my family don't share. It scares me, but it's also exciting. I see things differently to them, and in many ways my sisters are like strangers. I saw a film once when I was really small where a little baby was left in a basket outside someone's front door and I wondered if that was what had happened with me. When I asked Mammy she laughed.

Mammy. Mammy. Mammy. Always thinking of Mammy.

It's amazing how a person can be altered in a split second. Now my life feels completely wrong, out of sorts. The one person who made me feel connected to the world outside of myself is gone. I keep expecting to see her in the kitchen, her favourite place. But then I remember she's dead.

Dead and gone.

I feel empty and like it can't get any worse, but deep down I know it hasn't hit me yet, that it will get much worse. I have so many questions, questions I wish I'd asked her when she was here. But when she got sick it was too late to be asking her complicated questions. We had more important stuff to talk about. She wanted to talk about my father all the time. She missed him so much. I miss him. Now both of them are gone and the empty space in me has doubled.

Mammy had a plaster for every sore. But now she's gone and I need a plaster more than ever.

1
Standing Outside The Gate

Alice Cooper is here in London. Ah try to get ma head around this new information as Ah sit and look at the face on the screen. Years have passed but Ah still see ma Alice in there. Ah still see her; every bit of what Ah've known is contained in those eyes. Sure, a lifetime has passed since I last saw her, which will have added to the pool of energy that is this woman now, but the point is: she is contained in those eyes. 'We' – us two – are contained in those eyes.

In ma hand Ah hold a ring. It's the only thing Ah've kept all ma sorry life – well, besides the miserable bag of bones Ah drag from A to B. When we were both fifteen we decided that we would declare ourselves man and wife. That was the day she told me she was carrying ma baby. Ah look at the copper band in ma hand and Ah notice that ma palm is sweating and Ah'm shaking. There's so much of that girl still all over me. It must be love. Ja.

Ah look again at the information under the picture on the screen. It tells me that somehow, in a world as large and varied as the one in which I live, we have made our way to the same part of it. But then there are no coincidences in this life. The events of the last six months have shown me that. What are the odds of finding maself on the same island as a half-brother Ah did not know existed, an encounter which then led me here to London to ma father's house and now to Alice. Life is indeed very ordered. And who knows what else might be up its omnipotent sleeve.

It's almost four months since Ah came to London, four months since Sid Vicious died. Ah let that fact settle and

Ah feel the deep sadness that found me the night Ah lost him, when ma best friend died in ma arms. He had died saving me. He had died and led ma blood father right to me. Then the cat was out of the bag. Ah discovered Ah'd lost not just a friend but a brother. If someone else was to tell me the story of these events Ah would tell them it was too fantastical to happen in real life. And yet it all happened to me.

Ma life is ever changed. Ah'm narcotic free and Ah've vowed to make something of maself. Initially, ma sober ship had been captained by maself alone, but when Ah got to London ma father suggested that Ah seek out the help of the folk at a home-grown rehab group called Never Again, which had come to his attention due to its success rate amongst his peers. Since then, they've been helping me steer ma ship into a brighter future, and as Ah look at the only girl Ah've ever loved – as she smiles out at me from her Facebook profile – Ah wonder if maybe she will be a part of that future.

Ah make a decision. Ah will contact her, but not yet. First Ah must make sure that ma recovery is well and truly at large in ma dailies and that Ah can be trusted. Never Again dictates that Ah should give maself six months before making any other sudden changes in ma life, so by that measure Ah've three to go. Ma computer tells me we have just passed into the third day of December. In three months it will be the third day of March, just after our birthdays. Alice and Ah are both children of the same February. Ah came into the world a short three days after she did, yet Ah had to wait a further nine years before she was led into ma life for her short stay. But perhaps Ah can make it right. Perhaps we can come together in our thirty-third year and set about spending the rest of our lives together.

Ma brother appears and sits across from me on his bed, which is now ma bed. 'What do you say, Sid Vicious!' I ask him.

'I say go for it, Denzel!'

'Ah thought you would boet.'

'You're stalling.'

'Na, Ah'm not.'

'Yes you are.'

'Ah have to wait until Ah'm sober a good six months.'

'Well, make sure you don't wait any longer. Life's too short. I should know.'

'Ah take your point, little brother.'

And Ah really do. His life had been taken when we both least expected it. Ah catch ma reflection on the screen of ma laptop. These days it takes a minute for me to recognise maself. Ma appearance is significantly altered. Gone is the long wild hair Ah'd worn forever, cut away shortly after Sid's death. Somehow it felt like a necessary change, a way to mark the beginning of a new life, or at least a new way of being in the only life I have.

Ah look at Alice's picture once again. The Denzel of before would have left the past lie sleeping, for sure. But he's no longer here, so Ah decide that Ah'll go back, all the way back, and see if Ah can awaken Alice.

*

I look at the name on the parcel and wish for the millionth time that my parents had known enough about rock music to see how much hardship it would cause to call the youngest member of the Cooper family Alice. Actually, that was just the beginning of a life of getting things wrong when it came to their only daughter, but I won't get started on that one. Instead I look on the bright side: in only three months I'll have a different surname, thanks to Robert Shaw.

'More wedding stuff?'

The voice belongs to my future husband.

'I imagine so,' I reply just before I tear the box open.

Robert makes his way to the coffee pot for his morning fix. He doesn't touch me on the way past. He's not very tactile in the morning, but I've got used to it – to that and a lot of other things. Robert will make a good companion and support me financially, but I know I can't depend on him for anything emotional. He's safe and that's what I crave most of all these days: to be safe and secure. Our relationship isn't one of the world's great love stories, but the reality is I'm a woman of a certain age and I don't want drama, especially after the huge commotion of my early romantic life. Supposedly that was true love and it hurt me badly. Love is for books and movies; real life is about making sure you're protected and secure.

I look at the white card telling me that I will marry on Sunday 6th February – my birthday – at 4 p.m. in a church in North London, with a reception afterwards in Alexandra Palace. It will be a small affair, more for the benefit of Helen, Robert's mother, than anything else. The guests will be mostly Robert's family and friends. I've conceded to invite my own parents. After years of disappointing them, it seems that I'm giving them just what they want: to see me married and sufficiently distanced from the possibility of doing anything else that might shame them. That my future husband is a well-off professional man and is footing the bill for a fancy wedding will also have pleased them no end. My lovely family.

And what do I want? I've forgotten. I've even forgotten exactly when I forgot what I wanted. This is my life; this is how it has showed up – Robert, my home – and I accept it. Robert will look after me and I know I need looking after.

'Are those the invitations?' Robert asks, now sitting opposite me with his coffee and toast.

I nod my head and hand one his way.

'Very nice!' he says. 'I suppose tonight we should get them sent out so that we know a final number.'

'Good idea!'

'I'll be working late, but perhaps you could make a start on them and I'll join in when I come home.'

'Ja, no problem,' I reply. 'No problem at all.' I've mostly lost my South African accent, but the occasional 'ja' seems to slip out every now and then.

Robert finishes his coffee and leans towards me.

'I'm marrying the prettiest girl that ever walked into the Famous Royal Oak.'

'That's probably true,' I say and smile as I remember the night he's referring to. I'd been drunk – very drunk – and was with my best friend Jo, who was in an even worse state. We'd both noticed Robert, but the alcohol made me more confident than I usually am and I flirted outrageously with him while Jo looked on in disbelief. I'm not sure what it was – maybe I'd seen the potential, my future as it is now. Sure he was handsome – so were a lot of men – but he was different – *is* very different – to anyone else I'd met. And that's precisely why I'm marrying him.

Robert takes a last look at me before he leaves. 'I love how you look. You know that, don't you?' he says.

'Yes, you might have told me once or twice,' I say.

'Well, I love how you look.'

Jo had once remarked that Robert was marrying his mother and there's no denying that I have more than a passing resemblance to Helen Shaw. Yes, that's what men do – they marry their mothers. And women their fathers? Not true. He's nothing like the man who raised me. Robert loves how things look and I look good sitting in our beautiful home. I look the part; we look the part. Then there's the sex stuff.

I'd found his porn just after I moved in and curiosity had taken me further. Although I'm no prude and had watched porn before, what I saw disturbed me and I thought about ending it with him then. But our sex life bore no resemblance to what I saw. It still doesn't. What he does in his fantasy life is no concern of mine – at least, that's what I tell myself. It's a small price to pay. Maybe every man is a bit of a pervert beneath it all.

'And I love how we look,' I reply.

The right answer. He smiles his perfect smile and tells me he'll see me later.

'Yes you will.' I'm his security too.

He blows me a kiss and I blow him one back and he leaves without touching me. Sometimes I wonder if he's afraid that touching me in the daylight hours will make me less shiny for the general public.

I look back at the invitations. This is really happening. At one stage, I'd sworn I'd never get married, never do the white wedding thing. But never say never, isn't that how the saying goes? And where are all my dreams? Gone. Dreams are for dreamers and Alice Cooper is a realist.

Tonight, I'll post out the invitations alone and I'll be a long time asleep by the time Robert gets home. As usual. And that's fine. I never much mind spending time alone, and it's not like I need him.

I've only ever needed one person: Denzel Anderson. It still feels dangerous to dwell on him for too long. I tell myself his name is no longer in my heart, but my head is another story. He's been coming into my thoughts too much in recent times, since I began to plan the wedding to be precise, and now I find myself wondering what he would think if he were here and could see me doing this – this very thing I said I'd never do. Crazy Denzel Anderson – everything that Robert is not. He'd hate Robert, and Robert would be completely floored by my taste in men back then.

But I'm not the same person any more. That Alice is dead. She died after her love left. She had to. It was the only way she could have survived what happened next. Her death is the reason I exist – reincarnated with a different life ahead of me, and not a bad one as it goes. Soon to be married to a wealthy man, I'm living in a million-pound house, despite having a job that pays me very little but which I love – a job I should be making my way to right at this moment.

And so I let go of my past and take the next step into my future.

2

Addictions And Routines

Ah sing to maself as Ah take the first steps of the day; it's a familiar tune Ah think might belong to The Beatles. A new day. Another one that will begin here in the house of ma newly acquired father, Tim Harris. After Sid's death Ah travelled back to London with Tim and he offered me a place to stay. A home, the very thing Ah've needed for a long time – all ma life maybe – and here Ah am in Borough, London, England. Ah've never been the greatest fan of London, but Ah have to admit, the city has grown on me these past four months and now that Ah've found out Alice is here, the place smells even sweeter. Thinking about Alice makes me smile. The future; ma future; our future. Please, let it be. There seems to be a Beatles theme running through ma head this morning.

First thing – the thing Ah do every morning – is a set of martial art formations Ah'd learned from Bob, a roadie Ah spent time with on a Roger Waters tour. We would practise first thing every morning and then spend the rest of the day getting high. It kind of defeated the purpose, but we didn't know that at the time. There are five formations in all and they can take from ten minutes to a few hours to work through, depending on how much you want to put in and get out. This morning Ah land somewhere in the middle and ma practice is longer than anticipated. While Ah do the formations Ah imagine maself as a Japanese warrior in another time – a Samurai. This has been a long-standing fantasy of mine and Ah sometimes wonder if it's the ghost of a past life, but then

Ah'm not sure if we are here more than once. Ah guess Ah'll know for sure one day.

Ah'm a martial artist and have practised off and on ma whole life. Ah'd been told Ah'd a knowing and an instinct for it, and Ah believed that. The point is Ah get the philosophy, and not in a detached sort of way, but like Ah know it already. Or maybe it's because it just makes sense to me, at a deep level. It means Ah can protect maself, or Ah would have ended up dead, for sure. Ah think about Sid Vicious and, as Ah always do when that night on the beach comes floating into ma memory, Ah wish he had stayed away. Ah could have handled it.

'I had to do it, you know.' Sid looks at me from across the room. He's sitting cross-legged on the windowsill with his back to the wide-open window, thanks to ma need for ventilation.

'Ah'd tell you to be careful you don't fall out, if you weren't already dead,' Ah say.

He smiles. 'I had to do it,' he repeats.

'Ah know, boet. But Ah wish you hadn't. We could be here together now and Ah could be teaching you how to defend yourself.'

'It was my time.'

'Ja ja! You always say that.'

'Because it's true and you have to realise that and stop blaming yourself.'

'Show me how, Sid Vicious?'

He disappears and Ah come back to ma formation and remember what Tim, our father, had said to me back in Ibiza: that Sid had saved ma life and Ah was not responsible. But Ah *feel* responsible. Guilty as charged. The Tao tells me that Ah should use guilt to guide me away from injustice, and as Ah do ma final formation, Ah practise with this intention, that each move might lead me through ma guilt and guide me away from injustice.

Ah finish up and sit cross-legged in the space, just being with what is happening now that Ah've stopped being in motion. Ah sit and, breathing in, close ma eyes. Ah feel the charge of the energy around me, still moving. The realisation hits me, as it always does in these moments of contemplation. The flow moves regardless of whether or not Ah move along with it. Ma struggle, when Ah move against it, is down to me, but if Ah just surrender and move with it, it will carry me with such ferocious momentum. The Eastern warriors knew all about surrender and the power therein. We in the West see it as a weak position and fight this ridiculous battle that we'll never win. We end up fighting ourselves, chasing our own tails like giddy dogs. Giddy! That's a great word and Ah vow to use it today as Ah go about ma business. And now, as ma mind grows giddy, Ah decide to leave the space until tomorrow.

Ah get dressed for the day and then Ah look out the window, out into Borough Market. This is most certainly one of the nicer parts of this city and not like the shit-holes Ah'd found maself in during ma earlier visits. The memory of ma brother is beside me once again.

'Imagine what it might have been like if somehow we had grown up together, Sid Vicious. That would have been sweet. Ja?'

'It wasn't always sweet here, Denzel.'

'Na. Ah'm sure not, but it would have been nice to grow up with ma brother.'

'The rain would have driven you crazy.'

'Ja!' Ma belly rumbles telling me it wants compensation for the effort it has given overnight.

'Ah'll see you later, Sid.'

'See you, Denzel.'

Ah take maself downstairs and have some breakfast, sitting at the round table that Ah've come to love. Ja, every table should be round. Ah guess King Arthur and his knights knew what they were on about. Afterwards Ah head outside for a smoke. This is the only poison Ah'm allowed these days and Ah enjoy it all the more for that. Tim finds me mid cigarette on his way out from his studio, which is the flat below the one where we live. Handy.

Ma father is a musician and a very famous composer, Ah discovered. Sid had once mentioned that in the days before Ah knew we shared a father, a father who has now offered to put me up and to whom Ah'm grateful. He's also given me a substantial injection of cash that will enable me to take the time Ah need to dry out. Ah didn't want to take his money, but he assured me that it was ma rightful compensation for all the years of ma life he had missed. That was how he put it, so formal and all. He is a strange man, Tim Harris, and getting to know him is going a long way towards explaining how Ah maself have turned out.

'Good morning, Denzel.' Tim smiles his half smile, and not for the first time Ah wonder if he ever allows his mouth to travel the whole distance across both sides of his face.

'Good morning, Tim,' Ah reply.

'You're off out somewhere?' he asks, and for the first time today Ah contemplate what Ah might do with ma day.

'Ja,' I say. 'Ah reckon Ah'll take maself into town before Ah go to ma meeting tonight.' It's Never Again day, which means it's Wednesday here in London. Wednesday had been pub night in Ibiza. Very different times.

'Right. I'll see you later,' he says and waves goodbye before disappearing through the door from which Ah'd just arrived.

'Ja, Tim. See you,' Ah say.

Later, Ah take the Tube into Leicester Square and stand underneath the billboards for a little while and take it all in. This was the first place Ah'd visited all those years ago when Ah first came in search of ma father. Ah was angry, so angry with everyone and everything. The time had not gone well and the only good memory Ah took away was the feeling of being under this billboard watching the world pass me by. Today, Ah let the world pass me by just as Ah'd done then. When Ah've drunk ma fill from the people-watching cup, Ah decide that Ah'll go see a movie. Ah've been seeing a lot of movies recently and am enjoying getting reacquainted with the cinema, a friend from a long time ago. Today Ah see the first half of the last Harry Potter film. It does the trick, and there's a nice surprise when Nick Cave and The Bad Seeds appear on the soundtrack and the whole damn song is played all the way through. A nice touch. Ah remember Nick fondly; many years of listening pleasure has this man extended ma way.

Afterwards Ah get some food before Ah hotfoot it all the way to Euston Road, to the building where Ah can be found every Wednesday night with ma fellow ex-abusers. This group has been a real eye-opener and it has made me see maself in a different light. Ah've decided that Alice or no Alice, ma life choice to be single has been the right choice. Some of these people have caused immense suffering to their nearest and dearest, and now many have to endure the recovery too. Ma oh ma, the only thing worse than being a recovering addict must be living with one, Ah imagine. Ja, Ah'll make sure Ah'm well and truly clean by the time Ah reconnect with Alice. She deserves better, for sure.

When Ah get to the building, Clive is already there. Clive is English, and although he's a fair bit younger than me, he's an old head on young shoulders. We found each other at the first meeting and formed an alliance, for we have much in common. He's as odd as two left feet, something Ah've heard others proclaim about me from time to time. Right now, he has his back to me and is listening through earphones to what I know will be the music of David Bowie, for sure. If there's a bigger David Bowie fan in this world, Ah've yet to meet them. Ah wonder if David Bowie is aware of the adulation this man holds for him. If not he should be, and his fan club should give Clive some kind of award.

Clive sees me and beckons me over. As soon as Ah'm within reaching distance he hands me one of his earphones. Ah take it and listen as David Bowie's backing singers croon 'Doo do doo do do doo; Doo do doo do do do doo' into one of ma ears while Clive sings into ma other. We sway from side to side and Ah can't help maself when Mr Bowie begins to sing. I join in with the full of my gusto. The boet on reception looks at us like he might want to tell us to shut up, but of course he doesn't. This is London where, Ah've discovered, most people communicate through facial expressions and look totally shocked by words escaping from the mouths of complete strangers.

When the song finishes, Clive reclaims his earphone and asks after ma welfare.

'Ah'm good,' Ah tell him. 'How's about you?'

'Not bad, Denzel. Still on the straight and narrow, which is an incredible stretch for the universal imagination, but there we have it. I'm looking forward to tonight, I must say,' he replies.

'Ja – Kim is speaking tonight, ja?'

Clive nods. Kim is another one of our group. Tonight he must talk about the last time he used. Each week, one of us must speak. So far, three of the six have spoken. Clive had been last week, and what he said struck a chord with me. His own reasons for stopping are similar to mine: a tragedy. For me a brother, for him a best friend. Death gives a whole new perspective to drug abuse, for sure. Although we shouldn't really be discussing other members outside of the group, Clive and Ah have decided that Kim's story will be a knock-out.

'It's always the quiet ones,' Clive said and Ah knew exactly what he meant. Ah guess we would both find out tonight, for sure.

'When are you up?' Clive asks.

'Next week,' Ah reply.

He nods his head.

Billy joins us without a word. Billy is the youngest in our group and one of only two women in our motley crew. She is another quiet one, and Ah reckon there's a story there too. Billy reminds me a lot of Holly, a girl Ah knew in Ibiza – the same tiny features and short black hair. Ah think about Holly and feel sad. She had just hooked up with Sid before he died. Big love and then it's all over. Poor Holly, left behind. Ah wonder how she's getting along and make a promise to maself to contact her. It might be time for me to see how she is and whether she needs anything from me. Ah'm responsible.

Next comes Iain, the oldest in the group. Iain is Scottish and looks about seventy, but he swears he's forty-five. Iain's aged look is another incentive to keep us all on the straight and narrow. He's been battling addiction for thirty years. His was the first story we heard and it left us all cold. This is his final attempt to get clean, he says, because if he goes back again that will be it. He didn't sound all that confident and tonight he looks about as disillusioned as it's possible to look. The idea is that we all succeed together – if one fails we all fail, the exact opposite to divide and conquer Ah suppose.

'Hello,' he says.

'Hi Iain,' we all say in unison, and as if our salutation has in some way forced the situation, the door of the room that will hold us for the next few hours flies open.

'Hello Wednesday night,' says Gloria, our group leader, a big smile upon her face. This woman is one of the happiest Ah've ever encountered – real happiness, not that put-on kind of happiness that a lot of people try to palm you off with. Ah genuinely like Gloria. She shared her story with us on our first night. She was as bad as any of the rest of us and has been sober for forty years. It gives me hope. It also suggests that she might be approaching a time of life that means she is looking spectacularly good and carrying the age baton with true grace. She makes us a lot of promises, but Ah trust her and believe her – as she says, she's the living proof that this whole thing works.

We all move indoors and sit down. We sit in silence, waiting for the final two members to arrive. They do eventually, one at a time. First comes Sharon, the other girl in our group. She's a lot more talkative than Billy, sometimes a bit too talkative, but Ah guess it balances out the lack on Billy's part. And lastly, Kim who Ah've mentioned already. What Ah didn't say before is that Clive dislikes him vehemently and Ah'm not really sure why. Personally, Ah've no opinion of him. The boet has never done anything to me. Live and let live, a new motto for a new sober Denzel Anderson.

'Good evening folks. Now that we're all here shall we begin?'

Each week Gloria says this and each week she makes it sound like a real question, as if she might actually refrain from starting if one of us said No. As usual we all nod, and she launches into what is in store for us this evening.

First things first, a little 'share' by everyone in the group. How are we all doing today? Mine is short and sweet in which Ah basically say that despite the obvious – the obvious being that Ah'm attempting to live ma life without the assistance of a substance on which Ah had come to depend – Ah'm fine and dandy. And mostly everyone swears to be okay, or at least that's what they're saying – everyone except for Kim, who's going through a bad time. This makes me even more eager to hear his story. Ah think Gloria is too because today she breaks protocol and tells him that if he'd like to launch into his story now he should feel free. And so he does.

Ah sit and wait with the others and catch Clive's eye, which seems to say, *just wait for this boet.*

'The last time I used was tree months, tree days and four hours ago.'

Kim wipes his brow as if he's sweating, even though he isn't. This is a habit of his, Ah've noticed. Kim is from Jamaica, or at least his parents are – he was brought up here – and he reminds me of Bob Marley. He's a lot blacker, for sure, but he has the same features and the locks. He's a very cool-looking man and looks like Ah'd like to look if Ah'd been born Jamaican. Not for the first time Ah wonder if he can sing. He has a lovely speaking voice, but Ah've discovered that doesn't always lend itself to a good singing voice, for sure.

'I was not alone,' he continues. 'Although I've used alone, dis time I was with Carrie, my wife's sister.' This is the first time Kim has mentioned his wife. 'Actually my ex-wife's sister, to be precise. We did a few lines and we had sex. Jus' the way I like it with her. Have liked it with her since we first began. Carrie is married to my friend Lincoln and I started sleeping with her even before I met my wife, her sister. We've always had dis ting and neither of us could help it, you know. When she left that first day I told myself I would never do it again. Never. Never Again.' He flashes a smile that goes a long way to explaining how he could come to be sleeping with the two sisters. 'And den I found my way to dis meeting. It's been hard to not use but it has been harder to not see Carrie. I don't love her, dat's the crazy thing. I love Annie, my wife, but she's straight – don't even drink. And de funny ting is dat Annie left me because of the drugs. She's no idea about Carrie an' me. If she had, she'd kick both our asses.' He smiles again but it falls quickly from his face. 'She said she'll have me back if I clean up my act. And Carrie is still using and still hounding me. It's as if she is coke personified, encouraging me to come back for one last time. And all the time I'm getting the full support of Lincoln. He keeps telling me I'm great, dat it will all work out with Annie and me. And I been sleeping with his wife since before he married her. Even gave her her first line. Lincoln has no idea – he's never done a line in his life. He's a good person and yet he's picked up people like me. And Carrie. I guess like dey say, bad things often happen to good people. But I want to be different. Dat is why I'm here. To be different and to get Annie back.'

Kim stops talking and everyone stays silent. Ah'm thinking, *what an asshole*. Ah'm no prince, but this story makes me think Ah'm one of the good eggs because Ah couldn't imagine in a hundred years doing what this boet has done. But like Gloria says, we're not here to judge. It's very tempting in this situation however. So much for live and let live!

'Thank you, Kim,' Gloria says. 'I know that was very hard to say and I admire your honesty. Anyone who has ever taken drugs has done things that they're ashamed of and would like to pretend never happened, but it's by facing up to these things that we can move on. More than anything you need to move on. What you've done is in the past. Here at Never Again we are concerned only about now. Today. The only place we can be different.'

Kim nods his head. Good on Gloria, saying all the things he'll have wanted to hear. Ah'm thinking, *poor Lincoln and Annie for having such bad taste in people*. There's a part of me that would like nothing more than to take ma arse out of this room and find both of them and tell them what's what. They deserve to know. Kim looks my way and Ah smile, but inside Ah'm thinking, *asshole*, but also that Ah'd still like to look like him if Ah were Jamaican.

The meeting ends and Ah make ma way to the Costa Coffee around the corner where Clive and Ah'll go through the events of the meeting. This has become our ritual. Ah'm surprised that we don't ever see any of the others perched in here doing the very same thing. Tonight Clive is sitting waiting outside, cigarette in hand and two cappuccinos lined up.

'Thanks Clive!' I say, joining him.

He nods. I roll a cigarette.

'I told you Kim's story would be good,' he says. 'Fancy that, shagging his best friend's girlfriend and then marrying her sister. It's like an episode of Eastenders.'

Ah can only guess that Eastenders is an English soap.

'Ah know Gloria says not to judge, but Ah have to say it was hard tonight. Ah hate hearing things like that. Ah mean, your best friend's missus.'

'Yeah, I know,' Clive says. 'It makes me feel like Tracy hasn't had it so bad with me.'

Tracy is Clive's girlfriend. In his story he's revealed all the times he's let her down in the past thanks to his love of charlie. And all the times she's forgiven him. Clive is on his last chance with Tracy and all credit to him, he's determined to succeed. He said it helps to think about her at the times when he feels his own sorry ass isn't worth the effort of abstinence. Ah know what he means. Perhaps ma decision to contact Alice can help me during the times where Ah could so easily write maself off.

'So you all set for next week,' he asks me.

'Next week?'

'Your story.'

'Ja,' Ah say, 'Ah think so.'

'It's really therapeutic,' Clive says, 'just talking. Ah bet even Kim feels better. I never liked him, you know.'

'Ja, Ah caught that vibe.'

'So what are you up to this week?' Clive asks.

'Ah've no idea,' Ah tell him.

'That's always a good thing in my book,' Clive says and launches into a recital of his pre-Christmas plans with Tracy.

As he talks about Tracy, Ah begin thinking about Alice and what she might be doing before Christmas. Ah'd gone looking through her Facebook profile but there wasn't a whole lot there. For the life of me Ah hope she's single and not hitched. Now that would be a catastrophe. As Clive tells me that he'll take Tracy and Ben, his four-year-old son, out shopping this weekend, the first time in Ben's life that they'll do this as a family, Ah think about telling him about Alice, but Ah decide against it. Somehow it feels like Ah should keep Alice all to maself, at least until she's back in ma life where Ah hope she will belong. Ah let the early-stage idea incubate in ma imagination in the hope that it'll develop its own arms and legs and become a real live notion in ma near future.

*

'Not much time left, Alice,' Kate says and looks at me expectantly.

I wonder for a moment what my work colleague and friend is talking about, and then I realise it's the wedding. Of course! That's all she talks about these days.

Kate lives in Muswell Hill too, and is married to Frank, who coincidentally is Robert's oldest friend. They are both local Muswell Hill boys and actually went to the school where Kate and I teach. Due to the major overlaps in our lives Kate and I have become friends, although she isn't really a person I would have gravitated towards naturally. She likes to talk about Frank's money a lot in a way that I find quite vulgar. Yes, it's true that Robert earns over four times what I do, a figure that's constantly growing while my salary remains minuscule by comparison. I'm grateful for his wealth, but I prefer not to talk about it. When I mentioned Kate's obsession with money to Robert, he said he thought it might be because they are having problems getting pregnant. He might be right, especially as Kate has never mentioned her fertility issues to me. She tends to tell me about what's good in her life while omitting the bad. If she can't have children I feel truly sorry for her.

Robert and I plan to have children. We're both agreed on that. I want babies – I've always wanted babies – and as I think about the children in our future I think about the lost child of my past. I go there only fleetingly.

'Are you listening, Ali?'

'No – I mean yes. There's not much time left. I'm sending out the invites tonight.'

'And we are dress shopping tomorrow, yes?'

I nod my head.

'I can't believe how laid back you're being about your dress,' Kate says.

'It's only a dress.'

'It's your *wedding* dress! Sometimes you're a mystery to me!'

I shrug my shoulders. Kate looks up at the staffroom clock.

'Time to go to the little people,' she says and knocks back the remainder of her coffee.

'Yep, the little people,' I reply and follow her lead.

I make my way to the room that will soon fill up with four-year-olds. I love this job and have done since the beginning. Back then I shared a house with Jo and the commute had been a bit of a nightmare, but now that I live just a short walk away it's easy. It was because of this job that I was in Robert Shaw's local pub the night we met. The rest is history and now the Famous Royal Oak has become 'our' local pub.

I teach the toddlers here. I could easily work my whole career with this age group. I feel privileged to get to spend time with so many little ones every day. The children in my class are mostly from good financial backgrounds, unlike at my last school where the problems of poverty and neglect weighed heavily on them, and eventually on me. Too heavily. So I escaped to the middle classes where the problems felt more surmountable. I believe that these early school experiences have a profound effect on children for the rest of their lives – that is how important my job is – and I remember this as I go through my days, especially when I'm in danger of getting lost in the routine. I want to give each and every one of them the best start I can. I want to make a difference. Today the children are filled with Christmas cheer as they count down the days to Santa's visit, and in the interim, I mostly fill their little lives with nativity play rehearsals, my favourite thing in the entire school year.

'Miss Cooper?'

The voice belongs to Ben, the smallest boy in my class and the youngest. Although I don't openly do favourites, I have to confess that he's my favourite. But I'm careful and keep it hidden, for I know the damage this could do if it were to become evident. I've met his mother Tracy, a single mum whose parents supported her and helped her to raise Ben, like my own could have done if they'd wanted to. Ben is the proof that it can work.

'Yes, Ben,' I say and crouch down until I'm at eye level with this tiny boy.

'Can we wear our costumes now?' he asks, his eyes growing huge in his head.

'No Ben, not now. But later on, when we rehearse. Okay?'

'Yes, Miss Cooper,' he says and smiles, and at that moment I'm putty in his hands and could so easily change my mind were he to ask again.

We do our morning lesson and I work through my lunch to finalise the set for the nativity play. This will allow the children to have more rehearsal time, but it also means I can avoid Kate. I don't feel like talking about the wedding again. After lunch we rehearse and it's heaven watching the children give it everything they have. They deliver their lines with the whole of their hearts, and as I watch, I wonder how it is that we all start out like this yet lose it so completely. Here in this room I connect with their innocence and in so doing, I remember my own. It swells inside me, recognising a place where it can safely emerge without fear of exploitation. Most definitely there isn't a better job than this.

The day ends and I walk the short distance home. Christmas is alive and well in Muswell Hill. I love this time of year more than any other. What's not to love! Lights, Christmas songs, happy people filled with festive spirit. I pass woman after woman pushing expensive prams and hurrying their older offspring home. I imagine the me of the future with Robert's children. This thought gives birth to the me of my past, and again my little boy comes into my head. I named him Denzel, after his father, even though his father had long gone. How different my life could have been if only his father had stayed – or if only I'd listened to him and we'd run away. If only, if only … but there's no point in thinking like that now. I'm too lost in my past these days. If I'd known that agreeing to marry Robert would have resurrected all these emotions I might not have so readily accepted his ring.

I've never told Robert about that part of my life and I never will, because I know exactly how he would react. My past would not sit nicely with his present-day expectations. Although there's much about Robert Shaw I don't profess to know, let alone understand, of this I'm completely sure: if he knew that I'd fallen pregnant as a teenage girl, his opinion of me would shrink to nothing. As would his mother's. Helen's view would be much the same as Sheila Cooper's had been: my 'mess up', as my mother called it at the time. Then we never spoke about it again. Any of it. It was as if it had never happened. But it had happened, and I'd never forgotten.

At home, I eat alone, and just when I'm finishing up, Robert calls. Another late night, as usual at this busy time of year, and so I take advantage of the time alone. I pamper myself by taking a long, hot bath. I watch as the water washes over my body, this body that I've lived in for thirty-two years. Much about it has changed, but underneath I'm still that girl who wanted nothing more than to fall in love and for it to last forever. That might sound incredibly last century and I'd never in a hundred years admit it out loud, but that was what I'd wanted more than anything, what I'd hoped for – that I would fall in love and that that love would carry me through my life. And I had found it; I'd fallen in love, but it had abandoned me. Disappeared. And afterwards, there would never be love again – not like that. I suppose I hadn't looked all that hard really. Love like that would only have meant more pain.

In a few short months, I'll turn thirty-three, Denzel following me three days later. I remember his birthday every year. I wonder does he still remember mine. Probably not. I'm a sentimental fool. Denzel's life has moved on, I bet. 'But where are you? How are you?' I say into the rising steam as I turn on the hot tap once again. I'd heard a rumour that he had left South Africa and I wondered if he went to find his biological father, the father who had abandoned his pregnant mother (just like he had done to me). He had wanted us to run away and I'd talked him out of it. But I never thought my parents would react the way they did. Or that he would leave – without me. If he had come back for me I would have gone with him – of course I would have! – but he didn't. What does any of it matter now anyway. It's just fantasy; reality has played out differently. The life in which I find myself now is as far away from my teenaged life as it's possible to get. What a fool I'd been really!

But still I wonder – I can't help myself. Does he think of me? I close my eyes as the heat in the bathroom draws me more deeply into my fantasy. Would I want him to think of me? Yes I would. I'd want him to remember, just as I do, and to still feel the significance of those years. Then it would mean that those feelings were real. And although we hadn't made it together, we had both experienced a love that most people only dream about – true love. Wouldn't that be something? Wouldn't that mean everything? And would I like to see Denzel again? The thought alone terrifies me, but yes I would. To feel those feelings again. Just once. Yes.

I don't love Robert in that way. I never will. But he is safe and he is sound, and my future will be secure and steady with him.

But to have those feelings again …

'You're still with me, like a bad penny, asshole,' I say out loud, letting the South African in me escape. I imagine him smiling now. He would like that: Bad. Penny. Asshole. We used to say that we were one and the same, that we belonged together, that no one else had the measure of us like we had the measure of each other. I remember telling him once that it was our destiny to be together, and he had warned me that he was way too shallow for deep sea diving. I had remembered his words and wrote them down, as I recorded much of what he said, constantly mesmerised with his way of verbalising how he saw the world. Soulmates, that's what we were, a word he dismissed as too simple for a concept so complex. As I lie here alone I remember his smile that made me melt, and the gap between his two front teeth that had been handed down to him by Wendy Anderson, his mother, a woman with the most beautiful smile, despite everything.

The front door opens, snapping me out of my daydream. Robert is home. I've spent a lot longer in my tub than usual. He comes into the bathroom and takes a long look at me.

'Can I join you?' he asks.

'Sure,' I say and pull my knees up to my chest to make room for him.

I watch as he removes his clothes. He's a handsome man with a beautiful body, which he's sculpted to perfection at the gym. It should be easy to love a man like this. I wait for that feeling to come, that joy you feel when the one you love is close by. But it's not there; it never will be. Regardless of what might be best for me, the truth is: the person I really love is not in this room.

3

Social Plans And Wedding Dresses

Turnmills is dead! Ah'm flabbergasted! It was the nightclub where Ah'd spent much of my London time on past visits, the place where Ah'd stumbled upon ma Ibiza idea and which had taken me to the island that might have saved me. Ah'd just told Clive that Ah'd plans to revisit it once ma self-imposed purgatory was done when he'd given me the bad news.

'When? Why?' Ah ask.

'A few years back. And yes, I know it's a shame. But such things happen. Like when Bowie ended Ziggy Stardust. Just like that! It was all over.'

'So is there another alternative? What are the other clubs like?'

'I'm not sure, mate. I'm not really a clubber any more, even before Never Again. Anyway, it's probably best you steer clear of those places while you're sober. Really, don't you think?'

'Ah don't know, boet. Maybe. Ah miss the music though – the buzz. Ah see that Chemical Brothers are playing Brixton Academy soon. Ah think Ah might venture to see them.'

'You're serious! Won't Gloria love that! You're on the road to sobriety and you see a band called Chemical Brothers!'

'Would you fancy it?'

Clive shakes his head. 'No! Best I stay away. I don't want to put extra temptation in my way. Are you sure it's a good idea for you?'

'Ja! It'll not be a problem,' Ah tell him and Ah think Ah'm sincere but then Clive looks at me as if Ah might be in denial. Maybe this is the opportunity Ah need to score and get high and Ah don't even know it maself. But Ah don't think so.

'Honest!' Ah say to reaffirm my answer.

'Honest is a dirty word when it comes from the mouth of a junkie!'

The word 'junkie' echoes through my brain. It's a word Ah've only ever used to refer to other people – Ah've never viewed maself as a junkie. But perhaps that's denial itself, alive and kicking in the heart of me. Ah'm sure other people have thought of me in those terms. Tim had been the one to suggest Ah join this group of ex-junkies so maybe Ah was more of a junkie than Ah like to believe. And although it's feeling particularly easy for me to stay clean, not like those desperate early days, maybe Ah'm getting complacent way too quickly. Na. Ah'll go to the concert, for sure. Ah know ma own limits.

'So how's it all going at home,' Ah ask Clive, wanting to move the conversation away from maself.

'Like a charm. I took Tracy and Ben out Christmas shopping. She's a great girl, and Ben – I can't believe Ben sometimes. Given everything … I think I'll buy her a ring for Christmas and make it official. Finally. She'd love for us to be a family. She doesn't say it and she's still frosty, but I guess she still isn't sure that this time I mean to stay straight. It could just be the same old Clive making the same old promises, the ones she trusted lots of times before. As I watched Tracy and Ben take a trip to Santa's grotto in Brent Cross I realised that this was what I wanted, and no amount of charlie is worth losing that for. Victor dying was such a blow to me and it put everything into perspective. You know, we'd been friends for forever.

We grew up together. We did everything together – even started using together – and him signing out, well it was a sign of what's to come. Victor had a girlfriend – Mandy – and a kid, a little girl. Things broke down between Mandy and him shortly after the kid was born and he missed a lot of her growing up. She was born within a month of Ben. Yep, Victor and me really did do everything together. But the one thing I don't want to do is to end up like him. I've a lot of life to live.'

Ah smile at ma friend and raise ma coffee cup by way of a toast.

'Is there someone in your life, Denzel? You've never mentioned anyone so I assumed not, mate. But maybe there is.'

Ah think about mentioning Alice now, but decide against it again. Ah'll keep her close to ma chest, like a set of poker cards, for fear that Ah'll produce a losing hand when Ah eventually lay ma cards on the table.

'Na,' Ah say. 'Ah've done the female race a big favour over the past decade and left them to it. Ma life's been a single one for the most part.'

'But you have sex, don't you mate?'

'Ja, of course! But Ah pay for it.'

'O-kay … I want to say that's very noble of you but it sounds a bit fucked up.'

This makes me smile. 'Ah've never paid anyone, but I've been with some women that really should have been charging.'

He winks at me. 'It's probably just as well you're not with anyone. Although I have to say, if there wasn't Tracy I think I'd be finding this sobriety thing a lot harder. But I suppose we're all different and that's what makes the world go round. Listen mate, I'll love you and leave you –

I've got plans with Tracy at early o'clock tomorrow – but I'll see you next Wednesday?'

'You will indeed!'

'And I'll hear your tale.'

'You will.'

'And call me if it's all too much with them chemical boys. Yeah?'

'Ja. Thanks Clive.'

He leaves me and Ah watch as he walks out of the café. In another setting Clive and Ah would be raising hell together, Ah've no doubt about that, and Ah can sense that he's as much of a head-the-ball as Ah am … was. Our addictions are deep and have the potential to kill us both dead. This Ah know for sure, as does ma new friend. Sid Vicious didn't have this streak. It wasn't in his make-up even though we were cut from the same cloth, him and me. But somehow the addictive gene was mine and mine alone, brought in from somewhere – ma mother's side most probably, although Ah might ask Tim that very question in the near future, when we eventually have a heart-to-heart. Somehow right now we skirt around the side lines of most things. Ah wonder if that's because of the people we are, or is it just how it goes in the early stages of father–son relations. Ah guess time will tell.

When Ah get back to Borough, Tim is sitting at the kitchen table waiting for me. He looks about as serious as Ah've ever seen him look and Ah ask him if everything's okay.

'Take a seat,' he says, so Ah pick a place at the round table and wait for him to begin. Maybe a heart-to-heart is coming. Be careful what you wish for.

'We're going to have a house guest over Christmas,' he says.

'Sure, Tim. Do you need me on the sofa?'

'No. There's loads of space here. His name is Bill.'

Ah wonder if this is another brother about to be revealed to me. 'Okay!' Ah say and wait for him to fill in the gaps, but he doesn't.

'Great! Is there anyone you want to invite for Christmas – from your group maybe?'

Ah think about Clive and his plans with Tracy and tell him na, but thank him for the thought.

'So we'll be three,' he says.

'Right!'

'Right!'

Ma father leaves me there in the kitchen and makes his way back to the studio, and Ah wonder who this Bill is. Ja, Tim Harris is an odd man, for sure, and that's saying something coming from me, given ma terms of reference!

*

'We're all so looking forward to the wedding, Alice. I can't tell you how much your father is talking about it.'

I listen as Sheila Cooper gushes at the end of the phone.

'So have you found the dress yet?' she asks.

My parents had offered to pay for the whole wedding but Robert had refused. Then, after much debate, he'd allowed them to fund the dress, and so a hefty amount of money had been sent to my account to cover the cost. Their contribution was a small price to pay to get their fuck-up of a daughter hitched, the one who had nearly ruined the good Cooper name.

'Not yet,' I reply, not wanting to tell her that I'm going later today.

'You're leaving it a bit late, aren't you?'

'Do you ever hear anything about the Andersons?' I ask, wanting to change the subject and at the same time rattle her cage.

The name plops down in the distance between us.

'No, of course not. Why do you ask? That boy is disappeared, do you hear me. You haven't told Robert. Please tell me he doesn't know!'

'Relax, Sheila. I haven't told him.'

'Why do you upset me? Always. You can't help yourself, can you?' My mother's so good at playing the injured party. 'Just forget it. Ja!'

Sheila Cooper begins talking again as if the last exchange had never happened. My mother has an amazing ability to do this – to move on as if pieces of a conversation have erased themselves. It drove me crazy when I was growing up.

'So we'll come the week before the wedding and we can stay at a nearby hotel? Can you look after that, Alice? Ja?'

And there she goes again, Sheila Cooper at her finest. This is my cue to say 'no, of course not. You'll stay with us.' And just like that it's decided. My parents will travel over with my two brothers, they will all stay here in Muswell Hill the week before the wedding and then they will stay on and have an extended holiday while we enjoy our honeymoon. On the positive side, I suppose the house won't be left unmanned while we're away. In any case, Robert would never let them stay in a hotel. He's slightly deluded when it comes to family. The telephone conversation with my mother ends on the superficial note it had started on: 'Behave yourself. Your father sends his love.'

I find Robert in the front room watching television. He works hard and weekends are when he allows himself serious time off. One of his rules is that he will happily work crazy hours during the week but weekends are his own. Sometimes he brings work home with him at the busy times, like now, and I suspect that his work laptop will come out at some stage over the next couple of days, but he's never spent a Saturday or Sunday in the office like a lot of his fellow partners do.

'That was Sheila Cooper,' I say.

'Why do you always call her that?' he asks.

'Because it's her name,' I reply and smile.

'You know what I mean.'

I shrug my shoulders.

'Are they all booked in?' he asks, turning down the volume on the TV.

I nod and sit beside him on the sofa. 'So, my whole family are coming.'

'Great!'

'My mother offered to stay in a hotel,' I begin.

'No, no – they'll stay here. We have the space.'

'Ja, I said that.'

'Good!'

'Thanks,' I say.

'Don't be silly. Of course your family will stay here. I think it's pretty decent of your parents to allow their only daughter to get married here in London and not insist that we all fly over there.'

The idea had been briefly mentioned when our engagement was announced, but I'd made it clear then that I would not be travelling back to my homeland to get married and Sheila had backed down rather quickly. Her awkward daughter was getting married at last and she didn't want to upset the apple cart. Sheila Cooper knew how capable I was of messing everything up. And now I'd mentioned the Andersons, just to make her a little more anxious. I couldn't help it. I got extreme pleasure from making her remember a time she would rather forget.

'What are you up to today?' Robert asks me. He catches hold of a stray lock of my hair and moves it back behind my ear, wanting to fix me up so that I'm perfect. I remember someone else stroking my hair. The memory flickers but doesn't linger.

'I'm meeting Kate,' I say.

'Of course – wedding dress shopping!'

'Yep.'

Robert kisses my forehead and I leave him to it, watching the day's football, his favourite Saturday viewing.

An hour later, I'm walking down the King's Road with Kate on our way to find my wedding dress.

'I've already seen my bridesmaid dress,' she says and winks.

'Oh you have, have you?' I say and roll my eyes. 'What colour is it?' I ask, as if the roles were reversed and it's Kate's wedding we are shopping for.

'Purple, of course. My best colour.'

We get to the shop she's talking about, exactly the type that Kate likes to frequent – pretentious and expensive. If it were up to me I'd go to a local charity shop and buy a recycled dress, but this wouldn't go down well with my friend, not to mention Robert or my mother. I've got very good at pleasing the people around me. Imagine that, Denzel Anderson, your Alice, who never pleased anyone but herself – or you, even though she would never have admitted it.

'My God! This is it!' Kate says as she grabs hold of a dress only five minutes after we get inside the door. She holds it out so that I can see it fully. 'This is your dress, Ali.'

I look at the bundle of white material she's clutching and feel nothing. 'It looks good,' I say.

'And I bet it's your size,' Kate says. 'It's just meant to be.'

'Ah, a good choice,' chimes a shop assistant who appears out of nowhere.

'Can she try it?' Kate asks.

'Of course,' replies the shop assistant and we are ushered into the fitting room.

The two women chat away like long lost friends as I try on the dress, hidden behind a pristine curtain. The material feels really beautiful and finds every curve of my body, as if it had been made to measure. There's no price tag, which means that it's uber expensive, but money is no issue, of course. I pull back the curtain and both women begin to gush. Kate has found an ally in the overly friendly shop assistant. Things would have been very different if Jo had come with me instead of Kate. But Jo would never have come dress shopping with me, today or any other day, no more than she would have ever agreed to be my bridesmaid. I hadn't even asked.

'Stunning!' the shop assistant says.

Kate begins to cry. 'You look beautiful, Ali! Really beautiful!' she eventually says.

'I'm getting married!' I say, stating the obvious as I catch my reflection in the mirror. And there she stands, looking back at me out of the glass, the woman I'd once vowed I would never become.

4
Past Tenses

Tonight is ma night. Ah sit and wait for Gloria to call upon me to speak and the events that are happening in the rest of ma life fall away. Ma main attention is on what Ah'll say. Ah hate speaking in public like this and do ma best to avoid it, but Ah guess avoidance isn't an option here. Last night, Ah attempted to write out what Ah'd say, but it had sounded forced and elaborated upon, so Ah decided that Ah'd do ma own speaking in the moment. Ah would tell the truth then, for sure. The truth never needs no forward planning.

'So Denzel, when you're ready!'

Gloria smiles and ma heart beats so hard in ma chest that it feels as if it'll obstruct ma ability to speak further up my throat. Ah take a long drink of water from ma glass to pace maself.

'Ja!' Ah say eventually. 'Ah'm really nervous tonight.'

'It's never easy for any of us,' Gloria assures me and smiles.

Ah raise my eyebrows by way of a thank you and somehow, in spite of ma anxiety, Ah begin to speak, letting the words tumble out of ma mouth.

'Last August, a good friend of mine died. He died in ma arms after he was stabbed by someone Ah knew because of ma connection to narcotics. My friend was called Sid and Ah liked to call him Sid Vicious, but there was nothing vicious about him. Na. He himself wasn't a drug user. That, Ah suppose, is irony. What Ah didn't know at the time was that this friend that Ah'd randomly stumbled upon was ma half-brother. Sid and me, we shared the same father. The crazy thing is, neither of us knew about the existence of the other, yet somehow we met in Ibiza. We found each other by pure chance, some would say. But me, Ah think we were meant to come together, as sure as we were meant to be born.

'Anyways, Sid Vicious had fallen in love only a few short moments before he was killed, and it was the real deal – that kind of love that everyone searches for – you know, the kind where everything before and after pales into insignificance and you know this is the one you've been waiting for, for sure. His girl was called Holly and Ah had the job of telling her that this boy, who had just appeared in her life, had disappeared again – been taken from her. Ah saw Holly and it was a desperate state of affairs. She didn't want any details and she had only one request – "Let's get off our heads" – that's what she said, and given that Ah'd caused this awful thing that would change her life forever, Ah did just that. She had a stash of charlie. The crazy thing is that Ah didn't realise that Holly used but she must have, given the amount that was there. Ah think maybe she had stopped and she was saving it just in case she needed it, just in case there came a time such as we found ourselves in at that moment. So we got off our heads and we danced like two crazy people, and then she grabbed a hold of me and we stayed like that, locked together and moving like one body, holding each other up. Eventually we collapsed onto her sofa bed and we slept, wrapped around each other, neither wanting to be alone to feel the loss we knew we would surely feel.

'Ah woke the next morning and left her. Ah left her looking as sad and sorry as Ah've ever seen anyone look and Ah made ma way back to ma hostel room. Ah was leaving Ibiza. Ah'd had enough. But back in the hostel, the place where Ah'd brought ma friend – ma brother – to stay, Ah met ma father. He'd come to Ibiza to gather up his youngest son's belongings and bring him back to London in a wooden box. That's when Ah realised that ma friend Sid Vicious was also ma little brother. Ah'd met ma father once before but it hadn't gone well. He hadn't told me anything about his family, about Sid – and Sid hadn't mentioned him by name, nor had Ah, or we would have known. Sid died saving me, so Ah decided that somehow out of this awful mess maybe something good could happen. Maybe life was giving me another chance, saying Denzel, you can turn it all around if you really want to. So Ah took maself back to the stretch of beach where Ah'd lost ma brother and Ah made a promise that Ah would not use again. For sure. So Ah came back to London with ma father. He was the one recommended Ah come here, and Ah did and Ah've been clean for the longest time ever in ma sorry life.'

When Ah finish Gloria lets ma words fall into the silence. Eventually she thanks me and salutes ma bravery. We don't discuss what Ah've just said. There's no need; we tell our stories to get them out, that's all – and because it helps, so Gloria says, and Ah'm really beginning to believe it does. Ah look across at Clive and he smiles at me. Ah'd told him a little of ma story but now he knows it all.

We finish up the meeting and Ah head to Costa. This time Ah'm first there, so Ah get the coffees and sit outside waiting for Clive.

'Nice one, mate,' he says as he sits opposite me. 'Can we talk about your share?'

It's required that you ask the person's permission before you talk about anything that has been shared; then they have the option to say na. But Ah want to talk, so Ah nod ma head.

'Ah don't know if Ah would fully believe it if it hadn't happened to me. But it did.'

'And you had no idea he was your brother?'

'Na.'

'I know what you mean about things happening for a reason. It's all mapped out in front of us.'

Ah nod ma head.

'So we were meant to be two drug fuck-ups,' Clive says. 'If we hadn't, the world would have stopped turning on its axis.'

Ah laugh.

'And now it's time for us to stop and stay stopped,' Clive adds.

'For sure!' Ah reply and we bang our coffee cups together by way of a liquor-free toast.

*

'So you have the dress!' Jo exclaims sarcastically.

I nod and smile at my oldest friend, Jo Mitchel, who I met when we were children. We had shared all the significant parts of growing up together. It was thanks to an invitation from Jo that I finally escaped from Sea Point and came here to London. She knows me really well. There's only one other person that knows me better.

'Ah guess you're really doing this,' she says.

'Ja. In a few months I'll be a married woman.'

'And I'll still be single.'

Jo has quite possibly the worst luck in the world when it comes to men. She seems to attract losers and has slowly resigned herself to the fact that she's better off alone.

'You don't know that,' I tell her, trying to beam some optimism her way.

'Oh but I do. But not to worry – there are worse fates that could befall a girl. So, I've bought you a special Christmas present – tickets for a gig. It'll quite possibly be our last outing together with you as my single friend.'

'Great! Tell me who, when and where.'

'Alice Cooper, we are going to see the wonderful Chemical Brothers on December thirteenth.'

'Brilliant! That's amazing. In Brixton Academy, ja?'

Jo nods her head and smiles.

'Thank you. Thank you. Thank. You.' I hug her.

'It's my absolute pleasure. Robert will be cool about it, ja?'

'Of course! I see nothing of him in December anyway. It's the busiest time of year for him.'

'Great, it's settled then!' Jo goes quiet for a moment, then says, 'You'll never guess who tracked me down.'

'Who?'

'Jaspar Downey.'

'No way! He's here?'

'No. He's in Manhattan, but he found me on Facebook. You see, my friend, this is the beauty of Facebook, like I told you when I finally got you to join. Is Robert still complaining about it?'

I nod my head. Robert is even more anti-Facebook than I am, but unlike me, he won't be swayed.

'How is Jaspar?' I ask.

'He's good. He was asking for you. And you'll never guess who he bumped into last summer?'

I somehow know what's coming next but still I ask: 'Who?'

'Denzel Anderson.'

'He's in Manhattan?' I ask, trying to sound disinterested.

'God no! He was in Ibiza. Jaspar said he was in a right state and working in some club called Amnesia. Jaspar spent one night with him there, which all but wiped him out. Apparently Denzel told him that he'd found *his* island and he was on a mission to make sure he died there in the not-so-distant future. Nice, ja? Ah guess things worked out for him just about as well as we predicted they would.'

'I'm sorry to hear that about Denzel,' I say.

'What do you mean! It's poetic justice,' Jo replies. She'd been the friend I'd needed so desperately back then when he'd left. 'He did you a favour, Alice. Seriously, if you'd got lumbered with that loser you'd be in an awful way.' Jo smiles and waits for me to agree but I don't.

'So what's Jaspar doing in Manhattan?' I say.

'He's working for a bank, but he's thinking of coming over here for a bit. That's why he contacted me. He said he sent you a friend request as well but heard nothing back.'

'I don't go in to my account that often.'

'Jesus Alice, why not! That defeats the whole purpose of being there.'

'Email keeps me busy enough.'

'Yeah, but Facebook is great. You get to see how everyone is doing without having to enquire.'

'It's lazy friendship.'

'It's modern friendship. God, you're like an old, old person sometimes! Just like Robert.' She grimaces, probably sorry that the comment about Robert has slipped out; Jo mostly keeps her thoughts about him to herself.

'So we're heading to Brixton Academy on the thirteenth,' she says turning the conversation back to a better place.

'Yes,' I say. 'And thanks again.'

I get the feeling she might be regretting having brought up Denzel after a lifetime of not mentioning him. She'd been surprised when Denzel left, maybe even more surprised than me. We both thought he would never in a million years run out on me, but we were just kids, believing that my match with Denzel was something special – the kind of relationship that every teenage girl dreamed of. But then it had all gone horribly wrong and I'd become just another statistic – a pregnant teenager – and Jo had gone through the nightmare with me.

'So what do we do now, Cooper?' Jo asks.

'I'm not sure. You want another drink?'

'I wouldn't say no, if you can stay on for another bit.'

'Why not! I fancy one for the road.'

I get the drinks in and we tuck into our third and final glass of wine for the night. Then I say goodbye to my friend and make my way home. It's late when I get back, but Robert is still not there. This is later than usual, even in December, and it isn't like Robert not to have let me know what he's doing. But of course he has! I read the text message I missed earlier – he'll be very late as they've run into problems.

I think over the conversation with Jo and decide to log in to Facebook to find Jaspar. His friend request sits patiently amongst my notifications. I accept it and head straight to his profile. His picture looks familiar, and I instantly remember the boy I'd known in Cape Town. I send him a short message and am just about to log out when, before I realise what I'm doing, I begin typing in the search bar. I press enter. The search begins and I feel a charge of energy that makes me wonder if we're already connected somehow. Perhaps the connection has been there all along, in spite of everything. The screen fills up with Denzel Andersons – who knew there was more than one? I scroll all the way to the end. The last entry is the only one that has no picture and I know it's him. I just know it. The Denzel Anderson that had once meant the world to me – maybe still does, if I'm honest – is on Facebook. Losing him had almost killed me before. Can I bear to venture back there? I click the account and discover it's even more sparse than my own. Yes, this is you, and if I want to, I can connect with you right now. Just the thought of that makes me shiver.

I sit for the longest time, the cursor resting on the request button, and then I feel tremendous guilt. What am I doing! I think about Robert Shaw, my present and soon-to-be future, and yet here I am, hovering over my past and considering unearthing something that had once almost destroyed me. I quickly log off and put a safe distance between us once again. However, I'm left with a feeling that I might just have sent a subliminal message across some other less visible network.

5

The Gate Opens

'I would have thought you'd have left by now,' Sid Vicious says to me as Ah sit outside the window and smoke.

'Just about on ma way, little brother.'

'Your first meeting since you told them the whole story?'

'Ja.'

'Did it help?'

'Ja. It got me thinking about Holly.' It's the first time Ah've mentioned her. Sid Vicious doesn't reply so Ah change the subject. 'You used to smoke out this window just like this. Ja?'

'Of course. It would be almost criminal not to.'

'Ah know what you mean.'

'You're doing great, Denzel.'

'Ja?'

Ma phone rings and Ah don't recognise the number so Ah don't answer it. They don't leave a message. 'Ah wonder who that was!' Ah say.

'It wasn't me,' Sid Vicious says and smiles.

'You're funny. Ja!'

'And you're just plain weird.'

'Kettle and pot, boet!'

Ah'm seeing Chemical Brothers tonight. This is ma one and only Christmas present to maself. Ah'll go to Never Again and afterwards venture to Brixton Academy, the best venue in all of London, Clive has assured me. Ah'm excited. Ah'd seen Chemical Brothers in Ibiza when they played Amnesia and they were up there with the best that ever graced the club. Tonight Ah'll see them at a place where Ah'm not working. It'll be great for sure. Clive has refused to come, proclaiming that it might be detrimental to his recent sobriety, but Ah've no worries. A good concert will do ma soul the world of good.

But first, ma meeting. Ah hot foot it to Euston Road.

Tonight, Billy joins me as Ah wait outside Never Again. She smiles and Ah smile back.

'Can I talk about your share,' she asks. These are the first words she's ever uttered to me. Ah nod.

'It was unbelievable,' she says.

'Ja! For me too,' Ah reply and grin.

'I'm really sorry about your brother,' she says. This girl really reminds me of Holly.

'Thank you. It's your turn tonight, ja?'

'No, next week,' she says and then buries her head in her notebook, letting me know that our conversation is finished.

Ah hear a familiar voice behind me singing a David Bowie song. Clive is in the building, for sure.

'Hey mate,' he says. He looks at Billy but she keeps her head down; he looks at me and rolls his eyes.

'So are you all set for the Academy tonight?'

'Ja, Ah'm well excited, but unfortunately Ah'll have to pass on our after-meeting coffee.'

'Of course!'

'How goes it anyway?'

'Good, Denzel, good. I saw Tracy and Ben today and it was great. She's still a little cold but I guess that's to be expected. I've a lot to make up for. Ben is great. Cute as a button. He took my phone today and was whizzing around it like he's been using it his whole life. It's incredible how he picks everything up, just like that.'

Ah nod ma head, but really Ah'm playing a guessing game of huge proportions here. Ah can't remember the last time Ah was around a child, other than in passing. It makes me feel a little sad about that fact when Ah hear Clive talk about his son, and for a brief moment, Ah think about ma own child. Ma son. Ah've always imagined that Alice had a boy back then because sometimes Ah get a strong feeling that there's a part of me walking around on this planet. Ma boy. He would be a teenager now.

The door opens and Gloria greets the three of us and ushers us inside our weekly meeting room. In hardly any time, the others arrive and we get started. Tonight, we all share about how our weeks have been, and congratulate ourselves and each other for our respective sobrieties. Sharon is up tonight and Ah prepare maself for the verbal onslaught. Sharon talks any time, every time, all the time, speaking like her mouth is on the run from something much bigger. We hear that the last time she used she had been with her ex boyfriend, and it had left her feeling worthless and like she simply had to turn her life around. She talks for a long time and gives us more background than we need, veering off to her unhappy childhood and the first time she used. If Ah'm to be honest, Ah switch off mostly. In addition to liking the sound of her own voice, Sharon is one of those people who's hard to follow because she tells you facts you don't need to know but leaves out whole chunks of information that make her story meaningless. While she speaks on, Ah think about the concert tonight.

When the time comes to leave Ah'm out of there like a shot from a sniper rifle and make my way to Brixton. This is ma first time in this part of London and Ah like it from the start. It's probably somewhere Ah would gravitate towards living if it weren't for ma ready-made home in Borough. When Ah spy the Brixton Academy, Ah'm not disappointed. It's an amazing building, and even from the outside Ah can tell that it's especially built to house live music, whether it knew it or not. Ah find ma spot in the queue and smoke a cigarette. It's a long time since Ah've queued to get into a venue and Ah'm remembering ma charmed status while in Ibiza, ma Mecca now lost to me, given the events that had taken me away from there. It also puts two people in my mind, two people Ah need to contact: Holly and Titus. Titus had given me ma first job on the island and we had gone on to become friends. To ma utter surprise, just before Ah left he'd professed that Ah was like the son he never had, acting more sentimental than Ah'd ever seen him act before. Ja. Ah'll make contact for sure. But tonight. Music …

Ah get to the front of the queue in record time, given ma initial placement in the human tail, but now Ah find we are stopped and things are stuck for some time. And then – and not a moment too soon – Ah'm let inside. Wow! Ah love this spot. Ah go to the bar and for a moment Ah'm very tempted to grab a beer, but then Ah think about ma little group. Rules are rules. We all succeed together – that's what Gloria has drummed into our heads. It's all or nothing. And even though ma recovery is down to me on ma own, we're recovering en masse. Ah get it, Ah really do, and although there are things about the group Ah'd change, that isn't one of them. The point is, the practice has helped many get clean and stay clean.

Coca-Cola in hand, a take maself in towards the music. The support act has started. They are cut from the same cloth as Chemical Brothers and actually aren't so bad. It's only when Ah feel like Ah need to take a piss that Ah realise they're not that great. A strange but true fact is that when music is really good ma bladder assumes the almost superhuman power to contain itself and Ah find maself not needing the toilet for unbelievable lengths of time.

Ah'm sure there's no scientific explanation for this, but it's true nonetheless.

Ah first see her when Ah'm on ma way back from the gents and Ah know her immediately. She has her back to me but Ah know without question that this is the only girl Ah've ever loved. Alice Cooper is within touching distance. It takes me by surprise and Ah'm about to make maself known to her when Ah see the girl standing next to her, another blast from ma past. Alice and Jo Mitchel, best friends forever, are standing talking and Ah lean into the wall and watch. Alice throws her head back and laughs. Ah remember her. Ma whole insides begin to well up and Ah've an incredible urge to take the half dozen steps that would put us back together again. But it's not time. Not yet. For now Ah just look at her. Ah want to see her face. And then, as if she's heard ma inner thoughts, she turns around and looks in ma direction. Ah swear Ah begin to melt there and then and am thankful that there's a wall behind to steady me. Ma heart begins to hammer as if Ah've been using again. Ma Alice. For a moment Ah think that she's seeing me, as she doesn't look away, but then she brings her attention back to Jo and Ah realise it was ma overactive imagination. Ah'm unnoticed.

The two girls begin to move towards the music and Ah follow. Ah follow close behind but not close enough that Ah might be discovered. As the first bars of 'There's No Path To Follow' begin to play and the two people who are known to the world at large as Chemical Brothers take their places on the stage, Ah'm only marginally aware, as all the time Ah'm watching Alice. Ah watch her all through the concert. Ma eyes move from the huge screen on the stage that is producing amazing graphics back to this girl, and a few times she looks ma way but she doesn't see me. She doesn't feel the weight of ma stare. She couldn't, because if she did she'd travel the short distance and be with me. At times it feels so compelling, this desire to go over and take her in ma arms and kiss her, to kiss away all the fucked up years and go back to when we were teenagers and in love and that was all that mattered. But Ah don't. This isn't the time. Or the place.

The concert ends and Ah remain standing, letting Alice Cooper get swallowed up by the crowd. Ah'll find her again in a few short months. Just you wait for me, girl!

*

I wait for Jo outside, allowing myself to come down from what I've just witnessed. I'd forgotten how good that band is live. I'd seen them about five years ago with Jo and they'd blown us away then, as sure as they've just done now. I've never taken any of the club drugs I've seen at large around me over the years, but something about Chemical Brothers makes me think that they have subliminally placed something in the music that recreates that same high. As I wait, I watch the people passing by. Clearly I hadn't been alone in my appreciation: everyone else looks as happy and high as I feel. This is what I love about seeing live music. The actual event morphs into the before and after, the build-up as you travel there, the drinks beforehand in the company of other people heading to the show, and then later being a part of the crowd leaving, all feeling the same buzz.

My jeans are actually damp, which isn't surprising. Jo and I had danced. We both love to dance, and many of our fondest and finest memories are of us dancing around like fools. We would make up routines when we were kids and then Denzel had come along. He wasn't like the other boys back then. He wanted to join in with us, the girls. And when I'd suggested that the boys would think he was a sissy, he'd told me that he didn't care about the other boys, he only cared about me – if I thought he was cool, then that was all that mattered. And just like that I was under his spell. Just as I'm thinking about Denzel, I see a man in the distance. He's wearing a hoodie so his face is concealed, but the angle of his head lets me know that his gaze is upon me. It's not for the first time tonight. During the concert, I caught him staring at me on a few occasions but I'd ignored him, not wanting to invite unwelcome attention. But now as I watch this stranger looking my way, I get a fantastically crazy thought. Could this possibly be …

'Cooper!'

My attention shifts to my friend who's beckoning me over, so I begin walking, quickly glancing back at the hooded figure. But he's disappeared. I get a chill down my spine. Denzel Anderson is in Ibiza, I remind myself.

'That was electric?' Jo shrieks.

'Ja, it was amazing. Really amazing. Thanks Jo.'

'My pleasure. I have to get the best out of my single friend while she's still single, don't I?'

I think again about the man I've just seen.

'Imagine,' Jo continues, 'you'll be a married woman this time next year.'

'But nothing will change,' I tell my friend. She shrugs.

'I think it will, Alice. I think everything will change. People say they won't hang up the single version of themselves when they marry, but they do.'

'Well, I'll be different,' I say, reassuring myself as much as Jo.

When I get home Robert is waiting up, channel-hopping. He turns the television off as soon as I come in.

'How was it?' he asks.

'It was amazing!'

'And Jo's okay?'

'Yeah, she's great. Said to say hello.'

'Hello back!' Robert says by way of a response. 'Do you fancy a glass of wine?' He offers me the bottle.

'Yep.'

He grabs a glass from the side cabinet and begins pouring, filling first my glass and then topping up his own.

'Merry Christmas,' he says raising his glass and toasting the space in front of him.

'Merry Christmas,' I reply.

'I'm starting to feel it now, Ali. Finally.'

'How was the office party?' I ask.

'Very Christmassy actually, and one of the better ones we've had. It's a shame you couldn't make it. Everyone asked after you.'

I wonder if Sally asked after me. 'Sorry, but the gig tonight was a present,' I say.

'I know. It's fine,' Robert says and takes a sip of wine. 'Oh, my mother rang. She's coming this weekend – wants to talk wedding stuff with you.'

Of course he wants to change the subject. He might have to talk about Sally. I'd found out about Sally six months ago and said nothing to anyone. I saw a message on his phone that told me everything. I didn't know whether it was a full-on affair, but the message made it clear that they'd had sex. In fairness I'd been snooping and deserved to find something that would hurt me. That's what happens when you go looking for trouble – you usually find some. A bit like when I'd found his porn – I'd gone looking for that too.

'That'll be nice,' I reply. Robert smiles.

Kate is forever telling me how lucky I am to have the mother-in-law on side. Her own is a nightmare. But I know how to play the Helen Shaw game, having played the Sheila Cooper game for so long; both of them follow similar rules. There had been a girlfriend before me that Helen hadn't approved of but I was perfect, she was forever telling Robert. And I'd become very good at being perfect. Helen is particularly excited about the wedding and I'm allowing her to have an active role, given that my own mother is, thankfully, on the other side of the world. For now.

'When's she coming?' I ask.

'She said Saturday afternoon, if that suits you. I told her you'd give her a call in the morning.'

'Sure,' I reply.

Robert runs his hand over my arm all the way up to my shoulder and pulls the strap of my top down so that my shoulder is exposed. He reaches over and begins kissing my neck. I think again of the hooded stranger at the concert.

Robert is an attentive lover and knows how to push my buttons after all these years. But he is tame, restrained. I used to wish our sex life could be a bit wilder, that he would experiment more. But then I'd found his disturbing porn collection, so I hadn't encouraged him. Deep down I want wild sex – no, something more than wild sex – passion, which only comes from really longing for someone, from connecting with another body that emanates an opposite charge. I've known a lot of sex, but most of it has lacked that kind of passion. Of course, I've only ever really wanted one person. There's no point denying it.

I close my eyes and as I pull my soon-to-be-husband inside me, I'm thinking of Denzel Anderson.

'I love you,' I say, opening my eyes and wanting it so desperately to be true. How simple my life would be if I could just love this man.

Robert stops and looks at me with searching eyes, as if he knows my lie. He says nothing as I feel him go soft. Eventually he falls out of me, his erection lost.

'I'm sorry,' I tell him not knowing what else to say.

'Why are you sorry!' he says looking at me as if I repulse him.

I'm quite taken aback by what I see in his eyes. He rolls off me, stands up and leaves me there in our front room, my legs wide open and feeling like it's all my fault. I sense a very real fear beginning to grow – a fear that he knows exactly what I'd been thinking, that somehow he had read it all from my bodily responses and from my mind. I'm afraid he knows what is only beginning to dawn on me – that I really want to be with someone else.

6

Revelations And The Nativity

Ah've seen her and now Ah cannot for the life of me stop thinking about her. There was that moment outside the Brixton Academy when she was most definitely seeing me and creeping towards me, but then her attention had gone back to Jo Mitchel and Ah'd disappeared. As Clive talks to me about Bowie's collaborations with Iggy Pop and explains why they are like nothing else before and nothing that will come after, all the time Ah'm thinking of Alice. Ah'd seen her picture on Facebook and recognised her. But Ah would have recognised her anyway. She was still the girl Ah loved – *still* love, present tense. Ah'm sure much of what has happened in the last chunk of her life has altered her, as Ah know it has altered me. Yes, the meantime will have altered us both, but Ah pray that we can find each other somewhere beneath it all, still intact, still there, still the same. Still in love. Soulmates. Still. For now, dear Alice, Ah'm believing in soulmates in the hope that you are mine.

'You're somewhere else, mate,' Clive says, intruding on my thoughts.

'Sorry, boet. Ah'm back now.'

Today, we'd agreed to come to Costa a few hours before our meeting, as Clive has plans with Tracy directly after and we didn't want to miss our weekly catch-up.

'Anyway, you can hear Bowie all over "Lust for Life". Personally I think he gives Pop more credit than he's due. Don't get me wrong, Iggy Pop is a talented bloke, but let's face it – there's only one David Bowie.'

'Ja,' Ah say and nod ma head. Ah'm not just humouring him; Ah happen to agree.

'So anyway, how were the Brothers?'

'Fantastic, Clive. It's a shame you didn't make it.'

'Did they do their old stuff?'

'Ja, they did everything and played for over two hours.'

'That was a more than fair offering.'

'Ja, Ah thought so too.'

'It's nice to go to gigs alone,' Clive says.

'Ja!' Ah reply.

Ah've gone to most of ma gigs alone and it's never been a problem, although Ah would have liked to have been with Alice for that last one, not just watching her from across the room. And there she is again in ma head, where she's taken up residency. Ah get a burning desire to tell Clive, but again Ah decide against it. The point is, she's in ma imagination right now; the reality has yet to manifest. Ah get a strong feeling that the actions Ah take between now and then may greatly affect the outcome. More than anything Ah don't want to jinx the event that might just prove to be the most significant love event of ma life. Plus Ah'm way too sentimental at the moment. Ja, best Ah say nothing and keep ma internal world internal.

'Still, you missed a good time,' Ah tell him.

'I don't doubt that. And now here comes Christmas fast and furious. Are you a willing participant?'

'Ah haven't really celebrated for a lot of years,' Ah reply shaking ma head and realising that Ah can't actually remember the last time. Ah reckon it must have been when Ah was with the people who grew me and that won't have been anything to swoon about. Ah cast the memory from ma head space: these days are for the now and the what-next. That is what Never Again tells us.

What's done is done and best forgotten, and Ah agree wholeheartedly.

'I feel the same,' Clive says, 'but this year it will be Tracy, Ben and me, and I'm planning to go all out with the celebrations. We're with her family, who all hate me for obvious reasons. I have a lot to make up for. But I think me showing up sober for Christmas dinner might just be a way to start making amends. You're in Borough with your pops?'

This is the first time Ah've heard anyone refer to Tim Harris as ma 'pops' and Ah like it. Ah nod ma head.

'Just the two of you?' Clive asks.

'And someone called Bill.'

'Family?'

'Ah don't think so.'

'You don't think so?'

Ah shrug ma shoulders.

'I suppose given all the surprises you've had in the past year anything's possible! Yeah, I'm in the spirit all right, although the songs aren't helping much,' Clive says, nodding towards the speakers pumping out the Christmas medley that's playing in the background.

'Boet, they're everywhere,' Ah reply. 'Seriously this country loves these tunes.'

'Don't I know it. It's the same every year all through December. Some places even manage to squeeze them into November too. It stinks! But there's one exception to the rule.'

Clive raises his eyebrow and Ah know without question there's a David Bowie reference on its way. He doesn't disappoint and before long he's telling me how 'The Little Drummer Boy', a collaboration between his hero and Bing Crosby, is a great tune, despite being incredibly corny. Ah admit that Ah've never heard it and within ten seconds of showing some curiosity Clive has placed his headphones over ma ears and Ah hear the song in question, which, although most definitely corny, is the rose amongst the thorns, for sure. Ah listen to the end and then return ma ears to the coffee shop.

'Great, yeah?' he asks.

'Yeah. And that's not such a bad tune either,' Ah say pointing ma finger to the speaker where Noddy Holder is screaming 'Merry Christmas Everyone'.

Clive looks at me as if Ah've just farted. 'Mate, I'll do my best to forget you ever said that.'

We make our way to our last Never Again meeting before Christmas. Although we're not late, we are the last to arrive; everyone is seated already. All of us are punctual each week, Ah guess a testament to how dedicated everyone is to their sobriety. Tonight we'll hear the final story: Billy's. Gloria has left her until last maybe because she is the youngest. Her story gets me. It's the nearest to ma own. Her sobriety is connected to her little brother too, but unlike mine, he is still alive. She nearly lost him when he OD'd at a party and that had changed her outlook forever. A promise was made – he won't use if she doesn't. The end. She finishes her story and Ah take a deep breath. Ah hope for sure that she remains sober, her and her little brother. And us all. Billy looks at me, and Ah smile at her and feel a bond, not just because of the group and what she's just told us. There's something more. Ah don't know what exactly. Maybe it's because she reminds me of Holly, and thoughts of Holly always take me back to Sid.

The group finishes up. Clive says goodbye and rushes off to see Tracy. As Ah'm leaving Ah see Billy outside. She stops and smiles, saying nothing.

'Permission to speak?' Ah ask and she nods.

'Ah'm glad your brother made it,' Ah say, not sure if these words are appropriate but they are the ones that come.

'Thanks. I'm sorry yours didn't,' she says and Ah thank her.

She remains standing with me, waiting for something and then Ah think Ah might know what.

'You wanna go for a coffee?' Ah ask.

'Yes please.' she replies and our feet start to make their way to the nearby Costa.

Billy extends the necessary courtesy: 'Can we talk about your share?'

'Of course!' I say.

'So you really had no idea he was your brother,' she asks, holding her coffee cup as if it might be in part responsible for keeping her upright. She reminds me so much of Holly it's uncanny, and for a split second Ah forget Ah'm in London and travel back to Ibiza. It's a weird feeling and it makes me shiver.

'Are you okay?' she asks.

'Ja, Ah just got a chill up ma spine.' Ah return to her question. 'Ma brother and Ah were born in different parts of the world.'

'But somehow you both made it to Ibiza – you found each other. It's extraordinary. But also I think it was inevitable, like you said. You were meant to meet him. Everything in our lives happens because it's meant to. Lou Reed once said that.'

'Ja, and a lot of other people.' Ah smile at Billy. This is the most Ah've ever heard her talk and Ah like it. 'You look very much like Holly.' Ah'm just about to fill in the dots when she beats me to it.

'The girl Sid loved.'

'Ja. You remembered!'

'Of course. Your story stayed with me. Our stories are similar.'

'Ja.'

'We have a lot in common, except I got to keep my little brother. I'm sorry you lost yours. I can't imagine ...' She stopped,   having run out of words.

'Ja. Thank you. It means a lot that you say it. So how is your little brother doing?' Ah ask.

'He's good and clean. He promised me and he only makes promises he keeps, he's forever telling me. Unlike me. I've broken a lot of promises down through the years.'

'Haven't we all,' Ah say and smile. 'Don't beat yourself up. Ah think between the seven of us in that room there's no shortage of broken promises. Ja?'

'I suppose.'

'No suppose about it. And how about you?'

She looks at me and her expression tells me she wants clarification.

'Will you stay clean?' Ah add.

'Absolutely. I keep wondering how I'd have felt if I'd lost my little brother that night and it's enough to let me know I'll never use again. Never. I'm sorry,' she says again.

'If you keep apologising, girl, I'm gonna think you had a hand in what happened out in Ibiza.' This makes her smile. 'It's funny being here with you tonight. Ah usually come with Clive after each meeting.'

'You and Clive are tight.'

'Ah suppose so. Ah've come to enjoy our weekly coffees as much as the meeting.'

'But you don't tell the others.'

'Na. It wasn't planned or anything. We just found each other here on the first night and we made it a ritual.'

'What's he like?' she asks.

'He's a nice boet,' Ah tell her.

'He's a nice what?'

'Boet – I'm guessing you don't know too many South Africans.'

'That's where you're from? I wondered.'

'Ma accent didn't give me away?'

'No, it's not really that obvious.'

'What is really obvious when you think about it?'

'Lots of things – lies, drug addiction, love. But not your accent.' She smiles and Ah smile back. And then there's silence.

Ah'm about to ask her if she minds if Ah smoke when her phone rings, making her jump. Not me, though – Ah guess Ah've a greater noise threshold since ma time in the clubs. She answers it and Ah take out ma tobacco and begin rolling a cigarette in anticipation. Ah can tell that there's a boy on the other end and as Ah watch her, Ah remember that she's only twenty. Although she's older than her years, she's just a young girl when there's a boy on the phone. It makes me smile. Ah think about Alice and wonder what she might have been like when she was that age. Did she still speak like a girl even though she believed she was a woman?

'You can go ahead and smoke,' Billy says and Ah realise that she's back with me and the call has ended. 'But only if you roll me one too.'

'For sure,' Ah say and begin rolling her another as the first cigarette now sits comfortably between ma lips, too late to be offered up to ma company.

She watches as Ah go to work and Ah'm reminded of a cat Ah used to stay with. Well, it was more its owner Ah stayed with rather than the cat. The cat would watch while Ah carried out jobs that Ah thought would be boring to my feline friend, but still it watched, unfazed, without taking its eyes off me. This is how Billy watches me as Ah roll her cigarette, as if Ah'm showing her something of grave importance.

'Do you think about charlie a lot?' she asks me

'Ja,' Ah say as Ah hand over the cigarette. She thanks me. 'But not as much as when Ah was using and Ah remind maself about that.'

'I know what you mean. I was really bad – worse than all my friends put together. I would sniff through stacks. That's what caused my little brother to OD. He was competing with me and thought he could do more than his big sister.'

'What's your brother's name,' Ah ask. 'Sorry if Ah missed it earlier but Ah don't think you mentioned it.'

'No, you didn't miss it. If I'd mentioned it you would have remembered.'

And then Ah know with full certainty. For sure. 'His name is Sid, ja?'

'Yes,' she replies. 'His name is Sid.'

*

I watch as the children tell the story of the baby Jesus and how he came to be. The hall is aglow with proud parents and I dip into my own future to imagine sitting here watching my own kids. It fills me with a nice feeling. When it's all over, Ben finds me and tugs at my sleeve.

'Here, Miss Cooper,' he says and hands me a brightly wrapped present.

'Thank you, Ben,' I say

His mother appears from behind. 'He wrapped it himself, didn't you,' says Tracy.

Tracy is much younger than me, probably no more than twenty-one. She's a single mother, but tonight she's with a man who is not introduced. I suspect he's Ben's father.

'And a very fine job you did too,' I say, looking down at Ben.

'Thank you, Miss Cooper. Have a great Christmas and I hope Santa brings you all you want.'

'So do I, Ben. And I wish you the same.'

'That's my dad,' Ben says, pointing to the man and confirming my suspicions. It draws the man closer.

'I certainly am,' he says and extends his hand. 'I'm Clive.'

I shake the hand of the young man whose face does not belong in this crowd of middle-class parents. Although his eyes suggest he's only in his early twenties, the rest of him looks older than his years. Withered, the way a drug habit withers. I think about Denzel, who would probably have this same haggard look as he sat wasting away in Ibiza. Shortly after the concert I'd rejected my fantastic notion that it had been him at the Brixton Academy. He was all set to burn himself out in Ibiza – wasn't that what Jaspar had said? – so hardly in any fit state to find his way to London to a Chemical Brothers concert. It was too far-fetched.

'Please to meet you, Clive. I'm …'

'You're Miss Cooper. Ben's told me all about you.'

I look down at a smiling Ben. The admiration is mutual. For a split second I think about baby Denzel and wonder if he would have looked like this little cutie when he was four. I decide he would have been just as lovely, with the same gap-toothed smile as his father.

I wish the little family a lovely Christmas and leave them to begin packing away the nativity set. It takes my mind away from my past. However, when I catch sight of the trio leaving – Clive and Tracy with Ben between them, firmly gripped in place by their hands – my heart aches.

The teachers ensure that all the parents and children have left the school and then head to a nearby pub for a last drink before Christmas break. The long holidays are a great perk of my job and give me plenty of time to get everything ready for Christmas Day, which will bring Robert's family to ours, along with Jo. Jo and I have spent every Christmas here in London together. Come to think of it, we spent quite a few together in Sea Point as well.

'Merry Christmas, Alice – your last as a single girl,' say James, teacher of the ten-year-olds.

The rest of the group join in the toast and then we break up into our usual smaller groups.

'You should see the dress,' Kate tells James. 'She's gonna look stunning, is our Ali.'

'Is Hockney coming?' James asks. Carl Hockney is the headmaster of the school.

I nod my head. The RSVPs have started to come back and my boss's had been one of the first to arrive.

'Great! So I get to spend a weekend with him too,' James says.

'Yes, we all will,' I say.

'But at least you'll be in a nice frock,' he replies and winks.

If it were my choice I wouldn't have invited him. Of course, if it were my choice, I wouldn't be having this fancy wedding at all. But I'd done my duty and asked my boss. Of course, I had. I might not have officially changed my name just yet but I'd become Alice Shaw quite some time ago. The thought depresses me and I knock back my half lager.

'Someone's thirsty,' Kate says.

'I'm off actually,' I say. 'I told Robert I'd be home straight after. We have some wedding stuff to do.'

This is a complete lie. The truth is that nice as Kate and James's company might be, I don't want to be here right now. I want to be alone. They reluctantly let me go and I head for home.

When I get back, Robert is already there, much to my surprise, with a chilled bottle of champagne and two glasses. He pops the cork as soon as I enter the lounge.

'Are we celebrating?' I ask.

'Christmas is coming. Has no one told you?' he says.

'Sure, but in all the time I've known you, I've never seen you open a bottle of champagne to celebrate Christmas. Spill Robert Shaw!'

He smiles.

'Alice Cooper soon-to-be Shaw, we are going to New York in the New Year,' he says and hands me a glass.

'For a holiday?'

He shakes his head. 'For at least six months, but with the possibility of moving there if we like it. The firm is setting up an office over there and they want me to run it. Imagine, Ali – New York. A Manhattan flat! Just imagine it!'

Yes, I can imagine it. Robert and I had gone to New York a few times and we'd both loved it, but to go there to live is a massive deal.

'This is very sudden,' I say.

'Not really. Well, I've known about it for a while but I didn't want to tell you until it was final. It's great news, isn't it? I can't wait to tell Mum and Dad.'

'So when's all this happening?' I ask, beginning to feel like a mere spectator in my own life.

'Well, there's no reason why we can't go straight after the honeymoon. A new marriage and a new home.'

Robert beams as he says this, but I feel a sense of dread settle in the pit of my stomach. This does not feel like good news at all.

'You don't look very happy about it,' he says.

'I'm just shocked, Robert. Like you said, you've known about this for a while, but it's the first I'm hearing about it. It's a big deal – a huge deal – and it'll take me some time to get my head around it. I mean what about my job? I'll be leaving mid year and I don't think I'll get a job over in New York so easily.'

'But you don't need to get a job. I've told you, Ali – I can more than afford to support you, and anyway we both want kids pretty much straightaway. The plan was you would leave your job then.'

'Sure, but I'm not pregnant yet, Robert, and maybe it won't happen as soon as we'd like.'

'Well, why don't we start trying now?'

'It's true I want children, but I also want to work. A few years off work isn't the same as quitting altogether. I love my job.'

'Because you love children and when you have your own …'

'Robert, you're not listening to me. I love my job. I don't think I want to go somewhere that I can't work and in the process leave my children here stranded without a teacher. You really should have spoken to me about this first.'

'Come on, Ali! It's Manhattan. You loved it when we were there!'

'Yes, for a holiday. Staying for six months would be a different affair.' As would being completely dependent on you, I think to myself.

Robert squeezes his champagne glass and lets the smile slip from his face. I can tell that he's furious but holding back. This isn't the response he'd hoped for and his expression isn't one I'm used to; I usually let him have his own way. His face seems to darken and I see something almost sinister in it that sends a chill down my spine. I wonder what might be coming next.

'You'll come round,' he says. His earlier smile returns, but it never reaches his eyes.

7

It's Beginning To Look A Lot Like Christmas

It's Christmas Eve and Ah've no plans, so Ah ask Tim if Ah can spend the day with his record collection. The man actually has a record collection – a real vinyl collection. He says 'Yes, of course' before he heads off to the studio and leaves me to it, just me and a wall of music. Ah'm in ma element and as Ah'm looking through the records Ah imagine Sid Vicious doing this very same thing as a teenager.

'You would have done this when you were here, ja?'

'Yes,' ma brother tells me as he comes to stand beside me at the wall of music, past and present. 'I passed some of my happiest times here,' he says.

'It makes me feel warm inside to think that Ah'm doing what you would have done.'

'You've gone very soppy, Denzel. It must be love.'

'Ja, and losing your brother. That'll turn a grown man soppy for sure.'

Ah yawn. Ah'm tired, as Ah'd given most of the night to lying awake, thinking about Billy and our earlier conversation.

'What do you think it means, my connection with Billy?' Ah ask ma brother.

'Do you honestly think I've any idea?'

'Na, but Ah thought it was worth asking just in case.'

'Sorry, I don't know.'

'Ah guess we'll all find out what's what when the time's right for us to know.'

'Just like with us.'

'Ja, just like with us.'

'Now go and get lost in some music and stop worrying about things you've no business worrying about.'

'For sure, Sid Vicious.'

There are a very impressive number of albums on this huge wall. Ah'm beginning to realise that it will take more than just one day if Ah want to make ma way through them all and give all this fine music the attention it deserves. Ah do a quick scan: everything is alphabetical, and properly alphabetical at that. What Ah know of Tim Harris thus far is further proved – ma father thrives alongside order. A multitude of names float by me, a great number Ah don't recognise, but the ones Ah do please me no end: Air, Bach, Beethoven, Bjork, Kate Bush, Johnny Cash, Nick Cave, Bob Dillon, Depeche Mode, Dire Straits, The Doors, Brian Eno, Ella Fitzgerald, Handel, Jimi Hendrix – ma hero. Ah stop, tempted to linger, but decide to move on – Janis Joplin, Nat King Cole, Dean Martin, Sergio Mendes, Ennio Morricone (that one goes on for miles), Mozart (that goes on for miles and miles), Sinead O'Connor, Paganini, Pavarotti, Pink Floyd, The Pixies, Prince, Queen, Diana Ross, Frank Sinatra, Nina Simone, The Smiths, Vivaldi, Tom Waits. Here Ah stop and go no further. Ah pick up an album and make ma way to the turntable. A few minutes later ma ears are filled with the sound of 'Singapore', the first song on ma favourite ever Tom Waits album. *Rain Dogs* had first been brought to ma attention by Mick, a fellow roadie when Ah was touring with Black Sabbath, and Ah'd been hooked from then on. Mick was forever treating me to excerpts from Tom's huge back catalogue as we worked together, and as Ah recall, he could do a respectable impersonation of the man. Ah'd quickly got maself a copy of *Rain Dogs* as well as a number of Tom's other albums, but Ah always came back to this one. Ah even went so far as to learn the riffs to some of ma favourite songs on the album and play along on ma guitar. Ah can actually hypnotise maself by playing 'Diamonds and Gold' over and over again.

Now Ah'm hearing these amazing tunes for the first time on vinyl. It makes me want a guitar again and Ah think about the many guitars Ah see in the charity shops windows Ah pass on ma way to Never Again. Maybe one day Ah'll stop and buy one. Ja, Ah want to play this song again and sing along. Ah don't have no voice but Ah'd always sung along to Tom's tunes when Ah played them, assured by the man whose sound follows nobody else's. It encouraged me to sing Denzel style. Ja, maybe Ah'll get me a guitar for Christmas. Ma old guitar was back in Ibiza with JJ at the Okay Hostel – actually it was probably in America now, assuming JJ had taken it back to his homeland.

Ah spend the day lost in music, only breaking for cigarettes and food, and Ah listen to every Tom Waits album in ma father's collection. Most Ah've heard before, but a few not, although today everything feels new to me and Ah realise that this is the first time Ah've listened to music so intensely without using. It makes me think about charlie and the times Ah'd had with Mick. He was a crazy son of a bitch. He could sniff through his body weight and still function after a fashion. Until he couldn't. Didn't. He'd gone in his sleep. He just didn't wake up after a heavy night. Ah always thought that, as exits go, that wouldn't be a bad one. A lot better than how it had been for poor Sid, that was for sure. But the point is Ah guess we don't get to choose our end. It's written as it's going to be.

Ah'm just about to sign off for the night when the front door opens and Ah hear the sound of voices. Shortly afterwards Tim comes into the room where Ah'm setting the Tom Waits records back where they belong.

'You enjoyed yourself Denzel?' he asks.

'For sure. What a collection!'

'Ah his vinyl!' Ah hear the voice first and then another face appears through the doorway.

'Tim always had an impressive stock. There are more downstairs, you know – and probably more in places we'd never think to look. Hello, I'm Bill,' the stranger says, extending his hand ma way.

He has a slight American twang but Ah'm guessing he's another Englishman, or maybe an American who has spent a lot of time in England. Ah shake his hand and tell him ma name. He's about the same age as ma father, so that rules out ma other brother theory.

'Yes, I've heard a lot about you,' Bill says and smiles. 'And I'm very much looking forward to spending Christmas with you.'

Ah smile and nod ma head, but can't bring maself to reciprocate, for the truth is Ah hadn't given it all that much thought.

The three of us stay in the room and remain silent for a long time, which begins to feel uncomfortable, but still nobody speaks nor attempts to flee. Finally, Bill does something that tells me more about ma father than Ah'd known up until that moment – he places his hand on his shoulder in a way that lets me know without a shadow of a doubt that they're more than just good friends. Tim looks at me, waiting for a reaction, so Ah simply shrug ma shoulders and smile. Ma father is full of surprises. That's for sure. He smiles back – his half smile – and they leave me with an invitation to join them in the kitchen for some tea. Ah decline and say that Ah've worn maself out. Then Ah make ma way to ma room to find the sleep Ah couldn't quite pin down the night before. Tonight it comes and Ah sleep all the way into ma first Christmas in London.

*

The days have passed as quickly as running liquid through a funnel and I find myself in Christmas Eve without really knowing how I got here. Perhaps I'm still shell-shocked after Robert's announcement about our future. We haven't spoken about it since the night he prematurely cracked open the champagne. Meanwhile I've been wondering if staying here in Muswell Hill might be an option, although I'm not looking forward to that conversation with him.

'What are your plans today, Ali?' Robert asks as we sit and have breakfast together.

I blush as if he might just have read my thoughts. I've felt this way quite a lot recently, like he might be able to dip into my head and pull out the information he needs.

'Just some last minute shopping to get us ready for tomorrow,' I answer.

'It's not like you to leave things until the last minute,' he says and I wonder if there's suspicion in his voice or is it simply that I'm being paranoid.

'It's nothing major,' I reply as light-heartedly as I can manage.

'Of course. Anyway I'd better get myself out of the house. The sooner I'm at work the sooner I can get back and our Christmas can begin.'

He leaves. I clean away the breakfast dishes and then head into the Broadway to shop and lap up the lovely Christmas vibe that has everyone full of cheer and excitement. I miss the children already and I know without question that the idea of me going to New York isn't feasible. I can't leave mid year. As I walk and think again about Robert's actions, I begin to feel angry. How could he consider making such a decision without consulting me, and then to tell me I'd come round to the idea – expecting that I will, like I always do. I haven't told Jo yet, but I already know her reaction will be similar to mine. Really, if I'm honest, this is typical Robert and nothing new. He's forever making decisions for me because I have allowed him too – that's really what I'm angry about. Robert had made the New York decision because he knew he could, and he's expecting me to follow his lead, because I always do.

We'd discussed the prospect of marriage and children very early in our relationship, but what had not been discussed was how all those things would happen on Robert Shaw's terms. I am now the sort of woman I once swore I would never become – like Sheila Cooper; each day it feels like I'm stepping further into her skin. Oh my God, how had I let this happen! Unable to deal with thoughts of turning out to be the same woman as my mother, and knowing that as I grow older I'll see more and more of her in myself, I decide that I'll be different. For one thing I'll be a better mother, without question.

Retail therapy is always a good way for me to forget my troubles and so I throw my agitated mind into the experience. Before long I find myself in Crocodile Antiques, my favourite shop, which always has something different and quirky. Today I find some tree trimmings that will sit nicely on the discreet little artificial tree I'd found in John Lewis that not even Robert, with all his misgivings about Christmas, could find fault with. I also fall in love with a wooden calendar that is manually operated, making time recording a physical affair. It reminds me of the calendar at school that I get the children to change each day. Now, I'll have my own to move forward at home. Afterwards, I make my way to The Scullery, my second favourite shop, where I find a turkey baster and a few table decorations. For dinner this year we're entertaining Robert's family – his mum, dad and younger brother – and Jo, of course. I wonder if we'll ever break that tradition in the future. I hope not.

Before I head home, I go to Caffè Nero to have a coffee and enjoy the Christmas music that's playing in the background. I'm a secret lover of all those cheesy songs, and harbour a lot of Christmas spirit, considering that I'm surrounded by people with a limited supply of festive cheer. I sit with my coffee and mince pie and listen as Nat King Cole sings 'The Christmas Song'. There's a young couple at the next table. They look very much in love as they openly canoodle, oblivious to everyone else in the room. They probably believe that this is how it will always be, and part of me feels a duty to go over and tell them not to take it for granted but to enjoy it while it lasts. They stop kissing and he whispers something in her ear that makes her laugh. I watch them until the girl notices my intrusion and throws me a dirty look. I turn away and in an attempt to let them get back to the intimate moment I've just invaded, I leave.

Back at home, I do a few last minute preparations before Jo arrives. As I potter around the apartment, I remember the young couple and my mind goes back to my own teenage love story. I remember a time when I was as carefree with my emotions and I wonder if that feeling would still be there if Denzel Anderson were to come back into my life. Would we be able to pick up where we'd left off? I couldn't imagine myself being able to keep my hands off him in much the same way as we had been back then. I remember that uncontrollable longing, that feeling of wanting to touch someone. A charged energy flows through my body at the mere thought of it. I'm getting married and yet I'm fantasising about a boy from my youth, a boy who more than likely no longer exists. But what if he does still exist somewhere beneath the messed-up man that Jaspar found in Ibiza, just like the teenage Alice is still inside of me, despite the passage of time and the heartbreak? And what if I were to find him? Oh my God, am I actually thinking these things! Stop right now before you mess everything up, Alice Cooper. These are dangerous thoughts.

The ring of the doorbell lets me know that my friend has arrived.

'What's going on, Alice!' Jo says when I answer the door.

'It's Christmas Eve, I've been told,' I reply.

'Well, it's lucky I brought this then,' she says and produces a bottle of Chablis.

I step aside and let her in. She leaves her bag down, then heads straight for the kitchen where she gets two glasses and beckons me into my own front room. I love when Jo is like this – the real Jo – who appears when it's just the two of us and disappears when Robert is in the room. That she isn't comfortable around my soon-to-be-husband is pretty obvious. She can't hide it from me – I know her too well. She pours me a glass of wine, then one for herself and we toast our evening.

'I'm so happy not to have to think about work for the next few weeks,' she declares. 'I've a new client starting soon that I think might be a bit of a nightmare so I'm going to make the most of my time off.' My friend is an interior designer and often has to deal with some demanding characters.

'I miss the children,' I say and this immediately reminds me about New York. 'Robert's dropped a bombshell.' I take a drink before I continue, leaving Jo hanging on for a bit. 'Apparently we're moving to New York,' I say eventually.

Her jaw drops open. 'Fuck off!'

I shake my head.

'When?' Jo sounds a bit bewildered.

'After the honeymoon.'

'But how? Why?'

'His firm want him to set up a new office over there.'

'I don't know what to say, Alice! I should be happy for you and somewhere deep inside I'm sure I am, but I'm sad for me. How do you feel about it? To be honest you don't look over the moon at the prospect.'

'It's a shock.'

'Robert said nothing to you before?'

I shake my head.

'So?' Jo asks.

'I don't want to go. I don't want to leave my job. I love London. And I haven't even begun to think about leaving you. I mean, we've lived in the same country since we were kids.'

Now it's Jo's turn to nod her head.

'God, Alice! … Maybe I could move too. That way you'll have a baby sitter when the baby Shaws come along.'

'Would you like to live in New York?'

'Well, Jaspar is quite taken with the city.'

'Is he now! You two are in communication a lot.'

'Ja, he messages me a few times a week.'

'Mmmm.'

Jo smiles.

'He's nice, ja. You know I always had a soft spot for him. And he looks bloody good!

'If his Facebook profile picture is a true representation, then he looks very good,' I assure her. 'Has he mentioned Denzel again?' The question pops out before I have time to stop it.

'No! … Alice! Man, have you been going to that dark place again?'

'No,' I say a bit too quickly and feel my face reddening.

'I'm just sorry I mentioned him in the first place. I've been beating myself up big time. But I only wanted you to know that he was in a right state and show you that you had a lucky escape, ja?'

'I know, Jo. Jesus, calm down. I only asked a question because I'm curious. He's history. It's been, what? … nearly twenty years, for God's sake.' The truth is I know exactly how long it's been since I last saw him.

'Ja, but there was a lot of history,' says Jo.

'And that's what it is – history,' I reassure her.

She nods her head. A knowing look passes between us; we've been through a lot together.

'Where is Mr Shaw tonight?' she asks in an effort to change the subject.

'You can guess, can't you!'

'Work?'

'Yep, a few last minute things to do before the holiday.'

'I'm not complaining. It's nice to have the place to ourselves,' she says and winks as she pours another glass of wine. 'Merry Christmas, Alice Cooper!'

'Merry Christmas, Jo Mitchel!'

8
Family Christmas

Ah wake up in Sid's bed and sit up.

'Merry Christmas, Sid!' Ah say.

'Merry Christmas, Denzel,' he replies from across the room. 'It's snowing.'

Ah get out of bed and join him by the window.

'I never saw a white Christmas in my life,' my brother tells me.

'Me neither – well, up until now.'

We stand together and watch the falling snow gather on the ground. Borough market looks proper beautiful, for sure, like a scene from a movie.

'Today, Ah will make contact with Holly,' Ah tell ma brother and his image fades away, leaving me alone in his bedroom.

Ah call after him but he's gone. Holly has been especially on ma mind given the Billy association. Ah'd found her on Facebook, thanks to our mutual friend Pia, best friend to Holly and girlfriend to Marco, one of ma bad associations in Ibiza, the one who had been largely responsible – aside from me, of course – for what had happened to Sid. Holly's Facebook account is under her full name, which Ah hadn't known before. Her profile was as Ah'd expected it to be – artsy and craftsy. Ja, Ah'd found Holly Du Plessis easily enough, which astonished me considering the billions of us that are on this planet. Ah'm only recently beginning to see the real benefits of social media. Everyone can connect so easily now. Of course, that could be a real bad thing as well, but for now it's a blessing. Today Ah'll send ma first message. Ah'd wanted ma first Facebook contact to be with Alice, but now Ah desire my first contact with her to be in person, however that happens. Ah reckon Ah don't need to know the how, for even though right now we are apart, Ah believe the universe is conspiring to put us together. Ah mean, hadn't it already sent us both to the Brixton Academy. Ja! For sure.

Ah sit out on ma windowsill and smoke a cigarette, watching the snow fall and imagining ma little brother sitting here doing this very same thing when he was growing up while Ah was in Sea Point with ma messed-up family. Judging from the little bits Ah've heard, Ah think his upbringing was a similar bed of roses to mine. For sure. No wonder we found each other in Ibiza and became friends. No wonder at all. We were cut from the same cloth and our lives brought us together once we'd survived our turbulent childhoods. 'You survived that horror but not our reunion, little brother.' But your time was your time, like you keep telling me. That's what the Tao says as well: everything has an order, a natural order. We must all flow from one moment to the next and life and death are part of that flow; we are constantly walking with death every day. When Ah first read that it fucked ma head up. One of the reasons Ah vacated the land of books was that Ah was forever reading heavy shit that messed with ma mind. It wasn't a good pastime for someone with ma deep tendencies. Best Ah keep things light. The exception to ma reading ban is the Tao – heavy but necessary.

And music helps, for sure. The more Ah come to know ma father the more Ah begin to think this is something Ah've inherited from him. Ah know Ah'm in the company of a deep thinker too. Ah can feel his heaviness as sure as Ah can feel ma own. Sid Vicious had this too. However, given that his mother killed herself, Ah think Sid might have been at another level, spawned from two deep thinkers. Ah've been saved by the presence of ma mother in ma biological equation. Wendy Anderson is about as shallow as a puddle in mud. She doesn't run deeper than surface – never has and probably never will. The only thing Ah had in common with ma mother was her womb, and once Ah was out of there, we were done.

Ah get dressed and hear sounds coming from the kitchen. Tim and Bill are awake and Ah join them. We are celebrating Christmas to the sound of Beethoven. Somehow this doesn't surprise me. Ah hadn't been expecting a mainstream Christmas, musically or otherwise.

'Good morning!' Ah say.

Both Bill and Tim say good morning in unison, then look at each other in surprise and smile, enjoying the joke. It makes me feel warm inside and Ah realise that these two men might just be in love, for real. They are big men behaving like little boys, which is a sure sign. It's amusing to see Tim like this. Ah wonder if Sid knew his father was gay and if maybe it had something to do with why his mother killed herself. It sure can't have helped. Ah return from the backstory quickly. For the first time in maybe forever Ah'd like to have a Christmas far from the darkness, as Ah share it with ma father.

'How did you sleep, Denzel?' Tim asks. It's the same question he asks every morning.

Ah give ma usual answer. 'Very well thanks.' Ah've been sleeping the best sleeps of ma life as Ah make the journey back from drug addiction.

'Help yourself to some Bucks Fizz,' Bill says.

'Denzel doesn't drink,' Tim interjects.

Bill looks at me and raises his eyebrow. Ma face isn't the face of someone who has lived a sober life.

'I'm in a programme,' Ah explain. He nods and gives me a knowing look. 'I'll have some coffee though.' Bill serves me and then invites me to help maself from the platter of cheese, smoked salmon, caviar and breads. Breakfast is a posher affair this morning than Ah usually have in this house.

'Bill has expensive tastes,' Tim tells me as if he's read ma mind.

'Ja, for sure,' Ah say. Ah'd only ever had caviar once before, with Titus of all people. Ah remember him now and it makes me smile. Ah'll call him today and wish him a Merry Christmas, for sure.

'He can also navigate through this kitchen in a way that's beyond my comprehension, so he'll be cooking the meal.'

'You want a hand, boet,' Ah offer. 'Ah'm no chef but Ah can fetch and carry.'

'Thanks,' he replies. 'I might just take you up on that.'

Tim looks uneasy, unsure of what to say next, so Bill comes to his rescue.

'So, Denzel, how has your father been treating you?' he asks.

'Very well,' Ah reply. 'Providing this lovely roof over ma head in a nice part of the capital city.'

'Yes, Borough is great,' Bill replies.

'So what's on the menu?' Tim cuts in.

'What do you think, maestro? Turkey! You're not vegetarian, Denzel? God, tell me you're not vegetarian!'

'Na! Ah'm a meat-eater for sure,' Ah say and he looks relieved.

'Turkey and the full works, now that I've a decent workspace. I love this kitchen. It's soooo much bigger than mine in New York.'

'How long have you been in New York?' Ah ask.

'Years now,' he tells me. 'A lifetime.' A look passes between the two men. 'But maybe I'm coming home,' Bill says his eyes remaining on Tim.

Ah like the feeling in this room. Despite the fact that Ah've spent most of ma life on that other path, the one that goes in the opposite direction to love, Ah'm still sentimental. Alice. Alice. Alice. So much can happen. Thoughts of a future with her terrify me for two reasons. It's quite possible that she might not want me. It's also possible that Ah'll get another chance but Ah'll mess it up again. Ah start to feel heavy and then Ah remind maself that it's Christmas and Ah smile ma biggest smile in the hope that the rest of ma body will take the hint.

Ah help Bill in the kitchen while Tim prepares the room where just the day before Ah'd listened to Tom Waits. He transforms the place into a space worthy of the amazing dinner that Bill's preparing, producing a dining table and chairs from somewhere. He sets the table for four. Just before we begin eating Ah'm about to ask Tim if we're expecting someone else when he raises his glass and says a single word – the name of his youngest son. The three of us toast Sid, the person who had brought us all together. Ah watch as ma little brother takes his place, a huge smile on his face.

*

The door bell rings at 2 p.m. on the dot and its sound brings me back to the present. I've been staring out the kitchen window looking at the snow. It's amazing and I would have liked nothing better than to go out and have a snowball fight with someone this morning, but given my fiancé's complete unwillingness to participate and Jo's fragile state it's not an option.

Robert's family are the most punctual I've ever met. When they say a time you can set your watch by them. I open the door and Helen Shaw is the first person I see.

'Hello darling,' she says, air kissing me and then looking me up and down from head to toe. 'You look beautiful, Ali, as always.'

'Thank you. You too, Helen.'

'Isn't this weather amazing! The first white Christmas I can ever remember.'

'Yes, it's fantastic,' I reply.

Next comes Robert's father, Angus, who kisses my cheek and then looks me up and down, but in a different way than his wife had done. Although I do my best to hide it, Angus Shaw gives me the creeps and I always feel a little bit uneasy when he's around me – or any woman for that matter. I'm sure Helen must notice her husband's behaviour. I wonder if she ever reacts. Lastly comes Keith, Robert's younger brother, who looks like he'd prefer be anywhere else. He half-heartedly hugs me and then drags himself into the front room to see his brother. At one stage, I'd tried to get Keith and Jo together but it'd never worked out. Jo had actually quite fancied him but her feelings didn't appear to be reciprocated. Then Keith met Aisha, his current girlfriend, and the idea left the table.

Robert fixes everyone a drink and we toast the day. I head into the kitchen to put the final touches to the meal. Helen has brought dessert and it looks amazing, like all things Helen Shaw creates. She's a wizard in the kitchen; Robert is forever telling me this, as is Angus when he's near to any kitchen. Keith isn't so obvious in his maternal adoration, but he's just as much under her thumb as the other two. Helen Shaw loves 'her three boys' and prides herself on being the perfect wife and mother. And this is the standard she sets for her sons' partners. Apparently, I passed her inspection with flying colours, but like I said, I play the game well.

I look out the window and before I can stop myself I'm heading for the back door. Once outside, I find my way into the garden and not wanting to stop making deep footprints in the snow, I continue walking all the way out of our back garden to the front of the house and into the street. There's hardly anyone outside and I enjoy the solitude. This is romantic weather and I think once again of Denzel. I wonder what he's doing this Christmas and if he might be wondering what I'm doing. Our last Christmas together had been at Sea Point. We'd left our respective family gatherings and made our way to the beach to exchange gifts – always music. That was what we both valued above everything else then; we discovered new bands and shared new treasures with each other. Then we'd gone for a swim together, exploring each other's bodies and working our way towards what would happen a few months later –the thing that changed everything.

'Jesus! Helen Shaw always looks at me like I've just fallen off the back of a truck!' Jo says as she joins me outside.

I laugh. 'I won't insult your intelligence by suggesting you might have misread the situation.'

'Na, don't bother. And it's a good thing you can cook, given how those two men are gushing about her dessert. Apparently it's the best ever made and worthy of an award!'

'Shush,' I say. 'She might hear!'

'What? Does she have bionic ears as well!'

'I wouldn't be surprised!'

'Fuck, Alice, I've such a hangover. We should've stopped at that first bottle of wine.'

I nod although I'm feeling okay. Last night, I'd been drinking slowly because I was afraid that if I got really drunk I'd talk about Denzel again and confess that I'd been thinking about contacting him on Facebook. So I'd paced myself and let my friend drink most of the wine.

'We should go back in,' I say.

'Do we have to?'

I don't answer but simply walk and eventually she follows. We're not long back in the kitchen when Helen comes to join us. Jo and Helen exchange what could loosely be described as smiles; only *I* know better than to call their grimaces smiles.

'Can I help with anything, Ali?' Helen asks.

'Alice has it all under control,' Jo replies, emphasising my full name. Robert and his family have always insisted on calling me 'Ali', something that Jo dislikes. It also doesn't help her strained relationship with Kate, who has picked up this habit too. Personally, I'm not that bothered, which was what I told Jo when she mentioned it after a few bottles of wine a while back.

'Ja, Helen. Please – go and make yourself at home. I'll be in shortly to do presents,' I assure her.

'Great. I'll keep an eye on the drinks, shall I?' she offers.

'That would be great, thanks,' I reply and she makes her way back to 'her three boys'.

Jo rolls her eyes. I smile and am thankful that Jo isn't quite so expressive about her dislike of Robert. I wonder if Helen knows yet about New York, and then Jo asks that very question.

'I don't think so or she would have mentioned it,' I say. 'I've a feeling he may make the announcement today ... Let's do presents,' I add quickly wanting to escape the conversation.

'Fan-bloody-tastic!' she says sarcastically.

'You behave, Jo Mitchel,' I say.

Once dinner is done and we're all sitting digesting our food, Robert coughs loudly and I know what's coming next.

'Ali and I have some big news,' he announces.

I'm just thinking that this is a very poor choice of words when Helen finishes my thought.

'You're not pregnant Ali, are you?' She says like it might be the worst fate that could happen to a soon-to-be bride.

'God no,' I say. I look fleetingly at Jo and know that we'll both be thinking the same thing, remembering a time when I'd given a different answer to that same question.

'No, Mother,' Robert says. 'At least, not yet. I'll wait until I've made a respectable woman of her.' He winks and I can almost feel Jo's need for a sick bucket right now. 'We're going to New York,' he says, beaming.

'What do you mean?' Helen asks, which reveals that she isn't the only one who has been excluded from Robert's decision.

'Ali and I will be moving to New York after the wedding.'

Helen looks at her eldest son as if he's just spoken to her in a foreign language. It's the first time I can ever remember her being lost for words.

9
New Year's Resolutions

There's a call from Clive on New Year's Eve and an invitation which Ah graciously accept. Later, when ma father awkwardly invites me to accompany him and Bill to a gala, Ah'm glad of the other plans – best they have a little time alone to celebrate the New Year. That's how Ah would like it should Alice and Ah get back together, and Ah think about the potential for next year's celebrations if things work out according to ma plan. But this year Ah'll spend it with Clive. Ah get to his place at 9 p.m. He lives in a dodgy-looking neighbourhood and Ah pass a number of people Ah recognise to be dealers on ma way to his front door. Ah wonder how Clive does, living alongside all this temptation, but Ah suppose he's thinking of his son and it's enough to keep him on the straight and narrow. A promise of a future unlike his shitty past is enough. Ja, for sure.

Ah knock on his door. Two minutes later it flies open and Ah hear 'Let's Dance' playing in the background.

'Hey mate, you just missed the boy!' he says.

'Ah shame! Sometime soon, ja?'

'Absolutely!'

Ah hand him a bottle of fizzy water and a couple of plastic champagne flutes Ah'd bought in a pound shop earlier today. Ah'm becoming obsessed with pound shops these days; Ah can spend hours in them finding stuff. Most of it Ah need, but a lot of it, Ah must confess, Ah don't and Ah just buy it because Ah can for a pound. Ah guess ma obsessive nature is taking another avenue, but as long as Ah keep ma spending to pound shops, Ah shouldn't break the bank.

Clive smiles at the gesture.

'Something to toast in the New Year!' Ah say.

'Great, mate!'

'I've just made some coffee,' he tells me as Ah take in the strong aroma.

'Ja, that smells like some good brew!'

'It's the best. Tracy bought it for me in a speciality shop near where she lives. She's living with her parents in a posh part of town, a lot better than this shit-hole. It's unbelievable I managed to father a child with such a great girl despite the fact that I was in an awful state when I first stumbled across her. But I suppose Ben was meant to happen.'

'You believe that, boet?' Ah ask.

'What?' he asks, stopping mid coffee prep to look in my direction.

'That children are meant to happen.'

'Yep. I think coupling is merely a way of getting us here. We're not in control at all. That's why so many people get into such bad pairings and then wonder how it all happened. The power lies with the next generation, even before they're born. We make the problems they'll solve.'

'That's some heavy shit,' Ah say.

'Well, life is some heavy shit,' he replies and laughs.

Ah nod ma head and he gets back to pouring the coffee into two multicoloured mugs.

'Ah never thought about it that way, but maybe you have a point. Have you heard of the Tao Te Ching?'

He shrugs his shoulders and shakes his head.

'It's an Eastern text that speaks about everything having a natural order,' Ah explain.

'That's exactly what I'm saying.'

Ah take a look around the flat. 'The place is in great condition,' Ah say.

'You should have seen it six months ago.' Clive rolls his eyes. 'It was in a right state – like a mini crack house. If Tracy had seen it then, I doubt she'd let Ben come like she does now.'

'She never came here before?'

'No, I tried to keep a lot of my addiction from Tracy – well, the stuff I could hide. Of course, I couldn't hide anything, not really. She could see it all over me quite easily.'

'Ja, Ah know that drill,' Ah say. 'Ah remember an old school friend found me in Ibiza and his reaction told me Ah was in a bad way. Ah don't remember a lot about the night we met except that he was looking at me like I was a pane of glass about to fall out of a window frame and smash into a million pieces in front of him.'

'I know that exact look! It's nice not to see it on Tracy's face these days.'

'Ja, for sure!'

Ah take ma coffee from him, hand him over a cigarette and we light up. 'So this is ma last night as a smoker,' Ah announce.

'Fuck off!'

'Na, Ah decided Ah'll give it a go. What the fuck have Ah got to lose. Ah might as well go the full hog.'

'Fair play to you, mate. I'm not even considering it right now.'

'Well, Ah'll try,' Ah say. 'One day at a time, sweet Jesus, as the country woman said.'

'Tammy Wynette. My pops was forever playing Tammy. 'Stand By Your Man'. I'm sure my poor mother was wishing she hadn't. I got a lot of my bad shit from him but at least I missed out on his bad taste in music. Bowie has a new album coming out soon I heard.'

'Ja!'

'About time too, but I guess better late than never. So do you fancy watching a movie? I've got a Cohen Brother classic if you're up for it.'

'Ja,' Ah say. 'Ah'm always up for anything they do.'

We watch *No Country For Old Men*, which doesn't disappoint. It ends just in time for us to open the bottle of fizzy water and toast the New Year.

'Happy New Year, Denzel,' Clive says. 'May it bring you all you wish for.'

You too, Clive,' Ah say and take the cigarette he offers.

'I thought you were giving up.'

'Mañana,' Ah say. 'Tonight is still tonight.'

'That kind of talk will get you killed,' he says, and although he smiles, Ah pick up the serious undertones. We are peas in an abusive pod.

New Year's Day comes and Ah stick to ma word. Ah don't smoke and it's hard, maybe even harder to stop than the other substances on ma long list of things I've had to steer clear of. By the evening time, Ah'm nearly crazy. And then ma phone rings – the one Ah haven't used since Christmas Day when Ah'd tried to call Titus. Ah'm full sure it's him so Ah answer.

'Denzel!' the familiar voice says.

'Titus! How goes it?'

'Good! Sorry I'm only returning your call now but there was some business I had to take care of over Christmas.'

'No holiday for you then.'

'Na. You should know by now, Ah don't do holidays.'

'Ah forgot.'

'It's good to hear from you. It's been a while.'

'Ja, sorry.'

'No need to apologise. We're talking now, ja?'

'Ja. Happy New Year.'

'Is it? Let's just wait another while and see. I'm London-bound.'

'Lekker. It'll be great to see you.'

'Ja – and you. I'll call you on this number next week, ja, and we'll catch up?'

'That sounds great.'

'Till then, Denzel.'

He hangs up and Ah get a lump in ma throat; the tears begin falling shortly after. Not smoking is making me soft. Ah let the tears spill until they're done. No booze, no nothing with Titus in town. Ja, that will be interesting! All the same, it will be great to see ma old friend. Ah eventually fuse together again and decide to do something to take ma mind of ma lack of nicotine. Ah log into Facebook to see if there's anything from Holly. Ah'd messaged her Christmas night, and then Ah'd taken a good look at her art. There was a lot on the net and Ah'd been pleasantly surprised. Ah'd no idea she was so talented – and why wouldn't she be: it turns out her father is a big-shot artist. Ah'm delighted to see an unread message in Facebook and ma stomach does a little turn. Ah click into the communication and begin to read …

Hi Denzel

Belated Happy Christmas
And
Happy New Year!

This is a surprise, a pleasant surprise. Thank you for your message and for your concern.

And also for staying with me that black day in Ibiza. I wanted to thank you back then but you left too soon. And then I wanted to be away from that place and those people too and I begged Pia to come with me but she stayed. Imagine.

I am so happy to hear you are clean and now living in London, home of Sid. Your friend would be very happy for you. I think of him often and I think somehow he looks down on all of us. It has been so hard to love someone and have them taken away so quickly, but I have many memories in me and my work. I paint in Paris all the time and I am getting ready for a show to exhibit all the portraits I discovered in Ibiza. There are three of Sid that I'm told are wonderful. I think they are too, but of course I think all the pictures that come into my studio are wonderful. Somehow I couldn't think bad of any of them!

The exhibition will be January 27th and it will be super great if you can come to Paris. Yes??? Thank you for getting in touch Denzel and let us keep this connection. We have something in common, someone that neither of us wants to forget. Yes???

Ciao for now,
Holly
kiss kiss

The message reaches me and Ah begin to cry again. Sentimental detoxing fool. Ah blow ma nose and answer.

Hi Holly

It is great to hear from you and that you are living in Paris and painting. I saw your work on the internet. You are a talented lady. I don't know much about art but I can recognise beautiful pictures and yours are beautiful, for sure.

Our connection is firmly fixed as far as I'm concerned and Ah will be there at your exhibition. For sure. Until then, keep Paris warm for me ;-)

Happy New Year!

Denzel

And there it is! Ah will go to Paris. Ma first time in Paris. Na! Ah remember Ah'd been there on a Roger Waters tour. Ma poor frazzled head. There's so much blurred in there. But the fog is clearing. For sure.

The day after New Year's, Ah head back to ma little group. As usual Ah meet Clive out front and as usual he's listening to David Bowie. Today it's 'Diamond Dogs', and he gives me a listen through one of the earphones and we both sing along to the end.

'How's it going with the smokes?' he asks when David has finished.

'Not a one.'

'Good for you! And you're still sober?'

'Of course!'

'Me too. My first ever – well, since I can remember.'

'Ah know what you mean!'

'Amazing. I never thought I could go back.'

'Me neither,' Ah assure him.

'But it would have been nice to get fucked just once,' he says and looks at me with eyes that Ah recognise, addiction at their centre.

'That kind of talk could set off a lot of sirens, Clive.'

'I know, Denzel, but what's the point in denying it.'

'Sure,' Ah say. 'But be careful not to stay suspended there for too long.'

'I know, mate. It's a dangerous place.'

The meeting does what it needs to do and after a few hours with my addicted friends and fellow survivors, Ah feel ready to go out into the world again for another week. Afterwards, Ah go to Costa with Clive and we have our usual cup of coffee. He smokes; Ah don't. Instead, Ah touch the nicotine patch, now a permanent fixture on ma arm, from time to time for reassurance. Ah'd wondered if Billy would join us after our chat last time but she doesn't. It seems that Billy and Ah are back to how it was before, and except for the fact that both of us know we spent a significant evening together, it's as if it never happened. But Ah guess she's doing what she needs to do, as are all six of us – the dregs of society trying to make themselves into a healthy stream again, free-flowing and pure as we once were before it all got screwed up. The amazing thing is that we've come this far. Four months. An eternity for us all. Two months to go, Alice. Just two short months. Hold on girl.

*

Jo pours the Prosecco and wishes me a Happy New Year, even though the actual moment is nine hours away.

'I can't believe you're blowing me off for a bloody gala!'

'Me neither. If I had my way I wouldn't be going. It was Robert's idea.'

'Don't go, Alice!' she says, and although I know she's joking, for a split second I think about it. I really think about it. Robert would be furious.

'What's a bloody gala anyway!'

'I'm not quite sure,' I admit.

'You should come out clubbing with me.'

'You've no idea how tempted I am but ...'

'You have to go Robert's way,' she cuts in.

'You don't like Robert very much, do you?' This is the first time I've ever asked her outright and she goes bright red.

'What kind of a question is that? He's not my cup of tea, but I'm not marrying him. I can see that he's good for you.'

'Really?'

'Of course. He looks after you and he's loyal to the core – which is all that matters really.'

I think about mentioning his affair but don't, not wanting to get into it right now – just like so much else that's running through my mind at the moment.

'So what are your resolutions?' I ask in an effort to change the subject.

'You know me, Alice – the usual stuff. More exercise, less alcohol and chocolate. Oh, and more sex. A lot more sex. The last year has been so rubbish. I only ever remember having less sex when I was small and having no sex at all.'

'Good luck to you,' I say.

'Ja! I'm hoping that Jaspar reappearing will start the ball rolling again.'

'You've asked him to the wedding?'

'I was meaning to check with you. Is that okay?'

'Ja. Sure.'

'Great! Thanks! My sex life just took a turn in the right direction,' my friend says and smiles.

Later, I'm feeling tipsy as I finish getting ready. I'll need to take it easy tonight as I'm wearing a 1930s-style burgundy satin gown that I found in a vintage shop which requires the wearer to stay sober to prevent any wardrobe malfunctions.

'You look beautiful,' Robert says. 'Is the dress new?'

'Ja.'

His hand travels down the silk fabric at the front and finds skin and then my nipple.

'We don't have time, Robert,' I say, and the door bell rings as if backing me up. We haven't had sex since before Christmas and the truth is I'm not finding the prospect of it remotely appealing right now. He looks at me for a long time before eventually removing his hand from my breast. For the first time, he reminds me of his father and I get the same uncomfortable feeling I get when Angus Shaw is close by. Robert leaves the bedroom first and once the queasy feeling has passed, I follow.

'Wow! Guys, that's extraordinary!' Kate says in reaction to Robert's announcement about New York.

'Congratulations!' says Frank.

We're sitting at a table in a magnificently decorated hall in Alexandra Palace having just finished a fabulous five-course dinner. Very soon there will be music, courtesy of the London Symphonic Orchestra, followed by a firework display at midnight. Then a live band will dance us into the New Year. That, apparently, is what makes up a gala.

'Yeah, we're thrilled,' says Robert, looking in my direction.

I smile but say nothing. Inside I'm bursting to say no. NO! NO! NO! I don't want to go to New York. Right now, I don't want any of this. I don't belong here! I imagine myself dancing with Jo and wish I could somehow transport myself to wherever she is. No longer able to bear my surroundings, I excuse myself and head for the ladies. On my way, I pass by a door that's slightly ajar and get a whiff that lets me know that that's where the smokers congregate. A huge craving hits me and I follow my urge all the way outside. The smokers are mostly in couples but I spot a lone man and make my way over to him.

'Excuse me, could I possibly bother you for a cigarette?' I ask.

The man is in his mid fifties and very handsome. 'Sure,' he says and hands me a Marlboro Gold box and an expensive-looking lighter.

I take one and after lighting up, I inhale deeply. 'Thank you so much,' I say.

'That's quite all right. I must say, that's an exquisite dress.'

'Thank you. Happy New Year.'

'And you. Are you here with your fiancé?' he asks pointing at my ring.

'Yes.'

'He loves you very much judging from the size of that rock.'

'I don't know. Are you married?' I ask.

'No. I wouldn't mind being married, but I'm not sure my fella's the marrying type.'

'I'm not sure I am either.'

'Oh dear! When's the wedding?'

'February.'

'Well, you'd better get sure fairly soon or else break the news to the poor boy,' he says.

'Ja, good advice.'

'You're South African?'

'Ja,' I say. 'And you sound like an American.'

'No, I'm an Englishman, but I've lived in New York for a long, long time.'

'An Englishman in New York.'

'Yes, quite,' he says, deliberately sounding very English.

I smile.

'I'm Bill,' he says and extends his hand.

'I'm Alice.'

We shake hands and I find it very reassuring, like this is a man I could trust.

'You don't usually smoke,' he says.

'Na, only on social occasions.'

'Me too, and when I'm under stress.'

'And there's that too.'

'So, Alice, why are you getting married if you're not the marrying type.'

'I don't know,' I tell him. 'I was sure before, but now it doesn't feel right.'

'Do you love him?'

'No.'

And there it is. It feels good to say it out loud to someone.

'Okay. I feel compelled to mention that it's maybe not such a good idea to marry someone you don't love. I'm told it helps if you love your partner, especially after the honeymoon period.'

'Or maybe it's the best idea not to love them. Maybe love is actually what makes marriages fail,' I say.

'No. I'm not convinced. I'm a romantic and I'll stick with my sentimentalities, thanks.'

'You love your partner?'

'My dear, more than I can say. I always have. We've been apart for a long time, but now it looks like we might be getting a second chance.'

'That's great,' I say. Talk of second chances brings Denzel to the front of my mind.

'Ali!' The voice is Robert's and it's close to my ear as he wraps his arms around me from behind. 'I thought I'd find you here having a sneaky cigarette ... Hi,' he says to Bill. 'Has my soon-to-be wife been bumming cigarettes from you?'

'Ah, you know her so well,' Bill says.

'There's no one who knows her better,' he says and pulls me inside with a lot more force than is needed.

It makes me wonder how much of our conversation he might have heard.

10
Parental Connections

Ah wait in the hotel lobby for Titus and get a feeling of excitement in the pit of ma stomach. Ah don't think so much about Titus but this feeling lets me know he means a lot to me. Ah haven't seen him since that awful morning in Ibiza and it makes me want a cigarette. Ma abstinence has spanned seven whole days and although the patches are working a treat, there's a whole other part to the addiction going on outside of the physical craving.

The door flies open and Ah can tell it's Titus even before his familiar frame is revealed. He spots me immediately – not difficult, as Ah stand out in this posh establishment. Ma friend travels in style.

'Denzel!' he says and smiles his big smile.

'Ja! It's me!'

He hugs me and delivers two slaps to ma back which Ah return automatically even though it's an age since Ah've been called upon to deliver this salutation.

'You look good. Ah like the new cut,' he says.

Of course! Titus hasn't seen me without ma hair.

'Ja, thanks boet. It's good to see you. You look like you've been spending some time with the sun.'

'Ja, just been to Joburg for a while and thought Ah'd stop off and see you before heading back to Ibiza. See if Ah can bring you back to the small island with me. Have you eaten?'

'Na,' Ah say, checking in with ma newly awakened hunger. Ma appetite has grown without cigarettes.

'Great. Let's have some dinner. The food here is good,' he says and leads me to the dining room.

Titus is known in this hotel and he's well looked after here, in much the same way as he is in Ibiza – in much the same way he's looked after no matter where he goes, Ah'm sure.

We get to our table and he's about to order a bottle of wine when Ah tell him Ah'm clean. He looks at me and sucks down on his teeth.

'Is that so! No wonder you look so good. Ah'm shocked, I won't deny it.'

'Me too, most days, but then the odd time Ah forget about it – at least for a while.'

'So where are you staying here and what have you been doing?'

Ah remember that Titus knows nothing of the revelations that saw me leave Ibiza.

'Ah'm living with ma father.'

He raises his eyebrows. 'That's another shock, Denzel! You're out to surprise the shit out of me tonight.'

'Ja! There's one more, but maybe Ah should wait until after dinner.'

'You've met Kylie Minogue and now you're getting married!'

The name Kylie Minogue coming out of Titus's mouth makes me laugh. 'Ja, that's it for sure,' Ah reply.

Titus moves closer to me. 'Ah tell you what, let's at least order and then you can continue on your quest.'

We both order steak in the same raw state and Ah have a Coke while Titus has what Ah know will be a fine wine.

'So spill the beans,' he says.

'Na, Ah'm not getting married to Kylie, boet. Sorry to disappoint you.'

He raises his hand slowly and spreads his fingers as if he's drawing the words out of ma soul, his signal for me to proceed. It's a gesture unique to Titus that Ah've forever loved and forgotten.

'Just after Ah saw you that last time in Ibiza Ah went back to the hostel to get ma stuff and in the process Ah bumped into Sid's father. It turns out he just happens to be ma father too.'

The drinks arrive before Titus has a chance to react. He thanks the waitress. She smiles at him and tells him not to hesitate to call her should he want anything more. He thanks her again, says he will keep that in mind and doesn't take his eyes off her until she's left us to it. Just before she heads into the kitchen she turns back and smiles at him. He looks at her from over his sunglasses and smiles. Quite the charmer! Ah've never noticed this side to him before.

'So that must have turned you inside out. You'd no idea?' he says.

'None. It's hard to believe, ja?'

He nods.

'If someone were telling me Ah'd be sceptical as fuck, but somehow it happened.'

'Ja, it's extraordinary, but the world isn't such a big place really. So how is it here with your father?'

'It's good. It came at the best of times. The worst of times and the best of times.'

'Charles Dickens wrote that,' Titus says.

'Ja?'

'And I know what he meant. ... So I won't be able to entice you to come back with me?'

'Na, Titus. Not this time.'

'But maybe in the future?'

'Who can tell? Ah mean, in this life anything can happen!'

'Isn't that so!'

'How have you been?' Ah ask him.

'You know me Denzel, same old same old.'

'Business is good?'

He moves his head from side to side. 'I get by.' He smiles his crocodile smile.

'And what about Marco?'

Ah feel compelled to ask about him even though Ah'd promised maself Ah'd let Titus bring up the asshole who had set the chain of events in motion that had led to the death of ma brother.

'Ah've severed ties with Marco. Too much of a liability.'

'Ah'm glad to hear it.'

'You know, there's a job for you when you come back.'

'You sound like you expect that Ah will.'

'Na, I'll rephrase and say should you choose to come back. I don't expect anything, Denzel. Expectation is a sure way to lose sight of what is actually happening and I can't afford to do that in my line of work.'

Titus owns a company that provides equipment and maintenance to many of the clubs around Europe. In addition, he supplies his clients' venues with the best Class A drugs available. It means he is a very wealthy man and well protected. There are a lot of very powerful people with their paws firmly dipped in his ventures.

'Thanks, boet, but Ah think Ah'll stay here for now,' Ah say.

'And is there a wife on the horizon?'

Ah shrug ma shoulders. 'Maybe.'

'Best you keep that one under wraps until I need to buy a suit. Don't go jinxing it,' he says, reiterating ma own reservations about premature talk.

We finish our meals and while Titus has a glass of the finest port, Ah sip on a Cherry Coke, an old favourite of mine that Ah haven't tasted in years! Ah leave Titus in the hotel lobby just as the waitress from earlier sits across from us at the bar. Looking very much off-duty, she smiles at ma friend in a way that lets us both know he'll get lucky tonight. Ah leave him with the same promise as last time: to stay in touch.

When Ah get back, ma father is sitting at the kitchen table.

'I want to talk to you, Denzel,' he says.

Ah take a seat. 'Ja, for sure!'

'Tea?' he offers and Ah say yes, not because Ah want tea but because Ah've come to know that it makes him feel more comfortable to sit with someone when there's a pot of tea close at hand.

'Ja, please.'

He makes the tea and Ah sit and wait in silence. Tonight there's no music in the kitchen. Ma father puts the tea in the middle of the table and sets two cups in front of us. He lets the tea brew and then pours it, and only after we've taken the first sip does he begin to talk.

'Bill and I have known each other for over thirty years,' he says looking into his cup as if he's reading his tea leaves.

Ah just nod, expecting that he'll see the action from the corner of his eye.

'We were lovers before I got married and then we became lovers again years later.'

Still Ah say nothing.

'Does that shock you?' he asks.

Ah'm not sure how to answer, but Ah get the feeling that ma answer is of paramount importance. 'Not really, now that Ah've seen you together,' Ah say.

'But does it shock you to find out that I'm gay?'

'Na! That is your business boet.' The 'boet', hugely inappropriate here, just slips out and Ah realise Ah'm not as chilled as Ah think. 'To be honest it's a bit embarrassing talking to you like this because you're ma father, ja?'

Tim nods his head. 'I wanted to tell you because I've kept it a secret for so long. It has caused desperate unhappiness. My wife Penny knew I had affairs with men before we married yet still she married me. She also knew about all the affairs I had when we were married, even though I was sure I hid them from her. And when she died – killed herself – she left me a letter telling me that she knew about them all. She blamed me for her illness and her decision to take her own life. I told Sid the story the last time I saw him. I thought he knew. I thought he'd read the suicide letter when he found his mother dead, and that was my fault. It was all my fault and I spent my life blaming myself – until Sid told me to stop, that none of it was my fault.'

Ah've nothing to say. This is all heavy stuff, even bigger than all the stuff Ah hear in Never Again.

'There are definite parallels between us, Denzel. I'm not a big believer in coincidence or a fixed order. I write music, and although it's a very ordered process it comes out randomly. I've always viewed life to be like that. But what's happened over the last six months has made me question everything.'

'Ja, Ah know what you mean.'

'Of course! You of all people would. The last thing Sid said to me was that I should allow myself to be happy and I realised that the one thing that would make me happy would be to be with Bill. But I wanted you to know the whole truth. I made so many mistakes with Sid and look at how that turned out. Not very good at all. Rather bad,' he says.

Ah realise that this is Tim Harris's attempt at humour. Ah smile.

'You've never asked me about your mother,' he says.

Ah shrug. 'Ah figure it's the past.'

'I've always known I was gay. I knew when I met Wendy.'

It feels weird to hear Tim Harris talk about ma mother and call her by her first name.

'I think she probably knew too. I mean, everyone knew. I was fooling no one. I realised that afterwards. When your mother told me she was pregnant I offered to pay for an abortion, but she told me it wasn't my decision. She said she'd have the baby back in South Africa. I respected her for that, for taking responsibility when I wouldn't. Couldn't. I didn't offer to marry her because I was gay and at the time I really believed I would never marry. But that was before Penny. Somehow Penny convinced me otherwise. I should probably stop now but I'm glad I told you. It feels good to say all this to you.'

'Thanks,' Ah say, still a bit shell-shocked from the sudden onslaught of information out of the blue.

He nods. 'I don't ask you about your life, Denzel, but that doesn't mean I'm not interested. I'm just not very good at this kind of thing. But please, talk to me about anything, anytime you want.'

'For sure, Tim,' Ah say.

'Right, I'm glad we had this conversation.'

He stands up and for a minute Ah think he might be going to shake ma hand, but he doesn't.

'Me too, Tim.' Ah say. 'Thanks.'

He nods and begins clearing the table. This man is so steeped in ritual. Ah'm reminded of some of the warrior practices Ah've read about. Ah realise that ma father is a warrior. This is how he has survived everything.

Just as he's leaving – everything Ah've come to know about him tells me he will be heading back to the studio – he turns around and says something uncharacteristically spontaneous.

'Do you think you could call me Dad?'

This just about knocks the wind out of ma sails. 'Ja, Dad. For sure,' Ah answer.

In a short time, Ah've walked through a lot of heartache with this man, but now, for the first time, Ah feel like his son.

*

I look at the phone. It's time to ring Sheila Cooper and I feel my usual urge to run away and hide. My mother has had this effect on me as far back as I can remember. My father is a nightmare, but not even he can put the 'Sheila Cooper' kind of dread in me. She's forever pointing the finger and telling me how my life should be, and although there's been a slight change in her attitude since I announced that I was marrying Robert and doing what she's wanted me to do for a long time, she just can't break the habits of a lifetime. Before I pick up the phone, I remind myself that she's a long plane journey away. It gives me some comfort.

'Hello.' The voice that causes me such distress speaks into the receiver after a single ring.

She always answers immediately. It makes me wonder where the phone is positioned in the house that she can get to it so quickly. Or perhaps she hovers nearby, waiting for my call.

'Hello,' I say, and then it's her turn again.

Sheila Cooper always does most of the talking, which suits me fine. It's when she expects some participation from my side that the problems begin. My answers are never good enough. She's forever criticising me, and much as I like to believe that her criticisms don't matter, she still knows how to push my buttons.

'It's Alice,' she shouts away from the receiver, presumably to my father. 'Hello from your father,' she says, confirming my suspicions. 'So are you all set, ja?'

'For what?' I ask wanting to be facetious.

'Don't play the fool with me, Alice. Are you all set?'

'Yes,' I say.

'Good. We got your invitation but we won't be RSVPing. It's a waste of time and money, ja. They aren't the best invitations I've ever set eyes on but I suppose they're to your taste. I can't imagine Robert would have chosen them.'

Her statement is so loaded but I don't rise to the bait. It seeps inside where it will be added to the pool of reasons why I actively avoid my mother.

'I'm so looking forward to meeting Helen Shaw. Tell me, what's she wearing on the day?'

'I'm not sure,' I reply.

'What do you mean you're not sure! Have you not coordinated the bridesmaids' dresses with the mother of the groom? Alice, really! You tell her I'm wearing black and white. Let's make sure we don't clash. Your bridesmaids' dresses are still purple, ja?'

'Yes.'

'And have you found your dress?'

'No,' I lie.

'Aren't you leaving it a little late, Alice? I mean it's less than a month and we sent you all that money.'

'I still have plenty of time, Sheila. It'll be fine. Don't go getting your knickers in a twist!'

'Don't be so coarse! So we'll arrive the week before …'

'Yes, I can't wait,' I say sarcastically.

She begins to talk at me about what's going on in Sea Point and I switch off. Eventually I've had enough so I go to the front door and ring the bell.

'Sorry Sheila, there's someone at the door.'

'Okay. Look, I'll call you next week and by then you'll maybe have some good news about your dress, ja?'

I ring the doorbell once again.

'I need to go now. Goodbye.'

I hang up and let out a big sigh. As usual, I've successfully denied her access to what is going on in my life.

And what *is* going on in my life. Right now, everything feels really stale. It feels as if Robert and I are further apart than we've ever been before. I'm sure we're supposed to be closer than ever as the wedding draws nearer. In addition, I'm almost certain that he's having an affair with Sally. This in itself isn't the problem; the real problem is that I don't seem to care. In fact, it makes me happy because it means he hasn't been having sex with me. At the moment, the last thing I want to do is let him touch me. The last time we had sex was on New Year's Eve when we got home from the gala. He'd rolled on top of me just before he went to sleep. It had been quick and angry, almost like he was punishing me for something. It had convinced me that he'd heard my conversation with the charming Bill, the man who'd given me a cigarette and admired my dress. And if that isn't bad enough, I've decided that I'm not going to New York. I've yet to break the news to Robert. I'll do it tonight, I promise myself, and the thought alone makes me feel nauseous.

By the time Robert comes home, I'm sick with anxiety. He shouts hello but goes straight to the bathroom and is gone for a long time. When he reappears he's wrapped in a towel, letting me know he's just had a shower, probably to wash away the smell of Sally. He comes over and kisses me and I offer him a glass of wine, which he takes as he settles down on the sofa. I wonder if he knows what is coming next.

'Robert, I can't go to New York with you,' I say and wait for the fallout.

He takes a drink of wine and purses his lips. 'You can't or you won't,' he says.

I'm desperately uncomfortable with his tone of voice. He looks at me with stony eyes. This is a new side to my fiancé – Robert Shaw when he doesn't get his own way.

'Don't be like that,' I say. 'I teach the children at the school and I can't just leave mid year. It would really damage them.'

He raises his eyebrows and looks at me in a way that makes me regret my choice of words. 'Well, I've agreed to it now,' he says. 'So do I go on my own?'

'Maybe. I mean it's only for six months and I could come out to be with you over the holidays.'

'You've certainly thought a lot about this without mentioning anything to me.'

'In fairness, Robert, you arranged the whole thing without discussing it with me first.'

'I didn't think I needed to,' he snarls and my discomfort grows.

'But I love my job. You know that.'

His eyes darken, as if clouded by all the things he's not saying. I can tell that he's angry, yet he's choosing to hold it inside.

'Robert please,' I say and touch his arm in an attempt to reach him.

He pulls way, stands up and walks towards the window. He stands with his back to me for the longest time, making me wait. Eventually he turns his head so that I can see his profile and begins to speak. 'So you'll stay here, in the house. Is that what you're suggesting?'

'Well, yes,' I reply.

'It doesn't work out so well financially. If we both go we could have our mortgage paid.'

'But Robert, money isn't a problem is it?'

'No, of course not.' He's speaking through clenched teeth.

'I'll still be earning and can pay the bills here,' I say.

'On your great salary!' he says, sneering.

'Robert please,' I say again, not knowing how else to react. This isn't the first time I've felt financially insignificant but it's the first time he's made me feel so.

Again I reach for him but he pulls away.

'Have it your way, Alice,' he says.

He sits down and switches on the television to shut me out.

11
Internal v External Part I

Ah get another message from Holly and we instigate the plan of action that will take me to her exhibition. Ah've agreed that Ah'll fly into Charles De Gaulle Airport on the morning of the exhibition and stay overnight at her place. It's enough time to see her but short enough to minimise ma chances of falling off the wagon. And just like that, Ah will go to Paris. Ah'll share about this at ma next meeting because it's significant. Holly is the person Ah'd last used with and this might be construed as dangerous ground for me to be revisiting. Somehow Ah know it's safe, just as Ah'd known Ah'd be okay at Chemical Brothers. Ah feel self-assured in a way that Ah never have before – now Ah've a family: a father and the memory of a brother who feels like ma guardian angel. It's such a comfort to be able to talk to him about everything and anything – well, except Holly – but now that Ah'm going to see her I need to talk to him about it.

Ah try when we are in our bedroom, me sitting on the windowsill chewing a cocktail stick instead of smoking ma customary cigarette. Ah go straight to the point.

'Ah'm going to Paris to see Holly,' Ah say.

He says nothing for the longest time. Then: 'How long before you stop chewing those things?'

'Sid Vicious, Ah said Ah'm going to see Holly.'

He remains silent and Ah watch him staring out into Borough Market. Ah watch him until he fades away and Ah have to let it go for now. At least Ah said it out loud. Ah'd opened up the conversation. The next time Ah'll push more.

Ah think about seeing Holly. Ah want to check that she's okay. Ah want her to hear about ma connection to Sid in person. We've someone in common that we'll never forget. But somehow Ah also want her to know that he was blood, not for any other reason than that Ah want her to know. Staying with Holly overnight is necessary. It allows me to spend a good deal of time with her but not too much. Ah don't want to wear out ma welcome. Ah never wear out ma welcome. Lately, Ah've been thinking that maybe things might change for Tim – Dad – soon, that Bill might move in. Then, perhaps, it might be time for me to go. But for now, Ah'm happy to have this refuge while Ah dry out. Ah'm staying clean and this environment is helping with that. Everything helps me somehow. The universe is conspiring to keep me sober. Thank you sweet, sweet friend.

Ah'm just about to head into the room that Ah'm spending most of ma time in these days, going through ma father's record collection, when ma phone rings. Ah don't recognise the number, but thinking it might be Titus Ah answer.

'It's Denzel, ja!' Ah say.

At first there's silence on the other end of the phone. Then eventually: 'Denzel, it's Billy.'

'Billy?'

Eventually: 'Yes.'

'What's up?'

'Can we meet?'

'For sure. Just tell me where you are.'

Less than an hour later Ah'm walking by the Southbank. It's a cold day but there's a sun. Ah'm more tolerant of the cold when there's evidence of the sun. Ah need the sunlight; Ah need it to shine into ma dark spots. Ma bones need illumination, and although Ah stay in

London for now Ah wonder if it'll be possible for the long-term. It may be too cold for Denzel Anderson. But then Ah'm changing so fast these days that Ah'm not sure if Ah completely know who that is anymore.

Ah see Billy first – she has her back to me – but as Ah get closer, she turns around. Holly. She is so like Holly, and today her skullcap means that her long hair has disappeared and Ah see the full extent of the likeness. Ah remember Ah read somewhere that everyone has a doppelgänger in the world and this is most certainly Holly's. Or Holly is Billy's, depending on how you look at it, on who got here first. Ah'm guessing Holly but Ah don't know for sure. Billy's face tells me she's been crying hard. She lifts her arm up and waves at me in a way that would be more appropriate if Ah were a lot farther away.

'Thanks for coming, Denzel,' she says.

'No problem,' Ah tell her.

We stand there for a few minutes. She looks away from me out towards the river and eventually Ah have to ask her if we can move or go inside because Ah'm not built to stand in this cold. We head towards a coffee shop. Billy insists on getting the coffees because Ah came on her call and Ah get the feeling that protesting will be in vain. When she eventually sits down Ah let her take the time she needs before she speaks to me.

'Today is a bad day, Denzel, and I wanted to spend it with someone who understands,' she says simply. 'There's no big drama, just a need to use again and a feeling like I could all too easily. I thought of you and needed you to reassure me. Like that night in Costa, when you gave me your number and said I could call you any time.'

'Sure, Billy,' Ah say. 'Ah'm glad you called. For sure.'

'Do you have days like that, Denzel?'

'Ja! It's part and parcel, Billy. We just get through them. Put one foot in front of the other. You didn't join us in Costa the other night.'

'It didn't feel right. I don't really know Clive.'

'But you don't really know me,' Ah say and smile.

She smiles back. 'But somehow it's easy to be around you.'

'Maybe because you practise being around me,' Ah answer. 'We're all in this together. Ja! Like Gloria says. Ah don't know what's happened to me, Billy. Ah used to think that all people were assholes, you know, and Ah was very anti-social. But since Ah got clean Ah like other people better. Or maybe Ah like myself better. Ja, Ah think that's what it is. Ah thought Ah was a big asshole before, even though Ah would talk like Ah was the exception to the asshole rule. But Ah didn't like maself so much. Ah mean, how could Ah have, putting that poison into ma system. And ja, it's very seductive this idea that Ah could go back there and use again because it's familiar. Ah know how to dislike maself and other people. But it's the liking people that's new. It makes life a lot better, a lot brighter. Lighter. Enough with the fucking dark.'

'I'm very glad I met you, Denzel,' she says.

'Ja, me too, for sure. Ah recently found out Ah had a little brother and maybe Ah'm in line for a little sister too. You have a big brother?'

She shakes her head and Ah tell her that she has now. She smiles and Ah wonder who this sentimental fool is who has recently taken up residence in ma body.

*

I'm moving even closer to the date of my marriage and things are feeling worse than ever at home. I plan to marry only once so when it's done there's no going back. And yet I'm planning to marry one man when there's another at loose in my head! In addition, I've an awful feeling of dread, like something really bad is about to happen. Robert and I are pulling apart at a terrifying speed. Mostly I don't see him, but when I do our curt exchanges merely add fuel to the smouldering tension that has developed between us since I told him I won't be going with him to New York. He looks at me like he hates me and I know that there's no love in my eyes to douse his anger.

Denzel Anderson is unfinished business. He's still in my heart, even after all this time. Perhaps these feelings of first love never go away and I'll always be his for better or for worse, as if I'd married him all those years ago. And then I remember and wonder how I could have forgotten: when we discovered I was pregnant we had professed ourselves married. Sure, there hadn't been anyone official to tell us it was binding but we both declared it and believed it. We'd even exchanged rings. The ring! I kept it and I know exactly where it is. I head into our junk room, where Robert and I toss all sorts of things we no longer use but can't bring ourselves to throw away. There's a single cardboard box with ALICE stencilled on the front. Inside is my history before Robert, the bits and pieces I've collected along the way. Mementos. I begin emptying it and find old letters and pictures that I'd forgotten about, mostly souvenirs from my time in London, but right at the bottom there's a wooden box, an old jewellery box I'd brought over from South Africa with me. It contains my memories of Sea Point.

I open it and take a look inside. The contents of this box represent the first twenty-one years of my life, but there's not much in it. I'd needed to travel lightly. There's an old diary that everyone signed on the last day of school, a photo album, a seashell I'd taken from the beach the day before I left, some cassette tapes, all made and labelled by hand with personal messages of love and promises of forever, and then I see the little red box I'd come looking for, reassuring me that what I remembered was real. I open it and see the ring, the one Denzel had placed on my finger when we were fifteen. Tears begin to run down my cheeks as I recall the moment.

The engagement ring I wear on my left hand, the ring that cost Robert a small fortune and that he'd presented to me on a romantic weekend away in Venice, doesn't hold a fraction of the emotional charge that floods me now as my fingers touch the copper band that I removed when I heard my soulmate had left. The feeling is here now, strong and fresh, as if it had never gone away. Perhaps that's why I never experienced anything like it again – there was no room in me for it. It filled me up. I remove my engagement ring, and as I do I begin to tremble with a mixture of fear and anxiety. Perhaps what I'm doing will change the course of my life forever. I take out the little copper band with the Celtic design around the edge and put it on my finger.

Closing my eyes, I allow myself to drift off, back to Sea Point to picture the boy of my dreams. He was the most beautiful boy I'd ever seen and he fell in love with me. I'd ask him why he loved me and he always told me the same thing: he could make a list to keep me happy but the truth was he didn't know why; he just did. I felt the same way too. I remember how he looked at me and how, when his eyes locked on mine, I felt deeply connected to him, like we were one, opposite sides of the same coin. And then later, when I'd began to have sexual feelings, how his eyes would set a fire alight deep inside me and I actually ached for him.

The first time we'd made love had been at my insistence. I told him I couldn't go another minute without feeling him inside me and he'd asked me if I was sure. I was sure. Our energies were already connected and it felt like our bodies needed to play catch-up or I'd go crazy. What if I got pregnant, he'd asked. I'd told him I would be fine, not to worry. The sex had been painful and nothing like I'd imagined it would be, and when it was happening I began to feel afraid and not quite so sure of myself. What had I done – to him, to me? What would happen if our love for each other wasn't enough? And what if things didn't work out for us the way it was supposed to according to the magazines and movies, where love conquered everything and where its power alone would keep us safe? But the fear had left me as I watched him reach orgasm and then he'd cried. I remember his tears and how they'd made me love him even more. Afterwards he had held me and I'd felt closer to him than I'd ever felt to anyone else. I'd told myself over and over again that that was the only thing that mattered. Now, as I recall this, I feel a deep longing to experience that again.

I'd known I was pregnant straightaway. My body told me fairly quickly. I was afraid but I was also happy. It could work for us. We were in love. Sure, we couldn't do it alone but my parents would help us; they would give us their blessing. I'd actually believed that. Now, as I remember it all once more, I ask myself a question that I'd never dared to ask before: could it be, Alice Cooper, that you instigated the whole situation so that you would fall pregnant? Denzel had trusted me like he always trusted me, one of the reasons I loved him so much. No one on this earth had ever trusted me like that. No one. Denzel had reacted by giving me this ring that's now on my finger. He took me for better or for worse and declared we would be together forever. He had suggested that we run away, that he would take care of me somehow. But as usual, I'd convinced him to do it my way. Afterwards, when he was gone, I wished with all my heart I'd listened to him. We should have run, told no one and left Sea Point together.

Now I remember the last time I saw him – that awful night we told my parents, and Sheila Cooper had bawled and wondered how in God's name she could have given birth to such a slut. She said she'd never forgive me for doing this to her and Sam Cooper had told her to stop, to control herself. Then he'd started on Denzel, telling him to leave, that he was trash and not welcome in our family, that there would never be a baby. It was only then it hit me what a dreadful mistake we'd made. I wondered how I could ever have believed that my parents would help me. Denzel tried to fight our corner but my father hit him and I'd shouted at him to stop and he'd hit me too – the first and only time my father ever slapped me. Then Denzel had flipped and done something that doomed us from that moment on: he punched my father. It was the only time I ever saw someone hit the mighty Sam Cooper. And then my two brothers had appeared to defend the head of the family, and all three Cooper men had dragged the boy I loved out of the house while I stood watching, bewildered by what was happening around me.

Afterwards, the Coopers told me how it would be. I'd never see that boy again. I would go and stay with Sheila's sister in Johannesburg and have the baby. No one needed to know. Then I would come back and continue my studies. They'd make up some excuse. Abortion wasn't an option, even though Sam Cooper tried to argue that it was the best solution. But my mother insisted that I should be made to pay for my actions – that's what Sheila Cooper had said – and in that moment I slipped from disliking my mother to hating her. I left them arguing amongst themselves, sorting out my life between them. I just slipped away without them even noticing and wished that I'd listened to Denzel.

I went to my room and lay in bed, bewildered and wondering how we could find our way out of the nightmare. When my parents had gone to bed I'd heard rustling outside – it was Denzel climbing up to my room, just like he'd always done after my parents had sent him and Jo home. (He used to come back and kiss me goodnight and then leave, somehow managing to get past the security gate without setting off our guard dogs, Punch and Judy.) But that night was different to the others. That night, as he'd pleaded with me to go with him into the unknown, my parents heard us and Sam Cooper totally flipped out. He'd put a gun to Denzel's head and I'd been so scared because I thought he might actually kill him. He'd marched Denzel out of the house while my mother and I, united for once, pleaded with Sam to stop, to let Denzel go. And he did. Thankfully he did.

Denzel ran and he never looked back, not once. I'd watched as he cleared the gate and disappeared from my life forever.

Once a person is in your heart there's no removing them. Once you love someone, you always love them. My first love might just be the one and only person I need to be with now. I let the notion carry me back to the past, knowing that I need to leave my future waiting in the wings for a while. If I believe this to be true, and right now I do, I know exactly what I must do: I must see Denzel Anderson again, because maybe there's a place for him in my future.

12

Internal v External Part II

Ah'm on the beach, a familiar beach. This is Ibiza and Ah'm perched in the sand by the sea, watching.

'A penny for your thoughts,' comes Sid's voice from behind.

'You know what Ah'm thinking?'

Silence.

'Ah'm thinking about Holly,' Ah say.

Ah turn to face him and the blood begins to gush from his throat and Ah watch as ma brother tries to stop it with both hands, but to no avail. It spills all over me and Ah wake up with a jolt.

Ah'm in the music room with ma January blues, which Ah used to get in Ibiza but not as bad as Ah have them now. Ah guess this is the part of being clean and sober that sucks. Nothing to distract me from a messed-up reality, a grey and grim existence – the place where addiction begins. Or at least where it begun for me. And in these times what keeps me going? Alice. Only Alice. Ah'd drifted off listening to Jimi Hendrix, and now Jimi is gone and it's just me and the blues and the memory of ma bad dream. As Ah'm putting Jimi back in his rightful place, Ah spy a record randomly placed behind the others, probably the only stray in the bunch, a smaller seven-inch single that's got lost amongst the big boys. Curiosity gets the better of me and Ah begin to move the others out of the way until there's enough space to carefully prise the renegade vinyl free. Ma jaw drops as Ah turn it over and identify the single as 'Alice' by The Cocteau Twins. There's a single word stencilled onto the paper cover – SID

– and beside it is a date. Ah let ma hand run over it, imagining that he was the last person to touch this. It gives me chills.

Ah listen as the needle works its way across the vinyl and Ah remember how Ah used sing this song to the teenage Alice. Now as Ah listen, Ah realise that without knowing it Ah'd been singing about our future. The chills get stronger. We'd no idea what was going to happen, yet Ah'd deceived her – gone and left no shadow. The song ends and now the urge to make contact is strong. Ah want to say sorry, to beg her to forgive me and take me back. But then Ah realise that if she rejects me, if she tells me that there's no going back, well … Ah'm afraid of what Ah might do. Ah'm not yet strong enough to take that risk. If Ah'm to believe Gloria, and Ah do, Ah'll be stronger after six months. Then, Ah'll still have a lot of work to do but Ah'll have enough abstinence behind me to ensure that Ah'll get there. Ah decide to keep to the time frame.

Ah've told no one about Alice. Like Titus said, it might jinx it and it feels better to keep it to maself for now. Ah watch her via Facebook and Ah've seen that she's now connected with Jaspar Downey. Ah hope with all ma heart that they never get round to speaking about the version of me he encountered in Ibiza. We had all been in High School together. Ah'd gone as far as Ah could before Ah had to leave, but Jaspar and the others had gone all the way. He'd probably filled in a lot of the details for me that night in Ibiza but Ah don't remember much of what he'd said. It had been a damn uncomfortable experience, Ah recall that much, and afterwards Ah'd left him knowing Ah wouldn't see him again. What was the point! We were living different lives back then. But now? Jo, Jaspar, Alice – all still out there, existing, connected. Alice, Alice, Alice … the song runs through ma head.

Later Ah make ma way to Euston Road and Ah'm sitting thinking about Alice (as usual) when Clive finds me.

'A penny for your thoughts,' he says, reminding me of the Sid from ma nightmare and giving me the chills again.

'Ah was just thinking Ah miss Clive,' Ah say, smiling.

'Yeah right,' he says and raises one eyebrow, 'I'm not buying it, Denzel Anderson!'

Hearing ma full name outside an official setting is weird.

'Well, that's all you're getting for today, Clive Carpenter.'

'January sucks,' he says.

'It sure does. Ja! For sure!'

A while later we're all sitting inside the weekly room and Ah get the feeling that the January blues has engulfed our whole group. Even Gloria isn't her usual upbeat self. We all give our accounts of how January is affecting us and it's not pretty. We're all suffering. It's a joint affair, as if the vow we've all taken to abstain has bound us together emotionally and psychologically too. Everyone's story is a version of the same thing and we continually come back to the same starting place: addiction.

Tonight Gloria reveals a little bit more about the steps we'll be taking next. At the end of our six months we'll each get a mentor. This is a Never Again person two stages ahead of us. They'll have been mentored for six months, after which it's their turn to do the mentoring. They had started again like us and now operate from a place of freedom, transformed into something new, living a new way. When Gloria speaks ma blues lift and Ah really feel the possibility. Ah believe Ah'll make it. She's made it and others have made it. That's the beauty of Gloria's system; she's the living proof that it works. And

Ah'm beginning to believe, with the whole of ma being, that it's possible that Ah can live as part of the couple Ah'd walked away from all those years ago. Ah remember ma conversation with Sid back in Ibiza shortly before he died. He'd told me to find Alice again, just as he'd told our father to find happiness, which for him meant finding Bill. Ah'd told Sid it was too late, but Ah was wrong, totally wrong. Ma little group is the living proof that it's never too late. Never.

After the session, Clive and Ah go to Costa and tonight Billy joins us, much to Clive's surprise. And mine. Communication is stunted at first but eventually the conversation begins to flow as we get talking about tonight's meeting and express our curiosity about our mentors. Clive asks Billy about her Christmas and she tells him she was with family and friends. He speaks about his time with Ben and with Tracy's family, and then Ah remember his plan to ask her to marry him and Ah'm wondering why he hasn't mentioned it. Maybe he'd thought better of it for the same reason Ah'd not contacted Alice yet. Never Again advises that the only decision we should make each day is the decision to not use. It's good advice for sure.

Clive and Billy stop talking and we prepare to make a move, but just before we leave Ah propose a toast. 'Here's to sobriety and the decision to not use,' Ah say and raise ma paper coffee cup.

Ma two friends follow ma lead.

Back at home in ma room Ah sit and look out over Borough Market chewing ma way through another cocktail stick. Waiting.

'You're thinking about the beach.'

'Ja, Sid Vicious, Ah'm thinking about the beach.'

'There are certain things I can't talk about yet, just like Clive. You understand?' he says.

'Ja,' Ah reply but Ah'm not so sure Ah do and Ah wonder why he brings up Clive.

'All in good time,' he says just before he disappears, leaving me alone again.

*

Robert is working late again, so I sit alone and allow my idle hands to lead me to Facebook in search of Denzel. His profile is still as bare as a chestnut tree in January – no picture, no information – but as I glance down I discover that he has made contact with someone called Holly and she is very beautiful. I'm jealous, jealous beyond all rational thought. I go from Holly's profile to her website and discover she's an artist. I find one striking image after the next of this beautiful girl who has nothing of me in her. My first love has forgotten about me and our connection! Panic sets in and I prepare to send him a message. I click on the message icon and a box bursts onto the screen in front of me. I type:

Hi Denzel,
I miss you. Do you miss me?

Then I backspace, deleting the message. I do the same thing again. And finally, one last time.

Denzel Anderson I love you. Still
Alice x

I stare at what I've written. It's the truth. Or is it? I mean, I don't know him. The Denzel I knew was fifteen; the man behind the profile is thirty-two. 'Press enter to send,' the screen instructs but I can't. As before, I delete it backwards, character by character, until the screen is blank again.

I'm just about to leave the messages pane when one pops up from Jaspar. He's looking forward to the wedding. I can't bring myself to reply right now so I close the message and the beautiful artist flashes up in front of me again.

Who is this girl Holly, I wonder. Does he love her? As I think about them together my jealousy resurfaces. And yet the knowledge that Robert is having an affair doesn't have the same effect on me. I never feel worried about losing him because for me, there's nothing to lose. At least, not emotionally. My heart is quite safe. I look through Holly's pictures hoping to find one of Denzel and I'm reassured to find no evidence of a relationship, but I'm also disappointed not to see a present-day Denzel either. Finally, in a moment of desperation, I search for him by name on Google. I find nothing; he's anonymous.

My phone rings and it makes me jump. I see it's Jo.

'You made me jump,' I say.

'Na, that was your brittle nerves. Do you want to come out and play?' Jo asks.

'Yes please,' I almost sing, happy to be rescued.

'Come join me in Carluccio's.'

'What – in Muswell Hill?'

'No in Mars! Ja, of course in Muswell Hill, girl.'

'What are you doing here?'

'Just come, ja?'

I find Jo at a table tucking into a salad. A bottle of red wine and two half-full glasses are on the table.

'So what brings you to Muswell Hill uninvited,' I ask.

'I was invited, just not by you. You want some food?'

I shake my head.

'I have a job here at the moment. Designing a rather posh flat. It's paying a lot and they've given me a huge budget.'

'I should have been an interior designer.'

'Na, you should have been a teacher, Alice. You're good at it. So Jaspar is coming to the wedding.'

'Yep, I know. He Facebooked me.'

'Look at you spending time on Facebook!'

I smile, imagining my friend's reaction if she knew exactly what I had been doing on Facebook.

'Ja, I've a good feeling about this,' Jo says. 'He's even suggested that I might like to come out to New York to see him some time, and with you going over there – well, I think that just might be on the cards.'

'God Jo, I haven't told you! I'm not going to New York.'

'No way, Alice! What's happened?'

'I told Robert I don't want to go.'

'And he was okay with that?'

'Well no, but he accepted it.'

'Good on you! You shouldn't go if you don't want to.'

And I shouldn't marry him if I don't want to either. But I can't go there yet, not even with my best friend.

'So will he go on his own?' Jo asks.

'Yep. And I'll go over for a holiday. Maybe you could come too and see Jaspar.'

'I love that idea! It's not really the best start to married life for you and Robert though.'

'It's only for six months.'

'Does Helen Shaw know?'

'I've no idea.'

Jo pulls a face that makes me laugh. We sit in silence for a while both thinking our own thoughts until eventually she says, 'Have you thought anymore about Denzel?' She looks me dead in the eye.

'No,' I say and hold her stare. 'Like I said before, he's in my past.'

She nods her head and looks at me for the longest time as if she's trying to reassure herself that I'm telling her the truth. This is the first time I've lied to her since we were teenagers, and the reason I lied to her back then was the same as it is today: Denzel. Jo says nothing and pours us some more wine.

'Here's to the wedding,' she says and raises her glass.

'Yep, to the wedding.'

'Oh my God, look who it is!' I recognise Kate's voice behind me. 'Ali, you're out alone!' she continues as she comes closer. 'I mean, without Robert.'

When she reaches our table she smiles half-heartedly at Jo. These two girls have completely conflicting energies, so I don't push them upon each other.

'Well, she'll be making the most of her time as a single woman,' Frank breaks in. 'Hello beautiful,' he says and plants a kiss on my cheek.

'Hi Frank. You remember my friend Jo.'

'Hello Jo,' he says and kisses the back of her hand, a gesture which will have sickened both my friends, though for different reasons.

'How are the preparations for New York going?' Kate asks.

'You mean Robert's preparations,' Jo pipes up, not wanting to miss the opportunity of letting Kate know she's up to date with my plans.

Kate and Frank both give me a puzzled look.

'I've decided I'm going to stay,' I say eventually.

'What?' says Frank. 'Are you mad?'

'She can't leave the children, can you Ali?' Kate says, clearly relieved to have found a good reason for my behaviour. 'I couldn't either – even for somewhere like New York.'

'I'm sure Robert's over the moon about spending the first six months of married life alone,' Frank says.

'He understands,' I say. 'While he's there he'll be working flat out anyway – and I can always spend my holidays with him.' I shrug.

'You'll have plenty of time on your honeymoon first,' Kate says coming to my rescue.

Frank grimaces, reminding me that he knows his old school friend better than anyone else.

'Yes, he'll be delighted to have a break from me after so long,' I say.

Jo is staying very quiet. I could slap her for letting the cat out of the bag.

'We should go, sweetheart. A big day at the office tomorrow,' Frank says.

'Sure. Goodbye,' I say.

Frank blows me a kiss on his way out, Kate following closely behind saying she'll see me at school tomorrow. It strikes me that before I started going out with Robert, Jo and I would have called Frank a big dick. But now he's my soon-to-be-husband's best friend.

When they are out of sight I kick Jo under the table. 'What did you do that for?' I say

'I thought they already knew.'

'Well, they do now. And no you didn't, Jo Mitchel! You were trouble making.'

'Sorry Ali,' she says, holding her hands up in front of her as if I'm pointing a gun at her. I wish I was pointing a gun at her. 'I'm sorry,' she says again, a little more contritely.

When I get home Robert is sitting in the front room.

'Where have you been?' he asks.

'Jo was visiting a client close by so we met up in Carluccio's.'

He nods.

'Are you back long?' I ask.

'No, I just got in.' He yawns. 'Time for bed. Are you coming?'

'Yes,' I say.

I don't mention seeing Frank and Kate, but instinct tells me that I need tell him tomorrow, that it would be a mistake not to tell him. First thing in the morning, I promise myself.

13
A Trip To The Movies

Ah take myself to the British Film Institute at Southbank. Today Ah'll see a movie Ah haven't seen in ages: *House of Flying Daggers*. Ah'd never seen it on big screen but today, thanks to the people who make the decisions at this great film establishment, Ah'll get to see this movie supersized. Before Ah go in Ah think about having a cigarette outside and then Ah remember that Ah don't smoke any more. Ma oh ma! The power of a conditioned mind! Ah take some deep breaths as Ah look out over the river, settling for a fresh air hit instead. It's another cold day in London – bitter, but there's a bright sun making it possible to cope. It's the dull damp days that make me want to throw maself into the water with bricks in ma pockets. Today life feels good. Sober and good. And what better way to celebrate ma existence than to watch one of ma favourite martial arts movies.

As Ah'm watching the river Ah think about Sid. Ah remember the one and only studio session we had had in Ibiza the day we'd made a recording, a recording that Ah still have on ma computer but which Ah haven't been able to listen to yet. But knowing Ah can will do for now. He'd been down in the dumps that day and Ah'd called at his room in the hostel we shared. It was clear to me that it was something to do with Holly. Although he hadn't said anything, Pia, Holly's friend, had let the cat out of the bag. Holly had been painting Sid and we all knew what that meant. Holly didn't just ask anyone to sit for her. She'd asked me at one time. Ja! Ah'd never told Sid that. What would have been the point! Ah mean, nothing had happened. Ah'd been tempted, if Ah'm honest, but nothing had happened. Ah guess she'd seen enough back then to change her mind.

That day in the hostel he'd been so much in the doldrums. Ah'd recognised that heavy feeling, that brilliantly awful feeling in your heart when you're pining after someone. So Ah'd asked him to come with me to Amnesia to do some recording. But he'd convinced me to play something of ma own and reluctantly Ah had. Ah remember his compliments – so genuine but oh so hard to hear. It was impossible for me to take on board the idea that Ah might be any good. And then he'd offered the help of his father – our father. How close we had come that day to revealing our link! So close. Had he said his father's name Ah would have come to know that he was ma brother there and then. But he hadn't and he never knew. And he'd died and Ah'd watched him die without knowing this fact. But it had almost come to light that day.

As Ah sit and watch the Thames Ah wonder how that might have played out – if he'd said the name Tim Harris and Ah'd heard that name fall into the studio space in Amnesia. There would have been silence, and eventually, when Ah could have found it in maself to speak again, Ah would have said, 'Boet, it just might be possible that you're ma half-brother.' And Ah try to imagine his face if Ah'd have said that. What would have happened? How would our relationship have altered? Would he still have died? Might him knowing that have changed what happened?

Sid had hurried away that day and gone off in the direction of Holly's. Of course! Ah begin to think that had we had that conversation, perhaps he wouldn't have gone back to Holly's and then that might have fizzled out. Ah'm going back over history and trying to rewrite it, or work out other scenarios, and really it's a hopeless waste of energy. Like Sid is forever telling me, it was his time and so he died and led me to ma father.

And now Ah'm being led in the direction of Alice, for some reason. So that we might be together again, ja? If not, why are we back on each other's radars. If it doesn't work out, would Ah find someone else? Na! There's only Alice for me and if Ah've messed it up so badly with her – well, Ah've missed ma chance. There's no room for anyone else. It's Alice or nothing. Ja! And ma life will go on as before if it's not meant to be. But for now the point is Ah get a lot of comfort from the fact that there just might be a happy ending. It makes me feel good and warm inside, and Ah get a hit from that thought without the assistance of any substance that might kill me. Ma heart feels huge when Ah think of Alice – like it can love, and will love, again. For now it's the bestest feeling. Ah grab hold of ma happy ending and enjoy the prospect as Ah sit by the river preparing maself to see a movie Ah know has no happy ending. Now that, Miss Alanis Morissette, is well and truly ironic.

The movie is lekker on the big screen and once again Ah fall in love with this Japanese way of living – the beauty of its land and people, the colours with which both men and women adorn themselves, the warrior nation and their great fighting ability. So much grace, making fighting and dancing look like one and the same thing. Ah love that so much. Ah think about how long it is since Ah've danced properly and Ah miss it. The movie fills me with a sense of wonder and awe, and Ah watch the beautiful Mei. She is quite possibly the greatest warrior of the whole lot, and Ah'm reminded of Alice and how she had been the strongest one of us; she had always floored me with her courage. And then Mei meets the great love of her life and it turns to tragedy. Ah hope that our story is different and there's no third man waiting on the horizon to stick a dagger in ma chest.

At the end of the movie, Ah'm left altered. Ah always feel tremendously philosophical after Japanese encounters. The whole past life thing dances around me for a time because Ah've never known any Japanese folk in real life, despite my infatuation with the country. Nor have Ah ever ventured there. Well, Ah did as a roadie but that doesn't count as Ah'd been with Mick and we spent most of our time travelling inside with the help of mind-altering drugs rather than seeing the beautiful countryside. And now as Ah leave the Southbank still sober and aware of ma outer surroundings Ah have a skip in ma step. Just imagine how shocked poor dead Mick would be if he could see me now. Old habits might die hard, but they can indeed die. For sure.

*

I look into the mirror and see myself in my wedding dress. I have to admit I don't remember ever looking so good in any other dress, but so I should considering it had cost well over eight grand. This is the most expensive piece of clothing I've ever owned. I watch myself and wait for something, what I'm not sure – maybe a swell of emotion that lets me know I'm doing the right thing. But it doesn't come because the reality is, my heart is telling me a different story with a different outcome. It's incredible how quickly everything can crumble. To think that only a few months ago I felt solid in my relationship and sure of my decision to marry Robert. Now I'm filled with doubt and dread, and a growing fear that something awful is about to happen – has to happen – before I can escape. The phone rings and I shuffle across the bedroom to answer it.

'Hello,' I say.

'Ali?'

'Who else would it be, Robert!'

'You sound different. I thought I had the wrong number.'

'No. It's me. Are you about to leave?'

'No. Sorry but I won't make the movies. I have to get something finished for first thing tomorrow.'

'No worries.'

'Maybe Jo will go with you,' he says.

I hear a woman laugh at his end of the phone. 'Who's that?' I ask.

'Sally,' he says, offering nothing further to ease my mind should it wish to be suspicious.

'I'll see you later,' I say.

'Yes. Don't wait up.'

He hangs up without saying goodbye, his way of letting me know that we're still not okay. Things have been bad since I told him I didn't want to go to New York. And now I remember that I'd totally forgotten to tell him about running into Frank and Kate. He's probably seen Frank today for lunch so Robert will have heard it from him. I'm probably going to pay for that too. Needing a distraction, I decide I'll go to the movies on my own, but I'll travel further than the Odeon at the end of the road – I need to distance myself from my suburban life.

A few hours later, I'm standing outside the BFI in Southbank scanning the list of that day's screenings. Given the late hour, there's only a choice of two, but for me there's no competition. *House of Flying Daggers* is just about to start and I'm grateful for this bit of luck in an otherwise unfortunate day. I love this movie and had seen it on the big screen when it first came out. My love of martial arts movies is something that Robert knows nothing about. It's a love that was born out of my relationship with Denzel. When we were kids, we watched every Bruce Lee movie that had ever been made. I've often wondered what Denzel would have made of these amazing modern movies that have taken this mystical art and made it even more fantastical on the silver screen.

The movie begins and as I make my way through a huge box of popcorn, I reconnect with the characters. I love the heroine, Mei, for her beauty and great strength, and I'm totally caught up in her love triangle with Jin and Liu, two warriors with the same desire – to win the heart of this beautiful girl. Even though I already know how the story ends, I will Mei to forget her duties and leave with the man who is in her heart. But of course I know she won't. Her decision not to flee has heartbreaking consequences, just like mine had. How I wish I could go back to Sea Point and rewrite my history! If I'd known then what I know now I would have gone. The movie pulls me away from my own story and I get lost in the beauty and the colours as it heads for its tragic end. The heroine dies, having made the decision to save the life of her love, the only decision she could ever have made. It makes me feel sad and I cry, but more for myself than for the fate of poor dead Mei.

What do I want? The answer is clear to me, and no matter how much I try to hide from it or tell myself otherwise the reality sits squarely inside of me. I want to feel what I felt when I was a teenager, what I felt when I was with Denzel. I want to run away with him now and take our chances, forgetting the past and taking a leap for a very different future. We can't change what happened, but maybe we could start again. I resign myself to the fact that there might be a tragic end to all this, just like the last time, but then I realise that perhaps the most tragic ending is the one in which I marry the wrong person and don't take this last leap of faith. I have to know one way or the other.

Jaspar had seen Denzel in Ibiza and it didn't sound like he was having the greatest of times. This Holly seems to be in his life now, but what if Denzel is doing the exact same thing with this Holly girl as I am with Robert – building a life with one person while dreaming of being with someone else. I've had the same conversation with so many people who have stopped believing that having a real connection with someone else exists outside of fantasy. I'd even stopped believing myself and settled for the next best thing, consoling myself with the knowledge that at least I'd experienced this feeling once, even if it had only been for a short time. But what if it could be different? What if somehow that connection is still alive and waiting for me?

Amnesia. I remember it as I sit watching the closing credits disappear on the screen. The word appears so clearly in my mind that a part of me wonders if it might somehow have flashed up on the screen. Amnesia, the club that Jaspar had mentioned – that's where I'll begin looking. I'd almost contacted Denzel on Facebook but couldn't get any further because it was the wrong way to go about this. What could a few words on a screen tell him? Or me for that matter. The only way for me to know if this feeling is real is to see if I can feel it when I'm with him, put myself in the same place as Denzel Anderson and see if it still exists. I begin to feel sick with excitement as I see clearly what I'll do next – what I must do next. I'll go to Ibiza this weekend – somehow – and after that I don't know. Right now I don't need to know what will happen next; I just need to take another step in that direction and trust this feeling that is now in full flow, making me feel more alive than I have since I was fifteen. And if it hurts me again …?

'Excuse me.'

I look up and see a girl dressed in black.

'You need to leave,' she tells me

I miss my last train home so I have to take a taxi but I'm still in before Robert, who is without question screwing his work colleague. Suddenly I'm grateful for his infidelity, for it's going to make what I'm about to do much easier.

14

David Bowie And Nina Simone

There's a knock on the door and Ah hurry myself there. Ah know who it is already. Clive is coming to spend time in the music room Ah've told him so much about.

'Hey mate,' he announces as Ah answer the door. He spreads his arms as if he's about to give me a big bear hug but doesn't. Ah stand back and let him come in.

'Wow, this is nice. I wish I'd seen this place before I brought you to my shitty part of the woods,' he says.

'Boet, Ah've lived in some places you wouldn't even be able to imagine,' Ah assure him.

'Mmm. Well life certainly turned a corner for you,' he says and raises his eyebrows.

'Ja, this is true!'

'So where is it?' he asks. 'Show me the treasure!'

Clive is here because as Ah'd been working ma way though ma father's music collection, Ah'd found a rare copy of David Bowie's last show as Ziggy Stardust at the Hammersmith Apollo. Apparently, Tim is a fan – not as big a fan as Clive, of course; no one is as big a fan as Clive. Ah lead ma friend into the music room and he lets out a gasp of air as he spies the wall full of records. This is impressive stuff to anyone but especially to a music aficionado such as Clive.

Ah hand him the album cover and he takes it from me as if Ah've given him something very precious – the holy grail of music. Ah set up the turntable and in a few seconds we hear the unmissable sound of the needle as it moves through the grooves taking us to the start of the concert. We listen to the whole thing without either of us making any comment and the room is filled with an intensity only present when listening to something that is really and truly your soul's music. Although Clive had been too young to attend he knows every detail. Once again, as Ah watch ma friend, Ah see adulation at a new level, far above anything Ah've ever offered the artists Ah admire. For sure.

'That's probably one of the finest vinyl listening experiences I've ever had by far. I thank you, mate.'

'That's no problem,' Ah say.

'Can we do it all over again,' he asks.

'Ja, for sure.'

There's some music Ah can listen to over and over again and what Ah've just been listening to falls into that category. We listen again and Clive is satisfied.

'Ah could record it for you if you like. Ah'm sure ma father has some fancy-wancy equipment and could make it sound just like it does on the album.'

'That would be great,' he says, looking at me as if Ah've just offered to care for him in his old age. 'Although just to hear it is enough. I bet your father was one of the privileged people who actually went to the gig.'

I shrug my shoulders.

'You know what would be amazing, mate?'

Ah raise ma eyebrows, knowing what's coming next.

'Could I meet your father and talk to him about the gig?'

'Ah can ask him,' Ah say.

And just then, right on cue, the front door opens and Tim Harris returns home for his lunch.

'Is that him now?' Clive asks.

'Ja, it will be,' Ah reply.

Clive looks at me expectantly. 'Can I meet him now?'

'Boet, he'll be having his lunch now. Ah'll ask him after.'

'I won't take long,' he says and Ah realise that he won't take no for an answer. This isn't a side to Clive Ah've seen before, but then again Ah guess we're speaking about David Bowie.

'Boet, you're a fucking nightmare. You know that!'

'Mmmm, it's been said once or twice.' He grins.

'Ja ja!' Ah say and head out to see if ma father will talk to David Bowie's number one fan.

'Hi Denzel, are you okay?' Tim asks when I get to the kitchen.

'Ja!'

'Did your friend come?'

'Ja. Actually he'd like to met you, Dad.'

'He would?'

'Ja, he's a bit of a David Bowie freak and he wants to talk to someone who went to the last Ziggy Stardust concert.'

Tim looks a bit fazed.

'It can be another time if you like,' Ah say.

'No. It's okay. I'll make some tea and sandwiches,' he replies and busies himself.

A short time later the three of us are sitting around the kitchen table drinking tea and helping ourselves to ham and cheese sandwiches.

Clive puts his iPhone on the table and presses record. Ma father's expression doesn't alter but then Ah remember that he's used to having his interviews taped.

'This is just for your ears Clive, yes?'

'Of course, Mr Harris.'

'Please, call me Tim.'

My father's demeanour changes and his voice alters as if he's stepped into an acting role.

'So you were there,' Clive says, and now he sounds as if he's working for the NME. It makes me want to laugh.

'Yes I was, and it was an amazing concert. The best I'd seen Bowie in his Ziggy persona. He most definitely went out on a high.'

'Were you expecting the closing proclamation?'

'No, David told no one. I don't think even he knew he'd do it until that night. It was a complete shock to everyone.'

'And afterwards – there was a big party?'

'An insane party. His after-parties were always insane and filled with all the "it" people of the time. I went that night. In those days, it was important for me to mingle at all those sort of events. I'd an agent who would push me. I'm not naturally the most sociable person in the world. Those kind of affairs were always difficult for me.'

Ah listen as ma father talks to Clive and it's as if he's giving a press interview. He sounds very professional. But of course ma father has probably done this many times in his life. Ah listen and learn, just like ma friend.

'It paid off that night as David asked me to work with him on his next project.'

Clive moves closer to ma father like a tiger that has just spotted its dinner.

'You worked with David Bowie?'

'Yes. I helped him with some of his orchestral arrangements.'

'No way!'

'Yes,' says Tim and smiles.

'And are you still in contact with him?'

Ah know where this is going and so it seems does ma father.

'No,' he says. 'Bowie has most of his ties in America now. As you're such a big fan, why don't you take the album.'

'Are you serious?'

'Yes. It's not like I have a shortage of music in that room. And after all, I was there.'

'Thank you so much! I don't know what to say!'

'Thanks will do just fine. Now if you don't mind, I need to get back to work.'

'Sure. What are you working on at the minute, Tim?'

'A soundtrack for a new English director. He's a nice boy, very talented. The film is quite moving – at least I think it is. It's about gangs in the East End. A very different direction for me, but I believe it's always good to venture into the unknown as an artist. It keeps you evolving.'

'What's the name of the movie?' Clive says.

'So far it hasn't got a name. We're simply calling it "Project EastEnd" for now. Right, I must go.'

'Thanks, Tim. It's been great to talk to you,' Clive says and Tim leaves us to it.

'Thanks, mate,' Clive says to me. 'Your dad's a great bloke.'

'Ja, Ah think so too,' Ah say with pride. 'He's a great bloke!'

*

Nina Simone sings her way from 'Mood Indigo' to 'Work Song' as I walk to work with my iPod for company. I love Nina and have been hooked ever since I saw a documentary on BBC4 about her music and her life. She was such a warrior, fighting injustice with her voice and her piano. The force of Nina's piano solo propels me through the school gates where I'll begin to put my plan into action, which had overnight developed from a mere idea into a list of things to do. This morning I listen to her upbeat songs in the hope that they will keep me awake, as figuring out what to do next meant that I didn't get much sleep. I've decided to book my ticket from work so there's no evidence at home. I'm covering my tracks and hedging my bets. I'm telling myself that even if things don't work out with Denzel, I'm still going to call things off with Robert anyway, but I don't know how true this is – if it were, telling Robert I can't marry him should be top of my list. But for now I believe my own good press, which reads a little like this: I'll tell him after I go to Ibiza because if I tell him before I go there's a chance that I won't go at all – and I have to go. More than anything, I have to go.

Being one of the first to arrive today, there's a choice of staffroom workstations and I pick the one nearest to the wall, where there's less chance of anyone seeing what I'm up to. I find my way to the website and book my ticket just as Nina is breaking into 'See-Line Woman'. I'll fly to Ibiza tomorrow straight after work. When Robert eventually got in last night, looking like he had just had sex and wanted me to know, I told him that I was going to a spa in Herefordshire with Jo for the weekend and he had said that that was fine. We're in the middle of a cold war; things will blow up shortly, as they surely must, but I was thankful that my fiancé seemed to be willing to let them drag on for another bit. At the back of my mind, I'm also aware that Robert will be drawing up contingency plans of his own, plans which probably involve Sally. I wish him the best. But of course I do, for I'm getting ready to go to Ibiza and find my one true love! The hypocrisy of the whole thing is sickening, but right now I can't look at it too deeply or I'll rip up the e-ticket I've just printed out.

This is crazy, but it's the rest of my life I'm talking about and something is drawing me in this direction, something strong, like an invisible energy field that's linked to my future. Denzel Anderson doesn't just belong in my past. I have been carrying him around with me all this time, and this realisation means it's something I can no longer ignore – or control. All I need do is tick off each item on the to-do list and trust that it's leading me in the right direction. And in the meantime, I'm grateful for the distraction of work.

My morning sails along easily and I balance the tasks of allowing the children to play and ensuring that I can tick the piece of paper that tells the parents that their children are learning something. Even my little tots need to prove that they are learning. Sometimes I wonder if maybe the education system is sailing off in a direction that will eventually cause a whole part of humanity to be lost. We attempt to cultivate their imaginations in a certain way, but perhaps it would be better to let them grow their own. I'm always amazed at where my classroom goes when the children are steering the ship rather than following any agenda set by adults. This is something that Kate and I have long conversations about – how we would do education if it were down to us – and a lot of teachers share our unrest. However, as I head for lunch with Kate today, I know we won't be talking about school business. New York! New York!

'So spill,' she says as soon as I join her.

'I just can't leave the children, like you said.'

'But Robert must be furious.'

'Has he spoken to Frank?' I ask.

'God, he didn't tell you! Things *are* bad between you two, Ali.'

I shrug my shoulders.

'Frank called him when we came in from Carluccio's, even though I told him not to. When he got off the phone he said Robert was furious.'

Of course he was furious, but for some reason I was the only one who was blind to his fury. Our cold war *is* in full swing.

'It's odd because Robert hasn't lost it with me,' I tell her. 'I mean he's not happy, but he's doing this passive-aggressive thing that I've never seen him do before. Then again, I've never gone against him before.'

Kate suddenly looks worried – and guilty.

'What is it?' I ask.

'There's something you should know, especially since you're getting married in less than a month.' All at once I know what's coming next. 'Robert is having an affair.'

'I know,' I say simply.

Kate is clearly taken aback.

'Or at least I had my suspicions.'

'He told Frank last night,' Kate says, 'and Frank told me and made me swear not to tell you. But now that I'm here with you … I can't not say anything. I'd want to know, if it were me.' She stops dead, as if there's something else she wants to say but has changed her mind. 'What are you going to do?' she asks me eventually.

'I don't know,' I tell her. Of course I don't tell her about my trip to Ibiza.

As I leave the school at the end of day I listen once again to Nina, choosing a slower song, now that I no longer need to keep my energy levels high. 'Take Me To The Water' is one of my favourite songs, and it follows me on my pilgrimage, as I dream about finding Denzel Anderson sitting inside, waiting for me.

15
Crossing Over

Ah sit in front of ma laptop and feel as if a gigantic hand has come out of the screen and smacked me in the jaw. Alice is getting married in less than a month. Jaspar Downey has posted on her wall, tagging Jo, to say he's looking forward to coming over for the wedding – Alice's wedding. The words jump out at me. What had Ah expected? Of course she would be getting married. Ah was surprised she hadn't got married before. The idea that her life had stopped like mine had was the thought of a dumb fool. Of course, she's with someone, and now ma plans take on a whole new urgency. Ah need to make contact now. Ah'm about to send her a message when another thought comes into ma tormented head, one that Ah cannot push aside. Was Ah really going to do this – push ma way back into this girl's life now as she's about to marry someone else? If she's well and truly happy maybe Ah should leave her that way, especially if Ah love her. Isn't that what love is all about, wanting the best for the person. Maybe her not seeing me again is for the best – *her* best. But Ah have to know that she's happy and perhaps there's a way to do that without contacting her directly.

Facebook tells me that the person Ah need to contact is now online so Ah send a message.

'Hello Jo Mitchel, Ah see you're in London.'

There's nothing for the longest time. Eventually …

'Hello Denzel Anderson! Yes, I'm in London. How are you?'

Ah respond immediately.

'Ah'm good. Can we meet up?'

Ah press send before Ah get ice-cold feet. Alice is getting closer, Ah can feel it. There's a long wait.

Maybe Jo's been distracted. Or maybe she's just wondering what to reply. Ah'm instinctively drawn to the second idea and this is the one that leads me to a negative conclusion. Ah can almost hear the rusty hinges creak as Ah open the Alice gate. Then …

'Sure. When and where?'

'How about tomorrow night? Ah don't know London so good so you do the where.'

Another pause, but shorter this time.

'Okay. There's a wine bar in Soho called Le Beaujolais. It's on Litchfield Street just off Tottenham Court Road. 6.30pm?'

Nice one!

'6.30 it is!'

And this time no pause at all.

'See you then!'

'Ja, see you then!' I say out loud to the screen.

So there it is! The gate is open and on Friday Ah'll take ma first look through. Ah begin to feel very nervous. Ah take maself back to Alice's profile picture, ignoring the message below that led me to seek Jo out in the first place, and clutching the ring from all those years ago in ma hand. Ah allow maself to travel back there. Ah imagine a baby – a child. Our child. That thought alone sends an intense shiver down ma spine. Is it possible that this might just end happily?

'So you're taking the first step?' Sid says as he joins me in our bedroom.

'Ja.'

'You're doing the right thing.'

'Ah don't know Sid. What if it all goes pear-shaped? What then?'

'And what if it all works out and you get another chance?'

'Ja. That might be scarier. For sure. Ah was just thinking about our baby.'

'Your son.'

'Ja. Ah believe it's a son. Did Ah tell you about that in Ibiza? Ah can't remember.'

'I don't think so. But we talked about lots of things in Ibiza.'

'Ja, in such a short time. But of course there was a lot we didn't talk about.'

'Like Tim Harris.'

'Ja, like Tim Harris.'

'Well, we can talk about those things now.'

Ah think about Holly now and Ah begin to wonder if maybe Ah'm setting maself up for a disaster here. Ah mean, Ah'm seeing the girl Ah last used with and Ah'm taking this drastic action before Ah go. What if Ah see Jo and she tells me the one thing Ah don't want to hear? Then what? If Alice really is in love Ah want her to marry this man and live happily ever after.

'Regardless of what happens, life will go on,' ma brother assures me.

'Ja, and whatever is meant to happen will happen.'

As Ah look at ma brother his face begins to look very sad before he eventually disappears. Sometimes ma hallucinations seem so real that Ah think maybe it's more than wishful thinking and that somehow ma brother *is* with me, not just a projection of ma mind's eye.

Ah remember Sid's courage and how it paid off with Holly, and now Ah think about seeing her. We've been messaging for the last few weeks, talking about Sid a lot. Ah find this a comfort. Ma father and Ah rarely talk about him. Tim Harris has a different way of dealing with things, Ah suppose. He doesn't talk much, but every once in a while all these words come tumbling out of his mouth when you least expect them, as if they know that they need to come as quickly as possible through this small opening that will shortly be closed off to the world again. Perhaps we'll say what we need to say at one such verbal outing. Ah feel a connection to ma father and know instinctively that this is as new for him as it is for me. We're discovering how to have a father–son relationship. He didn't have that with Sid, and Ah didn't experience it with The Big Chief, for sure. A lot of the time you need to read between the lines to get what's going on in ma father's mind. Ah know this, and Bill, who's still at the flat and staying around indefinitely, knows this too. Ah've been watching as the two grow closer at a Tim Harris pace, slowly and deliberately.

Holly, on the other hand, writes unashamedly about Sid. Or maybe it's more apt to say she writes about the lack of Sid, about how we both talk to him and think about him, and how his death has shaped both our lives. We are altered forever. The more Ah correspond with this girl the more Ah'm looking forward to going to Paris to see her exhibition. She writes that she's keeping the work very guarded and no one, except her father and her agent, will see the pictures before the night of the exhibition opening. Ja, Ah'm excited to see her. And, of course, Ah'll tell her what Ah've not felt able to write down in an email. Ah'll tell her that Sid was not just ma friend. He was ma brother. For sure.

But before that next phase of ma life, Ah'll have an evening with Jo Mitchel. Oh ma sweet Lord Krishna! What have a done!

*

I lie in bed and look over at my packed bag. The fibs I've told my sleeping fiancé and his betrayal, now confirmed by Kate, hover between us, driving us further apart. The cold war continues. I'll fly to Ibiza to find a grown-up Denzel Anderson while Robert will more than likely spend his weekend with Sally. Even though our relationship has broken down, every moment brings us closer to our wedding day.

The alarm clock sounds but I keep my eyes shut. He sits up, waiting for me to stir, but I don't. Eventually he makes his way to the shower and I hear the sounds I have grown accustomed to. These days he leaves earlier and I stay in bed until he is safely gone. I can't face the prospect of trying to talk all this through. We're both ignoring the inevitable, but I'm feeling the strain as my head rests heavily on the pillow that has kept me company over the last few largely sleepless nights. Robert leaves without even a goodbye, despite the fact that he won't see me for the next two days. Another nail in the coffin of our relationship.

Despite the significance of this day in my personal life, it passes quickly, as Fridays generally do, the promise of the approaching weekend exciting everyone. I read a story to the children about right and wrong, couched in the language of a fairytale and promising a happy ending. The message this week is about telling the truth and I get the feeling that someone somewhere is wagging a finger at me. How good a liar I am! Robert's infidelity is no excuse. Two wrongs never make a right – wasn't that what Sam Cooper was always saying? It's a shame he never practised what he preached. I'm aware of my own hypocrisy as I tell this story to the children. How confusing it is to grow up!

Later, as I sit on the bus clutching my bag like a runaway, I get a text message from Jo telling me to enjoy my weekend away. She'd called me last night and sounded really shocked when I said I was going away alone. Her questions were understandable. Why at such short notice? Was everything okay between Robert and I?

'Of course,' I'd assured her. 'I just need a break before the Coopers arrive in town.'

That seemed to satisfy her curiosity. At least, it stopped her asking more questions. I wasn't ready to tell her the whole truth yet, especially as I knew she would confuse things and give me one hundred reasons why I shouldn't be doing this – reasons that are valid and would stop me in my tracks if I were to really think about them. I'll eventually tell her, but hopefully my gamble will have paid off by then and my actions will be justified by the presence of Denzel Anderson in my life once again. Jo is forever telling me that she would give anything to experience a real love connection with someone, so I've no doubt that she'll understand my actions, however extreme, and why I had to lie to her along the way. Of course, there's the chance that both she and Robert will discover my lie before I get an opportunity to explain, but that's a risk I'm willing to take, trusting that my friend and fiancé will not break the habit of a lifetime and choose to contact each other in my absence.

I get to the airport and as I wait for my flight to be called I get a tremendous sense of adventure. I feel more alive than I have done for a long time, like the girl back in Sea Point before she made the biggest mistake of her life and everything changed. It makes me feel even more determined to find Denzel Anderson. My flight is called, the gate announced, and as I follow the signs that take me closer to my future, I realise there's something even more important at stake here. Whatever happens, it might just be possible that I can let go of the great burden of my past once and for all. If that's possible then whatever other heartbreak might await me will have been worth it.

On the plane, I close my eyes and let my imagination run riot. I wonder how I'll find Denzel. Will I recognise him as the boy of my youth? Will he be as much of a mess as Jaspar had said? And if he is, how will I cope? I know nothing about drug addiction. What if he's too far gone to come back? Or perhaps he'll be clean and in love with this Holly. If he is, how will she react to me? Is he my destiny? Can we start again? Might Denzel come back to London with me in a few days? What if I were to decide to stay in Ibiza with him? Then what? I imagine myself into sleep just as the plane takes off, but my dreams are filled with Robert and the events of the last few weeks. Feeling paranoid and confused, I'm glad to wake up just in time to see the clouds break and Ibiza come into view. This is the dwelling place of Denzel Anderson. I'm crossing over into his world, and although I've no idea what will happen next, I get the distinct feeling that I'm heading for home, as if I were about to step back in time and find myself back at Sea Point.

16
Peeping Through The Gate Part I

Ah wake up on Friday knowing that ma whole day will be shadowed by the immense anxiety Ah feel about ma meeting tonight. It's been hanging around like a bad smell and today it's stronger, with less chance of me being able to distract it. Ah pack ma case, message Holly and do everything to try to take ma mind off it, including a visit to the music room. But today nothing is working so Ah take myself into Soho in the hope of finding a movie that can kill the hours before Ah go to meet Jo and find out a few things for sure, things like, have Ah fucked up ma life beyond repair? Is it so broken with ma Alice that it cannot be fixed?

The movie Ah choose is about as far away from love and the promise of love as Ah can get. It's a Japanese horror film showing at the Prince Charles, a lekker little movie theatre Ah find just off Leicester Square. A couple of hours in the life of a deranged serial killer will be sufficiently violent and gripping to carry me away. A short time later, Ah'm immersed in the twisted mind of some boet called Ichi. How someone can come up with this kind of stuff is beyond me and Ah wonder, not for the first time when Ah've seen these type of movies, what messed-up set of events a person needs to go through to write something like this. Ah mean, ma childhood was no fucking rose garden but Ah wouldn't even get close to thinking up some of this twisted stuff. My hours are passed in someone else's hell and it takes me out of ma own, the only reason for putting maself through such an ordeal. *Ichi* leaves me wishing Ah'd chosen something different, as Ah'm not sure what sort of damage this has done at a deep level, but Ah suppose the point is it took ma time and Ah'm left with only an hour and a half before Ah'll see Jo Mitchel.

Ah fill that hour at Caffè Nero, which is just around the corner from our meeting place. Ah eat a toasted sandwich and Ah count all my chews before Ah swallow, adding on an extra twenty chews so that the meal lasts one fifth longer. This is something that Ah've done since Ah was very small. It's often made me wonder if Ah might be slightly autistic or OCD. As Ah've grown older, many of these practices have intensified without any outside intervention, thanks to ma solitary nature. Wasn't Alice Cooper a lucky girl now that her no-job, no-prospects, OCD prince has come along to fetch her! These thoughts are not helpful and once again Ah'm thanking Ichi – he has saved me from ma annoying self, even if he might have permanently messed up a part of ma mind.

Ah get to Le Beaujolais at six fifteen, find a table and wait. This is an amazing wine bar and one Ah'd have loved to frequent daily before Never Again. Tonight Ah'm on the cranberry juice. In fact it might be the first time Ah've had a cranberry juice in such an establishment. The other thought that comes, prompted by the number of loved-up couples around me, is that this would be a great place for a romantic date. Ah wonder if Ah'll ever take Alice here. And now Ah wonder if she's ever come here with Jo – or with the man she is shortly to marry. Even the mere idea of that stings, and Ah have to admit to maself that despite all ma proclamations to want to see the girl happy, Ah really hate to think of her being with someone else. Soon Ah'll find out for sure.

Ah continue to crucify myself, hanging my heavy carcass up to weather ma own condemnation and abuse. A masochist lies at the heart of me, keeping the obsessive company. Lucky Alice! Ah wonder what the fuck Ah'm doing here. Why don't Ah just leave her the fuck alone! Ah had messed it up once before and yet here Ah am, back again – to what? To do it differently? But what do I know about loving anyone? Ah've spent the best part of ma life alone, looking after no one but maself. Ah've had no experience of loving anyone. How would Ah be able to transform into someone who can be one half of a good couple? The truth is Ah don't know. But then Ah hear ma brother tell me that Ah don't need to know – Ah just need to find my way back to her and everything will fall into place.

'Ah hope you're right little brother,' Ah mutter and take a huge drink of ma cranberry juice. Ah pat the patch on ma left shoulder by way of assurance that Ah have all the nicotine Ah need flowing into ma veins right now.

Then an extraordinary thing happens. A girl stands up and Ah can't help noticing – as does everyone else in the bar – that she's a knock-out, like she belongs in the movies, if she isn't already in them. She makes her way towards me and Ah'm full sure that she'll pass me right by or turn back, but she doesn't. Instead she stops at my table and begins to speak.

'Hi,' she says and smiles.

'Hello,' Ah say back.

'You look like you're waiting for someone. Here's my number if it doesn't work out,' she says in a smooth, self-assured American accent.

She hands me a card and smiles at me again before she walks back to her female friend at the bar. Ah hadn't noticed them before. Her friend waves at me and Ah wave back. It's the boost Ah need just now. It's so ridiculous that Ah wonder if Titus had paid her to approach me and might be hiding somewhere. The notion makes me smile. 'Just accept the compliment and move on, boet,' Ah can hear him say.

Ah forget the girl and let ma eyes go back to the door where they stay until Jo arrives. Ah recognise her immediately, having seen her at the Brixton Academy a short time ago. She passes by me at first and only comes back when Ah stand up.

'Hello Jo!' Ah say.

'Denzel?' She looks surprised. Ah guess Ah'm not the boy from Sea Point she remembers. There's something reassuring about the way she looks at me. It makes me feel a lot more relaxed about what Ah'm about to ask her.

*

Ibiza is much milder than the London I have just left. It's evening and yet I'm sitting outside on my balcony looking down on the marina at Ibiza town, dotted with lights and people. I imagine this place is packed in the summer months and I wonder what the Ibizan sun will feel like over the next few days. My sun-starved skin is desperately in need of some rays, something I've learned to cope with in London by taking frequent holidays to warmer climates. My hotel is great. The Pacha, which I chose because it was listed in the Expedia top five, will guarantee that I have luxury for the next few days. The promise of comfort drives me indoors and I lie on the huge bed, wasted on me alone. I think about sharing it with Denzel. The idea excites me and I let myself think it all the way through for the first time. If I meet Denzel and he feels the same way as I do, I'll bring him back here to my hotel room and sleep with him, make love with him.

I close my eyes and immediately feel the charge. The prospect alone unleashes a wave of passion. My mind takes me back to our first times on the beach at Sea Point. They were the best moments of my life, even though I hadn't known it back then. But life had turned sour very quickly.

My mobile phone tells me that I should make my way down for dinner very soon, and then the realisation hits me like a sledgehammer: if Robert Shaw decides to call me at any stage over the next few days he'll know I've lied. I'd totally forgotten about the different ring tone. But my panic is short-lived. I realise that I don't really care. While I'm here in Ibiza, I'm stepping back to a time before Robert Shaw existed for me, a time when it was just me and Denzel and we were separate from the rest of the world. I've come here in the hope that I find these same feelings very much alive in Denzel too, feelings that I know still exist in my own heart. If there is still an 'us,' then I'll find it, no matter the cost. That was the decision I made when I first booked the ticket here.

My plan is simple. Tonight I'll go to Amnesia. But first I need food. Even though I could easily go without, it's necessary. I sit up and look at my reflection in the mirror. Somehow I look different, more like an Alice from a long time ago, as if she's bubbled up to the surface, now that she knows she has a chance of true love again, of happiness, of going back and setting things right. I put on the red dress I've packed for this occasion. Not only is it my favourite dress but I remember it's a colour that Denzel loved. I'm suddenly remembering things that I'd forgotten long ago. They're coming back to me now as if they'd floated out of the small jewellery box that held my ring. I'd carried them with me from Sea Point and kept them until I was ready to reopen the box.

I remove my engagement ring and swap it for the copper band that had, until a few days ago, sat in that little box, forgotten. I take a final look at the engagement ring and get what almost feels like a premonition of me giving it back to Robert. I let it go and bring all my attention back to the little copper band that is now on my ring finger. 'I still do. For better, for worse,' I say into my empty hotel room, sending my words out into the universe and willing them to travel to Denzel so he knows I'm on my way.

Before directing me to the hotel restaurant, the receptionist advises me that I should take one of the taxis from outside the hotel to get to Amnesia. There are only a handful of people dining with me so my order of pasta and red wine comes quickly. The food is delicious and I clear my plate, despite my lack of an appetite. By this stage, I'm well and truly nervous so I calm myself by imagining the best case scenario: when I get to Amnesia, the club will be in full swing, but I'll spot Denzel the moment I walk in and he will see me too. And that will be that. We'll both know in that moment that we've found each other again.

Jaspar had told Jo that Denzel was in a bad way and I'm prepared for that. I might not be a junkie, but I'm equally damaged, lost in a life without him and settling for something less. No matter what our current states, we can bring each other back, rescue each other from our worthless lives. With him I was different and I will be different again. There's a part of me that only exists when we exist, and in coming here I have resurrected it. However, I've gone as far as I can go alone – the rest depends on him. We are soulmates. I believe this, and as I allow the romantic in me to escape, I realise that the sentimental side of me, the part I was sure I'd left back at Sea Point, has been travelling with me all this time.

I charge dinner to my room number and then go outside to find a taxi. There's one already waiting. I give the driver the name that will take me back to Denzel Anderson after all these years.

The driver turns and looks at me. 'Are you sure you want to go to Amnesia?' he asks.

'Yes,' I reply confidently, but I begin to feel paranoid about his concern. Is it how I look? Am I too old? Over-dressed? Under-dressed? Or maybe the club isn't the safest place to be. But Jaspar's been there.

The taxi pulls out and I sit back, trying to take comfort in the fact that at least he's moving now, despite his earlier concerns. It's only when we pull up outside a dark building that I begin to fully understand.

'It's closed!' I say and my heart drops.

'Si, until May, miss,' the taxi driver explains. 'You want to wait until then?' he asks. 'I can leave the meter running.' He laughs at his own joke but I don't join in. I'm on the verge of tears.

'No,' I reply. 'Please take me back to the hotel.'

So much for my great plan!

17
Peeping Through The Gate Part II

'You want a drink?' Ah ask.

'Yes,' Jo replies and asks me what Ah'm drinking.

Ah tell her cranberry juice and she raises an eyebrow.

'Ah'm drying out,' Ah say and she nods, as if this isn't surprising.

'I'll have a wine,' she tells me.

'A glass or a bottle?'

'Eh, a glass Denzel! Red, please.'

She smiles and Ah smile back, but there's an intense energy passing between us so Ah don't read too much into the gesture. We're not the friends we had been, for sure. Too much water under the bridge, as the saying goes. This will not be an easy conversation. We both know it. The bar is busy and it takes me quite a while to get served. Ah'm wondering if it was the best place to have met as it's starting to get full and loud and even Jeff Buckley's big voice singing in the background isn't managing to cut through this mass of sound.

Ah get her a Merlot. It's the most expensive wine on the list served by the glass and Ah realise that Ah'm buttering her up. She thanks me and sits waiting for me to begin. She knows why we're here – of course, she does – but Ah'll be the first to mention it.

'You know why Ah wanted to meet you,' Ah say and she nods her head.

'Of course, Denzel.'

'How is she?' Ah ask, finding Ah can't say her name now that Ah'm with someone who is in direct contact with her.

'She's very good, Denzel. Very good. She's getting married next month.'

All the wind leaves me like Ah'm an old bagpipe and someone just shot the piper. For a moment Ah don't know what to say.

'Ja?' is all Ah manage. It doesn't sound convincing and all the questions Ah had lined up in ma head seem irrelevant now – except for one, the one Ah'll regret not asking.

'Is she happy?' Ah ask, and as Jo nods Ah feel something twist in ma heart.

'What are you doing here, Denzel? Just when Alice is happy and getting ready to settle down.'

And there it is. Someone had to say her name sooner or later. Alice is happy with someone else. This hurts so much! Ah'm shocked by how much this hurts, and now somehow Ah can hear Jeff Buckley's piercing voice telling me what Ah should've done and Ah want to scream. So Ah do – internally, like when The Big Chief used to hit me and Ah'd not cry out. Somehow Ah'd learned to keep the screams inside. The problem had come when Ah'd tried to stop them long after the beatings had ended. Later they'd got louder until the only thing that stopped them was to use. Ah'd refused to let the bastard see ma pain, and now Ah won't let Jo see it either.

She's looking at me in a way that tells me she wants to hurt me because Ah've caused great pain. And now Ah just want her gone. Ah want to be alone but her glass is full, this meeting has only just begun. Ah think about knocking back the contents of her wine glass so she has no reason to stay, but then Ah think of ma little group, and Ah think of Sid. Ah think of being brave, of asking Jo if she's sure, but Ah can't because Ah'll scream if Ah open ma mouth. So Ah simply shrug ma shoulders and let her talk on.

What was Ah thinking! Can't Ah just leave her be? Ah had left her back in Sea Point. Ah had broken her heart. Ah want to stop her there to point out that Ah'd broken ma own heart into the bargain, but the internal screaming continues, silencing me. Now we're all grown up, different people. She hadn't recognised me when she got here, for God's sake. We're different now! Couldn't Ah see that? Didn't Ah know that? She tells me that Jaspar is coming to the wedding. Do Ah remember Jaspar? And all the Cooper family are coming over. They'll be arriving next week and they'll be house-sitting while Alice and her new husband honeymoon in Barbados, and afterwards they'll start a family. And just like that ma dreams come falling down around me, dreams of happily ever after, dreams of ma Alice no longer ma Alice – someone else's Alice – and Ah wonder, what the fuck kind of asshole am Ah to have ever thought it would work out any other way. Ah let Jo talk on and on, and Ah listen. Jeff Buckley is telling me to feel no shame and to fall in love. And right now there's nothing Ah'd like more than to snort ma way through half a dozen lines of coke and get completely out of it. All of these thoughts flash through my mind at lightning speed and it feels as if the outside world has speeded up. And now, in addition to Jeff Buckley, Ah can hear everyone around me, all the conversations at once, and for a minute Ah think Ah might be going to pass out. And Jo talks on and on, unaware that Ah'm melting down in front of her.

Suddenly she stops talking. Now it's ma turn to speak, but Ah can't, so we fall into a very uncomfortable silence, which probably lasts a long time but it doesn't feel like that for me. Eventually she tells me that she needs to be somewhere and Ah'm so relieved. She hasn't asked me anything about maself – nothing. She's not interested.

'Goodbye Denzel,' she says, and just before she leaves she tells me to leave Alice alone.

Happy Alice. Alice who is getting married. Alice who is going to Barbados on her honeymoon. Ah say goodbye. Ah don't know how but somehow Ah squeeze the words out. And then Ah'm alone with the voice of Jeff Buckley still coming at me. Ah sit there and look at her half empty glass of wine and ma hand travels to the stem. Ah grab a hold of it, Ah pull the glass towards me, and in that moment, Ah'm filled with such an impulse to drink Ah begin to shake. The fluid in the glass bobs from side to side. Ah could drink it and then follow it with the entire contents of this wine bar. Right now ma reasons for staying sober seem unimportant, trivial. By way of a defence, Ah remember Sid, ma father, Holly, Clive, Gloria, ma little group. Yet tonight the memory of all these people isn't big enough to cope with the idea that Ah must forget Alice, that Ah must let her be and leave her to her happily ever after that does not include me. Ah look at the red fluid that looks a lot like blood right now.

Drink you, asshole.

The voice is loud and clear and belongs to the part of maself Ah'm so desperate to deny. Ah'm sat with ma addiction and the desire is strong, stronger than anything else. A single drink will take me all the way back, and the last six months might as well never have happened. All ma sobriety will be swallowed up, gone. This time, failure after such conviction to stay sober, will carry me far away from ever trying again. Game over.

Drink!

The voice is louder, blocking out everything else around me and ma resolve weakens as the part of me that is still under its command comes all the way to the surface.

*

I wake up in a fresh white bed and immediately recognise that it's not my bed. I'm not at home. I've spent my first night in Ibiza and not found Denzel. But really, did I expect it would be simple? The answer is yes. I feel like a fool, having taken this huge leap of faith for nothing. But this is a small island and I have a full day left. Surely if Denzel is living here I can find him.

'I've come this far,' I say out loud and notice that I sound more South African than I have in a long time. Ja, I'm walking in my past.

Breakfast is served in my beautiful hotel room as I requested. I have it out on the balcony, watching the marina. Although it's not exactly summer, the weather is quite mild and for this reason alone I'm thankful I've come. It's such a long time since I've eaten outdoors and the sun looks promising, like it might just get strong enough later on to leave a lasting impression. This is the weekend away I need because when I get back I'll be facing a lot of changes. My relationship with Robert is ending, regardless of whether or not I find Denzel, and with that will come a change of home. I look down at the copper band still on my ring finger, my past pulled into the present, while my engagement ring remains out of sight, like the rest of my London life. Here in Ibiza, the sea's presence makes itself known, enticing me to come closer and not waste this opportunity to spend time with it.

A short time later, I stroll out of the hotel. Dressed once again in my red dress and wearing the copper ring, I am setting my intentions for the day and inviting a reunion with Denzel. The sea is something I have always missed about my South African home, and as I move close to the Ibizan sea I think about my hometown, Sea Point. That was where I spent most of my teenage years with Denzel; that was where we fell in love, talked about our dreams and what we wanted from our lives. We even made our baby beside the sea. And now, by the water's edge, I think about that baby. Baby Denzel. I look out into the distance and remember when I cried by the sea and let big Denzel go from my heart. I'd sent all my love for Denzel out into the sea where I hoped the vastness could contain it somehow. It had felt so huge and there was nowhere else for me to put it once he'd left. Denzel was gone and our baby was gone, taken away from me shortly after I pushed him into the world. All the tears I'd cried back then were carried away by the sea and it had felt like I'd cried my lifetime's ration.

I sit and let the emptiness of the ocean engulf me and bring me back to the now. I've run out of ideas, and then it hits me: I'll walk the length of the beach. If my love is to be found anywhere it's by the water. I stand up and begin to walk, and as I move I pray, something I haven't done for years. I pray that somehow I'll meet him here, that my Denzel will make his way to the sea front and find me here, that we'll find each other again by the sea. I walk for as long as I can and then, exhausted, I collapse into the sand where I just sit and wait.

'Come on, Denzel. Find me again. I've come this far. You walk the last mile,' I say eventually and keep right on waiting.

I stay on the beach all day, ignoring the need for food or water, but still he doesn't come. I sit on, despite the fact that the wind picks up and it becomes quite cold. Still he doesn't come. I watch the beautiful sunset – alone, waiting for my love. I stay until I can stay no longer. I drag myself away from the sea, away from all hope of finding the love I crave so badly.

Not sure where I am in relation to my hotel, I stop off at the first decent-looking restaurant I find. Thankfully it's almost empty and my food comes quickly. I eat and when I'm finished I decide to go to a bar for another drink. I've made my way to San Antonio, another area on the island which looks less flashy, and now I begin to think that perhaps this might be where Denzel would hang out, especially if he was as messed up as Jaspar had said. If he's not working he'll most likely be in a pub somewhere. And so with my new-found hope I go in search of a pub, a pub someone in Denzel's state might go to.

I leave the promenade and let my feet take me up the back streets. With a strange sense of certainty that I've found the right place, I go into a red bar with the word AQUI stencilled outside. It feels full of promise. Once inside, I find it all but empty, except for a few couples and a huge man parked at the counter. I quickly see there is no Denzel here, but something deep inside me makes me feel certain that this is his local. I decide to sit and wait.

18
Peeping Through The Gate Part III

Ah wake up with the baddest pain in ma head, which makes me suspect the worst, but then Ah remember – Ah'm still sober. Ah don't know how but Ah managed to walk away from the jaws of temptation last night. Ah'd felt the sharp teeth as they snapped at me, far too close for comfort. And today Ah'm so glad that Ah've a plane to catch. A distraction. Somehow ma sobriety continues. Ah get out of bed and begin ma formation. Today Ah'm detached, so ma practice is stale. But Ah go through the motions as much as Ah can in ma present state. Ah feel wooden, like an old puppet that someone has chucked away.

After breakfast, Ah say goodbye to ma father and Bill, and they both wish me well as Ah head to Paris. Sid had told our father about Holly and now he tells me to send his regards. Ah promise Ah will. Ma flight will get me into Paris about 3 p.m., so Ah should get to the exhibition in plenty of time to see the doors open at 5 p.m. Ah'll meet Holly there and tonight Ah'll stay with her. One thought comes into ma head: will Ah stay sober? Ah can't think about this now. Ah tell maself that the answer is contained in ma future and Ah leave ma future to take care of itself. *Remember the Tao, Denzel. One moment at a time.* It's helpful and diffuses ma tension so that ma head hurts less.

Ah switch off ma phone and let it drop into ma rucksack where it will stay for the next twenty-four hours. Then Ah chuck ma bag into the overhead bin. As Ah sit on the plane Ah'm struck by the notion that the last time Ah'd sat on a plane Ah'd been with ma father, and Sid had been on board too – in the wooden box we'd brought a week later to the crematorium. His burial had been a small affair, really small. Ma father and brother didn't move in large social circles, much the same as maself, and our family association was small, non-existent actually. Ah'd met no family. None. And no one had questioned who Ah was or why Ah was there. The only other person Ah'd recognised, because he'd come to Ibiza, was the really atrocious dancer. It seemed he was Sid's only friend, outside of me. He'd been there with his family – his parents, and his wife and child – and they'd filled up most of the seats.

Ah remember thinking his wife looked a lot like Pia, a healthy, drug-free version of Pia. Ah think about Pia now and wonder if she might be here at the exhibition, and Ah feel nervous because she'll have brought her huge cocaine habit with her. Addiction loves company, especially addiction that's been a long time sleeping. And Marco. Ah think about that fucker now and feel angry. Ah'd been surprised that Holly had never blamed me for what happened, but then maybe she didn't know the full story, something that will possibly change in the next twenty-four hours. A lot of things might change in that time. For sure. Ah guess Ah'll know if Ah can stay on the straight and narrow, if Ah'm going to make it long term.

Paris is fancy-wancy. Ah couldn't remember it being like this last time but then Ah couldn't really remember much about it at all. It's contained in the hazy period of ma life, that period that constitutes most of ma past. The taxi ride is filled with Frenchness. The driver is French, the music is French and the surroundings that we pass through are all French. Ah must stick out like a sore thumb in ma un-Frenchness. This is a beautiful city, for sure. As we're driving into the heart of Paris Ah see the

Eiffel Tower in the distance. Ja, Ah can understand why it gets all the good press, although it doesn't feel all that romantic to me, which isn't so surprising given the current state of ma love life. *Time to forget, Denzel. Leave her be.* Ja, Jo – if only it were that simple! For now, Ah accept the idea of letting her be. It's a start.

The taxi spits me out in front of a fancy gallery and Ah see Holly's name stencilled in big fancy black letters across a white background – it looks right; fitting – and beside her name is a copy of a print and a face Ah recognise: ma brother's. It's a picture so beautiful and vivid that it causes a huge lump of emotion to bubble up inside ma throat and pretty soon there are tears spilling down ma face as Ah look at a familiar face in an unfamiliar place. Ah stand there and gather maself together in this random street in Paris. Eventually Ah go inside.

At first Ah see her from behind and instantly recognise her, but nothing can prepare me for when she turns around. She is beautiful – elegant in a way Ah never saw her look in Ibiza. Her hair has grown longer and frames her tiny face. She looks older, as if the girl that Ah'd met in Ibiza has become a woman in the short space of six months. But a lot has happened to us both in that time. She sees me and smiles but doesn't come over, and then Ah remember ma lack of hair, which makes me look very different.

Ah follow her as she walks towards a group of three people, and then Ah decide to leave her be and look at the pictures. Ah'm still emotional from ma experience on the outside. Although Ah knew Ah'd see ma brother's picture, Ah'd not been expecting it to make me cry. But Ah guess ma emotions are heightened right now. Ah feel like a cigarette and so Ah press on ma patch, still there, still feeding me. Stubbornness will get me through this if nothing else. Ja, for sure. Ah make ma way around all her paintings. They're all lekker but the three in the centre have an extra vitality. The portraits of Sid are alive with love. Again they move me and tears begin to roll down ma cheeks. And that's how she finds me.

'My God! Denzel?'

Ah turn and look at her, the beautiful artist. Ah dab at my runny eyes.

'I didn't recognise you! You look so different without your crazy hair!'

This makes me smile. Ah want to tell her how beautiful she looks but Ah can't. Ah can't find the words. Ah can't speak. Ah gesture towards the picture. She hugs me, then tells me she'll leave me be. She needs to see about 'one hundred and fifteen people' but she'll find me again after the exhibition. Then she kisses both ma cheeks and she's gone.

Ah go from picture to picture and let her work suck me in – all the faces she'd encountered in Ibiza. Most Ah know or at least recognise from Pia's parties. And then the big shock comes. Me! There Ah am, seven feet tall, and Ah remember the time she sketched me. Ah look directly at what she'd seen in me. It unnerves me more than Ah'd have thought it possible for a picture to unnerve a person. But Ah suppose this is me! It's dark, really dark. Where the picture of ma brother contains love, this contains its opposite, and Ah wonder if she were to paint me now would the picture be a lot different, with more colour and light and not so much shade. Ah'd hope so, because the man depicted in the picture in front of me looks like he's travelled as far down a dark road as Ah person can go and still survive.

Ah look, and again Ah remember the time Ah'd gone to her flat and she'd spent all afternoon sketching me as

Ah'd drifted in and out of consciousness. Ah'd imagined for a split second what it would be like to fall in love with this very beautiful girl, and then Ah'd dismissed the idea, for how could any beautiful, decent girl allow herself to fall in love with someone as vile as me. She'd seen all that in me and got all she needed on that first day. She said she'd paint later and Ah'd left. Yes, she'd got the measure of me in that one sitting.

The picture is mostly red, and although red is ma favourite colour, Ah don't quite like this shade. Ah remember seeing a picture years before of a bullfight and the bull's blood was spilling all over the hungry-looking matador. This red is that same disturbing tone, a bit like the colour of blood as it's drying. This is the colour that Holly associated with me, in contrast to the beautiful blue tone that she attributed to ma baby brother. Ah sit there and watch maself for the longest time, seeing how Ah looked from the outside in Ibiza where Ah could never bring myself to look in a mirror. There had been no mirrors in the hostel, unlike in ma current home where each morning Ah come face-to-face with myself. In Ibiza Ah never did. Ah even managed to shave without a mirror, using only ma blurred reflection in a chrome surface as a reference point. Ah've never thought about this until now, and it makes me feel really sad.

At some stage in ma life Ah'd stopped looking at maself. It was mostly ma eyes. Ah hated ma eyes and what they told me. All ma sins were held in them. Here, in a gallery in Paris, Ah'm confronted by those sins, everything Ah was trying desperately to forget. All the bad things Ah've ever done are contained in the eyes staring out from this picture. Leaving Alice. Surviving afterwards. Abuse. Hatred. Fights. Prostitution. Anger. Then rage, great big waves of it. Wanting to make others suffer. Causing pain.

Blackness. Ah remember it all now, without the drug-induced haze that somehow made these things seem less horrible and destructive. They fell into an existence completely divorced from anything normal in this world.

And then Ah come to the worst memory of all, the one that's been buried beneath all the others: Ah remember the girl and Ah hate maself, the thing Ah'd done that made me vile. Ah remember how she'd looked at me. Her look told me Ah was past the point of rescue; there could be no redemption and Ah could not be trusted. It meant Ah never went with another woman again unless she was a professional and under no illusion about what she was getting and where it was all going.

The girl had looked a lot like Alice and that had been what had fucked with ma mind. Ah'd been high but it didn't matter - Ah'd done what Ah'd done. Ah punished her for the sins of Alice - for not coming with me when Ah left Sea Point, for not trusting me, for forcing me to break both our hearts. Alice had rejected me long before Ah rejected her, like ma mother had - and The Big Chief who Ah tried so desperately to please. And when Ah found my real father, ma last hope, he'd rejected me too. Ah would not allow it to happen again.

The girl had cried out, loudly at first, the same word - the one word Ah wouldn't allow maself to hear that night: No. No, no, no. Ah was done with people saying no. So Ah'd not listened. Instead, Ah'd taken what Ah wanted, what we both wanted - she'd come with me into the room, after all, and had to know what that meant. Afterwards she'd cried and Ah left her there. Ah could only recall in flashes what Ah'd done. When Ah'd finished raping her Ah'd listened to her cry. That was the truth. She'd told me to stop and Ah hadn't, and as Ah'd brought maself down on her with ma full force she'd eventually given up pleading with me to stop hurting her. Ah'd kept going until Ah was done. Somehow it had given me a sick pleasure. But it was a short-lived pleasure, one that made me feel like vomiting then – and again now as Ah remember it. Ah was scum, deep down where it really matters.

The girl who looked so much like Alice. Oh ma God! Ah remember her now and the guilt Ah feel for ma brother's death is swallowed up by the massiveness of this old memory, the one Ah've done ma best to forget. As Ah look at the picture Ah see it raise its ugly head, contained in the brush strokes. Holly had seen it and painted it, whether she knew it or not. It had come through ma pores and found its way onto her canvas. Here Ah am in paint form – a vile creature.

And now Ah'm remembering Alice and it's just as well that she's met someone else, someone better than me. Ah'm a nothing, unworthy and deserving of no one, and it's best that Ah remember that. The Big Chief had got so much wrong in his sorry life, but he'd been right about me. Ma mother too; she was right – Ah should never have been born. But Ah had been born and now Ah had to carry all these things, to live with them, even though Ah might be beyond redemption or forgiveness. No more, Denzel Anderson. No more hurting people!

Ah belong alone. That's ma punishment, and maybe if Ah can get through the rest of ma sorry life without inflicting any more pain, it may make amends. Ah really hope so because right now the idea that Ah can't ever make amends is the most terrifying thing of all.

*

I watch the man at the counter from a safe distance, drinking my beer while sitting at a little round table in the corner. There's one other seat across from me, awaiting the company I have come here to find. It strikes me, and not for the first time, how crazy it is what I'm doing, but then if Denzel shows up, my actions will be seen as phenomenally romantic. Of course, there's a good chance that he won't show and my behaviour, based on my delusions, will bring everything crashing down around me.

My eyes keep travelling back to the man at the bar, the man who looks like no one I've ever seen before. I hear his voice between two brilliant Pearl Jam songs that are playing on the jukebox. The deep gravely tone reveals him to be a South African, which doesn't surprise me as I had his full attention when I ordered, my own voice giving away our common place of origin. And then an idea begins to form. Birds of a feather flock together, so there's a good chance he knows Denzel. I have to talk to him even though the prospect is highly intimidating on every level. I take a huge drink of beer and make my approach, feeling like a small child about to ask an adult something that might get them into deep trouble.

'Excuse me,' I say, and the man turns around slowly. He looks at me through my own reflection in his mirrored sunglasses but doesn't say anything.

'Ah was wondering, do you know someone called Denzel Anderson?'

He says nothing for a long minute, as if he might be translating my question into some other language. 'Who wants to know?'

'I'm Alice,' I say realising that it's a long shot and probably means nothing to this man, but maybe, just maybe, it means something. He's waiting for more and I realise I'll have to confide in him to a certain extent. This man will tell me nothing otherwise, and I'm beginning to suspect that he could help me if he wanted to.

'I'm the mother of his son,' I say, and although this gets his attention, he still doesn't say anything for the longest while.

'Let's take a seat,' he says eventually and beckons me back to my table.

We sit for a while saying nothing and although I want to study his interesting face I don't. Also, I get a feeling that he's watching me like I'm a loaded gun. I don't want to do anything to send him away.

'He doesn't know? About the son?' he says eventually, and I look straight at him and shake my head.

'When he left I was pregnant.'

'He chose to leave?'

'I refused to run away with him, and my family threatened him so he left. I don't think it was his choice though.'

My drinking partner nods his head and I wonder if Denzel has told him the story.

'You're from Sea Point,' he says.

'Ja.'

'But you left a long time ago.'

'Ja.'

'And you haven't seen Denzel since then?'

'No, not since we were fifteen.'

'And the boy is with you?'

'Na, my parents decided I was too young to be a mother.'

'What do you want from Denzel now?'

'Nothing. I just want to see him … I still think about him and I want to know if he still thinks about me too.'

He lets the silence between us grow as if he's working out the best thing to do. I wonder if I might have said the wrong thing. And then eventually …

'He's not here anymore.'

My heart drops.

'He's in London.'

I begin to laugh and he looks at me over the rim of his glasses. For the first time I get a look at his piercing black eyes.

'I came from London to find him,' I explain.

'You're not a very good detective,' he says and I can almost feel him lightening up.

'No. Please can you help me find him?' I ask, hearing the desperation in my voice.

The lightness leaves him again. He looks down at his drink and sucks on his teeth in a way I haven't seen since I left South Africa.

'If you give me your details I'll get them to him.'

'Ja, that would be great,' I tell him.

I write my mobile number on a piece of paper and hand it to him.

'Na! Alice Cooper! Seriously?'

'My parents had no idea.'

'Obviously not,' he says and smiles.

I smile too. I watch as he takes out a little black book and copies the number into it. He hands the book to me and asks me to check it. I am struck by the neatness of his writing.

'Ja, that's it exactly,' I say. His thoroughness reassures me.

'I won't tell him about the boy,' he says. 'I think that would be better coming from you.'

I nod my head gratefully.

He shakes my hand. 'Good luck, Alice Cooper!'

'Thanks,' I say and he walks away from my table back towards the barman who has been watching us both intently.

They say goodbye to each other and he waves in my direction as he leaves. I suddenly realise he never told me his name. But the most important thing is that he leaves with my name and number and the promise that he'll take them both to my lost soulmate.

19
Closing The Gate Again

Holly comes and finds me once the exhibition is over.

'Shall we get out of here?' she says.

Ah nod. Although Ah've somehow pulled maself together again, ma hand had been desperately close to taking the champagne on offer at the opening. Luckily there was orange juice too, which Ah drank so much of that Ah might be in serious danger of becoming diabetic in the near future.

We leave. She takes me to a wine bar that's really quiet compared to where we've just been.

'Wow, is there something that Ah should know about this place?' Ah ask.

She looks confused. 'Like what?' she asks.

'It's a joke, Holly!'

'Oh, okay,' she says, still not getting it but not pushing for clarification either.

'Are you okay here?' she asks.

'Ja, fine.'

'What would you like to drink?'

'Cranberry juice,' Ah say.

She looks at me for a long time before announcing that we'll go back to her place. Ah wonder what she might have seen in ma face.

Apparently, her place is close by and in only five minutes we are in one of the most amazing flats Ah might ever have encountered.

'Woh!' Ah say as she opens the door.

'It's my father's.'

'Is he here?' Ah ask.

'No. He stays in a house just outside of Paris, so this is mine. Oh merde, I never introduced you to Papa did I! Sorry Denzel. It's been a crazy night – so many people to see, but I think it went well. I hate these sort of things, but I guess it's the price I have to pay if I want to be a successful artist.'

Ah nod ma head, but Ah'm not quite sure what to say. Ah don't recognise this Holly Ah'm seeing here outside of Ibiza, and Ah'm wondering if she feels the same about the Denzel that has turned up here in Paris.

'I'll make us some coffee,' she says. 'Please – have a seat. And please smoke, yes? There are no anti-smoking rules in this house.' She smiles.

'Thanks, but Ah don't smoke anymore,' Ah tell her. As Ah say it Ah tap ma faithful patch.

She backs out of the kitchen and turns to look at me. 'You've stopped smoking as well as everything else?'

'Ja,' Ah say.

'Merde!'

Holly makes the coffee while Ah watch. The flat is open plan so that the lounge, the dining area and kitchen are all in the same huge room. There are four huge windows offering an amazing view of Paris and the Eiffel Tower.

'This is an amazing flat,' Ah say.

'Yes. My papa has immaculate taste. It's a shame you won't meet him. He had to leave Paris tonight and so went straight to the airport from the exhibition. Initially he wanted to cancel his appointment but I told him not to. In a way I'm glad he's not around. He has very high standards. I need a little time before he tells me what he really thinks about the exhibition.'

'Na, Holly. Ah'd no idea how talented you were – are.'

She smiles. 'You saw your picture?'

'Ja,' Ah say but Ah don't want to travel down that road. Tonight Ah want to talk about Sid. 'The pictures of Sid really moved me.'

She nods. 'I still can't believe it. I'd only just met him. You meet someone special and have all these plans and then they're gone – just like that, snapped away right from under your nose.'

Ah nod and let her finish before Ah tell her what Ah came here to tell her. She is a part of this story and Ah want her to know.

'Why would life do something like that? It's unfair. No?'

Ah nod.

'Papa said life isn't fair and that I shouldn't make the mistake of believing that it is. I think he's right'

Now Ah think about Alice. And the girl Ah raped.

'Holly, there's a reason Ah came here. There's something Ah want to tell you. You know that Sid was ma friend.'

She nods.

'You know that he died because of me. Ja! He found me on the beach with a few of Marco's asshole sidekicks and came to ma rescue. That's why he ended up dead.'

She nods. 'It's not your fault, Denzel. I don't blame you, and you shouldn't blame you. Sid was your friend and he was doing what friends do. What you did for him the first time you met – he told me about when he was mugged on the beach and you came to his rescue. He thought so much of you, you know.'

Now it's ma turn to nod. 'Thanks Holly. It means a lot, you saying that, but still Ah feel responsible and that's why Ah've kicked the drugs and Ah'm trying to make something of maself.'

Alice floats into ma head but Ah quickly get back to ma story, the one in which Holly has a place. The reason Ah came here.

'There's something else Ah found out – a big shock. After Ah left you that morning with a plan to leave Ibiza forever, Ah went back to the hostel. There was a man in Sid's room. Ah didn't recognise him at first because he was so out of context and Ah'd never have dreamed in a hundred years ... He was Sid's father, but the reason Ah recognised him was because when Ah left South Africa Ah travelled to London to find my birth father and it led me to this man. This same man.'

'Oh my God!' Holly shrieks and her hand moves to her mouth. 'You and Sid were half-brothers?'

Ah nod.

'And Sid had no idea?'

'Nor did Ah. So when you talk about life being unfair Ah completely agree. It sent me a brother and then took him away from me before Ah even knew.'

We drink our coffee and then in spite of maself Ah talk about ma picture. 'Your picture of me was disturbing,' Ah say.

'It was how I saw you back then. But it's not how I see you now,' she says.

'So you think people can change?' Ah ask.

'Without question. You have. I have.'

'And Pia?' Ah ask, bringing up our mutual friend for the first time.

Holly shakes her head. 'Pia hasn't. She's still lost and I can't be around her anymore. It's too hard. And she can't be around me for the same reason.'

'You don't use any more?'

Holly shakes her head. 'No. After you left me in Ibiza, I had a really bad experience with Pia and decided I could

go one of two ways. I chose to take this road – the same
road as you.'

'The last time Ah got fucked was with you,' Ah tell her.

'It's so good that you've stopped, Denzel. You were on
your way to certain death. You know that?'

Ah nod.

'I'm glad you pulled it together.'

'Ja, me too.'

We fall into silence. Ah wonder what she'd think of me
if Ah were to tell her about the girl, the young girl Ah had
raped. Would she still say she was glad Ah'd pulled it
together? Could she bear to look at me then or would she
tell me to get out? Ah can only guess what her reaction
would be because Ah won't tell her. Ah can't tell her. How
can Ah ever tell anyone?

'It's good to be able to talk to someone about Sid,' Ah
say.

'For me too,' she says. She begins to cry and Ah watch,
feeling helpless.

'I don't think I'll ever feel that way about anyone ever
again, Denzel.'

Ah want to tell her that she will, to assure her, but Ah
can't because the truth is Ah don't think she will – no
more than Ah will meet anyone like Alice. Ah strongly
believe you love like that only once. But for now it's better
Ah don't say that out loud.

*

It's my last day in Ibiza. I pack my bag and lie one last
time on my hotel bed thinking about the events of the
night before and the strange man who may very well
bring Denzel back to me. It makes me smile, a smile that's

as wide as my face. For the last few days, I've felt as if he were there with me everywhere I've walked on this island and that 'we' are alive again. This island has reminded me so much of Sea Point. It has a feeling of the place we grew up, and I can see why Denzel was drawn here. It makes me believe that he has kept a hold of 'us' too.

So he's in London! Of course he's in London. I'd seen him that night in the Brixton Academy. I'd felt it but dismissed the possibility that somehow fate had put us together again without either of us having to do anything. Although he hadn't dared approach me, something else had happened between us, something that set all this in motion perhaps. I wasn't ready then, but I am now, and I pray that once he hears I came looking for him, he'll come find me. Everything depends on Denzel now, and then I get a bad feeling as I remember that everything had depended upon him once before and he'd left. So will he let me down again or will he come back? A knock on the door lets me know housekeeping is here and that it's time for me to leave.

A short time later, I'm in a taxi bound for the airport, taking in the scenery of this lovely island for the last time and wondering if I might ever return with Denzel. As I inhale the Ibizan air, I allow myself to believe that somewhere in my future he will bring me here to share his story and walk me through the years of his life I've missed. My new-found hope carries me all the way through my journey home and I only begin to think about Robert when the plane is making its descent into Gatwick. I look down at my engagement ring, now back on my finger but soon to be handed back to the man who had given it to me. Tonight, I'll tell Robert that it's over. The thought alone fills me with a sickening anxiety and I comfort myself by thinking that by this time tomorrow, everything will be done, finished.

I arrive back to a flat that tells me my secret is safe. Robert meets me at the door with open arms, and the promise of a bottle of wine and a home-cooked meal. This isn't the reception I'd been expecting and although I wish it was otherwise, as it'll make what I have to do harder, for now I play along. He kisses me and holds me, and I can tell that he knows we're not all right – it shows all over his body. Eventually he pulls back and looks into my eyes. It gives me a chill down my back. His eyes have the same stony stare they had the night I told him I wasn't going to New York with him. I get a bad feeling as I begin to imagine how they'll look when I tell him I'm not going to marry him either. He walks ahead of me, and I put down my bag and hang up my coat before following him into the candlelit room. I look around me and a wave of sadness washes over me.

Robert pulls out a chair, inviting me to sit down, pours me a glass of red wine and disappears into the kitchen. When he comes back he has two servings of spaghetti bolognese, my favourite meal. He's trying so hard and I feel tremendously guilty.

'Thank you,' I say, and I really mean it.

'So how was it?' he asks. 'Did you get what you needed?'

'Yes, thanks,' I say.

There's so much more to say but I'm at a loss to find the words. I don't know how to begin. I concentrate on eating, putting a small amount of food into my mouth and forcing myself to swallow what I have over-chewed. My appetite is gone and I realise I can't eat any more. I take a drink of wine and brace myself to say what I have to say. Now.

'Well, things here have been pretty dull,' he says. 'I've missed you, Ali.'

I smile, still unable to begin.

'This is when you're supposed to tell me that you missed me too.'

I look into Robert's eyes and I get a chill down my spine. 'I wasn't in Herefordshire this weekend,' I say.

Robert's eyes don't flinch.

'I was in Ibiza. I went there looking for someone from my past, someone I've never told you about because I couldn't bear to think about him, let alone say his name out loud. I'm really sorry, Robert, but I can't marry you. I don't love you and I don't think I ever will – I still love this person. Although I've tried to forget him I can't. I guess there are some loves that you don't get over or that you can't get over – or maybe you aren't meant to get over them because you belong with that person.'

Robert says nothing and I really wish he would.

'I'm so sorry,' I say again, not knowing what else to say.

He just smiles and I'm really unnerved by this.

'Robert …'

'Shut up, Alice. Just shut the fuck up!' he says and I do, because for the first time in all the years that I've known him I'm truly frightened of him.

20

The Wheel Turns

Ah had managed it. Ah'd stayed sober in Paris and it was all thanks to finding a sober Holly, the beautiful Holly that sits opposite me sipping coffee as we prepare to say goodbye. And then Ah'll be left alone with ma memory of the girl, who is now a permanent fixture, as if her ghost has been released inside of me.

'I'm so glad you came,' she says eventually.

'Ja, me too.'

'Are you okay?' she asks.

'Ah'm okay,' Ah say but it doesn't sound very convincing, not even to ma own ears.

'We've talked about a lot of things, but there's also a lot you didn't talk about, yes?'

Ah feel like she's reading me, as she had done when she painted me.

'Whatever it is, please don't let it pull you back down. You were close to death.'

And yet Sid was the one who died. How is that fair! And how is it that she can talk to me like this after everything.

'Just like Pia.'

Her eyes well up and a single tear rolls down her cheek. She lets it fall and although a part of me would like nothing more than to wipe it away Ah dare not touch her, afraid Ah might break her, given the things Ah've been confronted with this weekend.

'You think about Pia a lot.'

'Yes, we were the best of friends and although she's lost to me now, the friendship is still there. I think connections are like that. They remain, even if the person doesn't. Do you know what I mean?'

'Ja, Holly. For sure.'

But Ah wish this was not the case – that connections can be completely broken and forgotten – and now Ah'm remembering something Ah'd read somewhere or that someone had told me: that life is like a wheel and everything comes back around again eventually. It's a terrifying thought.

They announce that my gate has just opened for the flight back to London.

'Ah best go, Holly.'

She nods her head.

We both stand up and she hugs me as if this might be the last time she'll ever touch me. Ah allow maself to feel her as Ah've not dared to in all the time Ah've been here. There's so much here Ah can't look at and Ah wonder if she feels it too.

'Goodbye, Denzel.'

'Goodbye, Holly.'

'Stay in touch,' she says and catches both ma hands, as if that will in some way hold me to ma word.

'Ja, Holly. For sure.'

'Next time I'll see you in London.'

And then Ah remember. 'Hello from Tim.'

'Who?'

'Ma father.'

She looks puzzled.

'Sid told him all about you.'

She smiles.

'Please say hello back from me.'

Ah turn away and leave her with that thought. Ah don't look back because now Ah'm crying. Ah'm crying and in danger of howling if Ah don't get a handle on this.

Ah recall the practice Ah got during ma demented upbringing and bring it under control.

Sitting on the plane heading for London ma heart is heavy, but Ah'm assured by the fact that Ah'd not drunk a drop of alcohol, nor had Ah found ma way back into the land of charlie. Ah can go to Never Again with a clear conscience. But there's something Ah must take to ma friends in the circle. Everyone has admitted the worst of themselves and Ah've left out the worst bit of ma story. Now Ah must tell it. Ah need to lay it out on the table and look at it with the six people who made it possible for me to keep sober. Ah need to say it out loud. This is what Gloria has been telling me for forever and Ah believe her. What we don't tell stays inside and keeps us in prison, locks us away in its clutches and never lets us go. More than anything Ah want to be free of it. Before, Ah wanted to be free for Alice. But now there is no Alice so Ah guess Ah just want to be free for maself. Ah wonder if it's possible.

The connection Ah've made with Holly feels really important and Ah think about what she said in the airport about connections never being broken. We're in each other's lives now and we parted with promises that we would stay connected. Ah guess we are friends but it feels closer than that. It almost feels like we are family, linked together by the loss in our lives – the absence of Sid. Ah close ma eyes and wish her the best. And then Ah think of Alice, the girl of ma youth, the girl Ah might have spent ma life with if circumstances had been different. But they weren't and now she's happy – and Ah'm a rapist. Now Ah think of the girl and ma eyes fill up until the tears slip through the cracks and roll down ma cheeks. Ah sniff and, keeping ma eyes closed, Ah send an intention her way. Ah tell her that Ah'm so sorry and that if Ah could, Ah would turn back the clock and change what had happened. But Ah can't. Ah'm sorry. Ah say it, letting it run in ma skull like a mantra and hope with all of the life inside of me that somehow somewhere she can hear this and can find it in her heart to forgive me. Ah keep it going until we land back in London.

Just as Ah'm leaving the airport, Ah turn on ma phone and it beeps into life. It continues beeping and Ah see that there are seven missed calls, all from Clive. Ah register this fact and Ah'm worried that ma friend has fallen off the wagon. Cigarette. Na! Nicotine patch. Okay! Ah need to return his call. Ah tap the last caller number and wait until eventually …

'Hello.'

The voice throws me – it belongs to a woman. Now Ah'm scared.

'Hello. Ah was looking for Clive,' Ah say.

'Who is this?'

'Ah'm Denzel. From Never Again.'

'Oh right. I know who you are,' she says. 'Clive's mentioned you. I'm Tracy.'

'Ja, he's mentioned you too,' Ah say. 'What's happened? Where's Clive?'

'He's in the hospital, Denzel.'

*

I sit in silence and watch Robert. He looks like a cat about to pounce on something it wants to kill.

'I'm sorry, Robert,' I say again. What I really want to say is that I am scared, but something in the way he's looking at me makes me think this would be a bad idea.

He smiles. 'What exactly are you sorry for, Alice? That you opened your big fucking mouth and said something stupid? Something that could get you into trouble? Because you know you are in trouble now, don't you?'

I swallow hard. I'm really scared now and not sure how to talk to this person in front of me. It's as if Robert Shaw has been possessed by someone else, so any attempt to speak to the Robert I know would be a waste of time.

'Don't worry,' he says. 'I'll let you go. Eventually.'

I hate the way he drags out the word 'eevent-u-all-y' because it makes me feel even more scared. No, 'scared' isn't a strong enough word – I'm petrified and I get the feeling that this is exactly what he wants, that he might actually be enjoying seeing me like this.

'You can leave me. But first I'm going to have some fun with you. You've no idea what I like. What I would like to do to you! What I do to other people.'

As he says this he grabs hold of the edge of the table and squeezes it. It makes the hairs on the back of my neck stand on end.

'Robert …' I say, laughing nervously.

'Yes, Ali?' He's as calm as if we're discussing the weather.

'I saw the pictures on the internet,' I say, trying to stop whatever it is I sense might be about to happen from happening, but he smiles at me in a way that makes me feel like I've made a grave mistake.

'So you're a little spy as well as a liar, Alice Cooper! And to think I thought butter wouldn't melt in your sweet mouth. I thought I had you all figured out. But then you saw the marks on my back and said nothing and I wondered if you might know. Of course you did. It's not such a big deal for you, me being a stinking liar, because you're one yourself. It takes one to know one.'

'What marks on your back?' I ask, puzzled, and although my instincts are telling me I should stay very quiet, curiosity gets the better of me.

'Don't give me that! The marks that slut Sally put on my back. You know I've been fucking Sally at the office, don't you? Fucking her like the little slut she is, the way I've always fucked the whores I visit. You didn't know that did you? I have a supply of whores I see in a little backstreet in the city, sometimes more than one at a time – bitches that know what I like and give me what I like. It's amazing what these whores let me do to them. And all for money. You wouldn't believe it if I told you. But you? I thought you were different. I thought you could be my wife. But it turns out you're a little slut like the rest of them.'

Now my head is spinning and I'm thinking about the awful things Robert is telling me. He sees prostitutes and I'm wondering what diseases he might have given me, but then my mind whispers to me that this isn't the most immediate of my problems.

'And now I'll treat you like you deserve to be treated,' he hisses.

Before I know what's hit me, he has grabbed a hold of me and is pulling me by the hair up the stairs. The Bose home stereo system that is Robert's pride and joy is playing some hard electro music and playing it loudly, drowning out my screams and cries for help.

He drags me all the way up the stairs and into the bedroom, and eventually I stop fighting him as it's a waste of my energy. Robert is too strong, and instinct is telling me that this will be over more quickly if I don't fight. He said I could leave, so at least I know he's not going to kill me. But is this person who is dragging me into our bedroom like I'm a bag of rubbish someone I can take at his word?

'Please stop this,' I say, trying to somehow reach him. 'Please, Robert.'

He pushes me on to the bed face first and lies on top of me.

'Fuck you and your sorrys,' he whispers into my ear. 'You don't want to be with me? Fine. I'll be better off without you anyway, but I might as well have some fun with you before you go. If you ever tell anyone about this – well, I might just come back for more. And maybe I'll kill you next time.'

I freeze, paralysed by my own terror. I'm in the presence of a malignant force. The person I thought I knew isn't responding to me and I begin to wonder if he ever existed.

'I like pain, Ali. I like feeling it, but even more than that I like administering it. And now I'll show you how much. If you tell anyone I'll kill you – don't doubt me for a second, because I have killed before, and it was easy, Ali. Really easy. I broke the neck of a filthy prostitute when I was travelling after uni and left her dead in her room. I still think about it now, the glorious sound of her neck snapping.'

I begin to cry, no longer able to bear what he's saying. 'You're a monster,' I say between sobs.

Robert laughs as he wipes at my tears. 'Poor Ali is crying now. Well, let's see how much more you can take.'

'You're a fucking monster,' I say, but I'm sobbing so hard that it comes out all wrong.

He mimics me and laughs. That makes me angry and I start to fight back, but to my horror I discover that it's making him more aroused.

'That's it, bitch.'

I make a sound that I don't recall ever having made before – something worse than a whimper. More desperate. He turns me around, rips off my pants and forces himself inside me. I close my eyes and lie rigid.

'Keep your fucking eyes open,' he says, but I deliberately keep them shut.

'Careful Ali, you wouldn't want to do something that might get your neck snapped, would you?' he says and places his hands tightly around my neck.

Terror flashes through me. I look into his eyes, eyes I've looked into so many times before, but they've never looked at me like this. There I see something worse than hatred.

He punches me in the face, which sends a shot of fear and pain coursing down through my body. He continues to penetrate me, hard. I try to relax in the hope that it will hurt less and I'm giving that my full attention when he flips me over onto my front and pushes my face into the bed so that I can barely breathe. He sinks his teeth into my shoulder. The pain shoots all the way down my arm.

'You're a whore, Ali. You know that. You think you're so special, but you're nothing but a lying, dirty whore.'

I can feel his erection digging into me from behind as if it's made of something other than flesh and muscle. He anally penetrates me and sends a sharp pain shooting up inside me. It feels like I've been split in two. I sob into the bed clothes as I exhale the last of my oxygen, and pray that this will all be over soon.

He pulls out and comes all over me. I can feel it spurting on my bare buttocks, and then I smell it as I finally manage to lift my head to breathe. My relief is short-lived as he stuffs something into my mouth, something that I quickly realise is a condom soaked in blood and traces of excrement. I spit it out and dry heave, and although I don't look his way, I can feel his eyes boring into me.

'Get the fuck out of my house,' he says and leaves the room.

ADAM II

It's Aidan's birthday and we do something to mark the occasion. He's ten today and I'm his uncle, even though I'm closer to his age than I am to my own sisters. It's mad. We have a party and all of Tommy's family show up. Bernie and me are the only ones from the Sheehan side. Marie was too busy, of course. She puts herself out for no one. Mammy used to say that and she was right. It's seven weeks since Mammy died, seven weeks to the day and still I haven't cried. I wonder if I ever will.

We sing happy birthday to Aidan and he has a ball. It's great to see. He's a lovely boy, Aidan. Last night he asked me if he could tell people that I'm his big brother instead of his uncle, and I told him of course. I told Bernie after and it made her cry. She cries at the drop of a hat these days. She keeps asking me if I'm all right and I keep telling her I think so. But the truth is I don't know. I'm still all over the shop deep down; my insides are still trying to find their way back to the places where they rightfully belong. Bernie sent Tommy in to have a man-to-man talk with me last week. Tommy is grand but he's no help. I remember what Mammy said about him and she was right. He's not really the kind of man I want to grow up to be. I want to be like my own father – to make Mammy proud.

Everyone leaves and I go to my new room. I have homework to do but I don't care about that. My interest in school fell away as soon as I found out Mammy was sick, although I still manage to do all right. Mostly the teachers leave me to it, but there's this one, Mrs O'Carroll, who's got it into her head that she wants me to 'apply' myself. She went and told Bernie that I could be some kind of genius if I put some work in, but I couldn't care less. I'll leave school at the end of this year. As soon as it's over I'll head off, out into the world. I haven't told anyone this yet because I know there'll be blue murder. But they can't stop me from doing what I want to do. That's what makes me different to them. I don't need them, but they need each other.

I believe that we need no one. None of us. Mammy got very philosophical in the end and she told me this and I believed her. She stopped believing in God too – or at least the church. I understood that. She used to ask me to read to her and I would read her her favourite books, but then coming near the end she wanted to hear poems and I read her all the Irish poets, her favourites. Then one day on my way home from school, I called in to a charity shop and found a book. It was the title that caught my attention: *This Light in Oneself*. I bought it and began reading it in the hope that it would help me find the light in myself now that Mammy was leaving me. But as I read, I realised that maybe this book might help Mammy too. So one day, close to the end, I began to read it to her.

She never asked me about it or questioned what I was saying, but somehow it helped. I know it did. The book's a bit of a mystery to me and I get the feeling that there are things in it that might only make sense to me when I'm on my own death bed, so I keep it, just so I know I'll have it when I need it. I look at the book now, and opening it to the first page, I read out loud as I did when Mammy was alive. I like to imagine that she's in my room with me now, close by. This book made us feel close. It's the last thing she heard when she slipped away. That's the thing for which I am most thankful – although she was in desperate pain, pain I can't bear to think about, her last few days were peaceful and she died quickly. At least, that's how it looked from here. I was with her and I could let her go, and somehow this book I'm holding in my hand helped me to let her go. I believe that it's in some way responsible for the peace that was in that room. So Jiddu Krishnamurti, whoever you are, thanks.

I'm just about to become hypnotised by my own reading voice when there's a knock on the front door. It's too late for someone to be calling so I sense that this will be more bad news. Just what we need! I listen intently and hear Marie's voice. She's crying. I stay in my room. The news will reach me soon enough. Bad news is like that – it travels fast; good news takes its own sweet time. That is what Mammy would say.

So I sit and wait, and sure enough Bernie comes and knocks on my bedroom door. John is dead – a hit and run – and Marie is in bits. My poor sister, bad and all as she is. My poor sister – that's all I keep thinking now.

21
Emergency Rooms

Ah jump off the train at London Bridge. Tracy had given me the address of the hospital and said Ah should just come, suggesting that things are as bad as Ah'm thinking. Ah grab a black cab and proceed to a part of London Ah don't know. When Ah arrive, somehow Ah recognise Tracy – she is very Clive.

'He's still out,' she tells me as she takes me to his hospital bed, explaining to the nurse that Ah'm family.

The person in the bed doesn't look like Clive, and Ah remember thinking that same thought when Ah'd been in the ambulance with Sid. It gives me shivers.

'We brought him in early this morning,' she explains and begins to cry.

Why had Ah not kept ma phone switched on! Perhaps Ah could've talked him out of it. He had tried to call me, for fuck's sake, and Ah had not been there for him. Ah watch Tracy cry and let ma hand come to rest on her back by way of comfort. Ah don't know her well enough to offer anything more but Ah want to give her something.

'Do you want to get a coffee?' Ah ask, anxious to find out what has been going on but not wanting to talk about it within earshot of Clive, even though he's unconscious. Also if Ah'm honest, this is bringing back uncomfortable memories for me right now. Tracy nods and leads me to a little kiosk where Ah leave her at a table and get us some coffees. When Ah come back she's looking at her hands and Ah notice the engagement ring on her left hand. So Clive had proposed.

'This is all my fault,' she says.

'Na, you can't blame yourself, Tracy,' Ah say.

'No, you don't understand. It's because of me that he did this. He asked me to marry him on Christmas Eve and I told him I couldn't. He'd looked at me like his whole world had just collapsed and I thought it best not to tell him the whole truth – at least not for a while. This is the longest he's ever been straight and I thought I'd wait until he had done his six months, when he'd be stronger. You see, I've met someone else and I'm marrying him in the summer. Clive caught us together last night, but somehow I think he already knew something was going on. He called at the flat about an hour after I'd put Ben to bed. My parents were out so it was just me and Paul. When I answered the door he walked straight past me. I could tell he'd been using again just by looking at him. But he said nothing – just walked straight into the kitchen where Paul was half way through our evening meal. Paul guessed who he was and asked him if he'd like to sit down. He could see he was agitated. I asked Clive to remember that Ben was sleeping close by and then he turned around and looked at me. He reminded me of a ghost – there, but not there. And then he walked calmly out to the balcony and jumped. He was so calm … I never in a million years would have thought … imagined … I had a hard time stopping myself from screaming – the last thing I wanted was to wake Ben. Paul went down the fire escape and I called the ambulance. And somehow Ben slept through the whole thing. Thankfully.' She bursts into tears.

Clive what have you done, boet!

'Ah'm so sorry, Tracy,' Ah say and let ma hand rest on her arm.

'Of course, Ben knows there's something wrong. Kids have much better instincts than we do. My parents are with him now. This morning he was asking about his daddy. He was meant to be seeing him today and I couldn't tell him. I mean how can I tell him.'

Ah don't know how to answer that question so Ah stay silent. 'What have they said about Clive,' Ah ask eventually, needing to know.

'He's damaged his spine and they've done the best they can. But he might never walk again.'

'Na!' Ah say. 'But there's a chance he will, ja?'

She nods her head.

'At least he's alive,' Ah say and for this Ah'm so thankful. Ah'm not ready to lose someone else. Not now.

We walk back to Clive's room and the nurse tells us to go home, that there's nothing else we can do tonight. But he will need us tomorrow, in the morning when he wakes up.

'Can I give you a lift, Denzel?' Tracy asks.

'Na,' Ah tell her. 'You go back to Ben and Ah'll see you tomorrow. Ja!'

'Yes. Thank you,' she says.

'Ah'll walk you to your car,' Ah say.

'There's no need.'

'Ja there is,' Ah cut in and she lets me help her. She's a woman who Ah'm guessing doesn't find it easy to accept help. But today is different. Ah leave her when Ah'm sure she is okay to drive and Ah head in the direction of the taxi rank.

As Ah'm sat in ma taxi, homeward bound, Ah check ma phone and notice there's a voicemail. Ah listen, fully expecting Clive's voice, but instead Ah hear Titus and it throws me. He wants me to call him urgently and Ah don't dilly dally – Titus isn't a man who uses words like 'urgently' without real meaning. He answers almost immediately, suggesting he's been waiting for ma call.

'Ja boet, what's the matter?'

'There was someone out here looking for you, Denzel.'

'Ja?' Ah say and wonder what motherfucker is out for ma blood now.

'A girl called Alice Cooper.'

Ma head goes completely blank for a minute and Ah don't know what to do with this information.

'She wanted your details but of course Ah refused. Ah got the lady's particulars instead. She's in that same capital city as you. Ah told her she's not the best of detectives. Ja?'

This makes me smile.

'You got a pen handy?'

Ah tell him to hold on and ask ma taxi driver for a pen and paper.

'I'm driving mate,' he says.

'Well pull over,' Ah say, 'Ah'm paying ja!' It comes out more aggressively than Ah would've liked so Ah add that it's really important in a friendlier voice.

A few seconds later in a taxi parked in some back street in London Ah'm taking down the number of the only girl Ah've ever loved.

'Thanks Titus,' Ah say.

'She's a nice girl, Denzel.'

'Ja,' Ah say. 'She's a very nice girl. For sure.'

*

It's some time before I can move and when I eventually do, I get a shooting pain up my back passage. I attempt to stand up but then realise that I might need to wait a little longer. But I'm eager to get out and away so I try for a second time and although I'm slow, I'm successful and manage to find my balance. Moving from foot to foot is difficult. I'm walking like someone in splints. Just before I leave the room, I take off my engagement ring and lay it on the dressing table. I may have foreseen giving my engagement ring back but my premonition in Ibiza hadn't warned me about the rest of it. I make my way downstairs inch by inch. It takes the longest time, but eventually I get to the bottom where my coat and backpack are waiting for me right beside the door. I realise with a chill that Robert has set them there.

I can hear him laughing at something on the television in the front room and it makes me want to scream. He sounds like he always does, as if nothing out of the ordinary has happened. What a monster I've been living with all these years, without having had any idea! Opening the front door, I walk outside and choose not to close it behind me. I want to leave Robert Shaw exposed to danger, unsafe. Step by step, I walk slowly down the side street and out into the Broadway where I know there is a minicab office. As I approach, the two men in the office stare at me.

'Lady, you want the hospital?' one asks, confirming what I suspect – I look bad, like a victim of something. I wonder if I look like a rape victim.

'Yes,' I say. 'Please.'

As the cab takes me to the hospital, I feel detached from myself, as if this might all be happening to someone else. Perhaps I'm having a nightmare and I'll wake up soon. Or maybe I've imagined it – I mean this is Robert, my partner of nearly five years! How could he have done this to me – and confessed to murder! But it had happened. I'm not imagining the pain that is now shooting through me. He'd threatened to kill me if I told anyone, and I believe that he's capable of that.

The cab stops and I hand over a twenty pound note, telling the driver to keep the change. He tells me to take care of myself and I feel like saying it's a bit late for that. Inside, I am seen very quickly: I'm not sure how I managed to jump the queue as the young nurse ushers me into a cubicle. She pulls the curtain, as if she wants to hide what has happened to me from the rest of the world, and then invites me to lie down.

'The doctor will be along shortly, Alice,' she says in the loveliest Irish accent while placing her hand softly on my forehead.

I wonder how she knows my name and then remember the form I filled in somewhere along the way. Alone and only slightly conscious of the commotion that's happening all around me, I stare up at the white ceiling and wait.

The doctor, when he comes, looks very young and has a really kind face. He asks me if I'm in pain and I nod my head. After I confirm that I've not taken any drugs he gives me some painkillers. He examines me tenderly and tells me that although I'm badly bruised and cut I don't require any stitches. This makes me think of the poor girls who find themselves in a worse state than me after similar experiences. There are some tests that they need to run to check that everything is as it should be. The doctor doesn't need to explain the details – I know exactly what he's saying. It brings the condom to mind and the taste of it fills my mouth again. I feel sick and ask for some water, which the Irish nurse brings eventually. The doctor disappears but shortly returns with a woman he introduces as Jenny – just Jenny – and then we are alone, 'Just Jenny' and me, with a hundred questions.

First, she assures me that everything I tell her is in confidence and that she won't take any action without my consent. She asks me if this is clear and I nod my head. Physically, I am starting to feel better, now that the painkillers are beginning to take effect. Mentally, I feel numb and sloth-like.

'Who did this to you, Alice?' she asks.

I think about lying but then remember that she's said everything is in confidence, so I decide to tell her the truth.

'My ex-fiancé.'

'And has he ever done anything like this before?'

I shake my head and then recall what he'd told me about the girl he'd killed and I shudder.

'Do you need a minute?' she asks me.

'I'm okay,' I reply.

'You can press charges, you know, and he'll be punished for what he's done. We have the proof to convict him if you want to go ahead. I could take pictures of your injuries right now and his DNA is all over your clothes.'

Suddenly I remember him ejaculating on me and it makes me feel sick again. Right now I never want to see Robert Shaw again. Ever. Of that I am certain. What this woman is suggesting would mean I'd have to see him again. He'd also threatened to kill me if I told anyone and now I had. I need to stop this process going any further. I shake my head.

'Thank you for taking the time to speak to me,' I say. 'I just want to forget this and move on. Please.'

Just Jenny looks at me and I can see the disappointment in her eyes. 'Are you sure, Alice? I can't insist that you press charges but I strongly recommend it.'

'No, I don't want to.'

'It'll help you get over what has happened. This man deserves to be punished.'

'How do you know it'll help me?'

'Well, it's helped many women in the past.'

'But has it ever happened to you?'

'No, but ...'

'Well then, don't tell me what's best for me now. Please leave me alone. Like I said, thank you, but please go now!'

She looks at me and nods her head. 'I'm sorry this has happened to you. It's important you know that none of this is your fault. Most of the women I see are savagely attacked by someone they know. You're in no way to blame.'

I nod my head. 'Thank you. I know you're trying to help, but please, I just want to be alone now – to sleep if that's possible. Can I stay here tonight please? I don't want to go home.'

'Let me go talk to someone,' she says and I thank her.

She returns with the lovely young Irish nurse. 'Yvonne here will take you somewhere to bathe and you can stay overnight,' Jenny says. 'Here's my card if you change your mind, or if you ever need to talk.' She hands me a thin piece of card.

I take it but I've no intention of ever contacting this woman again.

22
Waking Up

Ah sit and watch a motionless Clive who still refuses to look like the person Ah've come to know. His face is without any life, so much so that it scares me. Ah'm sitting at his bedside clutching David Bowie's biography, which Ah'd borrowed from ma father's library to read to ma friend. And this is how Clive finds me as he comes out of his post-operation slumber. He doesn't say anything so Ah keep reading. Ah read until Ah get to the end of the chapter and then Ah close the book and wait for ma friend to speak.

'Where's Tracy?' he asks.

'She's on her way,' Ah tell him. She had called me earlier to say that she'd be here after she'd taken Ben to school.

'You know everything?'

Ah nod ma head.

'I wasn't planning on waking up,' he says.

'Ja, Ah gathered that, but Ah for one am glad you did!' Ah say.

'Does Ben know?' he asks.

Ah shake ma head and watch the relief show on Clive's face. It makes me want to grab hold of him and hug him.

'I'm all messed up,' he says and Ah nod ma head.

Ah bring ma hand to rest upon his arm. 'Ja, we all are, Clive. Remember?'

'What am I going to do?' he asks and Ah'm about to say *just put one foot in front of the other* and stop maself just in time.

'Ah don't know,' Ah say. And it's the truth. 'Ah'm sorry Ah wasn't here for you, boet. Ah had ma phone switched off while Ah was away.'

'How was Paris?'

'It was hard and Ah remembered a few things Ah wish Ah hadn't.'

'You stayed clean?'

'Ja, but only by the skin of ma teeth.'

'I didn't,' he says.

'Ja, Ah kind of guessed.'

'I broke the rules.'

'Gloria will probably fucking kill you.'

He smiles a little. It's not his usual smile but it's a start.

'We have company,' he says and Ah turn around to see Tracy with the doctor. The time has come and Ah leave, telling Clive that Ah'll return with coffees.

As Ah leave Ah catch Tracy's bloodshot eyes. The girl looks worn through. Ah leave them to it, figuring Ah'll be needed later to help pick up the pieces. Ah go to the same kiosk where Ah'd sat with Tracy the night before. Today, Ah take three coffees to go and after unsuccessfully trying several arrangements that might enable me to get all three cups back to Clive's room in one go, the bemused waitress hands me a cardboard tray.

'Try this darlin'!' she says, smiling.

'Thanks. Ja!' Ah reply and return her smile.

When Ah get back to Clive's room the doctor has already left and Tracy is sitting beside a silent Clive. Ah hand the coffees around and wait for someone to speak. Clive looks done for and Ah can fully understand why.

Eventually he tells us he wants to be alone. Tracy says okay but Ah'm not so easily convinced.

'Ah can stay and read to you for a bit,' Ah offer.

He shakes his head. 'Please go, Denzel. Please.'

Ah nod, and Tracy and Ah go back to the kiosk without a word.

'I've never seen him like this,' she says after we've settled into the exact same seats we sat in last time.

'Ja, but Ah don't suppose he's ever jumped out of your kitchen window before.'

It comes out comically and we both laugh. Ah guess we need something light for a minute.

'What happened when Ah left?' Ah ask once the moment has passed and we've taken from it exactly what we need.

'The doctor told him he'd badly damaged his spine and there's a good chance he might not walk again.'

'But did he also stress that there's an equally good chance he will walk again?'

'Well … no.'

'Why do doctors do that! Why don't they give patients a lifeline, for fuck's sake.'

'Maybe he doesn't want to get his hopes up.'

'Right now Ah think that might be the most important thing. But all he's heard is that he won't walk again. Tell him that he might, for Christ's sake. Tell him that it's been known to happen. Raise his fucking spirits!'

She begins to cry. 'It's all such a mess. I don't know what to do.'

Ah shrug ma shoulders. 'Ah don't think there's much you can do, Tracy. Ah don't think there's much any of us can do. Where are Clive's family?'

'He doesn't see them anymore. They fell out a long time ago.'

'Maybe it's time they all made up.'

'I don't think so. There's a lot of bad blood.'

Ah nod ma head. 'Ah know that drill'.

'Hello Denzel!'

Ah recognise the voice and a few seconds later, Gloria reveals herself. Ah had called her earlier and she said she'd come to the hospital as soon as she could. And here she is, true to her word.

'Hi Gloria. This is Tracy.'

The two women shake hands and Gloria joins us at the table.

'I've just seen Clive,' she says.

'He's not good,' Ah say.

'No, but that's to be expected. How are you two?' she asks.

Ah'm surprised that she groups me with Tracy, but then Ah suppose Ah'm one of Clive's close friends and given that his family aren't in the picture this is beginning to feel like it just became a very significant thing.

'I don't know!' Tracy says. 'It's like I'm living in a nightmare.'

'I can imagine,' Gloria says. 'How's your little boy?'

'He's okay. He knows there's something wrong but thankfully he doesn't know what, and he didn't see anything so I can choose what to tell him.'

'I know it's hard but the truth might be best,' Gloria says. 'He'll find out eventually.'

'But he's only four!'

'I'm sorry,' Gloria says. 'You're his mother and of course it's up to you what you tell your son. I don't have any children.'

Tracy smiles slightly. 'I think I'll go now and come back later,' she says. Ah get the feeling Gloria might have rubbed her up the wrong way. 'I'll see you later Denzel,' she adds.

'Ja, Tracy.'

She throws a goodbye at Gloria. There's a definite vibe.

'Call me if you need anything,' Ah say and she assures me that she will.

Gloria waits until Tracy is gone before she speaks. 'I think I put my foot in it there.'

'Ja, you might have. But Ah think it might be the least of Tracy's problems just now.'

She nods.

'I think we should record Wednesday night's meeting and bring it here for Clive on Thursday,' Gloria says. 'He's still a part of the group and I want him to be included to the end.'

'Even though he broke the rules?'

'He used?'

'Ja.'

'And do you think he should be kicked out of the group for that?'

'Ah don't know, Gloria. You're the sober one.'

'So are you, or have you fallen off the wagon too?' she inquires.

Ah shake ma head. 'Ah nearly did last weekend but Ah managed to steer clear.'

'Of course! You went to see Holly. How was it?'

'It was hard.' Ah remember the girl.

'Have you used since you've been at Never Again?' she asks, looking at me with eyes that have been trained to spot a lie from a long distance, no matter how well rehearsed.

'No, but Ah haven't told you the worst of it. And Ah've been saving a little incentive to get me through to the end of the six months.'

'Let me guess. An old flame and a walk into the sunset hand-in-hand moment.'

'Ja!' Ah say. She knows.

'I did that too and it helped, but deep down I think I knew it wouldn't happen. In the same way you do too. Don't you?'

'Ja, Ah guess Ah do.'

'It got you this far, Denzel, but maybe it's time for you to walk on and away. We can never go back.'

Ah think about Alice now and the number that Ah have in ma back pocket, the number Ah've been too terrified to call.

'You should be proud of yourself that you didn't use with Holly.'

'She's clean too, which made it a whole lot easier.'

She nods.

'And this terrible secret you've been keeping – are you sure that it's all that terrible?'

Ah look at Gloria and Ah think about the girl, the girl whose name Ah never knew but whose face Ah'll never forget.

'Ja, Ah'm sure,' Ah answer.

'So you'll tell us all on Wednesday?'

'Ja.'

'Okay. I'm going to go back to talk to Clive.'

'Should Ah come with you?' Ah ask.

'No, but maybe come back later tonight. He's going to need us all, Denzel. You especially. You're close.'

'Ja, we're close.'

'Good. Sometimes all you need is just one close person.'

'Ja. For sure.'

*

I wake up early, a long time before the hospital's busy day begins again, and I'm amazed that I'd managed to sleep despite everything. I'd been allowed to stay in one of the staff bedrooms most probably used for emergencies such as mine. The bed wasn't very comfortable but I'd been grateful for the place to rest and for having the time to get my story straight before I called Jo. In the end, my body had been so exhausted that not even the images inside my head stopped me from falling asleep. My bladder is full so I prepare to sit up and although there is pain, it's not as much as I'm expecting. It's only when I begin to move that the real pain kicks in.

It takes a long time for me to get to the bathroom, for I'm moving like an elderly person to mitigate the agony of walking. Emptying my bladder is also a painful affair due to its close proximity to the areas of my body that are bruised and battered, and I dread to imagine how it will be the next time I need to move my bowels. The nurse had told me to expect constipation, that that was normal after my ordeal. I'd replied that none of this was normal, not for me, and she had apologised. Everyone is apologising to me even though it's pointless. I cry out as I wipe myself. Every little thing is so hard, but nothing can prepare me for the shock when I catch sight of myself in the mirror as I wash my hands. One side of my face is swollen and bruised – I remember that Robert had punched me, maybe more than once – but somehow I hadn't expected my face to look this bad. I shudder at the memory.

Back in bed, I'm thankful that I can rest for now, but I'm also aware that I'll need to leave the hospital shortly. I'll call Jo and ask if I can stay with her. It's five o'clock on Monday morning and I know my friend starts her working day at six so I can call her soon without feeling guilty. The Coopers are due to arrive in two days. I might still be able to stop them from getting on the plane, but I know that Sheila Cooper will come anyway and calling her now will only mean I'll have to talk to her an additional time. I decide I'll not worry about Sheila Cooper until she gets here. For now, I just need to call Jo. But what will I tell her?

As I sit and stare at my mobile I realise that I don't want anyone to know what has happened to me, and not because Robert has threatened me but simply because I don't want the people closest to me to know. I feel ashamed, but more than that I feel responsible in some way. I'd failed to see this coming. 'Just Jenny' had told me that it wasn't my fault but it doesn't stop me from feeling as if it is. I had closed my eyes to certain things in our relationship and failed to see that the man I was about to marry was a monster, capable of rape and murder. How could I have got it so wrong?

I begin to work out my story for Jo. I'll tell her that Robert and I had an argument, that I'd found out about his affair and he'd found out about my trip to Ibiza, the trip that now seems like it happened a long time ago. He'd got so angry that I left the house and I'd been mugged as I walked to a nearby hotel. I decide that this is the story I'll tell Sheila Cooper too. Stories ... Lies. These are the main elements in my life so far – why should now be any different?

My friend answers her phone eventually.

'Jo, I need to ask you a favour. Can I come stay with you?'

'What? Of course. But what's happened?'

'I'll tell you when I see you. If I leave now, will you stay there until I reach your place?'

'You sound really weird. Please tell me what's happened?'

Something in her voice makes it impossible for me not to tell her the truth. 'I'm in the hospital, Jo. I was raped,' I blurt it out.

'Oh my God. But where's Robert?'

My story of five minutes ago abandons me, and as I don't know what to answer, I say nothing.

'Jesus Christ! It was him, wasn't it? It was Robert! Look I'll come and get you. Okay?'

'Yes,' I say, realising I don't have the strength to argue. 'I'm at The Whittington.'

'Jesus, Alice! I'm so sorry. I'll be there as soon as I can.'

I get dressed – it's a slow affair – and when I'm finished there's a knock on the door. It's the same nurse from the night before.

'You're dressed!' she says, sounding unbelievably chirpy for someone who has obviously worked all night. 'I wanted to check you were okay. Do you have a place to go to?'

'Yes thanks,' I say. 'My friend is on her way.'

'That's what you need now, a good friend.'

'Why am I not crying?' I ask her.

'It's most likely trauma, Alice,' she says simply and softly. 'Sometimes it takes a little while to reach the surface.'

I nod my head. It makes sense. 'Sorry,' I say, 'I can't remember your name.'

'It's Yvonne,' she says. 'It'll take time. But you'll be fine again, Alice. I promise it gets easier.' She looks at me and I see more than compassion in her eyes.

'You were raped?' I say.

She nods her head. 'My uncle – just before I left Ireland. I never thought I'd get over it at the time. But I did. It got easier day by day until eventually whole chunks of time would pass without me remembering. And just like that it was as if it never happened.'

'I'm sorry, Yvonne,' I say.

'Yes, I am too. But it doesn't change anything. It doesn't stop it from happening every day of the week. You do what feels right for you, Alice. Do what you need to do to get through this and don't let anyone tell you anything different. Okay, pet?'

'Yes. Thank you.'

'No problem. Now, I must get home to my husband or our two little ones will have him driven crazy. They're a right handful these days. Do you know where you're going, Alice?'

'Yes. I think so.'

'Good girl,' she replies and gives me a big hug. 'Take care of yourself pet,' she says before leaving.

True to her word Jo is with me an hour later and she begins to cry when she sees me.

'Your poor face. I'll kill the bastard!'

'No. Please, just take me back to your place,' I plead, and my oldest friend takes hold of me and we leave the hospital arm in arm.

23

Coming Clean

Ah sit and look around the circle. It's ma turn to share and tell the worst sin of ma life. After tonight it will be back in this realm, no longer forgotten and hidden inside ma head. And maybe somehow Ah will be free. Tonight there are six of us and ma story will be committed to tape as Gloria has asked everyone's permission to record the night's events so that she can play them for Clive tomorrow at the hospital. Ah prepare maself to speak.

'There's something Ah haven't told here so far and Ah need to tell it because like Gloria says, and Ah believe her, Ah'll only be free from this thing when Ah've said it out loud. It happened the first time Ah was in London. Ah was eighteen and looking for ma father. Ah met a girl who looked a lot like someone from ma past. Anyway Ah was about as fucked as it's possible to get and although Ah know this in no way justifies what Ah'm about to tell you, Ah have to believe that had Ah not been fucked, it wouldn't have happened. Ah couldn't bear to think that a sober me would ever do such a thing – could ever do such a thing. The girl was young – probably a little younger than me or the same age – and if she told me her name Ah didn't hear it. She was ma past that night. We partied, we partied hard, and then we ended up in a house somewhere, alone. We kissed and she wanted to stop. Even before she told me to stop Ah knew she wanted me to stop. Ah could feel it, and even though Ah was high Ah knew but Ah made a decision. Ah raped her, and as Ah was raping her she told me that she was a virgin and she didn't want her first time to be like this, but still Ah kept going all the way to the end. Ah can't be sure what was going through ma head or why, but Ah think that somehow all ma anger at what had happened in ma sorry life, all ma rejections, became that girl's fault. Ah was going to take what Ah wanted and no one was going to tell me *no*, not this time. When Ah was done with her, Ah rolled off and turned over and listened while she cried beside me. Ah left her there. Ah left and did the only thing Ah could do to live with maself – Ah used and Ah forgot, and every time Ah used again, Ah forgot a little bit more. Ah'd give anything to go back and change it, but Ah can't. It's done – something that can never be undone. Not ever. Ah'd forgotten about that girl until this weekend and Ah don't know how Ah could have forgotten because now that Ah've remembered her Ah know she is with me to stay. Ah changed the whole course of her life and Ah don't even know her name. That's what Ah did, but Ah hope with all ma heart that it's not what Ah am. Ah couldn't bear it if it was.'

Ah stop and Ah feel a sense of relief for having said it all, even though Ah can't bring maself to look up to see who is looking at me. The three women in the room – how will they see me now? Ah wonder if Billy will ever want to go for coffee with me again and whether Gloria will tell me to leave. This is by far the worst story that has been shared in our group. Ah can say that objectively, even though it's ma story. Ah hadn't cried, even though Ah thought Ah would, and somehow that makes it worse. Ah keep ma head down and wait for someone to break the rules and say something, for Gloria to break her own rule and tell me to leave. But nothing happens. No one says anything and we continue to the next person. This is how the share works – you say what you need to say and then it evaporates into the circle. That's the rule, but Ah had committed a crime and Ah'd have thought that superseded the rules of our circle.

We work our way round the group and then we hear the sixth absent member of our group share through the medium of Gloria's iPhone. Clive tells us the whole story – about how he'd been hoping he could make things right with Tracy and his son, but when he found out she'd met someone else he couldn't bear it, so he used. And then he went to her house to kill himself in front of her, to punish her. He'd tried to end his own life but unfortunately he's still alive and he wishes he wasn't.

When he's finished there is silence and the recording stops. Ah'm left feeling cold because the person Ah'd heard on the recording didn't sound like Clive.

The meeting continues and everyone seems to be just the same. Ah wonder what awful secrets they must have that makes them so willing to let me remain here despite ma vile deed. Or maybe it's because we're all ex-addicts filled with shame and that cultivates a deep compassion for others, a high threshold of acceptance. The meeting ends with a promise that we'll meet our mentors next week. Ah remember Alice now and how under different circumstances Ah would be planning to make contact in three weeks as per ma original plan. But now Ah'm not so sure. She deserves better. Sure, she'd gone to Ibiza looking for me, but she doesn't know the things Ah have done. It'll be easier to let her have her happy ever after, far away from me.

As Ah'm leaving Billy asks if we can go for coffee and Ah'm so happy Ah could hug her. At Costa, Ah buy the drinks and join her at the usual table.

'Can I talk about what you said in your share,' she asks, following the rules.

'Ja,' Ah reply, glad that someone wants to talk to me about it, especially a woman.

'I think you were really brave to say what you did. I really respect that you talked and for what it's worth I believe it was down to the poison in your system, rather than you. I really do. We've all done things we'd never in a million years believe we were capable of.'

'Thanks Billy,' Ah tell her. 'It helps that you say that. It really does.' And it does. 'Like Ah said Ah couldn't bear it if it was a reflection of what Ah am deep down. Ah'd hate it if that was the real me that'll jump up every now and then to remind me of exactly who Ah am, no matter what Ah might have convinced maself.'

'Denzel! But you know what you did was wrong and you think about that girl with regret. Anyone with half a brain can see that you're truly sorry. Now will you give yourself a break and stop looking like you've just murdered someone and move on.'

'Thank you,' Ah say and shut up. Billy is on a roll tonight and Ah let her talk.

'Jesus, you don't know half the shit I've pulled over the years. But I have to forgive myself and forget it. To move on you need to forget it.'

'You're a wise one.'

'No! Just well schooled in forgiving myself. Speaking of which – poor Clive.'

'Ja.'

'Do you think he'll pull through?' Billy asks.

'Ah don't know, Billy. Ah hope so. Ah've gone to see him every day since it happened and he doesn't want to talk so Ah've been reading him David Bowie's autobiography. But at least Gloria got him to make that recording, which is something, although he sounded really weird. You should go see him.'

'I'm not sure I'd know what to say.'

'Ja you would. Like Ah said, you're a wise one.'

She smiles. 'I think Gloria is really fazed by it. It's the first time someone in her group has relapsed.'

'Did she tell you that?' Ah ask.

'No, but you can so tell – no?'

'Ah don't know.'

'In a way it makes me even more determined now. Do you know what I mean?'

'Ja, Ah feel that way too. It puts more on the line.'

'Plus I don't want to go back, Denzel, ever. However bad it gets while I'm sober I keep telling myself that at least it can't be as bad as when I was using. Everything was so stuck then. At least now I feel things are moving.'

'Ja, Billy, that's for sure.'

'How was your trip away?'

'It was great. Ah saw Holly.'

'How was she?'

'Sober, and coming to terms with what happened. It was lovely to see her again. You two could be twins, you know.'

She blushes, reminding me that she's a young girl. Sometimes it's so easy to forget.

'Maybe I'll meet her some day,' she says.

'Maybe you will.'

We finish up, leave and head our separate ways, but not before Ah hug her. It's the first time we have embraced and Ah feel the same kind of protective stuff for Billy that Ah feel for Holly – and that Ah felt around Sid. Maybe this is what normal families feel like, but Ah can't know that for sure.

*

'Alice, I am so sorry!' Jo says.

I have finally spoken after spending the last few days in bed, too brittle to face anything other than the soft pillow on which I'd rested my broken head. We are sitting at Jo's kitchen table and I've just given her a watered-down version of Robert's attack. Much of it I left out not because I don't trust this girl who has just proved herself to be a truly amazing friend, but because I can't bear to say some bits of it out loud. I just want to forget as quickly as I can and I remember what the Irish nurse said to me at the hospital. Yes, I'll do what feels right for me, and sharing the full horror of my ordeal does not feel like it will help me, or Jo for that matter. She doesn't need to know.

'You've been incredible,' I tell her, and she has been – taking time off from work to look after me and dealing with the people in my life that I can't face right now while giving me the space I need to readjust. 'I don't know what I would have done without you.'

'Well, you don't need to worry about that because I'm here, ja! And we'll get through this, Cooper.'

'Fuck, my parents arrive today,' I remember. Jo has agreed to meet my family who are expecting me to be their welcoming party.

'Ja. Do you feel up to coming with me to the airport?' she asks.

I shake my head. 'Sorry, I couldn't bear it – and to have to explain this.' I cup the right side of my face with my hand; it's still tender.

She nods. 'What am I supposed to tell them?' she asks softly.

'I don't want anyone to know what happened,' I say, unable to look my friend in the eye.

'Okay,' she says simply, surprising me.

'He's been having an affair. That'll do.'

'That's good.'

'It's true, Jo.'

'Since when?'

'A few months.'

'How did you find out?'

'Kate told me last week.'

'And that's why you went away?'

'Yes,' I lie.

'Bloody Robert Shaw! And to think I thought he was the best thing that ever happened to you. I want to kill him – seriously.'

She catches hold of my hand and I feel tremendous guilt. I'll tell her about Ibiza, I promise myself, but after she's seen the Coopers.

'Did you speak to the police?' Jo asks.

I shake my head. 'I can't put myself through that.'

She pats my hand. 'I wouldn't either for what it's worth.'

'I just want to forget it.'

'Of course,' she says, and again I'm surprised she's not urging me to put up more of a fight like 'Just Jenny' had. This isn't typical of my oldest friend. 'The problem is, your family are supposed to be staying with Robert. Do you think that's such a good idea under the circumstance? I mean it's all a bit messed up, no?'

'You're right. They can't stay there.'

'Do you want me to bring them here?'

'God no, Jo! Please no!'

'Okay! Sorry! Maybe I should take them to a hotel somewhere.'

'I probably should have called them and stopped them from coming at all, but I just thought that Sheila Cooper would come anyway and I couldn't handle dealing with her.'

'It's okay, Alice. Ja.'

My friend is looking at me full of concern now and I realise that I've begun shaking, like someone on the verge of a fit. I begin to feel nauseous and barely make it to the sink before I throw up the partly digested toast I had forced down earlier. Jo stands behind me and holds my hair back until I am done.

'It's okay, Alice. I'll sort it out. Let's get you back to bed.'

I let her lead me back to her spare bedroom. She tucks me in and kisses my forehead before leaving me alone with a promise that she'll sort everything out and that I shouldn't worry about anything.

As I lie buried beneath the duvet I take comfort in the warmth of my own breath. I close my eyes and he's there in my head, the monster who has come to haunt me over the past few days, so I open them again and look into the darkness. I wonder where my tears are. I wish I could cry – their absence seems partly responsible for this awful numbness that engulfs me. I begin to count my breaths like I used to when I was a child and couldn't find sleep. Somewhere past one hundred I drift away.

'Alice? ... Alice, I've made some soup.'

I open my eyes and see Jo's familiar face inches away from mine.

'Will you come and eat something?' she asks and I nod.

Five minutes later I find her in the kitchen with two bowls of hot soup sitting on the table in front of her. An automated voice from the radio tells us we are listening to 'Jazz After Dark', easy tunes that allow us to remain comfortably silent while we eat. I finish the soup slowly; it's the first substantial thing I've eaten in days.

'That was really nice,' I say.

'I made it myself,' she says proudly.

'Did you?' I ask.

'Of course not!' She winks at me. 'Marks and Spencer, darling!'

I smile.

'How were they? I ask.

'Concerned,' she lies.

'Angry,' I correct.

She nods. 'Your mother was demanding to see you immediately, but I told her she'd have to wait until tomorrow.'

'Sheila Cooper is a nightmare – my whole family are. You were much luckier than me in the parents pools. Thanks for dealing with them.'

'She's coming in the morning. I won't go into work until later.'

'You really are an angel.'

'Na, you'll owe me big time Cooper!'

'I realise that. Seriously.'

'I'm only joking! That's what friends are for. Isn't that what they taught us in the playground?'

'Listen, I need to tell you something you're not going to like.'

'Okay,' she says and looks at me searchingly.

'I wasn't in a spa last weekend like I said.'

She waits until I finally spit it out – that I had gone to Ibiza chasing after the past that I'd barely survived as a teenager.

'I don't believe it,' she says, shaking her head.

'I know you think I'm a fool but I can't stop thinking about him ...'

'No Alice, that's not what I meant! I saw Denzel Anderson here in London last Friday!'

'What?'

'He came looking for you!'

This huge news hits me and despite everything, my heart flutters.

24

Getting Back To Something Like Normal Part I

Ah get to the hospital first thing in the morning and find Gloria there already, sitting with Clive and playing the recording of the meeting from the night before. Ah join them just as ma recorded self is going through the motions. Ah guess this is how it's supposed to be. Ah'm meant to listen to ma crime again, the crime Ah committed. Ah'd given a lot of thought the night before to what it would be like if Ah was made to do time for what Ah'd done, if Ah found the girl after all these years and she decided to press charges. That would be justice, ja! Ah listen and ma cheeks redden. Ah'm ashamed and although Ah do feel freer for having told everyone in the group, Ah also feel tremendous fear that Ah've diminished in the eyes of the people Ah care about – especially the women in ma group. Billy said some nice words last night, but perhaps she just said them to make me feel better and to make sure that Ah don't fall off the wagon like Clive.

As Ah sit and listen, Ah wonder what Clive is thinking. He's listening without looking up, so Ah can't gauge his reaction. His face is blank and gives nothing away. It's the same face Ah've been watching for the past few days. The doctor has told Tracy that Clive's depression is natural and he has been prescribed anti-depressants. Ah just hope that this isn't feeding the addict. But Ah guess right now he needs something, and it's better it's prescribed than self-administered.

The recording finishes and Gloria asks Clive if he'd like to add anything. He shakes his head. He looks up at me and nods. Ah nod back.

'Do you want to say anything, Denzel?' Gloria asks.

'Ah'm curious to meet ma mentor,' Ah say.

'I bet you are. When are you getting discharged Clive?'

He shrugs his shoulders. Ah know he's been told but maybe the information hasn't registered.

'I'll bring your mentor here to meet you next week with another recording, assuming you're still in here,' Gloria says.

'Thanks,' he says without any emotion.

The three of us sit there for a while without speaking and eventually Gloria says that she has to make a move. But first, she invites me for a coffee. Ah promise Clive that Ah'll return.

'Ah brought David Bowie with me again,' Ah say, taking the book out of ma bag and setting it down on the table.

'Great!' he says but he sounds really flat.

'He's really not himself,' Ah say to Gloria when we're safely out of earshot.

'And he won't be for a long time. A suicide attempt takes a long time to come back from.' She says it like she knows first-hand.

We get to the kiosk and Gloria buys me a coffee.

'Permission to speak about your share, Denzel?' she asks and Ah nod. 'It was really brave of you to say what you did last night.'

'Thanks.'

'How do you feel about it today?'

'Ah feel relieved, but Ah'm also afraid.'

'What are you afraid of?'

'Of everyone seeing me differently now. And of having to seek out that girl so that justice can happen.'

'And what would that justice look like?'

'Ah'd be locked away for a very long time.'

'I think you've done enough of your own personal jail time and now it's time to let yourself out, to set yourself free. You did wrong, but your life begins now. You've the power to be different, and you are.'

'Thanks for saying that, but Ah worry that Ah am that person, the one who did that awful thing. That deep down Ah'm that level of badness and no woman is safe with me.'

'Have you ever felt like raping someone else?'

'Na! But Ah've been with a lot of prostitutes.'

'I don't understand. What has one got to do with the other?' she asks.

'Well, with prostitutes, Ah can pretty much do what Ah want.'

'Okay, I see. But what about when you're with girlfriends?'

'Ah haven't been with anyone since that girl. Ah've been afraid of what Ah might do.'

Gloria was silent for a moment, then said: 'I think you've been telling yourself one thing when the truth is something very different.'

'Ja?' Now it's my turn to be confused.

'Perhaps you're not afraid of what you'll do in relationship but of what will be done *to* you.'

Ah feel very uncomfortable now, like she might be telling me something Ah don't really want to know.

'Everyone is afraid of something,' she went on. 'Do you believe that?'

Ah nod.

'And most people punish themselves for being afraid, in some way or other. I punished myself by using. And so did you. You see that, don't you?'

'Ja.'

'I've watched you closely over the last few months and I believe you're not what you fear you are. You're not bad, nasty or vile – or any of the words you use in your shares. You're just like the rest of us – afraid of being hurt because we've been hurt.'

Ma eyes begin to water and Ah dab at them with ma hand, hiding ma face away. Right now Ah miss ma long hair. For sure.

'It's time to forget, Denzel – time to make peace with what's happened to you, and with what you did to that girl. Then forget and move on.'

'But maybe it's best Ah never allow maself to forget so that it doesn't happen again.' Ma voice is barely more than a whisper, but Gloria catches it all the same.

'I believe the opposite to be true. We're not what we forget but what we remember.'

'Ah really like that. Who said that?' Ah ask.

'Well, there's only you and me here and you weren't talking,' she replies.

Ah laugh out loud.

She smiles. 'Maybe I read it somewhere – wherever it came from I really believe it and I want you to as well. It's the memory of addiction that keeps us addicts.'

'Ja, Ah suppose.'

'I'm an ex-user.'

Ah try to picture her a user but Ah just can't. 'But you should forget that now, ja?' Ah smile.

'Touché!' she says. 'I know I'm different now. Every now and then I remember the bad times – it keeps me humble. Sobriety is inclined to travel on a high horse if you don't keep it grounded. But mostly I forget the details of who I was back then because it has no relevance to who I am today.'

'Lady, you are filled with the wise cracks. Sitting with you is like an evening with Confucius.'

This makes her laugh out loud.

'It's spending time with people like you, Denzel, and all the other wonderful and brave souls I meet in Never Again, that gives me the blessing of insight. It keeps me alive and free. You're going to make a very good mentor,' she says.

That's unexpected!

'You think so,' Ah say.

'I know so. But anyway I'm jumping the gun. Let's keep you on this side of the fence for another while yet. So, now is the time for me to say goodbye. I've a lunchtime group, so Euston Road here I come. And remember to forget,' she says and smiles.

'Okay, Gloria. Thanks. For sure.'

'My pleasure, Denzel. See you next week.'

'Ja, for sure!'

She leaves and Ah watch her walk away – an angel. Ah know that might sound sentimental but as she walks away Ah get that feeling. She must be an angel. Ah mean just look at all the people she's helped and that she will help in her future. What else is she if not an angel? And Ah'd be a fool to ignore the advice of an angel.

She's right – Ah must forget. Ah close ma eyes as Ah'm sat in the hospital. Ah tell the young girl Ah'm sorry, that Ah'm truly sorry. And just like when Ah lost Sid and promised that Ah would turn this sorry arse of mine around, Ah make the same promise, but this time to the girl. It occurs to me that all these promises are really to maself. But somehow having these people at the receiving end makes them feel more solid. It's easier to feel a conviction for others rather than for myself, especially when Ah've fucked maself up left, right and centre. So ma promises are made to the people Ah've done wrong to, and Ah remember the Tao, which advises Ah do something similar – offer ma good actions up for the bad in the hope that a balance will be struck and karma fulfilled. Ah promise the girl Ah'll be a better person and make up for what Ah've done. It all begins now.

Ah head back to Clive's room and find him pretty much as we'd left him. Ah go and sit by his bed.

'Hey boet. You heard ma share.'

He shrugs his shoulders.

'Ah just spoke to Gloria and she told me to set maself free. Imagine that! Now there's a sobering thought. She said that we are what we remember, not what we forget, and that made sense to me. Everything starts now. Ja, for sure. We have to move on, boet.'

'Thanks for pointing out the parallels in our lives, Denzel, but you have full use of both your legs. I'm a fucking cripple. That's where we differ.'

His words take me by surprise and sound bitter as fuck, but at least now he's talking. It's the first time he's said the word 'cripple' out loud, at least to me.

'Ah know Clive, but there's a possibility that you will walk again. Ja! You have to hold onto that.'

He doesn't say anything. His eyes stare blankly at me and Ah wonder if that's down to the medication.

'Can you read now please?' he asks.

So Ah pick up the David Bowie book and begin.

*

In less than an hour, I'll see Sheila Cooper for the first time in three years. Robert and I had gone to South Africa for a holiday and had spent five days at Sea Point under my parents' roof. Everyone had got along really well – and why wouldn't they, having so much in common. It's me who has always been the odd one out. As I wander through these memories where past and present lock together, I remember that the man who had spent three weeks with me in South Africa, the man I was going to marry, is the same man who raped me and threatened to kill me a few days ago. It doesn't seem possible somehow.

I stare at my face in the mirror. It looks even worse now, and although logic tells me that it needs to get worse before it gets better, part of me is worried that I might never look normal again. Or *be* normal again. I still haven't cried, and although Jo isn't saying anything, I know she's worried. If the shoe were on the other foot, I'd be worried too. She feels terrible for sending Denzel away, even though I told her that I don't blame her. If I'd told her about my plan to go to Ibiza, then she'd probably have told me that she was going to meet Denzel, and perhaps I'd have gone with her. We had both lied to each other, allowing the past to cloud the present. And Denzel was as guilty as the rest of us, going to Jo rather than contacting me directly. All of us tripping over each other trying desperately to get it right this time.

Jo had told me that the Denzel she met was clean and sober, miles away from the one Jaspar had encountered. That had made me happy and reassured. Apparently he looked really good, a grown-up version of the person we knew back at Sea Point. He had wanted to meet up with me again and Jo had told him that I was truly happy and getting married, and that it was best if he left me alone. Yet all the time my friend had been professing this I was running around Ibiza trying to find the happiness she claimed he was in danger of destroying. It would be quite funny if I wasn't so worried I might lose him again, that he might disappear as completely as he had done before.

Perhaps we have all, by our actions, assured the same outcome as last time.

No, I refuse to believe I'll lose him again, not when we are this close to finding each other. He had come looking for me and knowing that makes me feel as if something good might come out of this nightmare. The man I'd met in Ibiza would tell Denzel I had come looking for him, revealing Jo's mistake and propelling him to contact me. We have to find each other again or what will any of this have been for!

I bring my attention back to my battered face and begin to apply foundation in the hope that Bobbi Brown's claim to even out any skin tone is true. My face is still tender so I move slowly and gently. When I'm finished I'm pleasantly surprised. I still look lopsided, but more like I've had a dodgy procedure than a beating.

The doorbell rings and I let Jo answer while I sit in her front room preparing myself for my interrogation. Sheila Cooper's voice prickles my flesh even before I see her and every part of me tenses up. I take a deep breath and wait. She walks into the room and I swear the temperature drops a few degrees. Jo follows behind her and stands in the doorway.

'Hello Sheila,' I say.

'What the hell is going on, Alice?'

Although my mother looks older, her manner remains unchanged: hard and unforgiving.

'It didn't work out,' I say.

'What do you mean it didn't work out! This isn't some Friday night date! This is your future. You manage to find yourself a decent man and this is what you go and do, and just before the wedding.'

'It's not like that, Mrs Cooper. Robert is in the wrong here,' Jo says, but Sheila Cooper ignores her and continues.

'If it's another woman, as Jo says, it's probably a last minute fling before the wedding. Men often do that. It's quite common and not something that has to destroy everything. Think about what you're doing – I mean, you stand to lose everything.'

'I'm not marrying Robert Shaw. I'm sorry that I brought you all this way for nothing,' I say, sounding rehearsed and mechanical.

'You're sorry, are you!' Her voice rises and I can see that she's furious. I've seen her like this many times before but she's always managed to do it without any witnesses.

'It's nothing he did, is it. It's what you've done. I know you well enough to know it's probably you who has messed it up.'

The words wash over me like water off a duck's back as I find the place inside me where I used to go when my mother got started. I stopped believing her a long time ago, telling myself that just because this woman gave birth to me it didn't mean she knew anything about me.

'That's it! You're the one who's been sleeping around! I mean, what could I have expected from you when you spread your legs to the first boy that came along and let him get you pregnant. You were a little slut then and you've grown up to be a whore now. How did I give birth to a whore!'

'Mrs Cooper!' Jo says, and I can see that she's horrified. She's in for quite a shock because I know that my mother has just got started.

'I'm sure Robert will have figured you out. Did you tell him about your pregnancy? Stupid girl! Did you tell him that you were a child whore or did he work it out for himself.'

'Enough!' Jo yells and I salute her attempt, but it falls on deaf ears.

'You mind your own business, Jo Mitchel. Do you hear me?'

Jo is completely taken aback with this view of the Sheila Cooper she's only ever heard me speak about.

'I won't let you talk to Alice like that,' she says.

'Oh won't you!'

'Have you forgotten this is my house.'

'And have you forgotten that she is my daughter.'

'She doesn't need this kind of abuse from you now. None of this is Alice's fault. She was raped, Mrs Cooper. Robert raped her. I'm sorry, Alice. I couldn't let her go on.'

Jo looks at me and I don't say anything. If I had the energy I'd slap her. Sheila Cooper is the last person I want knowing I was raped. I look at my mother, whose gaze remains locked on Jo. Eventually she lets her huge, hateful eyes fall on me.

'What nonsense is this! He raped you! Do you expect me to believe that you've been with him all this time and there's been no sex? You couldn't keep your legs closed before you met him! He raped you!' Sheila Cooper sniggers. 'I should've known you'd mess this up. I had the feeling you would and I was right. Out of all my children I don't know what happened to you. I've often wondered if I took the wrong child away from the hospital.'

'What happened to you?' I ask.

'Excuse me?' my mother says, shocked that I'm answering back, something I'd stopped doing a lifetime ago.

'All these years I've wondered what happened to you. What could have made you so hateful? What. Happened. To. You.'

'How dare you talk to me like that! You're the problem, not me. You've always been the problem in our family!'

'Please leave now,' I say, suddenly exhausted. 'I can't do this anymore.' I walk in the direction of the door wanting to get away from her.

'Don't you walk away from me, do you hear me!' She screams and grabs hold of me, and before I'm even aware of what I'm doing, I swing back my arm and punch her full in the face. It takes all my strength but the sense of satisfaction I feel afterwards is more than worth it. She cries out.

Jo and I are rooted to the spot, both of us shocked by my behaviour. Meanwhile, Sheila Cooper quickly gathers her things to leave. She stops when she gets to the doorway, turning her head slightly so that I see only her profile.

'You are dead to me, Alice, and to the rest of the family,' she growls. 'Do you hear me girl! You are dead to us all.'

Then she opens the door and leaves without looking back.

25

Getting Back To Something Like Normal Part II

Ah get back to the flat and find ma father up in the kitchen by the teapot. Not an unusual sight.

'Goodnight,' Ah say.

'Would you like some tea?' he asks. Another out of the blue heart-to-heart.

Ah say 'Sure' and sit maself down. Ah've been avoiding him since Ah got back from Paris because I feel he has a right to know that his eldest son, who is availing of his hospitality, is a rapist. Ah sit down and watch him, measured in all his movements and making them all matter. This is something Ah'd noticed about Sid too, although it was less pronounced in ma brother. But perhaps that's something that would have developed as he got older. Ah guess now Ah'll never know. Ah sit and wait for ma father to speak, giving him the time he needs, which is a great deal more than a normal person requires.

'Denzel, I need to talk to you about Bill,' he says eventually.

'Ja,' Ah say and realise for the first time that Ah haven't seen Bill around for the last few days. Ah've had other things on ma mind.

'He's going back to New York for a short time and then he's returning and is going to move in.' A smile crosses one half of his face.

'That's great news, Dad,' Ah say and smile back. And it is. This isn't the time to tell him about me being a rapist, not when he's giving me such big news.

'I want you to know that it in no way affects you staying here. There's room enough for all of us.'

'Thanks,' Ah say, but deep down Ah've been thinking that perhaps it might be good for me to leave. Well, actually that's not strictly true. Part of me had been planning that Ah would go and live with Alice. Stupid asshole dreamer!

'But Ah'd have no problem with moving out. Ah mean Ah've been here six months now.'

'And it's a small time frame considering you've been on this planet for over thirty years.'

'Ja, but you don't need to give me a home by way of retribution.'

'That's not how it is! I want you to live with me. That's the truth.'

'Sure. Ah'll stay on for another while if that's okay.'

'It's more than okay,' he says and the smile, which had almost disappeared, returns.

'Right, time to get back to it,' he says.

'Ja,' Ah say, standing up and taking ma cue. 'Ah'm made up for you and Bill.'

'Thanks, Denzel,' he says in an even softer tone than usual.

Then he pushes something in front of me, and for the first time Ah notice the notebook on the table, even though it's been there all along. My father has moved it into significance.

'I need to ask you something Denzel,' he says. 'A favour.'

'Ja, go ahead,' Ah say.

'I want you to read this and tell me if I should.'

Ah'm confused now and he rightly reads ma expression.

'It's Sid's and I'm not sure I can bring maself to read it. I think I might discover lots that I shouldn't know. It's a diary about his time in Ibiza, and since you were with him

I thought you'd be the best person to read it first and tell me if I should.'

Part of me wants to tell him to read it himself and face whatever is in there, but then another part of me is touched beyond words that he'd ask me to do this for him.

'Ja,' Ah tell him. 'Ah will. But not just yet, if that's okay. Ah think it's still a bit early. Ja?' Ah'm thinking of ma own sobriety.

'Of course. Whenever you're ready, Denzel.'

Ah leave ma father and go to ma room with a piece of ma brother in ma hands. Ah place the notebook reverently on top of the wardrobe.

'You're not ready,' Sid says from across the room.

'Na, not yet brother. Not yet. Will Ah be surprised?'

'I honestly can't remember. But you know how it all ends.'

'Ja! For sure.'

Ah feel like getting lost so Ah head to ma father's music vault. Tonight, Ah want to hear something new, something that Ah can get lost in but without the charge of memory, something that requires me to hang on to every beat. In ma father's eclectic music library it doesn't take me long to find something Ah don't know. A man called Astor Piazzolla graces the cover of an LP, holding one of the most beautiful accordions Ah've ever seen – not that Ah've seen many of them in ma lifetime. This is a piece of art.

Ah let the needle catch in the vinyl groove and close my eyes so that Ah get the full effect of those first few glorious sounds before the music begins. The sound instantly takes me back to the streets of Paris where Ah had been the previous weekend, but Ah'm not with Holly – Ah'm with Alice. Ah allow maself to imagine what it might be like if Ah were with her again – seeing her, touching her, smelling her. Ah listen to this music, which is in possession of me now. Ah feel this man's passion and his torment. The jarring sound of the strings and that accordion, an instrument Ah had not really appreciated before this, and Ah remember something Tom Waits said about a true gentleman being someone who knows how to play the accordion but doesn't. Ah think: Tom, you must never have heard what Ah'm hearing now.

The record comes to an end and Ah sit steeped in nostalgia until Ah eventually find ma way to ma laptop and onto Facebook. Ah look at Alice's beautiful smiling face: those green eyes that turn aqua the longer you look into them, the lips that Ah'd spent most of ma early teens kissing, the golden hair that fell down and tickled my face as she lay on top of me. Ah think about her and the memory is so strong that Ah swear Ah can almost smell her. And Ah hear her voice, a voice Ah still remember and will probably never forget. Ah'd once watched a movie about penguins and Morgan Freeman had informed me that they recognise their mate by sound; Ah've no doubt that Ah'd recognise Alice's voice in a crowded room. Ah think about taking that number from ma room and calling her and Ah begin to shake. Ah'm literally trembling at the thought of it, as if the room has just got really cold all of a sudden, and then Ah realise the truth of it – Ah cannot go any further.

Deep down Ah know she's better off without me. What would be the point of going there and uprooting her life? Plus Ah'd be risking ma own sobriety, because a rejection from her would probably send me over the edge. Ah couldn't bear it – to see her, to want to touch her and for her not to want me back. Ah couldn't bear to be disappointed. That would be too much. That would reinforce every fucked up thing Wendy and The Big Chief had ever told me about ma sorry arse and Ah have to believe that ma arse is worthy of being here. If not Ah will surely extinguish – fade away. Ah make the decision while Ah look at her face, until eventually Ah can't look any more. So Ah vow that Ah'll leave her alone. Ah go into ma Facebook account and close it down.

*

Today, for the first time since I got here, I leave Jo's flat. It takes a lot to get me outside and I can see how easy it would be to stay locked away for the long-term. But hard as it is, I manage it, walking at a steady pace and reassuring myself that I'll keep to the busy areas. Something has changed in me; I won't allow myself to take any chances. It's the first day I've felt capable of physical exercise and as I walk, I get stronger with every step. Although I've yet to face a lot of people, there's a great sense of relief that I'm finished with the Coopers. My mother, true to her word, has seen to it that no further contact has been attempted by any other family member. We're all better off – in this we're agreed.

I've heard nothing from Denzel, but I'm giving it time and not losing faith. This is all that is left to hope for. There has to be a reconciliation, because being together again would give some meaning to my life and bridge the nothingness between the past and the present. I remember the spirit of us, stronger together rather than apart, and I need that strength now. I clutch at the ring, now back on my finger, willing it to bring him back to me, like a gigantic magnet attracting only him.

It's not long before I get tired, so I stop off in a little café not far from Jo's. The girls behind the counter are friendly and after I pay, they offer to bring the coffee to my table. I accept their kindness gratefully. Seated at a cosy table in the corner, I watch a young couple. It reminds me of Christmas Eve when I'd watched another couple and the girl had let me know I was intruding. However, these young lovers don't notice me; they're too busy giving their full attention to each other. As I sit and watch, I resent their chance at happiness, a chance that was taken away from me. Right now, I wish with all my heart that I could go back in time.

In my wildest dreams, I'd never imagined that my life would come to this. Every day horrible things happen to normal people, things that make them no longer normal, and it's easy to believe that it'll never happen to you. But what do you do when it does? I thought I was protected, safe, secure, but the person I'd trusted with my safety turned out to be the most dangerous of all. Now I feel abnormal and no matter how hard I try to forget what happened or to make it all okay again I can't. I've been changed into someone else – some*thing* else – and I can't change back. Robert Shaw raped me, brutalised me; he might have killed me and no one could have stopped it.

'Just Jenny' had wanted me to press charges. She'd told me it would help me to get over it. She'd also told me that most women are raped by someone they know. Well, none of this helps me or reassures me. To know that I'm one of many makes me feel disillusioned and scared and I wonder how many more men like Robert Shaw are out there. How many women press charges? Not many I bet, and now I understand why. I just want to get on with my life and never see Robert Shaw again. I can't bear for more people to know about what happened and look at me differently, like I'm a victim. There's no desire to see him pay because it won't change anything, it won't erase the memory, and should I go to a courtroom and relive it then it'll be further ingrained in my mind, together with all the other unpleasant memories a trial would add to the experience. And how would I prove my case? No, I couldn't go through all that. I don't believe it'll help me to forget, which is what I want to do most of all. Maybe it's cowardice, but it feels more like self-preservation – it's the only way I'll survive.

Back then, when Denzel left me and then my baby was taken away, I'd eventually forgotten them both – and the pain that went with it. I forgot because I was forced to get on with my life and live it without them and because no one ever talked about it. It was as if it had never happened, and after some time I actually began to believe that. That was how I had survived. It seemed to be the only way I could survive things that would otherwise have killed me. Denzel always used to say I was the strongest person he knew, and I was, back then, when I was with him. Alone I'm not strong at all. I discovered that after he left and I'm discovering it now. I'm alone again and I can't be alone. Please don't let me be alone. I say this over and over again in my head until it begins to feel like a prayer. I repeat it until finally the tears I thought would never come begin pouring down my face.

26
Internal v External Part III

Ah'm with Alice and we are by the sea, but not by our familiar Sea Point. Now Ah'm with her in Ibiza on the sand where ma little brother died. We begin to kiss and undress each other until we're both naked with only skin separating flesh and bones that feel like they're of the same body. Ah tell her Ah love her and she says she loves me too, that she never stopped loving me. And then we're making love and Ah'm looking into those green eyes, trying to get deeper inside her. Ah come and as Ah do Ah close ma eyes and breathe her in, every last drop of her. Then she screams and Ah open ma eyes again. And it isn't Alice underneath me any more – it's the girl from London and she's screaming at me to stop. Stop. Stop. Stop. And then Sid is there and he pulls me off her and asks me what the fuck am Ah doing.

Ah wake up and feel as if Ah've been struggling for ma life even though Ah'm lying in bed. Ma breathing is heavy and ma chest rattles as Ah cough maself back into full consciousness. Ma bad deeds have collected inside of me and are in danger of pulling me under. Ah'm in the hands of ma addiction and now the only thing Ah want is to get out of ma tree – as high as it's possible to get – and forget all the awful things. Ah try to talk to Sid, but even that isn't working today. Ah can't reach him when Ah'm in this place.

Ma bad actions keep me tied to ma victims. Ah wonder if good actions have such strong roots and whether Ah'll survive long enough to get the chance to find out. Ah drag maself out of bed and over to the window. Ah swing ma legs out until Ah am sitting. Ah think about lighting up – a reflex thought. Despite everything Ah've managed to abstain from smoking. Ah don't quite know how but Ah have. Ah guess Ah'm a stubborn bastard. As Ah sit and watch, Ah begin eating ma way through a packet of Starbursts. Ma tooth, which has always been sweet, has become sweeter since Ah've become smoke-free and Starbursts seem to be the flavour of the month.

Ah wonder if Ah can ever move on from the things Ah've done, the things that haunt me. Sid would still be alive if he'd never laid eyes on me. Alice would have been happier too. And that girl whose face stays with me these days as Ah go about ma business. The people Ah meet perish. Poor Tim, not to mention ma little group on Euston Road – they've drawn the bad penny, for sure.

Ah'm twisted and have always been. Ah was born twisted. Ah don't believe Ah'm capable of this thing called love. In ma past, Ah seem to have continually punished the people who professed to love me. But Ah have to believe it can be different. Ah love ma father. Ah have to believe Ah do. Ah feel a tremendous warmth when Ah'm around him and sometimes Ah can imagine how it would have been to be small around him. Ah'm small around him still, and will remain so, no matter what ma age. The son. The child.

Ah've watched ma father closely and Ah've seen that he's in the grip of enormous guilt. Perhaps it's only because his eyes are clouded by his own wrongs that he can't clearly see mine. It's the reason he lets me off the hook, a hook on which Ah should be hung until all the life slides out of me. He somehow manages to afford me the forgiveness and compassion he can't extend to himself. How weird we all are, us human beings. And Ah can allow those around me to take a few tumbles, but when

Ah do Ah'm a worthless piece of shit with no hope of retribution.

And yet a list of people is forming – ma father, Bill, Holly, Gloria, Clive, Billy – people for whom Ah care and who care about me. It's possible that Ah will disappoint them all and be rejected. This is the most terrifying thing of all, and what Gloria touched on when Ah told ma fairy tale of prostitutes and potential future crimes. It terrifies me that they will discover how worthless and unworthy Ah am.

Ma battle for sobriety is a battle for someone Ah can never bring back, and ma hopes to make it right with Alice are a nonsense. Ah think about Clive lying in the hospital bed. Ah know how he got there and how easily Ah could follow him. Then the others in the group could fall, one by one, and eventually Gloria's faith would be broken by her inability to save. Her desire to right her wrongs by overcompensating for a past in which she has done as many bad deeds as the people she's attempting to save would go. In reality, all our lives are empty, though we seek to fill them with something other than the vileness that pumps through our veins.

Ah see a woman watching me from below and Ah stare back at her, thinking we might be sharing a moment.

'What the fuck are you looking at?' she shouts up, setting me straight.

Ah don't respond and Ah don't look away. Ah simply stare through her and let the heaviness of what is in me fall upon her. Ah refuse to look away.

'Fuck off,' she tells me and Ah understand where her animosity comes from.

But Ah don't fuck off. Ah stay there watching her until eventually she shouts 'Asshole' and takes herself away. Ah watch her leave and feel a sense of victory that she left first. This is the me that girl saw – the nastiness, all still in here however much it's contained. Ah feel it and it drives me indoors, back into the bedroom and under the covers. Ah'll stay here for the remainder of the day. It's the safest place for me right now. For sure.

*

I wake up terrified and struggling to breathe. For a minute I really believe I'm in my own bed lying next to Robert and I begin to panic. But then I remember I'm in Jo's spare bed and my breathing settles, although my heart is still thumping, way too fast for sleeping. This isn't the first nightmare I've had about Robert but it's the most disturbing one yet. It had started off like all the others: I relived the events leading up to the rape – me getting back from Ibiza, our meal and then him dragging me upstairs and into the bedroom. However, when the rape begins, Robert becomes Denzel and I'm as afraid of him as I was of Robert. He rapes me in the dream in the same manner I'd been raped in real life and that's when I wake up. The whole experience leaves me cold and wondering who had done what to me: who had loved me and who had hurt me; who would love me again now that this has happened to me. Everything is jumbled in my head, which begins to pound, as if the weight of what's happening in there is too much and the tension is in danger of ripping my skull apart.

Grabbing for the covers, I pull them over my head. Denzel Anderson, the man who changed my whole life a lifetime ago, has the power to come back and change it all over again. Yet in the dream it's Denzel raping me, brutalising me, and I get a bad feeling in the pit of my stomach. It's just a dream, but it makes me wonder about how it will be from now on. Will I ever be able to have sex without remembering what had happened? And what if my dreams are trying to warn me about a future danger, trying to warn me that to go back to Denzel might be a grave mistake, for he had hurt me before and could again. But I dismiss this worry because I truly believe that Denzel left me all those years ago because he was young and the prospect of what my father could do to him was too great.

So he has come back to find me. That's all that matters now. He has come back because he feels the same connection I do. It's at a deep level, so deep that whatever it is that ties us together is unreachable and, therefore, unbreakable. We are each other. I remember once telling him that, and he said he knew exactly what I meant. Those were the days when I was young and self-assured, and could easily make those kind of proclamations and believe that they would be true for all time. I'd been studying Wuthering Heights at school and I really believed that we were Cathy and Heathcliff but that we would have a different ending, a happy ending. I knew the bond Cathy spoke of; it was the same as my bond to Denzel. Years later, a quote from Rumi had brought only one person to mind, a quote that said lovers don't find each other, they are in each other all along. That was me and Denzel – in each other all along. A part of each other.

I reach for as many romantic thoughts as I can in an attempt to forget my nightmare. It helps but it's only short-lived. A great sense of shame about what's happened comes calling. It's my body that has been violated and it should be Robert who is ashamed for what he has done. Yet I feel as if I was in some way to blame. I don't know why I feel this and I wish I could stop feeling like this but I can't. The truth is, I feel as if I had in some way asked for this, caused this. And now I'm remembering that I had stopped fighting Robert, and I curse myself for not having tried harder, forgetting how scared I had been so that the stick with which I am beating myself hits me all the harder.

And then my mother's accusations return to haunt me in these early hours. All the things she said rattle around in my head and are far easier to believe in the middle of the night when I'm feeling low and alone. I had disgraced the family and myself. I had done the worst thing that a young girl could do and the whole world would know, thanks to the baby I gave birth to. That poor unwanted child – I think of him now and cry, using the pillow to stifle my sobs so that I don't waken my friend.

I'm upside down and outside in and nothing will ever be the same again. Physically my wounds are healing fast but it's the other deep scar, the one I feel but cannot see, that is getting worse and weighing me down. I am responsible. I am accountable. I am a victim. I am a coward. There are many brave people in this world and I used to be one of them – at least, I believed I was a long time ago. But now I'm not. I'm weak and afraid. I've only got what I deserve. This is all my own doing. And if Denzel does find me, I'll be embarrassed by what he'll find. His Alice is long gone, buried deep, no longer existing. And if that's the case, I'm in big trouble.

27
Getting Back To Something Like Normal Part III

Ah stand outside with Billy and wait for Gloria to call us in. Tonight there are six people inside waiting for us. We had seen them go in – our mentors, strangers who will help us to stay clean. Clive is still in hospital where Ah'd had just left him before making ma way here. Each day Ah go and each day it's the same thing. Ah read to him because he refuses to talk to me, or to anyone. He's completely switched off, and although the doctors say this is normal and advise that he needs time, if Ah'm to be honest Ah'm losing patience with him. Ah know that what has happened is a nightmare but this is worse than just being in the doldrums. He's given up and Ah can't just sit back and watch. Of course, it's down to him in the end, but Ah've a feeling that some Denzel stubbornness might help him take that first step – the hardest but most necessary step. Ah believe ma friend can come back even if he doesn't believe it right now, and maybe ma belief will be enough to get him through this.

Billy doesn't say much and Ah tell maself not to be paranoid. That's just how she is and it has nothing to do with last week. Ah remind maself about what Gloria said. It's time for me to forget. Ah've still not told ma father but Ah will. Somehow Ah need him to see me the same way Ah see maself and to know he'll not write me off even when he knows the worst about me, unlike Wendy and The Big Chief. As Ah think of them, Ah see their sneering faces while they profess that they always knew Ah was a no-good fuck-up. Ah've no doubt that were Ah to travel back to Sea Point for some insane reason, Ah'd find them the same, as if no time had passed.

Gloria calls us in and we all share. Tonight, there are more shares as the mentors go first and we have just doubled up in number, but everyone's share takes half the normal time, the mentors setting the precedent. Ah talk about how Ah feel about Clive. There's a wish to say something about Alice but that would take too long, for sure, so Ah say nothing. Today's a day for brevity. Ah give an update and we move along to a very upbeat Iain. Ah wonder what it can be that's brought this jazzed up version of him to our little club. Good for him anyways!

After the shares, we hear our mentors stories. All are different but similar, and with similar endings – enduring sobriety. They were us six months ago and we will be them six months from now. After that Ah don't know. But Ah guess for now Ah don't need to know. After the session, we go to a local bar and we each sit with our mentors. This is the first time we've been to a bar on Never Again time. Although Ah have been in several drinking establishments in that time, for some this will be their first since they have come away from their addiction. It would have been Clive's first time. Gloria sits with Clive's mentor, Alan. Ah watch them as Ah wait for ma own mentor, Peter, to come back with ma drink and imagine Clive sitting where Gloria is.

Peter returns with two Cokes. As cocaine was his drug of choice also, the comic element is not lost on me.

'Congratulations!' he says as he hands over ma drink.

'Ja, thanks.'

Ah reckon Peter is close to ma age. He's Irish, so also a fish out of home water like me.

'You've done well to get this far. We all have,' he continues. 'Gloria says it's one day at a time and it really is. There's no getting complacent.'

'How did you find Never Again?' Ah ask him.

'It was an intervention from the divine, I think. I had given up trying to give up and was really just waiting to die. Then I met Gloria. It seemed like a random meeting at the time, but when I look back it was too timely to be random. I was in a coffee shop and she sat beside me and started talking to me. A short time later I was at the Euston Road meeting. She's a very special lady.'

Ah nod in agreement.

'And how about you?' Peter asks.

'She helped some of ma father's peers get cleaned up and he passed me her way.'

'Cocaine was your poison?' he says.

'Ja, for sure and yours too, ja?'

He nods. We can recognise each other.

'All drugs are conniving but charlie must be the most deceitful of all. It took me a long time before I was fully aware of how bad I was.'

'Ah know exactly what you mean.' And Ah do.

'It still creeps up on me every now and then, but the good thing is I have abstinence on my side. I know I can do without it. Once you know that you're on your way. So, Denzel, you need to know that I'm on the end of a phone whenever you need me, and please take advantage of that. Okay?'

'Ja. Thanks, boet,' Ah say.

'But? … What?' he asks.

'Na, it's a South African word.'

'Okay, I don't know so many South Africans. What's it like?'

'Boet is like bro Ah suppose. Ah can't shake it off me, that habit.'

'Okay. Although I meant what is it like to be South African.'

'Ah don't really know,' Ah say finding it a strange question. 'It's just the same as being Irish but in a South African way.'

This makes him smile. 'I think mostly accents give people's origins away,' he says. 'But yours isn't so identifiable.'

'Ja, Ah've lived all over and picked up a few influences.'

'So accents aside, how are you doing with all of this?'

Back to business.

'Ah'm struggling right now to be honest. Life has taken a few turns and taken me away from where Ah thought Ah was heading.'

'Away from a happy ending?' he asks and Ah begin to realise that maybe Ah'm a typical human being after all, deep down at a level that counts.

'Ja, exactly!'

'Is it possible that abstinence alone can be your happy ending and the other things an extra bit on the side to make it all the sweeter?'

'Ah don't know? Perhaps as addicts we always want more.'

'But Denzel, you're now an ex-addict. That's fundamentally different from being an addict.'

Ah say 'Ja' but on the inside Ah'm thinking that right now, Ah will simply have to take his word for it, because in ma mind there really doesn't seem to be much of a difference between the two.

*

Time continues to pass as it does, despite my personal misfortunes and the feeling that life is somehow broken. Each day, I've taken steps that a few short weeks ago would have seemed little and insignificant but which now feel huge and important. I finally made contact with Kate, who had been trying to reach me since Mr Hockney gave her the news at school. Initially, Jo had told him I'd been mugged, the story I'd rehearsed for her ears, and a few days later I spoke to the headmaster himself. He had been more than sympathetic and told me to take all the time I needed. He suggested that they could get the temp who was covering my wedding and honeymoon period to come in earlier and he would see me back at school after my honeymoon. So then I had to tell him that the wedding was off and he said he was sorry and repeated that I take the time I need. Of course, I'm aware that the story has its holes and it invites huge speculation but it's the best alternative I can think of. Telling people the truth was never an option.

My conversation with Kate has led me here, to the little coffee shop where I first found the tears that had been lacking but which are now a part of my daily existence. I'm waiting for my friend, as usual. In all the time I've known her, Kate has never managed to turn up for a meeting on time. Today I'm grateful for her tardiness and use the time to gather my thoughts. It's important that I stick to my story and that Kate believes it. The last thing I want is for everything to come spilling out like it had with Jo. These days my behaviour is far from predictable – I mean, I punched Sheila Cooper for Christ's sake – so it's best that I tread carefully.

Kate arrives and spots me immediately.

'Ali darling!' she exclaims and then hugs me for what feels like a very long time. Eventually she pulls away and offers to get me a coffee. I shake my head, pointing to the cup in front of me, and she leaves to fetch her own. As I watch her queuing, I wonder what she knows. Our telephone conversation had been short and vague. She and Frank will have seen Robert and I wonder what he's told them. I'm pretty sure he hasn't told them the truth.

'So tell me, Ali darling, what happened?' she asks when she eventually settles herself.

'What has Robert said?' I ask.

'Just that you'd left him because of his affair and that the wedding was off. Frank said that Robert's in an awful state. I'm sorry. I shouldn't have said anything. Frank said I should have kept my big mouth shut about the affair. But Robert had no idea you were mugged. Frank told him and apparently he's been trying to call you. He's really worried about you, Ali!'

He's worried about me! I do my best to keep my anger in check and ignore the part of me that wants to erupt and set her straight.

'What's going on, Ali? We're all worried.'

'Sorry. I just haven't wanted to speak to anyone.'

'You were probably in shock. Did it happen in Muswell Hill?'

'Yes, but I really don't want to talk about it. I had to go through everything in the hospital and I just want to forget it now.'

'Of course. Your poor face. I can see the swelling, although your make-up's doing a great job. What brand is it?'

'Bobbi Brown.'

'Yep. That's the one I swear by too. It looks really natural but does a great job of concealing what needs covering up. Why won't you talk to Robert? He's worried.'

'I don't trust him,' I say simply.

I really can't trust him.

'I know you're upset but are you sure you want to call off the wedding? I mean, has Robert said he doesn't want to marry you?'

'I don't care about what Robert wants! I know now that I don't want to marry him. I could never trust him after what he did.'

He raped me.

'But is it all that bad? Really?'

'Yes!'

You've no idea how bad it is.

'Did he hit you?'

'No.' *Yes, after he had dragged me up the stairs by my hair and just before he buggered me.*

'I'm sorry, Ali. It's just a little strange. How he is and how you are.'

'He had an affair!'

And he sees prostitutes, sometimes more than one at a time.

'Frank had an affair before we were married,' Kate announces.

'God, I'm sorry, Kate! I didn't know.'

But Frank is not Robert. Trust me.

'No one knew – or at least Frank thought no one knew. But I did – of course I did. I think it's nearly impossible to miss. You knew, right?'

I nod.

'But I never confronted him and I married him. He still cheats now from time to time. And he goes to strip clubs.'

'I'm sorry,' I say.

But at least he's never hit you. Or raped you.

She shrugs. 'I just live with it. It's better than being alone. To be honest I don't know what I'd do without him. I'm not like you, Ali. I need to be with someone. You're stronger than me.'

'I don't think that's true.'

I know it's not true.

'Well I do – or you wouldn't have left Robert.'

'I had no choice. I couldn't stay.'

He's a rapist and a murderer.

'Because you know you're strong enough to be without him.'

'I don't feel very strong now.'

And I don't want to face him again because I'm afraid of what he might do next time.

'Are you sure you know what you're doing?'

'Yes.'

No.

'But you'll have to move out. I mean, you need to get all your things.'

'I know.'

And I can't bear to think about going back there.

'Have you spoken to Helen Shaw?'

'No.'

She hasn't called so I'm guessing she doesn't know.

'She'll be devastated. I'm surprised she hasn't been on the phone. I wonder what Robert told her.'

'If he told her.'

And if he did, he'll definitely not have told her what really happened.

'Is your family here now?'

'Yes.'

'How did they take the news?'

'I only saw my mother and she disowned me.'

Kate laughs. 'You're joking!'

I shake my head. 'Actually it's a good thing. If I'd known it meant I never had to see Sheila Cooper again, I'd have left Robert a long time ago.'

A long time before he raped me.

'You don't mean that?'

'I do, Kate. My family aren't the nicest of people. I'm better off really. How are things at school?'

Please let's talk about something normal.

'Your temp started early. She's okay.'

'Am I in danger of losing my job?'

At least tell me that part of my life is waiting for me unchanged.

'No fear.'

Kate goes silent and I let everything we have talked about sink in.

'How are you going to divide everything up? I mean, you have such lovely things,' she says eventually.

'I don't want any of it.'

It will be a constant reminder.

'Are you sure? It'll cost so much to start again!'

'I'll survive.'

I hope.

'So this is really happening, Ali?'

'Yes, Kate, it is.'

There's no going back.

'Oh my God!' she suddenly exclaims, making me jump. It's the most animated I've seen her since she got here. 'You won't get to wear your lovely dress!'

I really don't know how to respond to that.

28

Talk Of Forgiveness

Ah watch Bill from behind as he moves around the kitchen, the place Ah usually find him in the flat. He's cooking. Bill loves food and the food that he prepares loves him all the way back. Ma palate has been spoiled since his arrival. He leaves whatever he has just put into the oven to do its thing and upon turning around becomes aware of ma presence for the first time.

'Denzel! How's about a cup of tea?'

'Ja, for sure, Bill. That would be great.'

Ah sit at the table and let him serve up the tea in much the same way as Tim would. It tickles me.

'I've been drinking so much tea recently,' he says.

'It might have something to do with ma father, no?'

'Yes. He's quite the addict.' Bill smiles. 'So how are things going with Never Again?'

'Ja, good. Ah can't believe Ah've come this far. Sober for almost six months – Ah would never have thought it possible.'

'I felt the same way.'

Ah look at Bill and the penny drops. He is one of the fold.

'Cocaine?' Ah ask, but Ah already know the answer.

'Oh yes – big time. After I went back to the States I snorted my way through a small fortune. I ended up in an awful state.'

'Was that after you split from Tim?'

'Yep. That whole business was terrible. I knew Penny, and Sid. The idea that I was tearing a family apart – well, it never sat right with me. And then when Penny killed herself and Tim's reaction … It was too much. It just floored me. Ah couldn't believe that he wanted us to be over, but I also totally understood. I mean, how could we keep going? Did Tim tell you about Penny?'

'Ja, a bit,' Ah say.

'She was hard to read. It didn't help that she was an actress, I suppose, but I'd never have guessed that she suffered like she did. Somehow she was able to keep it hidden, but I suppose she was never going to be relaxed around me. That made it even worse, what we did, and the fact that she knew it was going on. I've often wondered if Sid knew too but apparently he didn't. Poor Sid! God, when I first heard about Penny I just kept thinking about the boy and how it must have been for him, finding her like that. I just didn't feel able to help Tim with any of it, so when he told me to go, I did. I'd probably stay if I could do it all over again. Hindsight teaches a lot of lessons, but hindsight's always too late. My biggest mistake was leaving and I think I knew that, especially when things started to go belly up in the States. We could have helped each other – perhaps. But I guess we'll never know. That was then and this is now. A fresh start.'

'Ja. You can't change the past. For sure.'

'True. But life always gives you another chance. You just need to be watching carefully. Nothing is ever unfixable.'

'You always believed you'd come back together?'

'I wouldn't exactly say I believed we *would*, but I believed it was possible. And I always knew I'd come back if I heard from him. There was never anyone quite like him afterwards. You never meet the same person twice – that's what my therapist tells me over and over. But the connection I had with Tim I never felt with anyone else, and I really did try to find someone. Once I got clean I put myself out there, but there was never anyone who hit the spot.'

'So you believe that you love only once?' Ah ask, ma own sentimentality bubbling to the surface.

'I don't know how it is for everyone, but that's what I've found. How about you Denzel? Is there someone special?'

A chance to speak about Alice. And finally Ah take the bait.

'Ja,' Ah say and take a deep breath, realising that this is the first time I'll tell the story since Ah had told Sid. 'Her name is Alice. Ah met her when we were nine back in South Africa and Ah believe Ah loved her at that very first moment. Ah can still remember it. She was like no one Ah ever met before. We were together until we were fifteen. Ah left her, pregnant and alone with a seriously intimidating family. Ah left her and ran, but not because Ah didn't want to be with her or because Ah didn't love her. Ah was scared, is the truth of it. We were both so young, kids who thought we were well and truly grown up because we were feeling a lot of grown-up feelings. Ah was scared of her father and her brothers, and of ma own step-father, even though back then Ah would have told you a whole other story. Ah left Alice to face everything. She was the brave one. But Ah still think about her, and Ah recently found out that she's here in England – Ah managed to make contact with a friend of hers. Ah'm still a coward – too afraid to take the direct route. Just recently Ah heard that Alice went looking for me in Ibiza. Unlike me, she went straight in for the kill. Ah'd called her friend, like a stupid schoolboy arranging a first date and afraid of the rejection, whereas she actually got on a plane and went looking for me. Ja! Her friend told me she's getting married. She's met someone decent and she's going to start a family with him. So ma story doesn't end like yours and Tim's, Ah'm sorry to say.'

'But I don't understand. She went looking for you?'

'Ah messed it up back then, Bill, and Ah hope she'll be happy in her future. That's all. And whichever way Ah look at it, her future would be better without me. Ah'm no good in relationships.'

'But why did you contact her friend if you thought that?'

'A moment of insanity. When Ah forgot who Ah was for five minutes.'

'You sound like your father, you know,' Bill says and Ah feel a surge of pride somehow, even though this is not ma finest moment. It feels overwhelmingly comforting.

'He said similar things to me when he contacted me again. But it was the action that showed me he still thought about me, as I did about him. It was enough to make everything else fall away – all the lost years. Perhaps your Alice will feel the same way. I mean, she came looking for you. If she was happy with her new fella, her future husband, would she have come looking for you?'

Ma heart warms to hear someone else call her 'ma Alice', as if it might be possible again. The plan was that Ah'd tell all of this to ma father, but Ah'm beginning to understand that ma father might not be partial to these types of conversation – moments with Tim Harris are stolen at the most unexpected of times – but here is his partner and the opening Ah need. Maybe he could open the pathway that leads to ma father. Ah think about what Ah'm about to do and could so easily shy away from – but Ah won't.

'Ah've done something Ah couldn't bear her to know.'

'We've all done things we're ashamed of and regret, Denzel.'

'Ja, but this is something Ah can never undo. And Ah don't think she could forgive me either.'

Bill looks at me as if he'd prefer Ah didn't go on, just in case he can't keep judgement from his heart. He wants to tell me that everything will be okay and that what Ah've done, however bad, is not unfixable, that Ah can have redemption, but he's hesitant. It compels me to continue. Ah realise Ah've come to trust this man in a very short space of time and Ah remember Sid and having this same feeling when he first opened me up.

'Ah raped a young girl.'

Ah let the words fall into the ether and wait for repulsion to cross Bill's face. It doesn't, but something else does instead. He's sorry for me, as if something bad had happened to me, as if *Ah'm* the victim. He doesn't say anything, so Ah go on.

'Ah was off ma face at the time and Ah don't remember much about doing it but what Ah can't forget is afterwards – how she looked at me. Maybe, just maybe, in that moment Ah was really who Ah am and the rest is just bullshit, just pretend, a farce.'

'Do you really believe that, Denzel?'

'No, Ah mean Ah don't want to believe that but Ah can't be sure it's not true, can Ah?'

'I won't insult you by saying it wasn't an awful thing you did, but you know it was awful and you're sorry. I think that should tell you all you need to know about yourself. You have to allow yourself to move on, allow yourself to do it differently. Isn't that what recovery is all about?'

'Ja. Ah just keep imagining what Alice would think if Ah told her, which Ah would have to. Ah mean, she'll have to know the man she's with and what he's capable of. Ah also want to tell ma father because Ah think he should know what his son has done.'

'You're being very hard on yourself, Denzel. Why tell her? Why tell Tim? Why tell me? What are you expecting? Really? That we'll all confirm your worst fears? Or that we'll all forgive you? There's only one person whose forgiveness you need.'

'Ja, but the problem is Ah don't know where she is. Ah don't even know her name.'

'No, Denzel, not the girl. You. You need to forgive yourself. What I've seen of you over the past month tells me you're a good person. Today. Now. That's all that matters. Nothing that you've told me tonight has altered that. Move on, Denzel. And for God's sake contact Alice. If you really love her, contact her. How can anything bad ever come out of telling someone that you still love them, provided that you do really love her? You need to be sure. Does that make sense?'

'Ja, Bill. It makes a lot of sense.'

The door opens and ma father comes into the kitchen.

'What are you two talking about?' he asks.

'Love, of course. Can you not feel the charge in the room,' Bill replies and winks at me.

It makes me smile, all the way through.

*

'So we're going out, girl. Put on some glad rags,' Jo announces when she gets in from work.

'I'm really not in the mood,' I tell her.

'Well I am, and I've been pussyfooting around you for long enough. You owe me, Cooper!'

My friend is right – I do owe her. So I put on my red dress, the one I wore in Ibiza when I went in search of Denzel. It almost feels like that was a different lifetime.

'You look good, girl,' she says just as we leave.

'So do you,' I say, returning the compliment.

We go to The Ploughman, a bar just at the end of Jo's road. It's quite full as it's a Friday night, but we still manage to get a table for two.

'I'm getting us a big bottle of red wine,' she says and I hand her twenty pounds.

'You get it but let me buy it,' I say.

She waves my hand away.

'Please.'

'Okay, thanks!'

She goes to get our drinks and I look around the pub. There are so many people and for a minute I feel almost claustrophobic. It's some time since I've been surrounded by people like this and it feels weird. A man looks at me and smiles; I look away. Something in me can't bear it and for a split second I think about running out of the pub. But I don't; I stay and stand my ground. Not wanting to face Robert is one thing, but letting a look from a complete stranger drive me out of a pub is something I refuse to allow.

Jo arrives back with the wine and two glasses. She pours and then we each drink.

'I so needed that,' she says.

'Ja. Me too.'

She smiles a sympathetic smile. 'I can't believe your mother's behaviour.'

'I told you, Jo, my mother isn't a typical mother in any sense of the word. She never was and she never will be.'

'What is it that makes her so?'

'I've no idea. I don't really know a lot about Sheila Cooper. I can't remember ever having had a single real conversation with her.'

'I was shocked.'

'Ja! Sheila Cooper can be quite shocking when you don't have the measure of her.'

'I'd always thought you exaggerated when it came to your mother. But when I saw her in full swing the other day, I realised you hadn't been. I couldn't believe all that stuff she was saying to you!'

'It's nothing I haven't heard before. You were blessed with lovely Mitchel parents.'

'Ja!'

'Listen, thanks for letting me stay with you but I should probably start looking for somewhere else to live now.'

'Really, there's no need, Alice. I mean, give yourself a chance. And anyway, I like the company. The flat's big enough for two.'

'Are you sure, Jo?'

'Of course I'm sure. It's just like old times, girl.'

It's so *not* like old times but I keep that to myself. The last time I stayed with Jo we were two young girls just out of Sea Point with plans to have the time of our lives in London.

'Do you want me to move out when Jaspar comes?'

'Why? For God's sake, stop talking about moving out. Jaspar will just have to stay in my room with me.' She winks and I smile.

'When's he coming?' I ask.

'Sometime next week.'

Next week, the week of my wedding, which isn't happening now. I'd finally picked up the phone today to tell everyone who needed to know – the church, the venue, the band – and it had all already been done!

Someone had got there before me – Helen Shaw most probably.

'I want to ask you something about Robert,' Alice says.

I shake my head. 'I don't want to talk about him anymore. Please! Forget him. He doesn't exist. It never happened. I can't stand it!' I blurt out, almost falling over my words.

'Okay, okay. I'm sorry,' she says softly.

'No, I'm sorry.'

I begin to cry and my friend puts her hand on mine. I'm sure the people around us are looking but right now I don't care. I cry and my friend sits with me and waits patiently, telling me it's okay. Eventually I stop crying and Jo squeezes my hand.

'There's something I need to tell you, Alice.'

I look at her, wondering what other surprises life might be about to throw my way.

'Do you remember Felix Peters?'

I think for a minute. Initially the name means nothing to me, but then I slowly remember. He's from a long time back. From Sea Point. He was a nerdy boy who had the hots for Jo when we were students.

I nod my head.

'Do you remember the night we went to the party at his parent's house?'

'Yes, the one when his sister showed up and booted us all out.'

She nods her head. 'Just before his sister showed up I was upstairs using the bathroom in his parent's room when he barged in and bolted the door behind him. At first I was really embarrassed and tried to pull up my pants really quickly, but then I got angry and asked him what he thought he was doing. He started to come on to me and I told him to stop. But he wouldn't. So I tried to leave. He caught hold of me, pinned me down, took the hand towel and shoved it into my mouth – and then he raped me.'

'Oh my God, Jo!' I start to cry again. 'I'm so sorry!'

She takes a long drink of her wine and then exhales loudly. 'So I understand if you never want to talk about it again.'

'You never told me!'

'I've never told anyone, Alice. I was too ashamed. And afterwards I felt somehow like I was to blame. Can you believe that!'

'Yes I can,' I say. 'I feel the same, although I don't understand why. I am so, so sorry, Jo. I can't believe I didn't notice that night. What was wrong with me?'

'You were drunk and enjoying yourself. Everyone was – except me.'

'Now I remember – you just came home with me that night like nothing happened.'

She shrugs her shoulders. 'All I kept thinking was I was lucky that I was on the pill so that at least I didn't get pregnant ...'

'Like I had,' I say, finishing her sentence for her.

She nods and has a guilty look on her face. 'I think it happens to lots of people, Alice, and they tell no one – do nothing. Just get on with it.'

'Do you think I'm wrong to do nothing?' I ask.

'How do you mean?'

'Do you think I should do something? Press charges?'

'I can't answer that, Alice. I think it would be a rough day in court.'

'I do too.'

'But whatever you decide to do, I'll support you. You know that, don't you?'

'Ja,' I say. 'I do.'

'Anyway. Let's change the subject,' she says.

I nod but then I backtrack. 'What were you going to ask me before I had my meltdown?'

'It's about what happened,' she warns me.

'Okay – ask away.'

'I wondered if you think you can ever forgive Robert.'

'I don't know, Jo. Have you forgiven Felix Peters?'

'No.'

We sit in silence and finish our wine and then there's a choice to be made. I leave it in Jo's hands. She eventually makes her way to the bar to get us another bottle of wine.

'Let's get pissed, Cooper,' she says and pours.

So we do, and for a little while we feel like the same silly, carefree girls we had been at one time. At the end of the night, we waddle our way the short distance home, arm in arm, each holding the other up and only splitting apart when we get to the front door. It takes Jo a long time to get the front door open, which makes us both giggle hysterically. Once we've stopped laughing, I hug her.

'You're my best friend in the whole wide world, Jo,' I tell her.

'Ja, Alice, and you're mine. Everything's going to be just fine, girl – like it always is.'

I hug her again. These are exactly the words I need to hear right now and I'm grateful.

29

The Next Step

Bill's questions have given me a whole lot to work through, and not just the Alice stuff, which has ma head spinning. Do Ah really love her, when all is said and done? Do Ah *really* love her? But now, in addition, he's made a proposal. He's going back to New York to sell up, and when he comes back here he's setting up a club and wants me to run it with him! He's been thinking about this for the longest time, apparently, and has the cash to make this happen – he's already accepted an offer on his Manhattan apartment and it's a small fortune. It's a huge proposal and Ah asked him to give me a little bit of time to think it over. That's where all of ma head space has gone since then, pushing Alice a little further back. But the truth is Ah'm stalling on the Alice front. Ah mean running a club is huge, but it's teeny tiny compared to getting in contact with Alice Cooper again. Just thinking about that sets off a whole lot of uncomfortable internal shenanigans.

Today as usual, Ah take maself to the hospital. Ah want to sit with Clive, talk to him. Ma conversation with Bill has given me a lot to think about but hasn't led me to a final decision. It's also given me an idea. Ah get to the hospital and see the lovely Irish nurse who is ma favourite of them all. She has a lovely warm smile that makes me feel like Ah'd want her near me if Ah needed nursing.

'Hello, Denzel,' she says and smiles.

Ah smile back and say hello, but Ah can't remember her name. Ah want to say Mary but don't as Ah suspect Ah might be wrapping her in an Irish package and sticking on what Ah think is an appropriate label. She doesn't seem the slightest bit bothered by ma inability to remember her name and leaves me to it.

'Hi Clive,' Ah say. 'Interesting times in ma life, boet. Ah met ma mentor, Peter, and he seems like a good sort. He's Irish and feels like a black sheep. It takes one to know one, ja? How was yours?'

'I don't remember,' he says.

'How so?' Ah ask.

'Oh what does it fucking matter, Denzel.'

'It fucking matters, Clive. It fucking matters a lot.'

'Maybe for you. But have you seen me lately!'

'Ja Ah have and Ah'm getting a bit fucking sick of it, boet, to be honest.'

Clive looks shocked but Ah've had enough of this sympathy business.

'Ja, what happened is shit and you fucked up big time, but the point is you're still here, for better or worse. You've a life to live, a little boy who needs you and Ah best friend who would like to see some hint of the person he has grown quite attached to.'

'Fuck you, Denzel,' he snarls.

'And fuck you too, Clive. Fuck you for using, and fuck you for throwing yourself out of a window in front of Tracy.'

'Get out,' he hisses.

'No, Ah won't get out. You get out.'

He begins to cry and Ah let him.

'Is this what you want?' he says. 'Happy!'

'Na, Ah'm a hundred thousand fucking miles away from happy, but Ah'm doing ma best to make the most of it. You have to as well – you have a son, boet. Have you forgotten?'

'He'd be better off without me.'

'You want to ask him that and see what he tells you? He loves his daddy, and he'll love his daddy even more when you show him that you can royally fuck up in this life but can bounce back. You can always start again and fix things. Nothing is unfixable.'

'Do you want to tell that to the girl you raped? Do you think she would agree?'

'Fuck you, Clive. Ah can't change that but Ah can change me. Ah can live a decent life to make up for it.'

'You really believe that? You're deluding yourself, Denzel. The things you do make you the person you are.'

'Na! A short time ago Ah'd have agreed with you. But not anymore. The people you love make you the person you are. The people you love.'

'Well, right now I don't love anyone.'

'And that, ma friend, is down to you. You've decided that, you alone.'

Clive begins to cry again and Ah leave him be. When he doesn't begin to speak again Ah pick up the David Bowie book and read. Ah read and eventually ma friend falls asleep and Ah keep reading until Ah get to the end of the chapter and then Ah watch him sleep. He looks more peaceful than Ah've seen him look in waking life and Ah'm happy that perhaps in sleep he's getting some comfort. Ah had been hard on him, but someone had to be. He's been feeling sorry for himself for way too long and it's in danger of becoming another bad habit that he might not shake easily.

The door opens behind me, the noise reminding me of a flip-flop on a tiled floor. Ah miss that sound, which Ah was forever hearing in Ibiza. Ah turn around to see Tracy and today she has a little person with her. It can only be Ben.

'Hello,' Ah say, scooting down to the bright-eyed blonde-haired boy who could only ever be Clive's. Ah can see ma friend all over the small boy's face, a mini Clive. Ben looks at me and then draws closer to his mother.

'Ah'm a friend of your dad's. He's told me a lot about you.'

This seems to alter something and he extends his hand to me in a way that makes me think of a little prince.

Ah smile. 'Ah'm pleased to meet you Ben.'

'What's your name?' he asks, his voice piercing into me in a way Ah'm not familiar with. Ah guess Ah don't have much to do with children.

'Ah'm Denzel,' Ah say.

'That's a funny name,' he says.

'Ja, Ah suppose it is,' Ah say and smile.

'Hello Denzel,' Tracy says, reminding me that she's there.

Clive opens his eyes and Ben shouts 'Daddy!'

Ah stand up, tell Tracy Ah'll leave her to it and say goodbye to Clive, who ignores me because he's lost in the presence of his little boy.

As Ah sit drinking coffee in the kiosk, Ah'm reminded of the son Ah could have had with Alice and again Ah'm haunted by Bill's words. Do Ah *really* love her? Ah wonder. Do Ah really love *anyone*?

Ah had told Clive that we are the people we love. It had come out of nowhere and Ah believe it to be true. But what do Ah know about love? Ah'm an emotional retard. The people who grew me knew nothing of love. And what did Ah know about anything when Ah was a teenager and claimed to be in love with Alice? Come to think of it, what do Ah know about anything now, a man in ma thirties? Ah had learned how to hate and be resentful and to hurt. Maybe that's who Ah am now. But had Ah truly loved

Alice Cooper? Ah can't know that for sure, but Ah have to believe that Ah had and that Ah could again before contacting her. For sure.

Ah feel a little tap to ma back and turn around to find mini Clive looking up at me.

'Mammy wants to know if you want a drink?' he says in his squeaky voice.

'Na,' Ah say. 'But thank you.' Ah watch as he walks over to Tracy's side. That boy is really cute.

They come and join me at ma table and Ben offers me a Jelly Baby. Ah take one and thank him. It's years since Ah've had Jelly Babies – probably not since Ah was Ben's age – but now Ah discover Ah like them and decide Ah might substitute them for the Starbursts that are no longer hitting the spot.

'These are nice,' Ah say, and Ben nods and looks at me as he bites through the top half of the little jelly man. The bottom half remains in his hand.

'You talk funny,' he says once he's finished chewing.

'Ben! That's not very nice,' Tracy says.

'Ja, but it's true,' Ah say and smile at him, 'Ja, Ah do talk funny.'

'Why?' he asks.

'Ah'm from a funny part of the world.'

He screws up his face and this makes me laugh. He laughs too.

'Drink your juice, Ben,' Tracy says.

'He's very cute,' Ah tell her and she smiles.

'Yes, he's a good boy. I'm very lucky.'

'Ja, Clive says so too.'

Tracy looks upset. 'I wish he would move on,' she says.

'Me too,' Ben says and we both look at him.

'You listen to everything, don't you?' Tracy says, and he nods and smiles.

'Do you think Daddy will move on soon?' he asks me. The way he looks at me makes me want to warn him, to let him know that not everyone will answer his questions honestly.

'Ah hope so, Ben,' Ah say. 'Ah really do. But Ah don't know for sure.'

He looks at me for a long time, as if what Ah've said is sinking in.

'I think he'll move on very soon, Mammy. Just in time for the wedding.'

Tracy begins to cry and Ben puts his little hand on hers. 'Don't worry, Mammy. He'll be all right.'

'Ah believe that, Tracy,' Ah tell her, 'and you should too.'

'Yeah, Mammy,' he says in his little squeaky voice.

*

Jo sits with me in Caffè Nero and we wait for Kate, neither of us saying a word. It feels really weird to be back in Muswell Hill, but it is necessary. Today I went to see Mr Hockney and told him I'll be taking the remaining holiday time as I need to sort out my life. He was very understanding and wished me well. Apparently they are happy with the substitute teacher, which makes me feel less worried for the children, and taking the full holiday will mean that by the time I come back to Muswell Hill, Robert will be in New York.

Today, I'm doing the hardest thing. I'm going to collect my stuff and I've enlisted both Kate and Jo to help. Safety in numbers. Jo had offered to go alone, but there was no way I was going to let that happen. I know what Robert's capable of; Jo had made her offer without knowing all the facts. There are things I know about that night that I'll never tell anyone, things that I hope I'll be able to forget in time. I had decided to ask Kate, knowing full well that Robert would be on his best behaviour in the presence of his oldest friend's wife. Although we're going at a time when he will more than likely be at work, I'm not taking any chances. Having others there also means I'm less likely to freak out when I see him.

I'd called him a few days ago and he'd sounded unbelievably normal, unlike me. Despite my best efforts, I came across exactly how I felt – nervous at first, then frightened. Hearing his voice again had made me feel sick but at least it had been a short call and I had done it. For me, these are all little victories that mean a great deal. I might not be pressing charges but neither was I going to allow Robert Shaw to become this terrifying bogeyman stopping me from getting on with my day-to-day life. I had to confront him and let him know that I wasn't intimidated – or at least pretend I wasn't. He told me he'd been expecting my call, that he would gather my things for me and I could collect them at my convenience. He sounded like we were doing a business deal and it almost made me laugh. I arranged a date when I'd call, told him I'd lock the door when I was done and push the keys through the letter box. We ended the call by saying goodbye. It had all been so civilised, unlike the last time we'd been together.

'Thanks for coming with me, Jo. Really thanks for everything,' I say.

'Ja, you owe me big time, Cooper,' she says and winks.

I smile. 'It feels weird to be here'.

She nods. 'Are you okay though?' she asks.

'No, not really. You?'

'Life is rosy,' she says and smiles.

I see Kate coming in. She spots us, waves and comes over.

'Shall I get a coffee,' she asks.

I say I'd prefer to get this over and done with, which is the truth, but also I don't want to force either of my friends upon each other more than I have to. As we three walk down my old street, one friend on each side of me, I see Jo's car parked outside the house.

'Perfect spot, Jo,' I say.

'It was there just waiting for us. The gods are conspiring to make this as easy as possible,' she says and links my arm.

'I really hope so,' I reply and turn to Kate. 'Thanks for coming to help.'

'It's the least I could do, Ali.'

'I really need you both, for moral support.' I link her arm, just as Jo had linked mine a few seconds before. 'Thank you both.'

We walk to the front door and I begin to shake at the prospect of going back inside. The chub lock is unbolted, which tells me that Robert is here, and I prepare myself, praying that I don't fall apart. Neither of my friends say anything, but knowing they're beside me is all I need right now. My heart beats a little faster as I put the key in the lock and do my best to push away the images that are flashing through my mind. I open the door and freeze. Robert is standing in the hallway. He looks straight at me and smiles, and I swear in that moment I hate him more than I've ever hated anyone in my entire life. Everything is contained in those eyes and that smile, and it tells me that he's not one bit sorry. He's wearing a look of sick victory on his face. But when he spots Jo and Kate, it simply falls away and he becomes the Robert with which the other two are familiar.

'Hello,' he says and smiles nervously.

Kate says hello back. Jo doesn't.

'I've gathered all your things together,' he says as he leads the way into the front room. I let Kate and Jo go first as I can't bear the idea of being too close to him.

'That should be everything,' he says.

I look at all my things packed in boxes and suitcases, and stacked in a neat pile in the middle of the room. It actually doesn't look like much and I wonder if that's because of how well it has been packed away or because I don't have a lot. A chill creeps up my spine as I find myself thinking about Robert Shaw going through my things, touching them, knowing what he did to me. I have to force the thoughts from my head. It's too much to deal with right now, too much.

Robert leaves the room and only then do I walk over to my stuff.

'We'll manage all of this in your car?' I ask Jo.

'Ja, of course we will. You forget I'm an interior designer. You've no idea the amount of stuff I can pack into that space.'

I take a look around the room and then out through the door to the stairs that I'd crawled down after my ordeal. I shiver. Jo grabs my arm.

'Are you really not taking any of your lovely things?' Kate asks.

'No,' I say flatly. 'Everything belongs in this house.'

'Except you,' Jo says and I smile at her.

Robert comes through the door suddenly and startles all of us. He hands me an envelope.

'This should square everything up,' he says.

I wonder how he thinks he could ever 'square everything up' with anything that would fit in an envelope. Feeling much braver thanks to the presence of my friends, I look him straight in the eye and try to find any hint of remorse or regret. But there's nothing. As I stare at him, he simply becomes the old Robert again and for a split second I begin to question whether or not what had happened had actually happened. Suddenly I can understand the women who go back for more after episodes of domestic violence. The man in front of me shows no trace of the monster I had seen. He's just Robert, someone who had taken care of me when I was sick and let me sleep on his chest at night. And yet he had done those other awful things to me as well. It's all so confusing. I hold his stare and wonder if he can tell what I'm thinking. He eventually looks away and that feels significant, another small victory for me.

'Goodbye Robert,' I say and I'm surprised by the steadiness of my own voice.

I hand him the keys to the house. He takes them, deliberately making contact with my hand. Somehow I manage not to flinch.

'Goodbye Ali,' he says and leaves the room.

30
Graduation: The End

This is the last meeting. Ah sit and look around me at the people who Ah've been meeting with once a week for the last six months. We're all here. Clive is by ma side. Ah wasn't sure he would come but he did. He got himself out of the hospital just for our session and Ah'm proud of him. Ah went to see him yesterday and dropped the club bombshell. Ah think it might have worked – well, he's here and Ah'm waiting patiently for his answer. His showing up tonight makes me suspect that it will be a yes. Ah'd had a chat with Bill and asked if his kind offer could be extended to someone else, so that Ah'd come into his club with a plus one, so to speak, and when Ah'd explained about Clive he'd been more than happy to agree. So the question was, would Clive take a change of direction and come and run a club with me? Ah told him to stop seeing himself as Ah cripple and get himself back up on his two legs. Ah believe he can do this, but the point is he needs to believe he can do it himself.

Tonight Gloria looks almost sad, like Ah've not seen her look before. Ah'm getting to grips with ma own future and what it will mean once Ah've left this place.

A while ago Ah thought there would be an Alice to come out to, but there isn't and Ah'm still not sure if that's the right course of action. Ma future is so unsure. Can ma sobriety be ma happy ending, like Peter said?

'Hey Denzel.'

Ah'm happy that tonight Billy salutes me in her usual fashion, given ma paranoia last time.

'Hi Billy.'

'How are you?'

'Ah'm okay. A bit sad that it's our last meeting.'

'Yeah, I know what you mean,' she says. 'Hi Clive. It's good to see you.'

Clive smiles at her. 'Denzel?'

Ah look his way.

'I thought about what you said.'

'Ja.'

'Do you think a couple of assholes like us can run a successful club?'

'Ja,' Ah say and smile. 'Ah think a couple of assholes like us could run a club like our lives depended on it.'

He smiles. 'Okay, so the answer is yes.'

'That's good news, ma friend,' Ah say.

We fall silent and Gloria eventually opens the share circle. Each of us talks and tells about what's going on for us at the moment. Then we sit and wait again in silence until Gloria eventually speaks.

'You've completed your first six months of sobriety and I am so proud of you all.'

She smiles and lets her beaming energy fall upon each one of us. Ah feel it rest upon me and I take ma portion.

'So you've made it. What does that mean? You're sober and you have been for six months. I can remember when I got to my first six months. I felt such a sense of relief as I really didn't believe I'd make it. Yet I had. However, I was told not to get complacent – just because I'd got this far didn't mean I was free. I was an addict and that meant I'd be one for life. That's the twelve-step way. But as you know, Never Again isn't about twelve steps. It's about that first step, which is always the next one you take. I don't believe we're addicts for life – I never have and I never will. Each of you is a person who has messed up. You found something that made you unbalanced and you continued to use it until it took over. That's physically what happened in your body, and it's the physical manifestation of the addiction that has kept you defenceless. The mental side of this is really very simple. When you feel like you want to use and use the way you did before, the answer is no. It's always no. This doesn't make you any different to other people. You're not a singled-out addict, it just means that you've crossed a line that anyone can cross. It doesn't make you a weaker person or a lesser person. Nor does it make you a stronger or a greater person. When you hear this exchange happening inside your head know that you're back in the cycle that caused the unbalance in the first place. And that is all it is – a cycle. Not a prison, where you'll be locked for the rest of your life. You're free, each and every one of you.'

Gloria looks at Sharon who is on her left. She lets her eyes remain with Sharon for a little time before moving on to Iain. She moves all the way around the circle until her eyes fall on me, and again Ah get the feeling that she's an angel. For sure. Once she's completed the circle, she begins speaking again.

'You leave here the same as anyone else and go back into the playground of life where the rules have not changed. How society works is still the same. Just because you walked away and changed yourself doesn't mean that the situations you walked away from will have changed too. More than likely, they're just the same. However, you will go back to them a changed person and you know the path you took before and where it led you. You had one problem before: you used. Now it's gone. The mentor you met last week is there just to remind you of this. You'll meet socially. You'll go out together into the places where you went before, the places where you felt in danger, and your mentor will remind you of this. Then after six months you'll be the mentor to someone else. After that, it's up to you.

You can continue to mentor at Never Again or you can get on with your life and think of us from time to time. It's your call. I can tell you that it'll make no difference to your recovery. You are responsible for your sobriety. You got yourself free and you will continue to keep yourself free. Not me. Not the group. Not your mentor. You. … I'd like to thank you all from the deepest part of me. It's been a great reminder of how incredible people are and the ability of the human spirit to rise above anything. You're all amazing and I salute your bravery – the courage that brought you here in the first place, that made it possible for you to share things you never dreamed you could tell another person. I salute your ability to listen and respect the rest of the group and to support other people going through the same thing. What keeps me sober and healthy is the knowledge that I'm human, no different from people like you, people who always manage to find their way here.'

Gloria looks at Clive and he begins to speak.

'I'm sorry I let everyone down.'

'You let nobody down,' Gloria says. 'You're here now aren't you.'

He nods.

'So I think that's a good place to end our meeting. Goodbye everyone, and take care of yourselves. It would be great to hear from you from time to time, so feel free to get in touch. Class dismissed.'

She smiles her big beaming smile and Ah realise that Ah'll miss this each week. For sure. It's the first time it really hits me. This is the end, the end of something that has been a significant part of ma first six months in London.

So now what happens?

*

I sit and watch Jo make the coffee. Jaspar is arriving today and she's noticeably excited. My journey, which had started when I opened the jewellery box containing my Sea Point days, seems to be continuing, and shortly Jo and I will be reunited with Jaspar. Perhaps today is the day Denzel will contact me and be a part of this reunion too. But I'm beginning to worry that he's not coming back, given that so much time has passed since I went to Ibiza and I've heard nothing. I'm worried that he'll be lost to me again, that he'll disappear like last time and turn up again in another seventeen years. However, I'm also aware that I've just been through something that has brought new gigantic fears to light. Trust. Can I trust him should he come back? Can I trust any other man for that matter? Just Jenny's words come back to haunt me. It's happening all around; women are raped all the time and it's usually by someone they know. I have to stop this now! How will my life be if I let fear govern my behaviour! I will not be a victim for the rest of my days, afraid of my own shadow. I refuse!

'Will you come to the airport with me?' Jo asks.

'No,' I say, having given the subject a lot of thought earlier. 'I'll leave you to it and see you when you get back.'

She nods and I know she's glad of my decision. This is a huge deal for my friend. I hope with all my heart that this is the start of a big romance for her.

'It'll be nice to see Jaspar after all this time. I'm feeling nervous, Alice.'

'Of course you are. But it's a nice nervous, ja?' I smile.

'Ja,' she says. 'I've been thinking maybe we should go on Facebook and message Denzel.'

'To say what? No, Jo. The ball's in his court now. I don't want to push it.'

'But what if that South African in Ibiza didn't get your message to him?'

'He did.'

'How can you be so sure?'

'I told him I was the mother of Denzel's son.'

'Wow! I guess that should do it.'

Jo falls silent but I know what she's thinking. I've opened a can of worms.

'So you should get a move on,' I say. 'Go and meet Jaspar.' I lift my arms in the air as I say his name and it makes Jo smile.

'What are *your* plans for today?' she asks.

'I don't know.'

'Are you sure you don't want to come with me?'

'Na, Jo. It's time you stop worrying about me and enjoy yourself. Okay?'

'Okay! But if it all goes tits up I'm blaming you, Cooper.'

'And I'll be here waiting. But for now, go and start making good on that New Year's resolution of yours!'

Jo leaves and I sit alone. I begin to think about Denzel. I wonder if maybe I *should* go on Facebook and connect with him like Jo suggested, but something stops me. I want *him* to find his way back to *me*. He'd tried once and I want him to try again. There's a part of me that wants him to make good what happened before. He had left me, for whatever reason. He had ended us by walking away, and now I want him to come back and pick it up again. He needs to find me and rescue me. It's sentimental and foolish, and not something I would ever admit out loud, but it's how I feel and what I really want.

I am alone, no longer engaged, and now I remember the brown envelope Robert had given me, which has remained untouched in my coat pocket. What has he given me to 'square everything up'? Finding the envelope, I look at it for a long time before I eventually open it. Inside is a folded piece of paper with something sellotaped to the front – it's my engagement ring. When I unfold the paper another slip of paper falls out and flutters to the ground. I get down on my haunches and look at the cheque lying face up on the floor – it's for £25,000. I'm shocked. Between this and my ring I have a tidy sum of money. Robert will have done this not out of any sense of duty or charity, but because he'll want to keep the house and get me off the mortgage as soon as possible. It's not much compared to the value of our house, but in fairness it is about equal to what I've contributed in the time I lived there. He's written two words on the page, which, although sinister, also fill me with a sense of relief. 'THE END'.

There's another thought that eats at me. This is a payoff for my silence. I know that. Potentially I could ruin his life by pressing charges. No, I'll take the money and I'll forget. The physical evidence of the rape has all but gone now, but most nights I have the same nightmare. I usually wake up crying, which feels like it helps, like I'm clearing out my insides of all the old emotional stuff in addition to salting my recent wounds. Now I never have to see Robert Shaw again.

Kate had called me and told me that he's going to New York ahead of schedule and will stay indefinitely, so I could go back to school earlier if I wanted to – but I won't. I'm going to take advantage of the time off. I might even go back to Ibiza, only this time for a holiday rather than to seek out my first love. I'd liked the place. It had reminded me of the things I liked about Sea Point. The sea would be good for me now. For a moment I allow myself to go back to the fantasy. I allow myself to imagine that Denzel might come with me and show me the island, and that we might begin again by the sea and make plans for our future. And become a family.

My thoughts take me all the way back and I begin to cry as I feel the loss of what has been denied – the chance to raise my son and be with the man I love. I imagine baby Denzel but in my fantasy he's no longer a baby – he's a boy on the road to becoming a man. I think about him, my son, and I cry in big sobs, taking advantage of the empty flat.

31
Happy Birthday, Alice Cooper

Ah do ma daily martial arts formation and then Ah head to the kitchen. Tim and Bill are chatting at the breakfast table where Ah find them most mornings. They say good morning and Ah reply and get the formalities of the day out of the way.

'Bill is leaving us today,' ma father says.

'Ja! It came along fast,' Ah respond.

Bill nods. 'I wish I could stay on for the awards but the timing just doesn't work.'

'The awards?'

'Yes. Tim, haven't you told Denzel?' Bill rolls his eyes. 'Your father is up for a BAFTA.'

'Ja! What's a BAFTA?'

'It's a load of nonsense, is what it is!' Tim says.

'Ignore him,' says Bill. 'It's the yearly celebration of the best of British talent in film and television. You should take Denzel with you!'

Ma father looks at Bill as if he's suggested something that he'd never have thought of in a million years. 'Is that something you'd consider, Denzel?'

This makes me smile. Ah'm still tickled by the social ways of ma father. 'It's something Ah'd more than consider. It would be great! When is it?'

'Tonight,' he replies and just like that Ah'm going to the BAFTAs with ma father.

'Great! Will Ah need to get dolled up?'

'Yes, it's black tie.'

'Oh! Ah don't have a monkey suit.'

'I'll lend you one,' my father offers. 'We're about the same size, I would say.'

'Fantastic! When do we leave?'

'About six.'

'Okay. I'll come back at about four. Ja? Now Ah must leave you to it.' Ah don't really need to go but Ah want to give them the remaining time to be alone.

'That will work,' my father says.

'Are you off to see Clive?' Bill asks.

'Eventually,' Ah reply. 'He's made up about the job offer. Thanks Bill.'

'And I'm made up to have the help. Exciting times!'

'Ja!'

'I'll most probably be gone when you get back, Denzel.' He stands up and hugs me, a proper hug.

Ah can feel ma father's eyes on us and can almost see his internal thoughts like they're sitting in a bubble close to his head. *How is this so easy for other people?*

'I'll be gone for about a month, just enough time to get everything sorted. I look forward to hearing all about *everything* when I get back.'

He raises one eyebrow and Ah know exactly what he means by *everything*. Today is her birthday and maybe it's her wedding day. Perhaps Ah'm missing the boat as Ah sit here. The lack of inclination towards action makes me feel that Ah've ma answer to Bill's question. Our distance and separation might have made a big love relationship impossible. Ah leave ma father and his big love in the kitchen. Outside, Ah'm just thinking about where to go when ma phone rings. It's Billy, who makes a proposition Ah'm happy to accept. It's a beautiful day in London and we will meet at the Southbank and sit by the Thames.

A little later as Ah sit watching the water, letting ma thoughts swarm around ma head Ah feel a hand on ma shoulder. The touch is so light that Ah don't jump. Ah turn around and see Billy, and just like so many times before, Holly comes into ma mind, with Sid not far behind.

'Hey Billy.'

'Hi Denzel.' She squeezes ma arm. 'Do you mind if Ah smoke?' she asks.

'Na! For sure,' Ah say and reach for a Jelly Baby in ma coat pocket. 'You want a Jelly Baby?'

'No,' she says and laughs. 'Jelly Babies?'

'Ja, Clive's son Ben reminded me how nice they are.'

'You're amazing, giving up the smokes.'

'Ja! Now Ah'm addicted to confectionary,' Ah say just before chewing through a purple Jelly Baby.

She laughs and lights up. 'The other night was really sentimental,' she says.

'Ja. Ah was sorry when it all ended. Ah'll really miss our Wednesday nights.'

'Me too,' she says.

'Ah'm going to the BAFTAs with ma father tonight,' Ah say, wanting to tell someone.

'No way!' she says and beams up at me. 'How did that happen?'

'Ma father's up for an award apparently.

'Yeah?'

'Ja, he's a composer. But Ah don't know what his award is for exactly. Ah'm assuming music.'

She laughs. Ah laugh too.

'I really like you Denzel,' she says.

'Ah like you too Billy.'

'I really hope we stay in touch now, even though we have no reason to meet.'

'But Billy we have every reason to meet. Ah feel linked to you. You know that, don't you.'

She looks at me and runs her hand across ma cheek in a way that Ah'd not expected. Ah'm lost for something to say. There's probably so much Ah should say, but right now Ah can't find the right words. Ah can tell that she's waiting for me to kiss her and Ah'm shocked that she could feel this way, especially given everything she knows about me. Ah'm also aware that Ah don't feel that way in return. She feels like ma little sister and Ah wonder if Ah should say that now in case this gets messy. What Ah'm thinking must be registering on ma face because she reclaims her hand and looks away. We both stand there awkwardly saying nothing. She finishes her cigarette, throws it to the ground and kills it dead with her left foot.

'See you, Denzel,' she says and walks away.

'See you, Billy,' Ah call after her but she's already gone.

Ah sit there alone and watch the water, only one person on ma mind. Ah wonder whether or not Ah should call and wish her a happy birthday. Right now Ah want to call for no other reason than to hear her voice. Finally Ah pick up the phone and call her number.

It rings three times and then she answers.

'Hello?'

Her voice fills the airwaves and Ah recognise it, even after all this time, just like those paired-up penguins Morgan Freeman had told me about in the documentary. For sure.

'Happy Birthday, Alice Cooper,' Ah say and wait.

*

It's my birthday. I wake up a year older but feeling no different than I did yesterday. I've slept for seventeen hours, all the way through, and I realise that Jaspar and Jo will have returned from the airport. Then I hear laughter outside my bedroom door. I wonder what happened last night between them, if they got together. I get dressed, making a special effort today as I have my full wardrobe at my disposal once again, and it *is* my birthday. My face is less swollen, almost back to normal, and I feel ready to start a new year in my life. I'm thirty-three and today should have been my wedding day, yet here I am, still single – happily single. And my friend is happily coupled up, I see, as I catch the two of them in an embrace that lets me know they've consummated their relationship.

'Good morning!' I say, wanting to alert them both to my presence.

Jaspar turns around and looks at me. 'Wow, Alice! I'd pick you out of a line-up. You look lekker!'

'You too, Jaspar!' And he is still the Jaspar of my teenage years; although older, he's still recognisable.

He pours me a glass of Bucks Fizz and Jo wishes me a happy birthday.

'Thanks,' I say and accept the early morning drink.

'Here, I've done some crackers and cheese so that you don't drink on an empty stomach and get hammered,' Jo says. 'And I hope you don't mind, Alice, but I've booked us a table for dinner tonight.'

'No, not at all. That'll be great! I've no other plans, now that I'm not getting married.'

Jaspar laughs but Jo doesn't. 'So what happened Alice? Jo is being very secretive,' he says.

'My darling husband-to-be was having an affair with someone at his work,' I say.

'Well, best you found out before he put a second ring on your finger. It's about time you took that off.'

I wonder what he's talking about and then I remember.

'That's not my engagement ring.'

He takes a closer look. 'Oh right!'

'What is it, Alice?' Jo asks and when the expression on her face changes, I know she's recognised it. 'Is that what I think it is?'

'What is it?' Jaspar asks. 'Would someone tell me what's going on?'

Jo looks at me.

'It's a ring that Denzel Anderson gave me back in Sea Point,' I explain.

'Did Jo tell you that I saw him?' says Jaspar.

'Ja. And did Jo tell you that she saw him too?'

'No! Now girls, you obviously need to fill me in on the story to date.'

'First, you tell me about when you saw him?' I say to Jaspar. 'Tell it all and spare no details.'

'You won't like it, Alice.'

'I don't care. Just tell me the truth. The whole truth.'

'He was in an awful state. He was working in this club, Amnesia – a great club by the way. Anyway, I stayed back and had a drink with him after. Then I tried to get his number but he couldn't even find his phone. I made an arrangement to see him the next day, but he never showed and I never saw him after that. He wanted to know about you though. How's Alice? Where's Alice? I told him I didn't know. He said he loved you, that you were the only girl he'd ever loved. But he was in a bad way. Seriously. He looked like someone who could check out at any time. When did you see him Jo? Were you in Ibiza?'

'Na. Denzel found me on Facebook and we met up here in London. He was stone-cold sober, drinking cranberry juice.'

'No way!'

'Ja. And he looked very healthy. He'd come looking for Alice. He's got himself cleaned up.'

'Na. I find that almost unbelievable, considering the state he was in back in the summer. Good for him! Really, the boy was out of control. So why did he meet you and not Alice?'

'I've been wondering that too Jaspar,' I say.

'He wanted to test the waters, I reckon,' Jo says. 'To see what you were up to, Alice.'

'So have you seen him since?'

'Well, that's the other part of the story you need to hear,' Jo continues. 'While I was meeting Denzel in Soho, Alice was actually looking for him in Ibiza.'

Jaspar begins to laugh. 'You're kidding!'

'I wish she was,' I say. 'I went to Ibiza without telling anyone I was going.'

'And you met Denzel without saying a word to Alice?' Jaspar says to Jo.

'Ja, that's about the size of it.'

'So are you back together again after all these years?'

'No,' I say.

'What happened?' Jaspar wants to know.

'I sent him away,' Jo says.

'Why?'

'Because at the time I thought Alice was happy with Robert.'

'Lord, girls, there are some serious communication problems between you two! So what's happened? Have you seen Denzel now, Alice?'

'That's the thing. He's disappeared again.'

'Find him on Facebook!' Jaspar says, rolling his eyes at us. 'Isn't that how everyone meets these days, rather than hopping on planes!'

'His account's closed,' Jo says and looks at me sadly. 'Sorry Alice. I tried to get back in touch with him but couldn't. I wanted to make this right.'

'It's okay. I mean there's still a chance he'll contact me.'

'How so?' Jaspar asks.

'I met one of his friend's in Ibiza and passed on my number to him.'

'That doesn't sound too hopeful,' Jaspar says. 'I mean if you can't find Denzel, the friend probably can't either. There's a good chance he's no longer sober either.'

'Jaspar!' Jo shrieks.

'No Jo, Jaspar's just saying what we're all thinking. Ja! I've lost him again.'

'He'll turn up,' Jo says. 'I mean it's your birthday.'

Jaspar looks at Jo like she has a screw loose and it makes me want to laugh despite everything.

'Ja, it's my birthday!'

We drink and afterwards there's silence, which is eventually broken by Jaspar.

'Do you realise it's almost fifteen years since we set eyes on each other.'

'No way!' Jo says.

'Yes, I worked it out. It was a house party just before we were all about to head off in different directions.'

'I remember it,' Jo says. 'Everyone was there – the old gang.'

'Everyone except Denzel,' I say.

'Maybe it's for the best Alice,' Jaspar says. 'I know Jo said he was looking good when she saw him in London, but earlier in Ibiza – well, it was frightening. Really, if someone had told me he'd been found dead on the beach I wouldn't have been shocked.'

I burst into tears, surprising myself as well as the others.

'Jesus, Alice, I'm sorry. Me and my big mouth.'

'No, don't worry Jaspar. I'm teary these days. It really doesn't take much.'

Jo looks at me with a deep pity that I resent. I don't want her pity. I want her to forget. I want me to forget. She moves towards me but I hold my hands up to keep her away. Now isn't the time for me to fall apart. I want to start my birthday year as I mean to go on. I struggle to pull myself together.

'So Jaspar, tell me about you?' I say, deliberately changing the subject.

'Well, I'm working as a stockbroker in New York and have been for the last three years. I love it over there. It suits me a lot more than Joburg.'

'You lived in Joburg for a while?' I ask, sounding almost normal again.

'Ja, but it got too much very quickly. It's a crazy life over there and you come to view it as the norm, forgetting how fucked up it is.'

'I couldn't live back in South Africa,' Jo says. 'Ever.'

'Me neither,' I tell them both.

'I'm glad things have worked out so well for you, Jaspar. Listen, I think I'll go out for some air. I've slept for an age,' I say.

'Don't you want your present first?' Jo asks.

'Present? You didn't need to, really.'

'Ja, but I wanted to.'

She hands me the most beautifully wrapped box. I haven't seen as nice a gift box since the last present she gave me.

'That's amazing,' Jaspar says. 'I'd be happy with just the box.'

Jo swells with pride.

'Ja, Jo does amazing things with wrapping paper and fabrics.' I say.

The box is tied up with a medley of coloured string and there's an artificial flower made from velvet ribbon in the left hand corner. Jaspar and I continue to admire the packaging until Jo, lacking in patience at the best of times, interrupts us.

'Open it, Alice, for Christ's sake!'

I begin opening it slowly, but speed up when I remember a time an impatient Jo took one of her gifts back and opened it for me, depriving me of the pleasure. The strings fall away giving me access to the silver wrapping paper underneath. I rip it away to reveal a velvet box. I open it and lift out a gold charm bracelet with a single charm.

'A wishbone for luck,' Jo says.

'I love it,' I say and can feel my eyes watering again.

'I remember you had one when we were teenagers and you lost it.'

'Ja! Thank you, Jo.'

I had collected charms through my teens and just a few months after the bracelet was full I had lost it. Stupidly, I had worn it while swimming in the sea and it had come undone and disappeared quickly. And now a vivid memory comes into my head. At the time I had imagined it lodged on the sea floor with an army of sea life wondering what it might be and then finding different uses for it – two fish holding it while another swam through, another using it as a seat and swinging on it.

'Shall I?' Jo asks and I nod. She fastens the bracelet to my wrist.

'And now for mine,' Jaspar says and hands me a bottle of Gold Tequila.

'Oh my God Jaspar!'

'You still drink this, ja?'

'Not recently, but soon,' I say and smile. Another piece of me to remember.

'I'd have brought a spliff but I wouldn't know where to begin looking.'

'I can cover that later on,' Jo says and winks.

'I was joking but why not! For old times' sake.'

I nod. 'But first I really want to get some air.'

'We'll see you later then. Dinner is booked for seven.'

'Great! Thanks. Thank you both.'

'It's a pleasure,' Jo says.

'And it's not over,' Jaspar adds. 'So Jo, shall we seek out some drugs?'

'Just don't go getting arrested,' I joke, although part of me is serious as I remember the strange times I am living through at the minute. Nothing would surprise me.

Outside, I walk in the direction of a little park that has a pond with some ducks in it. There are a number of women with small children. I take a seat and watch as the children feed the ducks pieces of bread. A memory comes into my head of when I was a small child feeding ducks with my father.

'Bottoms up,' the Sam Cooper of my childhood had said when they dived for fish, sticking their bums up in the air. It had made me laugh so hard. He'd been a happier man then, very different to the one I knew later.

I sit with the memory, feeling surprisingly content despite the many reasons I have for feeling gloomy. My phone rings and I answer without looking.

'Hello,' I say and wait.

32
Awakenings And Awards

Ah look at ma reflection in the mirror and Ah swear Ah almost don't recognise maself. Ah went for a hair cut today and so Ah look newly sharp, like the first time Ah had it all cut off after Sid died. Ah'm wearing ma father's monkey suit; it's one from a long time ago. Ah love it and, given the Armani label, Ah'm conscious that it might be the most expensive item of clothing Ah've ever worn. The last six months of ma life have seen me change in ways that Ah'd never thought possible and Ah realise something as Ah stare into ma own eyes – Ah like the man that looks back at me. For maybe the first time in ma life Ah'm feeling like a decent human being, like Ah'm worth something. Ah've spent a lot of ma years wandering and believing that the world would be a better place without me. It feels nice to think that maybe mankind might not be so unlucky to have me as part of the gang.

Ah'm sober – amazing, and better late than never. For sure. Ma sobriety makes me smile and Ah remember what Gloria said the night before about me being no different to anyone else. The stopwatch has been reset to zero and it all starts again here. Right now Ah feel like Ah'm worthy of Alice. Ah remember our telephone conversation and Ah smile to maself. We are going to meet up tonight after the awards – neither of us wanted to break our plans, but neither did we want to wait another day before seeing each other again. So we'll meet in Covent Garden after the awards ceremony. Ah was reassured by that and Ah'm glad because she'll get to see me in this get-up and hopefully believe me worthy.

'You look good,' Sid tells me from across the room.

'Ja,' Ah reply. 'Ah do. We haven't talked since Holly.' Ah wait to see how he responds.

'How was she?' he says eventually.

'She was great, Sid. Her exhibition was amazing. Her paintings of you were the star attraction.'

'I miss her,' he says.

'Ah know, boet. And she misses you. You were it for her, you know.'

'I know. And she for me.'

'Ja. Ah'm sorry little brother. If Ah could Ah'd rewrite the history book.'

'But that was never open to negotiation. It was my time. I had to leave for the story to play itself out.'

'You mean me and our father?'

'And you and Alice. And what's coming next.'

'Ah'm nervous as hell little brother.'

'Of course you are. This is huge, Denzel – the rest of your life.'

'Can you tell me how it works out?'

'No, but I can tell you that it'll turn out for the best, as things always do.'

'Ja. For sure.'

Ma father knocks on ma bedroom door and Ah tell him to come in. He looks around the room.

'Who were you talking to?' he asks.

'Sid,' Ah say.

He looks at me blankly.

'It helps me work some things out,' Ah explain and he nods.

'You look very flash,' he says.

'Thanks,' Ah reply. 'You too.'

'I first wore that suit when I was about your age. We're the same size.'

'Ja,' Ah say. 'Ah guess there's no doubt about my lineage.'

'No,' he says. 'I knew that the first time I saw you. Sid looked more like Penny, but you're a Harris,'

'Ah saw a lot of you in Sid.'

'Really? I never thought so.'

He leaves me for a bit, travelling on the inside, and then eventually says, 'I can't change how things were with Sid, but I'm glad I have the opportunity to make it better with you, Denzel. Thank you.'

'Ah think if Ah hadn't met you Ah might not have made it this far. Ah've never had a family. It's nice to have one now.'

'Yes, we're a family. Not a typical family, mind you.'

'Ja, but let's face it, we're too odd to be typical.'

He smiles his half smile.

'After the awards I need to meet someone, Dad. Is that okay?'

'Of course! It shouldn't finish too late, about eleven, and we can both make a sharp exit. No after-parties for me – I really don't like those things, but I have to play the game a little.'

'Ja, doesn't everyone.'

We settle into our black cab.

'Ah've been thinking,' ma father begins and Ah look in his direction. 'How would you feel about living in the upstairs flat? Ah mean Ah use it now just to store things but it's in good condition and – well, you could do what you want to it and it would be your flat, away from me but close by too.'

'Ah don't know what to say! Thank you! That would be great.'

'Great, it's settled then,' he says. For a moment he looks like he's about to say something else but he doesn't. It falls away.

Nothing could prepare me for our entrance to the BAFTAs. It's only then it begins to dawn on me that ma father is indeed a famous person. It's so easy to forget, given his closed-off life. But Tim Harris is at the top of his game and well known in this industry. Cameras flash and then someone asks who Ah am. He tells them Ah'm his son, and Ah don't know how but Ah manage not to make a big fool of maself and burst out crying. We enter the beautiful building and immediately champagne finds its way into ma hand. Ah do something that is about as out of character for me as standing in a monkey suit – Ah let the glass remain in ma hand but Ah don't drink it; there's no urgency. It's a new feeling – a free feeling – and Gloria's words come into ma mind. Ah'm no different to anyone else in this room, no matter what Ah might tell maself and what some people might want me to believe. Ah am free. Ah'm not that person Ah once believed maself to be – different, stigmatised, broken beyond repair. Ah don't have to find maself back in the dark place from where Ah'd come.

All these insights arrive at once. This is really possible. It's as if time slows and what is happening around me stops and there's only me and the glass and a voice inside ma head that tells me it's fine to take a drink, that if Ah drink Ah can drink in the present day. Ah can start again with this social drug and be with it in the same way as the people around me, knowing what Ah know about maself and ma limits and ma understanding of the drug. Ma heart pounds in ma chest and ma pulse speeds up. Ah take a sip. Nothing happens. Absolutely nothing. Ah don't drop dead and the scene around me doesn't disappear. Ah am safe. The glass remains in ma hand for the remainder of the time as ma name is passed from person to person, and Ah place it down, still almost full, without any regret when we're called into the main hall.

The amazingly lavish affair commences and although Ah see many people Ah recognise from the world of movies, there are so many more that are strangers. Ah feel like a child at the zoo for the first time, doing his best to process the medley of exotic creatures that surround him. Nominations are announced and then winners make their way to the podium. And then the biggest shock of all, ma father's name is announced as a nominee for best original score and he wins! The movie, a big British production, is lost on me, but it has swept the board. It's a surreal moment for me as Ah take in the hugeness of it. But the truth is: none of this is important. What matters most to me is that Tim Harris is calling me his son and has offered me a roof so that we can be near. Ah close ma eyes and thank whatever it was that brought Sid Harris and Ah together.

The show ends and then there are the interviews. Ah stand beside ma father as journalists and presenters talk to him, and then the host has a word and there's a camera on me while he inquires who Ah am, and ma father introduces me to the world as his son Denzel. They want to know if Ah'm a musician and ma father says he doesn't know and it makes the presenter laugh, but we both know it's not a joke. This is a subject we've never talked about – well, not yet – and as Ah wander around with ma father, seeing him in a whole different light, Ah begin to feel like this is just the beginning of our relationship and Ah'm excited about what has yet to come. It's a feeling Ah could easily hold on to forever.

*

I'm not sure why but I haven't told my friends my big news. We are sitting in a lovely restaurant that Jo has picked and I've managed to get through the past seven hours without telling them that Denzel Anderson called me today, that he's coming back into my life. I'm fit to burst but somehow I've kept it inside me as I've listened to them talking about their time together and let them tell me about the day they've shared. They didn't go to score drugs as they promised but found their way to Covent Garden instead and looked around the market. Tomorrow they plan to go to Madame Tussauds, which Jo has never visited despite living in this country for such a long time. I'm guilty of the same crime, if it is indeed a crime. Jo and Jaspar have the glow of two people who have started to have sex together. It's apparent by the little touches they give each other, demonstrating that they now share a new level of intimacy not present in the world of friendship.

As I sit and watch, I really wish the best for my friend and hope that this works out for her. I wait until the meal is just about over and the coffee has just been served before I begin the conversation that will include them in this new development in my life.

'Denzel Anderson called me today to wish me a happy birthday,' I say when a quiet moment presents itself.

Jo shrieks at the top of her voice.

'When?' Jaspar asks.

'This afternoon. After I left you, I went and sat in the park and he called.' Try as I might I can't keep the smile off my face.

'Cooper! Tell us more,' Jo urges.

'I'm seeing him tonight – after our meal.'

'Why didn't you invite him here?' Jaspar asks.

'Come on, Jaspar! I think Denzel and Alice might want to catch up without us getting in the way. So what did Denzel say, Alice?' Jo asks.

'Happy Birthday Alice Cooper!'

'I got that bit! What else?'

'Well, he asked if he was disturbing me – I wasn't busy getting married or anything and I said no. And then he said he was sorry. So I told him not to be sorry, just to come and see me and he said he would tonight. After the BAFTAs!'

'Wait a minute! The man I saw almost about to check out of life last summer is at the BAFTAs! How's that possible?' Jaspar asks.

'Apparently his father is up for an award.'

'That doesn't make any sense,' Jo says.

I explain that it's his biological father who's up for the BAFTA.

'I didn't know Denzel was adopted!' Jaspar says.

'Well, he's not adopted exactly. His mother came to London in the eighties and when she came back to Sea Point she was pregnant and alone.'

'Imagine – his real father is some big shot!' Jo says.

'Did you ask him who it is?' Jaspar asks.

'No.'

'Well, I have to hand it to him – the boy is full of surprises,' Jaspar says.

'Yes, he always was,' I say, smiling and trying to get my head around this recent turn of events. I still can't quite believe that in a short time I will be with Denzel Anderson again.

'So, very soon the old gang might be back together!' Jaspar says.

'Ja!' I reply.

'Well before you go, it's time for cake,' Jo says and waves to the waiters.

They bring the most decadent-looking cake I've ever seen – chocolate with an array of exotic fruit – and everyone begins to sing happy birthday. Usually I hate such displays, but tonight I'm in a great place so I simply sit back and enjoy the moment. It'll not be long until I see him, I remind myself, and my joy swells. I'm thankful there aren't thirty-three candles to blow out, just a dozen or so. I make a wish, one that will be no surprise to the people around me, and then I close my eyes and blow.

'To new beginnings,' Jo says just before she cuts into the cake.

33

In The Same Place

As Ah leave the BAFTAs with ma father, Ah hear a voice coming from behind. *Her* voice. Ah think maybe Ah've dreamt it but then Ah hear it again, and so does ma father. We both stop and Ah turn around slowly. Somehow Ah've found her. There she stands in front of me, ma Alice. This might be the scariest moment of ma life as well as the most precious. Ah want to move but Ah can't. Ah want to touch her, to hug her but Ah'm frozen by ma own inadequacy as a potential lover, a potential friend, as a man. She stands and watches me but without a hint of wanting to move things on. Ah guess she's remembering me too.

Almost two decades have passed and here we are, standing in front of each other once again. Our lives apart will have fleshed us out, but now as Ah look at her Ah'm remembering only our lives together that shaped me forever. The rest of time since then simply falls away. Ah love you, Alice. Ah still love you. Ah dare not say the words out loud, but for now they're written all over ma face, ma body. Ah'm hers. Ah always have been and Ah always will be. And she must see all this as she stands and watches me, reading the information from ma aura or some other energy field that isn't visible to the unloving eye.

She smiles. Her reply is in that smile. All Ah need to know. Ah move towards her, ma arms extending, making space for her in the place where Ah know she'll fit perfectly. Ah hold her; Ah wrap ma arms around her and feel her as if she's a part of me. Ma Alice. Ah say this out loud and she replies, yes. And somehow everything is forgotten and there's nothing to talk about. The events that tore us apart no longer exist. It's a new beginning. A new place to start again – together.

Ah feel something, something Ah've not felt in a very long time, something Ah'd felt so easily with this girl all those years back. This is love. Ja! Don't ask me to explain it, let alone understand it, but Ah feel it here as Ah pull her close to me. Ah love her and Ah know Ah won't lose her again. Ah'm never letting go.

We stand here like that for the longest time and eventually Ah remember ma father and turn around to look for him. But he's gone and Ah'm thankful. The time will come for introductions, but now isn't that time. Now it's just me and her. Ah kiss the top of her head, just like Ah always used to. Then Ah stand back and take her face in ma hands so I can look deep into those aqua eyes, still as mesmerising as they had been when Ah was a boy. That boy comes alive again as Ah gaze upon the face Ah've loved for so long. It turns me inside out.

'Ah'm so sorry, Alice,' Ah say.

She nods. 'Me too, Denzel. But somehow it doesn't matter now. We can forget it and move on, can't we?'

'For sure,' Ah reply. 'And you're not married?'

'Yes I am, as it happens,' she says causing the smile to drop from ma face.

She lifts her finger and shows me a ring Ah recognise, propelling me to find mine in ma jacket pocket.

Ah slide it onto ma wedding finger and she smiles.

We walk off together, finding our way to an empty public bench in the middle of the post-BAFTA commotion. There's a conversation we need to have.

'Ah've thought about the baby so much over the years, Alice. If only Ah'd stayed what might have happened. We would be a little family now. Ah always imagined it would have been a boy and Ah hoped he would have your courage. Ah'm so sorry that Ah left and that you had to go through all that without me. Ah was scared – your father and The Big Chief beat me so badly, Alice.'

She squeezes ma hand. 'Nothing made sense without you. But I got through it, Denzel.'

'Still, Ah wish it had been different. If Ah could go back Ah would do it differently. Ah would have taken you with me.'

'And I would have left with you when you asked.'

'Was there a baby?' Ah ask.

Alice looks at me with tears in her eyes. 'Yes, there was a baby, but he was born dead. My parents sent me to relatives in Johannesburg and the plan was that I'd have the child and return without him. But he died during labour. Maybe he sensed what he was arriving into. He wasn't wanted by anyone – except me. But I couldn't keep him.'

Ah hold her and let her cry in ma arms, and when she's finished Ah once again take her face in ma hands like it's the most precious thing Ah've ever held. Then Ah notice the bruising.

'Did he do this to you?' Ah ask, already knowing the answer.

'Yes,' she says and although Ah feel a rage inside Ah also feel a tremendous sense of shame. Ah'm desperate to be different, to move on. Ah'm the person Ah remember, the person who will love this girl from now on. Things only matter from now on. For sure.

'From now on, Ah will look after you, Alice,' Ah tell her and she nods just like the young girl did all those years ago. 'Ah love you. Ah really and truly do,' Ah say, and right then, any doubts Ah might have had disappear. It's the truth that comes all the way from inside ma heart where this girl lives, a strong feeling reassuring me that no matter what comes our way we'll be okay. And as Ah prepare to begin again with ma Alice, Ah almost believe that it's possible ma life might just be heading for a happy ending.

'I've only ever loved you, Denzel Anderson,' she replies, and just like that, life knocks me completely off ma feet.

*

I look into the face of a sleeping Denzel Anderson. The boy I love is now a man, a man I also love. He looks beautiful – all man but yet a sleeping boy. This is a face I trust, a face I love like I've known it for a hundred years. We just made love and it was how I remembered it. He was gentle and held me like we were both teenagers again; it was almost like it was when we first found each other sexually. The thing that was furthest from my mind was what happened with Robert and I'm grateful for the miracle. It's forgotten and I silently applaud my decision to leave it be. Denzel need never know, and he never will.

He lets out a single snore and I hold on to the sound of it. Despite a wish to let him sleep, I trace the shape of his face with my hand and then plant a single kiss on his cheek. He smiles slightly but remains asleep and I wonder what he sees in his dreams.

I wonder what the future holds. It's almost twenty-four hours since we met and much has happened. Reunions: Jaspar and Jo found us early this morning and we were all together for the first time in almost twenty years. Meetings: I've met Tim Harris, Denzel's father. Discoveries: I've learned that Denzel had a little brother called Sid who died last year. He died in Denzel's arms on the stretch of beach I had walked in Ibiza. And the man I met and who had passed my number on to Denzel is called Titus, an ex-employer and friend. The beautiful Holly was Sid's girlfriend and not the love rival I had suspected. Coincidences: Ben, my favourite pupil at school, is the son of friends of Denzel's, and yes, it was Denzel at the Chemical Brothers gig in December.

There was much to catch up with and we talked into the early hours of the morning before falling into a deep sleep. Then tonight we came back together and made love. Now, as I lie and watch him, I feel like maybe the horrible things that happened between us have disappeared, have been erased by our rekindled love. Now there is only a bright future filled with promise and possibility. Already the plan is that I will live with him in the flat above his father's. We looked at it today. It's beautiful and feels like a good place to start again. Meeting Tim has been enlightening. I can see that, other than his smile, Denzel hasn't taken much from his mother by way of physical attributes. He and his father are uncannily similar. I really liked Tim from first impressions.

I watch my love sleep under the dim lamp in my best friend's spare room and I give thanks to whoever has made this happen. I think again about baby Denzel, the son we lost, and wonder if we'll ever get another chance. Are there children in our future? I hope so, but for now my mind is tired and I decide to succumb to sleep. Just as I'm thinking about turning off the light, Denzel opens his eyes.

'When did you become a peeping Tom, Alice Cooper?' he asks and I shrug my shoulders.

He leans over and moves my hair back from my face, the way he used to do, and then he kisses me. I fall into him and let the kiss run through me. Afterwards we look at each other for the longest time and I feel compelled to ask the question that is running through my mind.

'What's going to happen now?'

'Well, we'll probably sleep. Ja?'

'You know what I mean!' I say and slap him gently on the arm.

'What do you want to happen?'

'How about you marry me for real so that I can escape from Alice Cooper once and for all.'

'That would suit me just fine, Alice Anderson! Let's make it official,' he says and smiles that adorable gap-toothed smile I fell in love with when I was a girl. 'But first – let's get some sleep, ja?'

I nod and then I notice the time – it's three minutes past midnight.

'Happy Birthday, Denzel Anderson,' I whisper.

'Ja,' he whispers back. 'It is. For sure.'

ADAM III

The whole Sheehan family are under the same roof for the first time ever. Marie has moved into Bernie's house. It's a good job Bernie's place is so big – we all have our own rooms. Marie is a nightmare these days and it's Bernie who takes the full brunt of it. Of course, it's awful that Marie lost her husband in the car accident, but she's milking the whole situation and taking advantage of her grief. She's so rude and cruel, especially to me. Sometimes I could slap her. I felt sorry for her at first, but now I think she's getting worse – more rancid – day by day. Bernie's so nice to her though. You wouldn't believe it! Tommy seems to feel the same way I do.

I'm just biding my time until the end of the school year when I can leave. I fantasise about just disappearing, running away. I have a Saturday job in my uncle Tommy's garage, and if I work through the summer holidays I could make enough money to be able to leave. I don't know where I'll go yet, but the way I see it, I need the money first before I make any plans. The only money I spend is on books and music. I even stopped my guitar lessons and keep that money too. I still play but teach myself. I reckon I've gone as far as I can with the lessons anyway. I love playing. It's helping me to stay sane in this insane situation, although I have to take my guitar into school and stay behind in a classroom to practise, as Marie hates the noise. We're all creeping around poor sad, sick Marie.

With every passing day she seems to get more and more angry and I feel all of her anger coming in my direction. She really hates me. When I confront her about it, she always tells me the same thing: I'm spoiled and Mammy ruined me. I really have to restrain myself from saying things to her that I know I'll only regret afterwards. Somehow I keep all the bad words perched on the tip of my tongue, itching to be set free. One day she'll push me too far and it'll all come flooding out.

Tonight, we're all gathered round watching the BAFTAs, pretending that everything is okay and we're not sitting with a sister who's as mad as a hatter. Marie is quiet at first, which is a nice change, but then she gets really agitated and begins to act all crazy. I'm just about to leave them to it when Bernie begins to hush her in a way that grabs my attention.

'I can't believe it, Bernie,' she says. 'It's him. That's him – the man who raped me.'

Bernie tells her not to be tormenting herself but Marie won't shut up. 'It's him, I'm telling you.'

Bernie puts her arms around her. 'Be quiet, Marie,' Bernie says. She tries to comfort Marie but Marie's having none of it.

'I'm sick and tired of being quiet,' she says. 'That's the man who raped me – there, on the telly. Why won't anyone talk about this! And why have I been forced to watch the little bastard I gave birth to grow up.'

Marie's glaring at me now.

'Marie!' Bernie screams.

As my mind tries to wrap itself around what Marie's just said, we're all moving in slow motion. My eyes move from Marie back to the telly and I look at the man she's pointing at – the man on the telly who shares my face. He's standing with his father, the host tells us –my grandfather, if Marie is telling the truth. As I watch him and listen to my sister's weeping in the background, everything begins to make sense – that feeling of not belonging, the tension amongst the family.

I go up to my bedroom. Now I know who I am, for better or worse. God help me! They say that bad luck comes in threes and this is the third blow. I close my eyes and see that face again, the face that looks so much like my own. I feel a rage build up inside me, the extent of which I've never before known. There's a knock on the door and I know it'll be Bernie.

I open the door and she looks at me. She's my aunt, not my sister.

'Are you okay, pet?' she asks.

I shrug.

'Marie's upset, that's all.'

'But it's true, Bernie,' I reply.

She nods. 'But please, put it out of your mind, Adam. Just forget it. Marie would be a lot better off if she could just forget it. It doesn't mean anything, you know that love, don't you? We all love you, pet, and always will. It doesn't matter to the rest of us.'

But it makes sense of my life. I was born out of a great pain, out of violence – everything I hate most in my world conspired to create me.

'Tell me you know that, Adam?' Bernie says looking at me with eyes full of fear.

'I know,' I say to ease her mind. She looks at me a bit longer and blinks slowly. 'You should have told me, Bernie. I deserved to know.'

'But how could we!'

And how do I live with this now? That's the question that hangs unanswered in the air.

THE END

About The Author

In addition to writing fiction, Kira Kenley is a singer-songwriter and teacher. She lives in London with her musical husband and their lunatic cat.

Her first novel *All The Way Back To Here* was published in 2013. *Awakening Alice* is the sequel, and the second part of The Harris Trilogy.

In *Adam's Apple*, the final part of The Harris Trilogy, Holly Du Plessis arrives in London with a plan to move on from her beloved Sid Harris and strengthen her connection to Denzel Anderson. However, the arrival of the mysterious Adam further exacerbates her loneliness and pushes her dangerously close to the edge. *Adam's Apple* will be available in 2015.

To connect with Kira visit kirakenley.com